FEARLESS

KENNY PORTER AND ZACH WILCOX

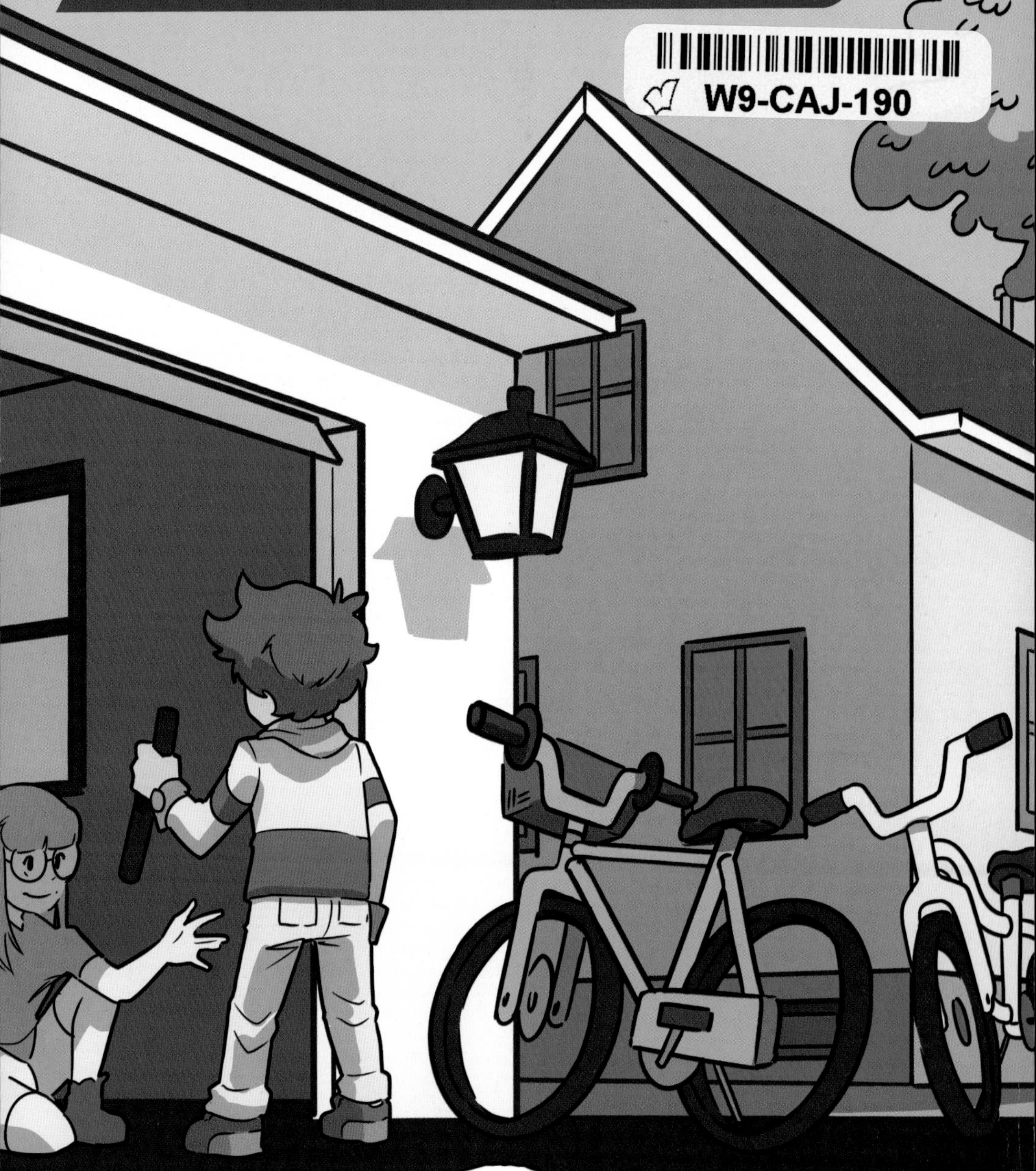

graphix

AN IMPRINT OF

SCHOLASTIC

All rights reserved. Published by Graphix, an imprint of Scholastic Inc., *Publishers since 1920.*
SCHOLASTIC, GRAPHIX, and associated logos are trademarks and/or registered trademarks of Scholastic Inc.

Library of Congress Control Number: 2020943278

ISBN 978-1-338-35588-8 (hardcover)
ISBN 978-1-338-35587-1 (paperback)

10 9 8 7 6 5 4 3 2 1   21 22 23 24 25

Printed in China   62
First edition, May 2021

Book design by Steve Ponzo
Creative Director: Phil Falco
Publisher: David Saylor

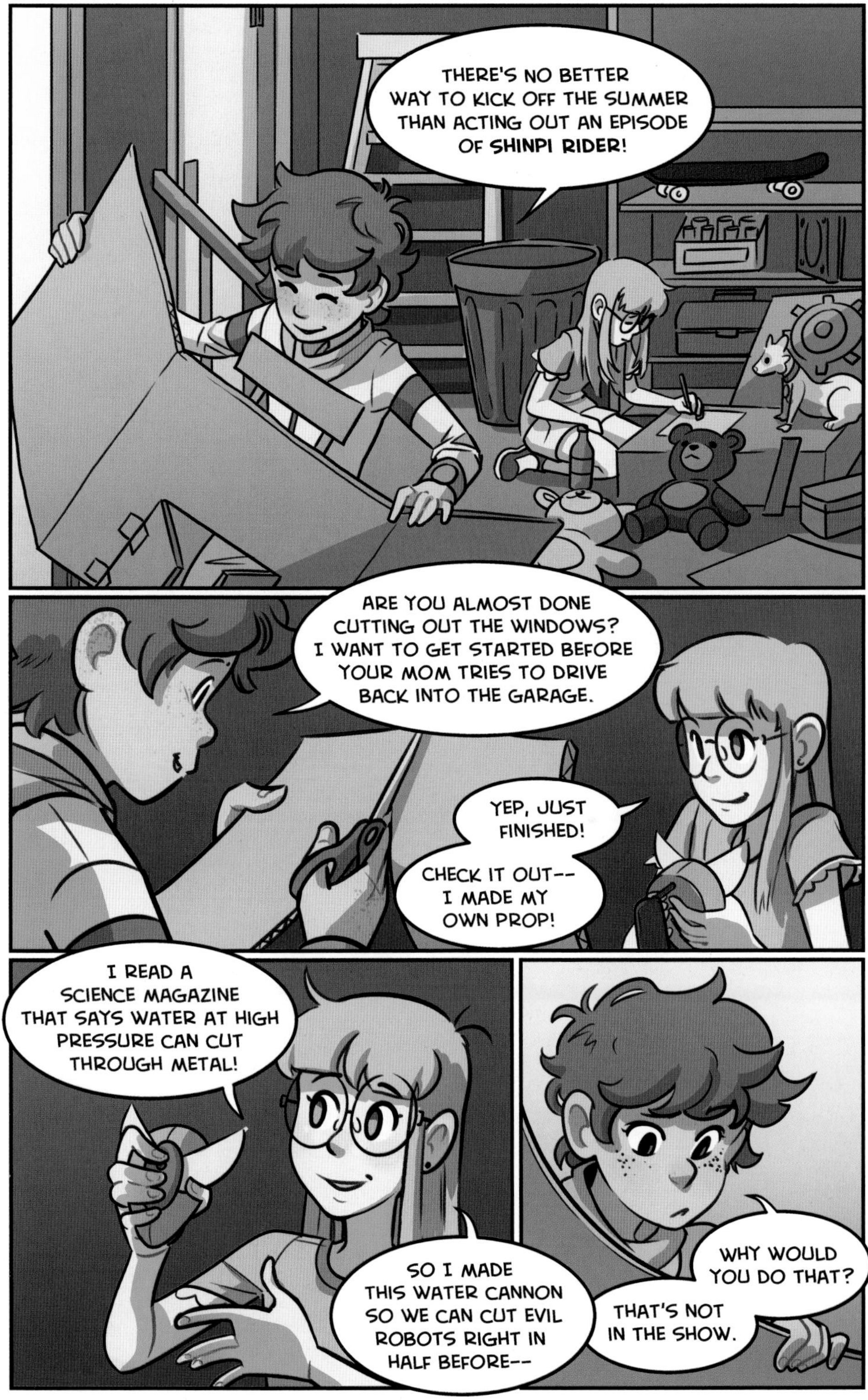
THERE'S NO BETTER WAY TO KICK OFF THE SUMMER THAN ACTING OUT AN EPISODE OF **SHINPI RIDER**!
ARE YOU ALMOST DONE CUTTING OUT THE WINDOWS? I WANT TO GET STARTED BEFORE YOUR MOM TRIES TO DRIVE BACK INTO THE GARAGE.
YEP, JUST FINISHED!
CHECK IT OUT-- I MADE MY OWN PROP!
I READ A SCIENCE MAGAZINE THAT SAYS WATER AT HIGH PRESSURE CAN CUT THROUGH METAL!
SO I MADE THIS WATER CANNON SO WE CAN CUT EVIL ROBOTS RIGHT IN HALF BEFORE--
WHY WOULD YOU DO THAT?
THAT'S NOT IN THE SHOW.

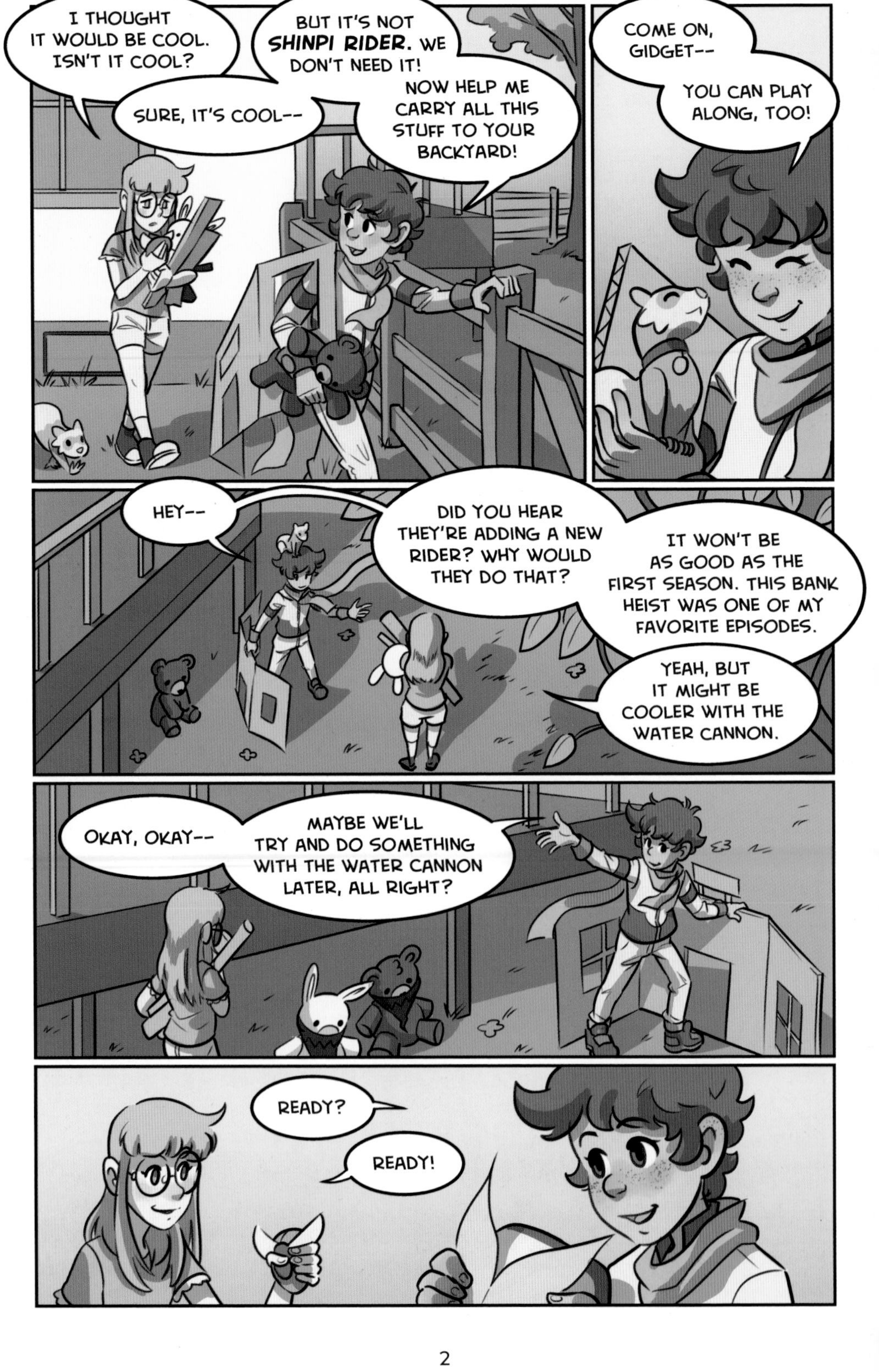
I THOUGHT IT WOULD BE COOL. ISN'T IT COOL?
BUT IT'S NOT **SHINPI RIDER**. WE DON'T NEED IT!
SURE, IT'S COOL--
NOW HELP ME CARRY ALL THIS STUFF TO YOUR BACKYARD!
COME ON, GIDGET--
YOU CAN PLAY ALONG, TOO!
HEY--
DID YOU HEAR THEY'RE ADDING A NEW RIDER? WHY WOULD THEY DO THAT?
IT WON'T BE AS GOOD AS THE FIRST SEASON. THIS BANK HEIST WAS ONE OF MY FAVORITE EPISODES.
YEAH, BUT IT MIGHT BE COOLER WITH THE WATER CANNON.
OKAY, OKAY--
MAYBE WE'LL TRY AND DO SOMETHING WITH THE WATER CANNON LATER, ALL RIGHT?
READY?
READY!

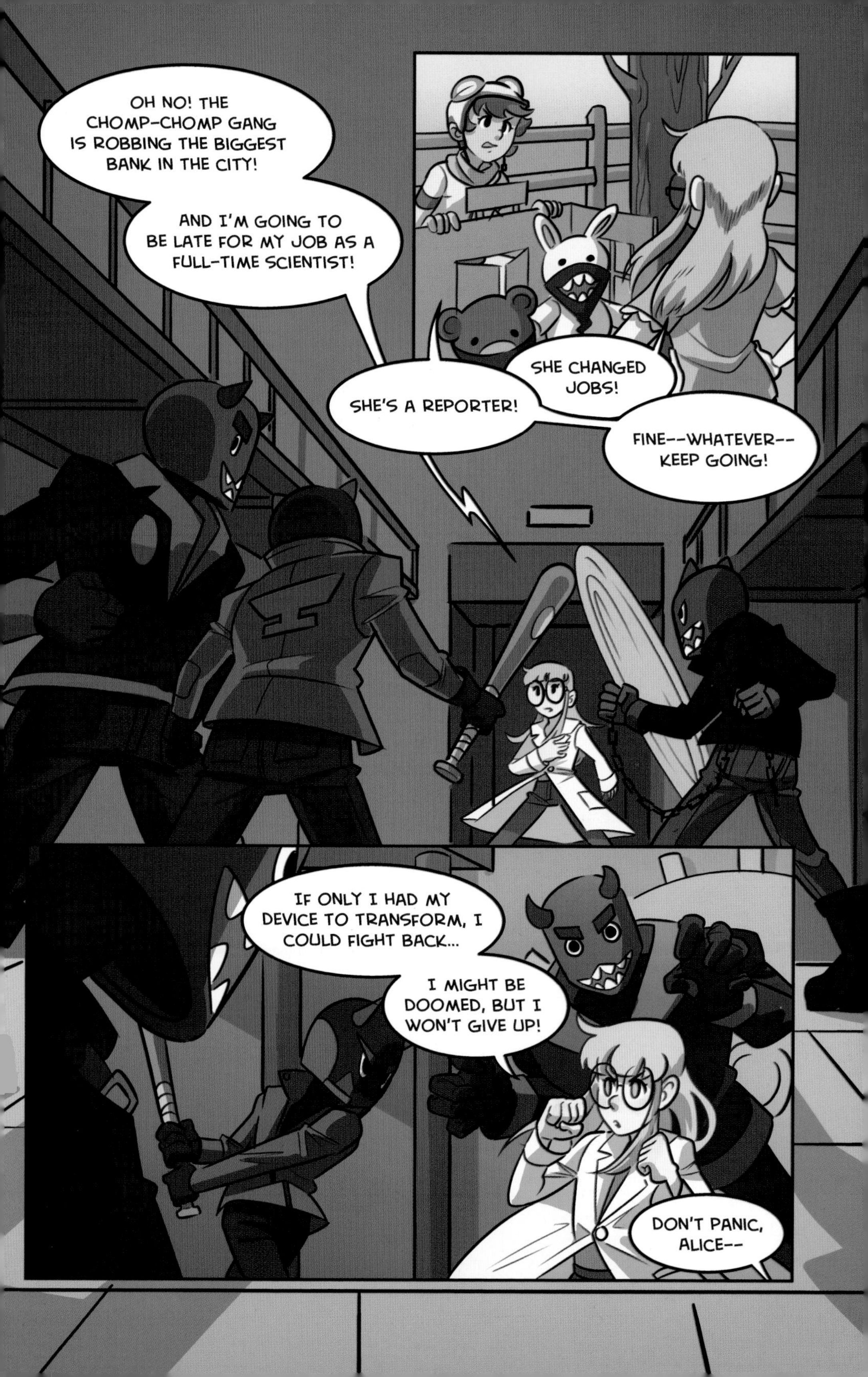
OH NO! THE CHOMP-CHOMP GANG IS ROBBING THE BIGGEST BANK IN THE CITY!
AND I'M GOING TO BE LATE FOR MY JOB AS A FULL-TIME SCIENTIST!
SHE'S A REPORTER!
SHE CHANGED JOBS!
FINE--WHATEVER--KEEP GOING!
IF ONLY I HAD MY DEVICE TO TRANSFORM, I COULD FIGHT BACK...
I MIGHT BE DOOMED, BUT I WON'T GIVE UP!
DON'T PANIC, ALICE--

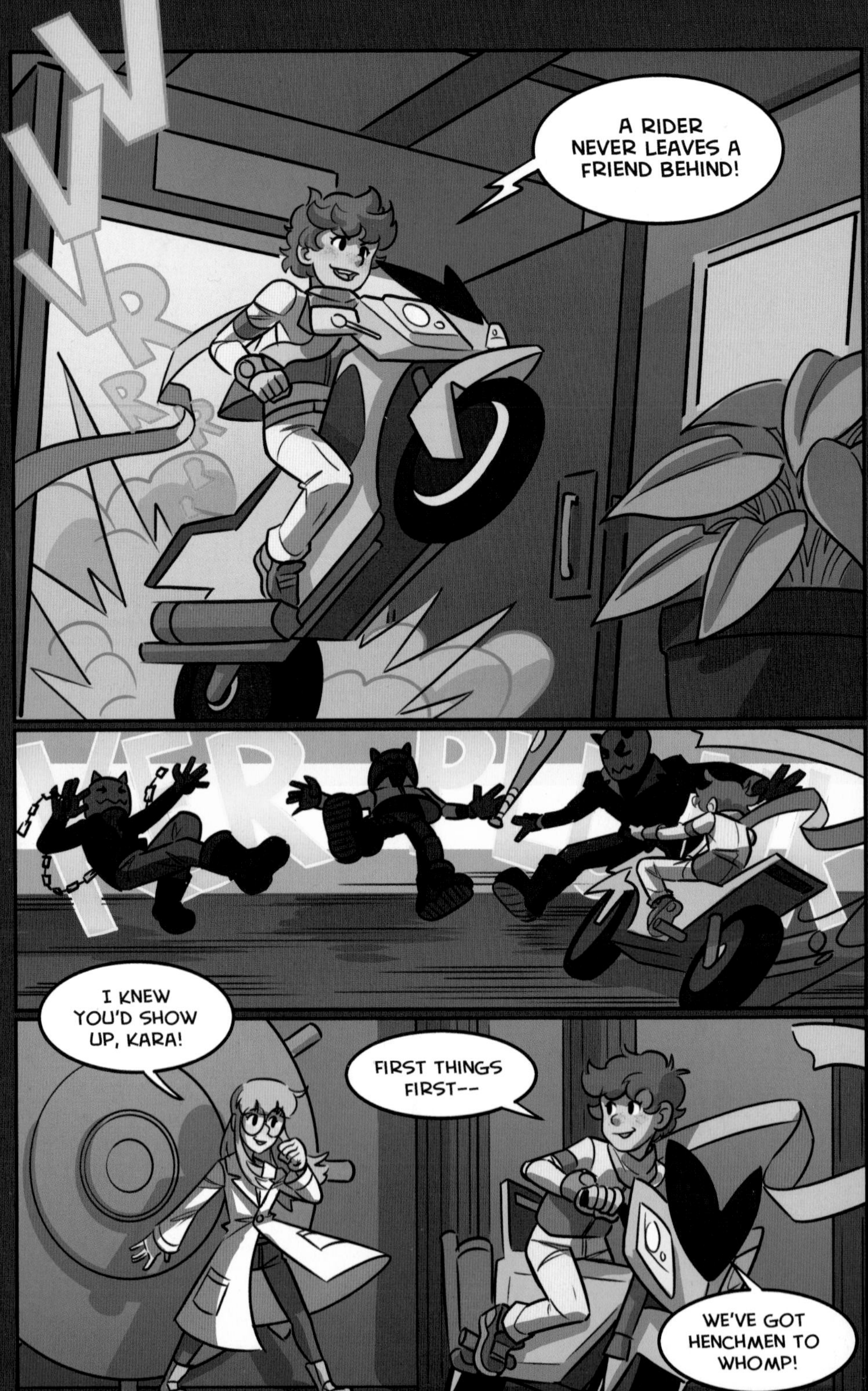
VVVRRRR
A RIDER NEVER LEAVES A FRIEND BEHIND!
I KNEW YOU'D SHOW UP, KARA!
FIRST THINGS FIRST--
WE'VE GOT HENCHMEN TO WHOMP!

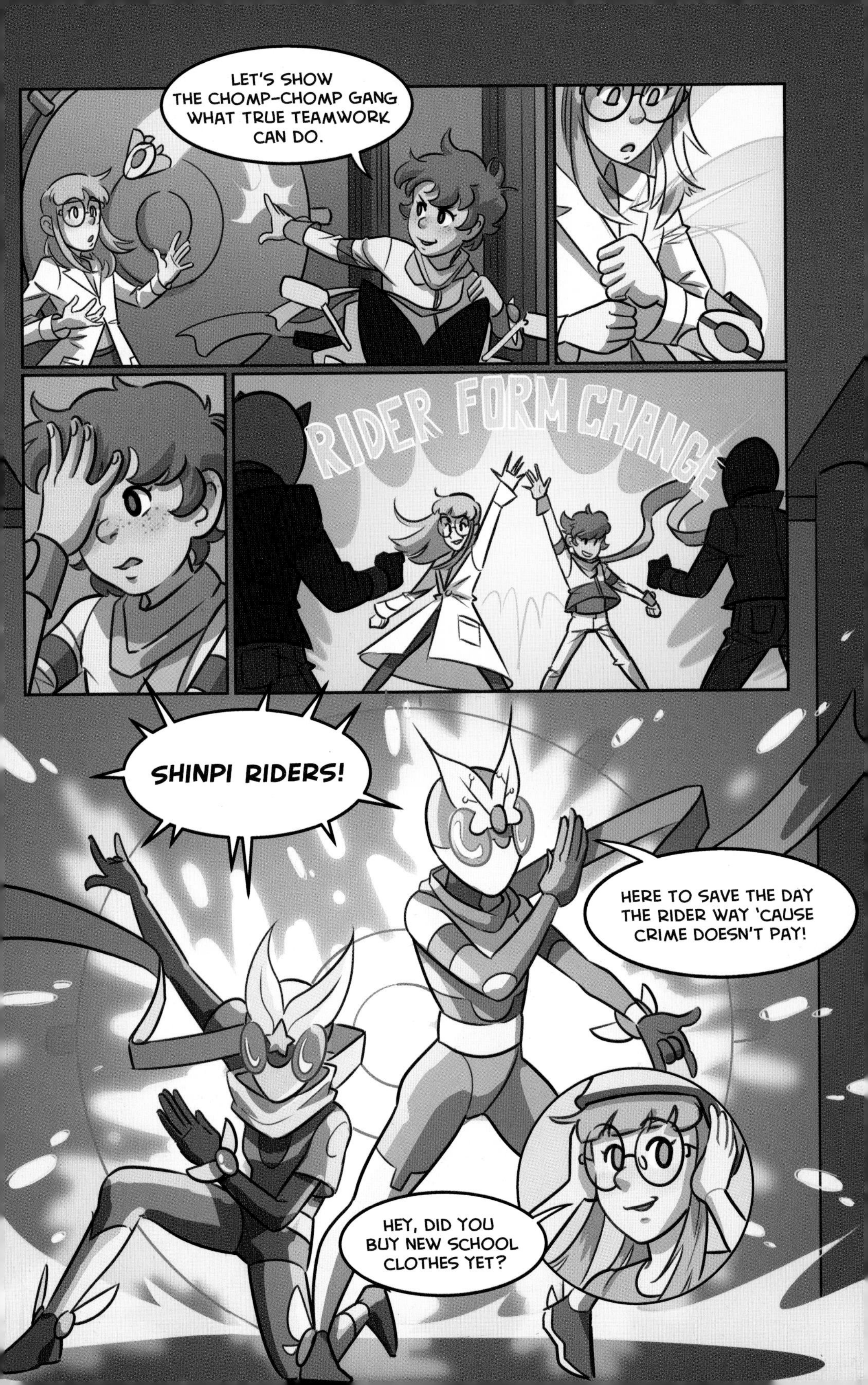
LET'S SHOW THE CHOMP-CHOMP GANG WHAT TRUE TEAMWORK CAN DO.
RIDER FORM CHANGE
SHINPI RIDERS!
HERE TO SAVE THE DAY THE RIDER WAY 'CAUSE CRIME DOESN'T PAY!
HEY, DID YOU BUY NEW SCHOOL CLOTHES YET?

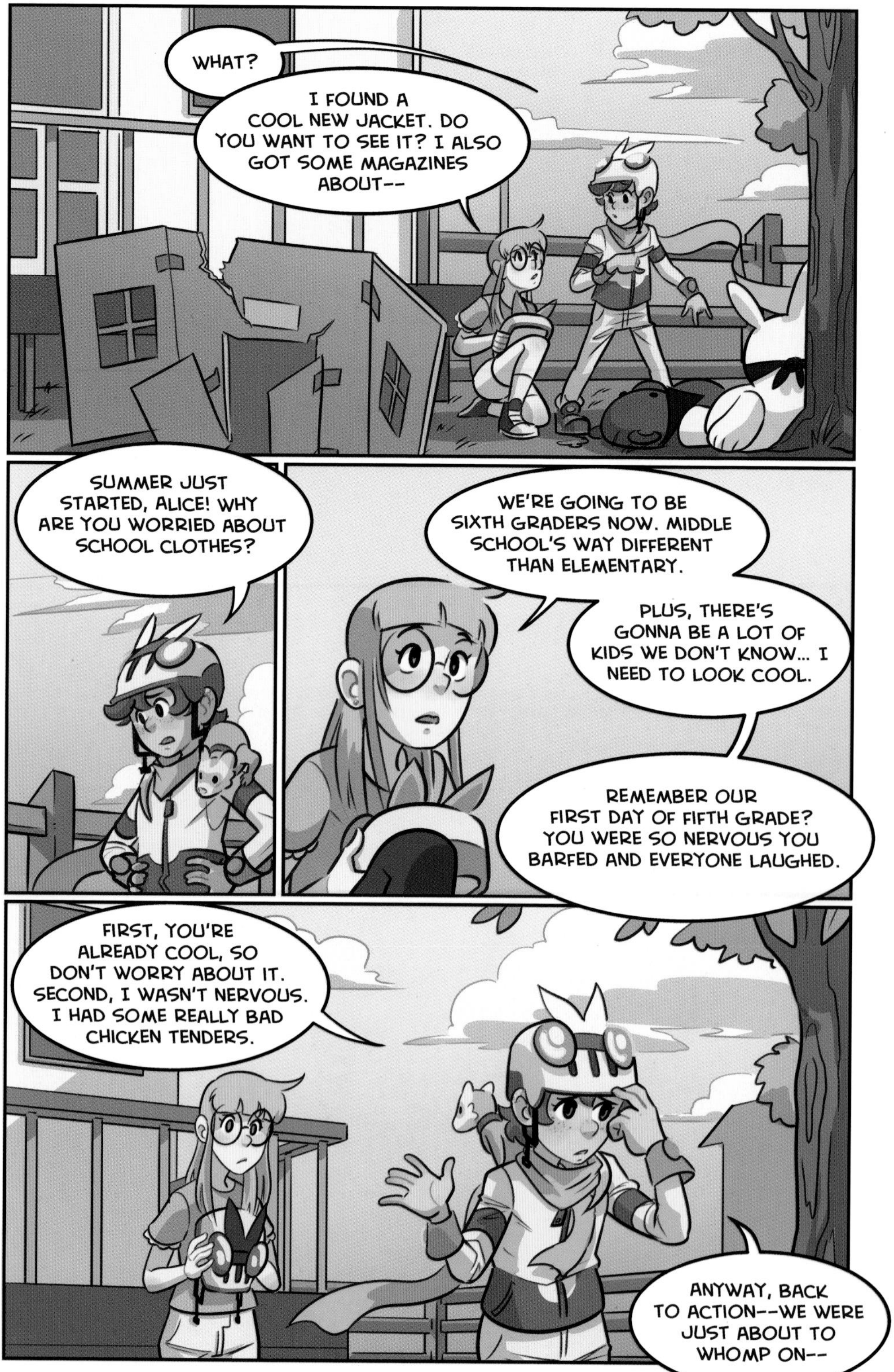
WHAT?
I FOUND A COOL NEW JACKET. DO YOU WANT TO SEE IT? I ALSO GOT SOME MAGAZINES ABOUT--
SUMMER JUST STARTED, ALICE! WHY ARE YOU WORRIED ABOUT SCHOOL CLOTHES?
WE'RE GOING TO BE SIXTH GRADERS NOW. MIDDLE SCHOOL'S WAY DIFFERENT THAN ELEMENTARY.
PLUS, THERE'S GONNA BE A LOT OF KIDS WE DON'T KNOW... I NEED TO LOOK COOL.
REMEMBER OUR FIRST DAY OF FIFTH GRADE? YOU WERE SO NERVOUS YOU BARFED AND EVERYONE LAUGHED.
FIRST, YOU'RE ALREADY COOL, SO DON'T WORRY ABOUT IT. SECOND, I WASN'T NERVOUS. I HAD SOME REALLY BAD CHICKEN TENDERS.
ANYWAY, BACK TO ACTION--WE WERE JUST ABOUT TO WHOMP ON--

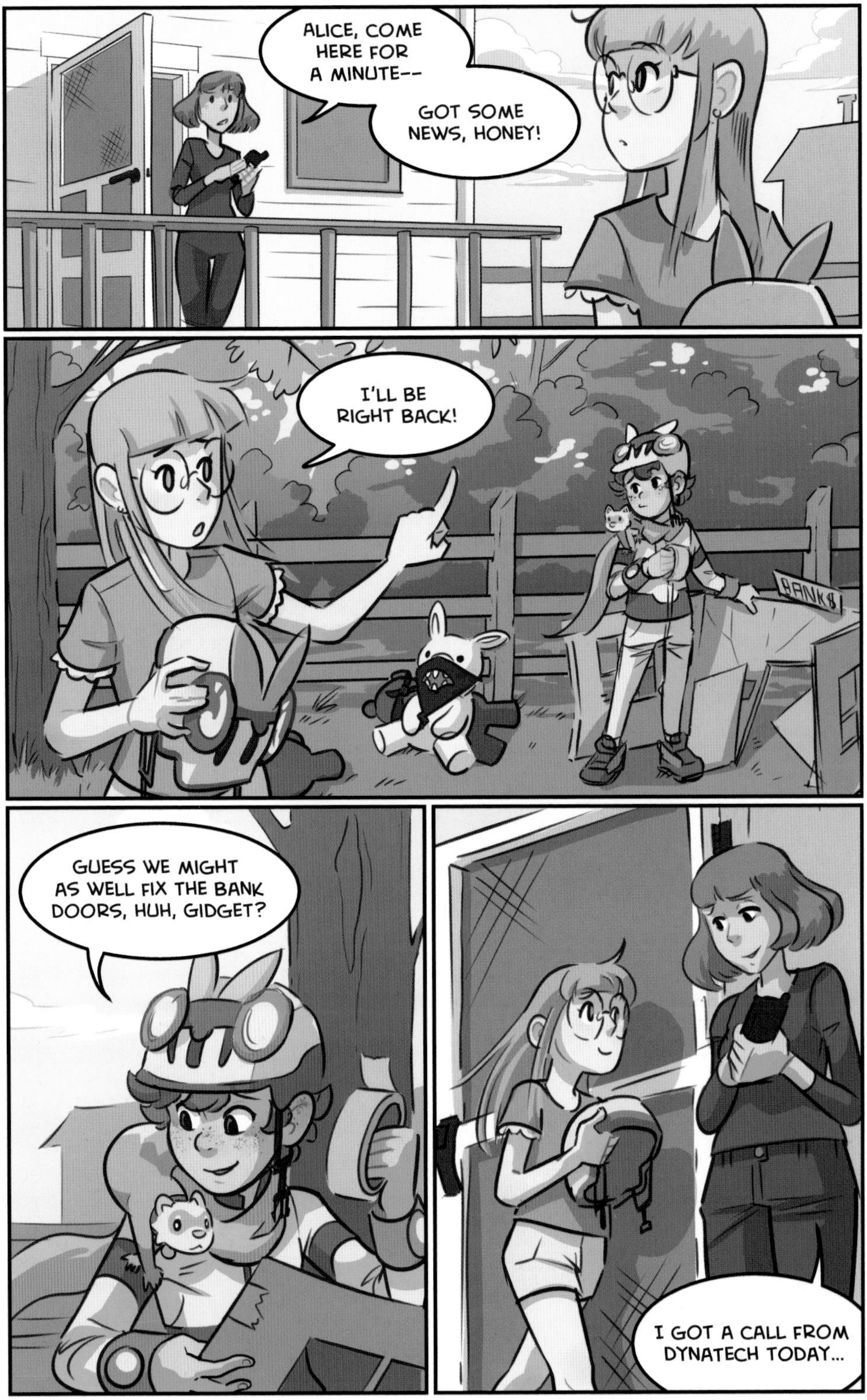
ALICE, COME HERE FOR A MINUTE--
GOT SOME NEWS, HONEY!
I'LL BE RIGHT BACK!
BANK
GUESS WE MIGHT AS WELL FIX THE BANK DOORS, HUH, GIDGET?
I GOT A CALL FROM DYNATECH TODAY...

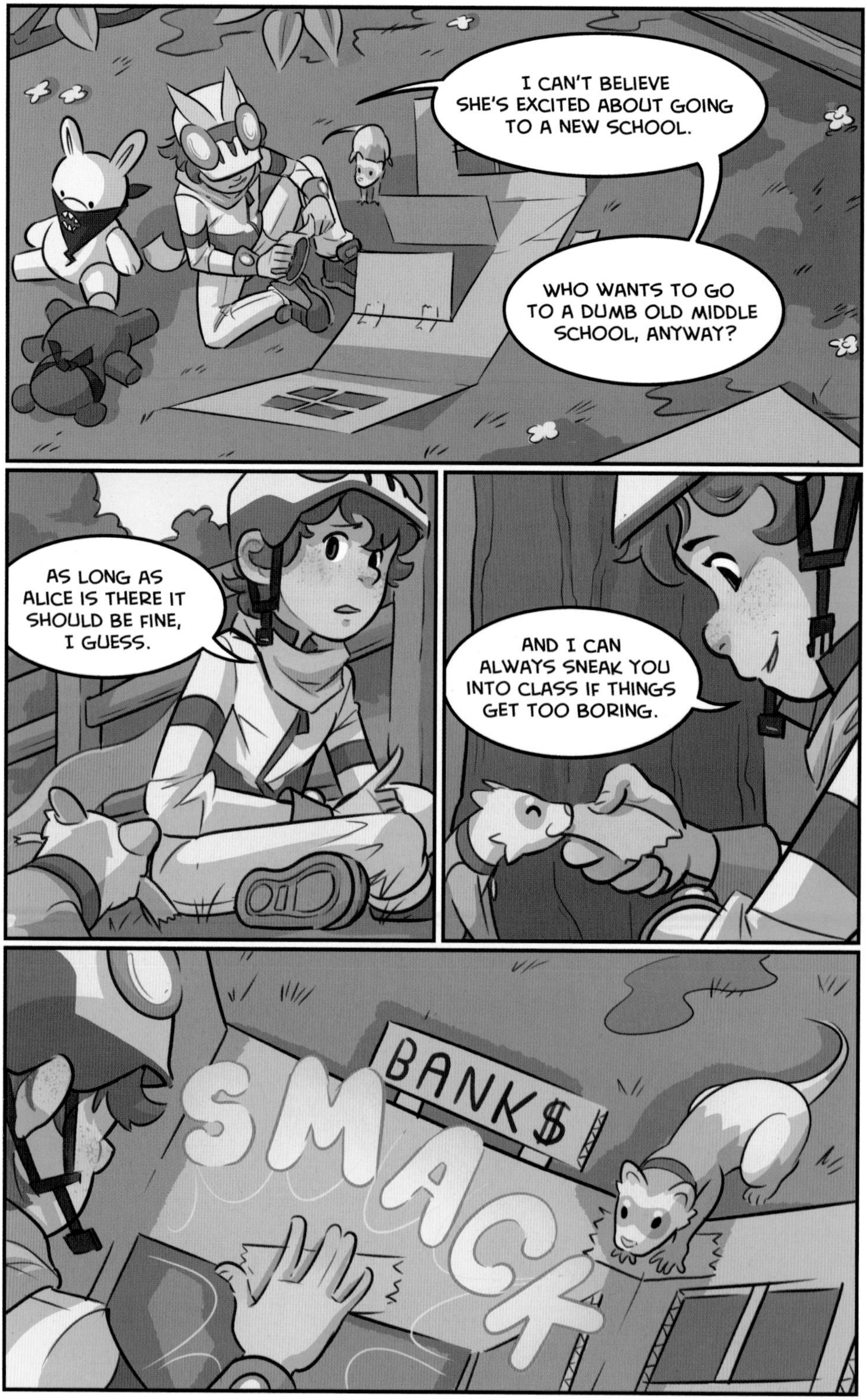
I CAN'T BELIEVE SHE'S EXCITED ABOUT GOING TO A NEW SCHOOL.
WHO WANTS TO GO TO A DUMB OLD MIDDLE SCHOOL, ANYWAY?
AS LONG AS ALICE IS THERE IT SHOULD BE FINE, I GUESS.
AND I CAN ALWAYS SNEAK YOU INTO CLASS IF THINGS GET TOO BORING.
BANK$
SMACK

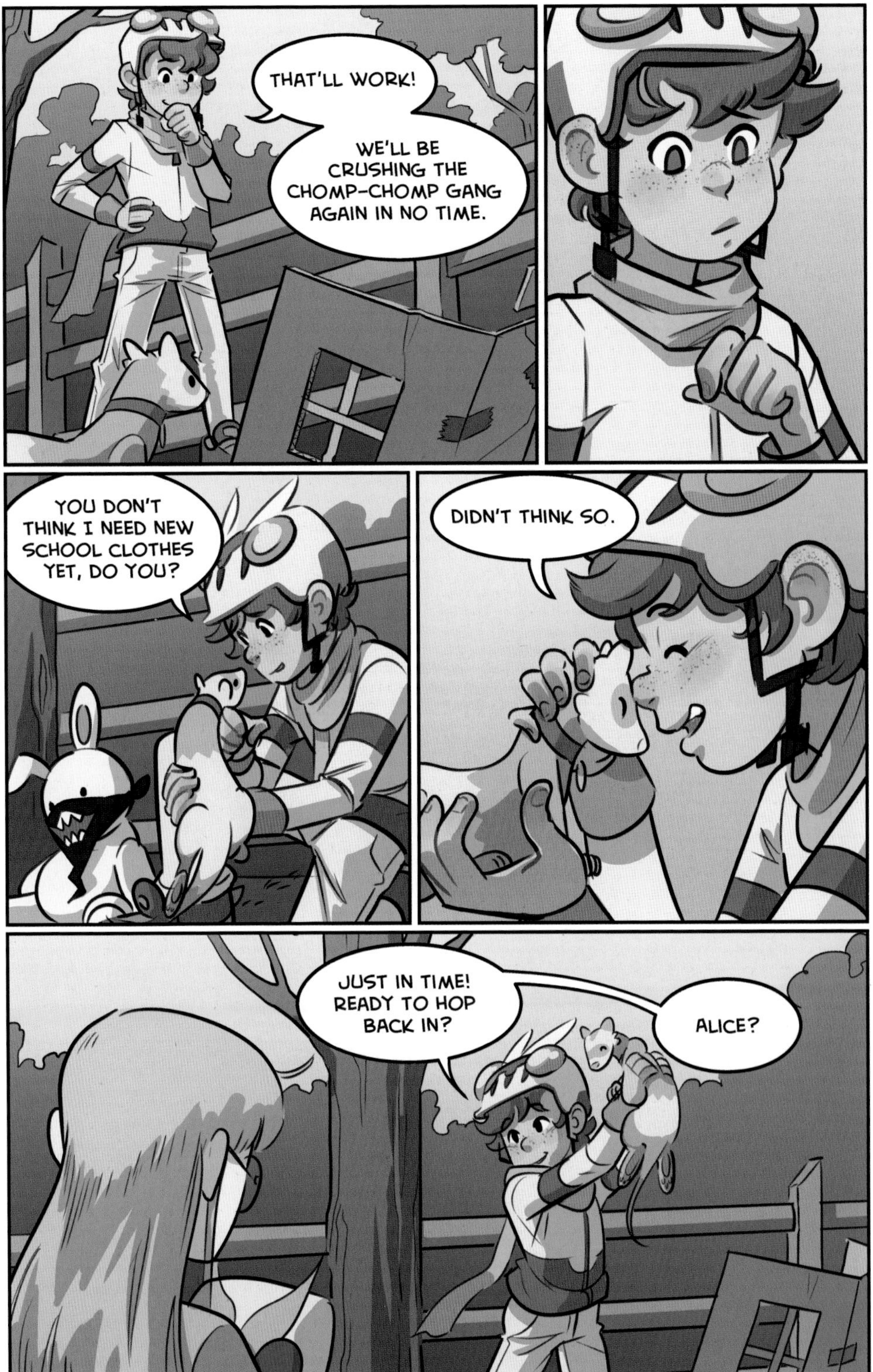

THAT'LL WORK!
WE'LL BE CRUSHING THE CHOMP-CHOMP GANG AGAIN IN NO TIME.
YOU DON'T THINK I NEED NEW SCHOOL CLOTHES YET, DO YOU?
DIDN'T THINK SO.
JUST IN TIME! READY TO HOP BACK IN?
ALICE?

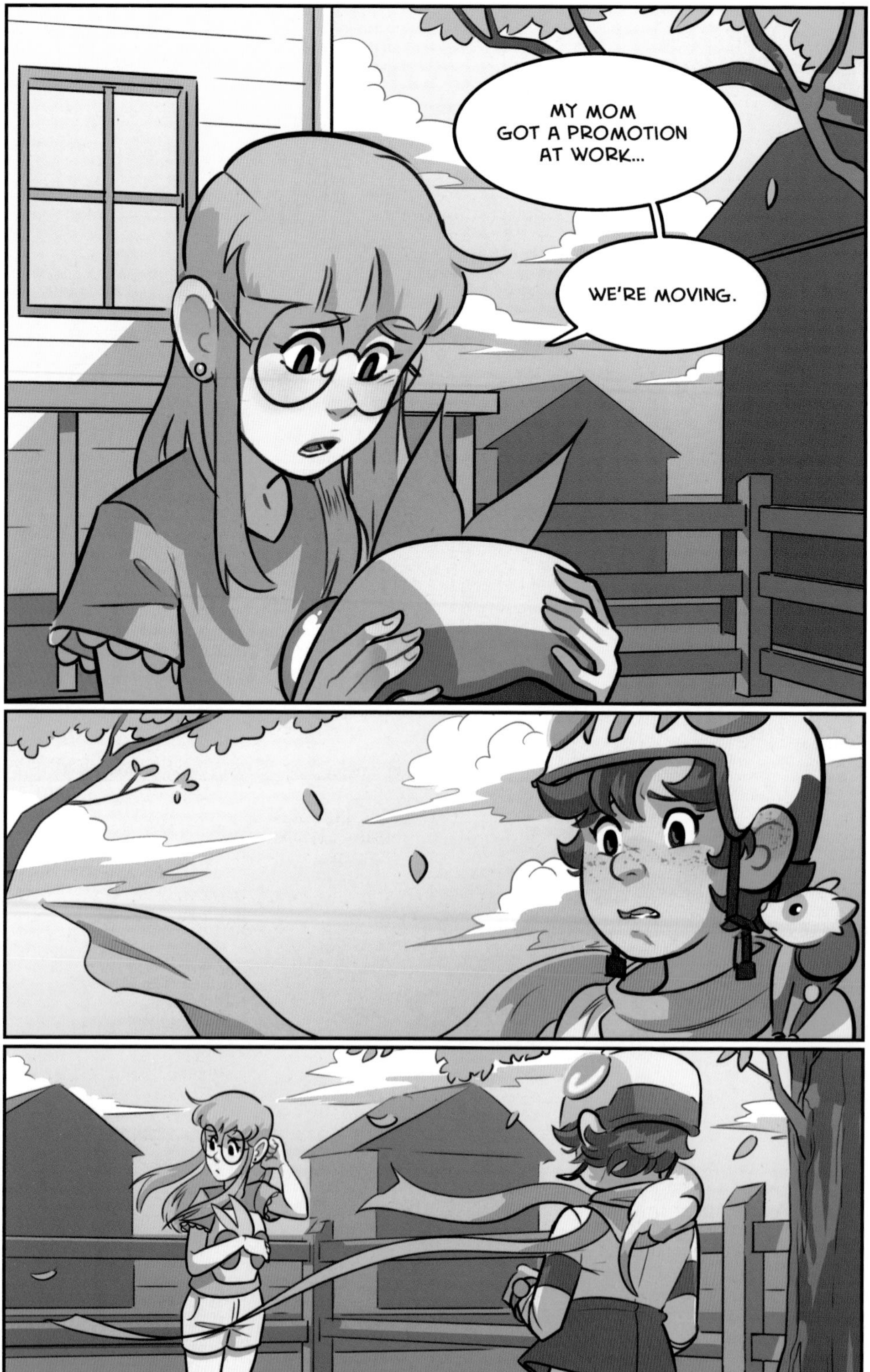
MY MOM GOT A PROMOTION AT WORK...
WE'RE MOVING.

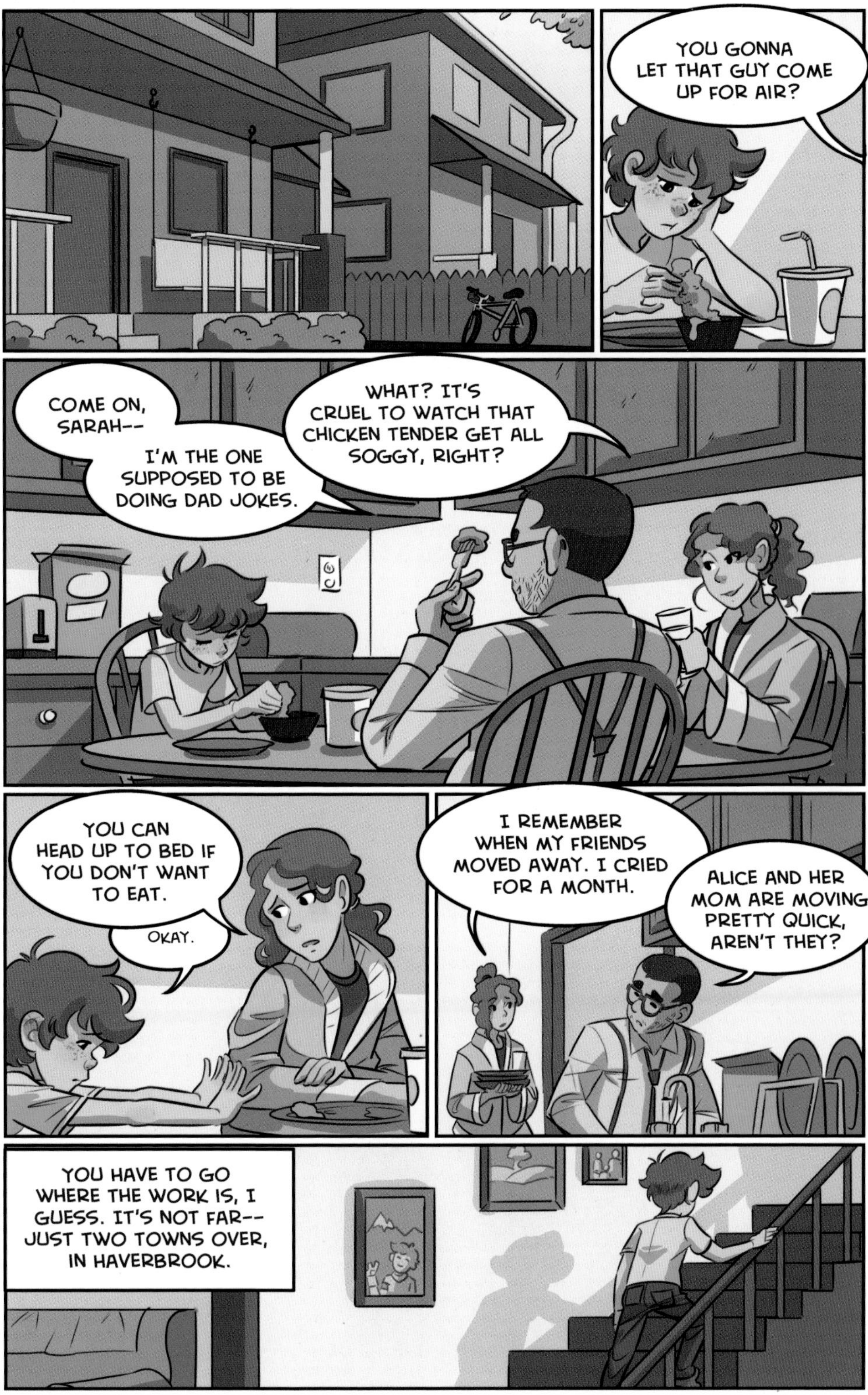
YOU GONNA LET THAT GUY COME UP FOR AIR?
COME ON, SARAH--
I'M THE ONE SUPPOSED TO BE DOING DAD JOKES.
WHAT? IT'S CRUEL TO WATCH THAT CHICKEN TENDER GET ALL SOGGY, RIGHT?
YOU CAN HEAD UP TO BED IF YOU DON'T WANT TO EAT.
OKAY.
I REMEMBER WHEN MY FRIENDS MOVED AWAY. I CRIED FOR A MONTH.
ALICE AND HER MOM ARE MOVING PRETTY QUICK, AREN'T THEY?
YOU HAVE TO GO WHERE THE WORK IS, I GUESS. IT'S NOT FAR-- JUST TWO TOWNS OVER, IN HAVERBROOK.

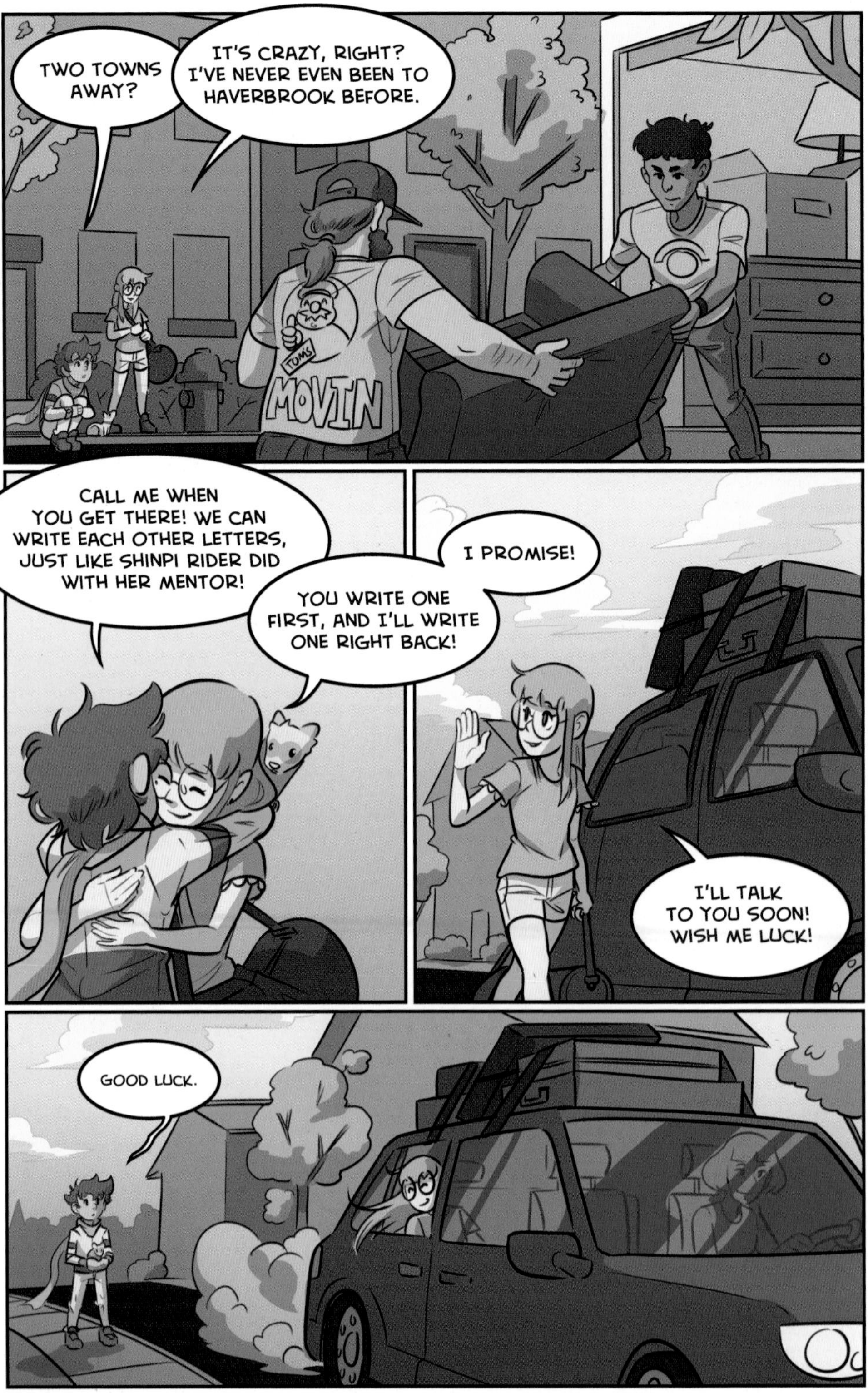

TWO TOWNS AWAY?
IT'S CRAZY, RIGHT? I'VE NEVER EVEN BEEN TO HAVERBROOK BEFORE.
TOMS
MOVIN
CALL ME WHEN YOU GET THERE! WE CAN WRITE EACH OTHER LETTERS, JUST LIKE SHINPI RIDER DID WITH HER MENTOR!
YOU WRITE ONE FIRST, AND I'LL WRITE ONE RIGHT BACK!
I PROMISE!
I'LL TALK TO YOU SOON! WISH ME LUCK!
GOOD LUCK.

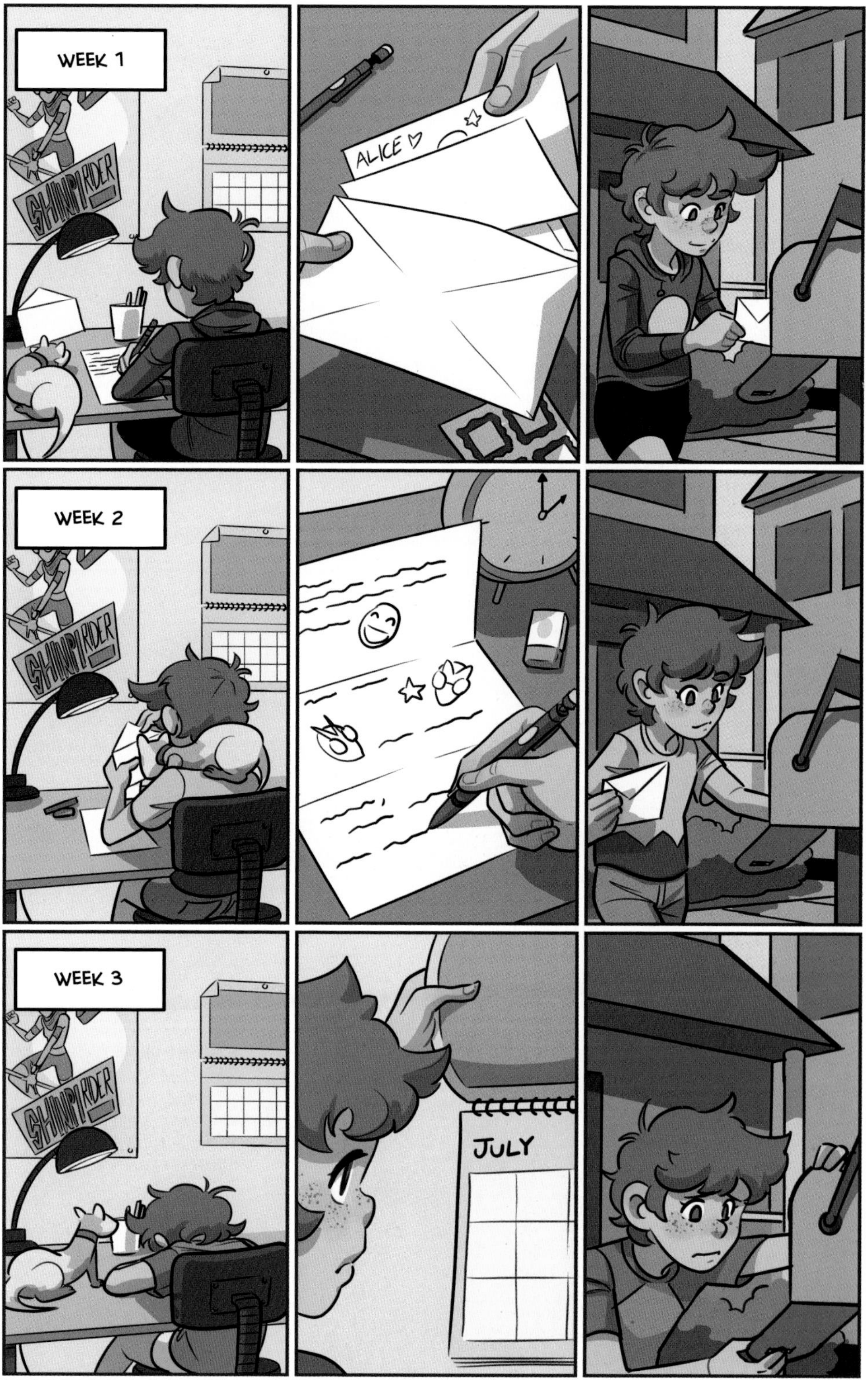
WEEK 1
SHINPI RIDER
ALICE ♡
WEEK 2
SHINPI RIDER
WEEK 3
SHINPI RIDER
JULY

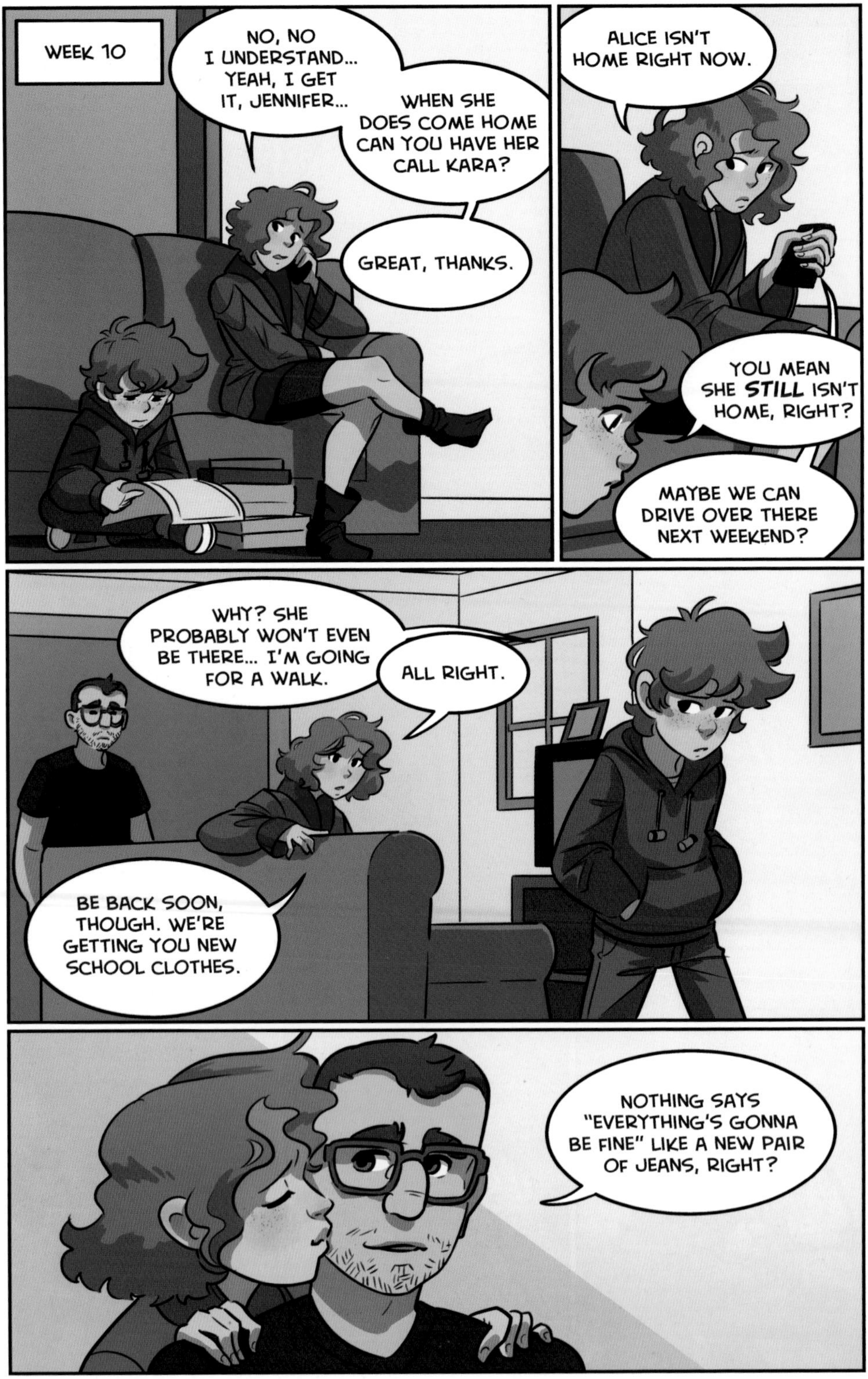
WEEK 10
NO, NO I UNDERSTAND... YEAH, I GET IT, JENNIFER...
WHEN SHE DOES COME HOME CAN YOU HAVE HER CALL KARA?
GREAT, THANKS.
ALICE ISN'T HOME RIGHT NOW.
YOU MEAN SHE STILL ISN'T HOME, RIGHT?
MAYBE WE CAN DRIVE OVER THERE NEXT WEEKEND?
WHY? SHE PROBABLY WON'T EVEN BE THERE... I'M GOING FOR A WALK.
ALL RIGHT.
BE BACK SOON, THOUGH. WE'RE GETTING YOU NEW SCHOOL CLOTHES.
NOTHING SAYS "EVERYTHING'S GONNA BE FINE" LIKE A NEW PAIR OF JEANS, RIGHT?

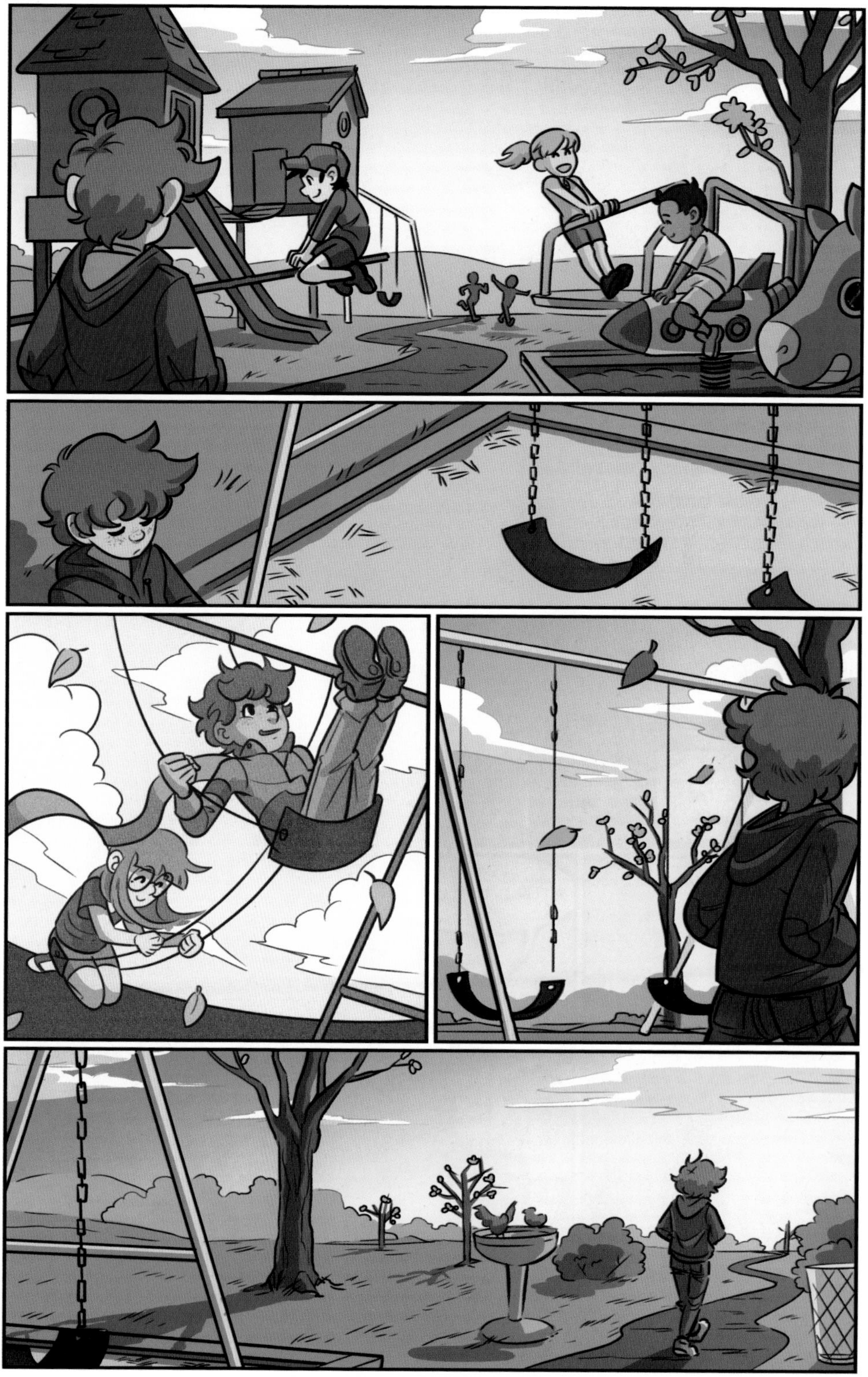

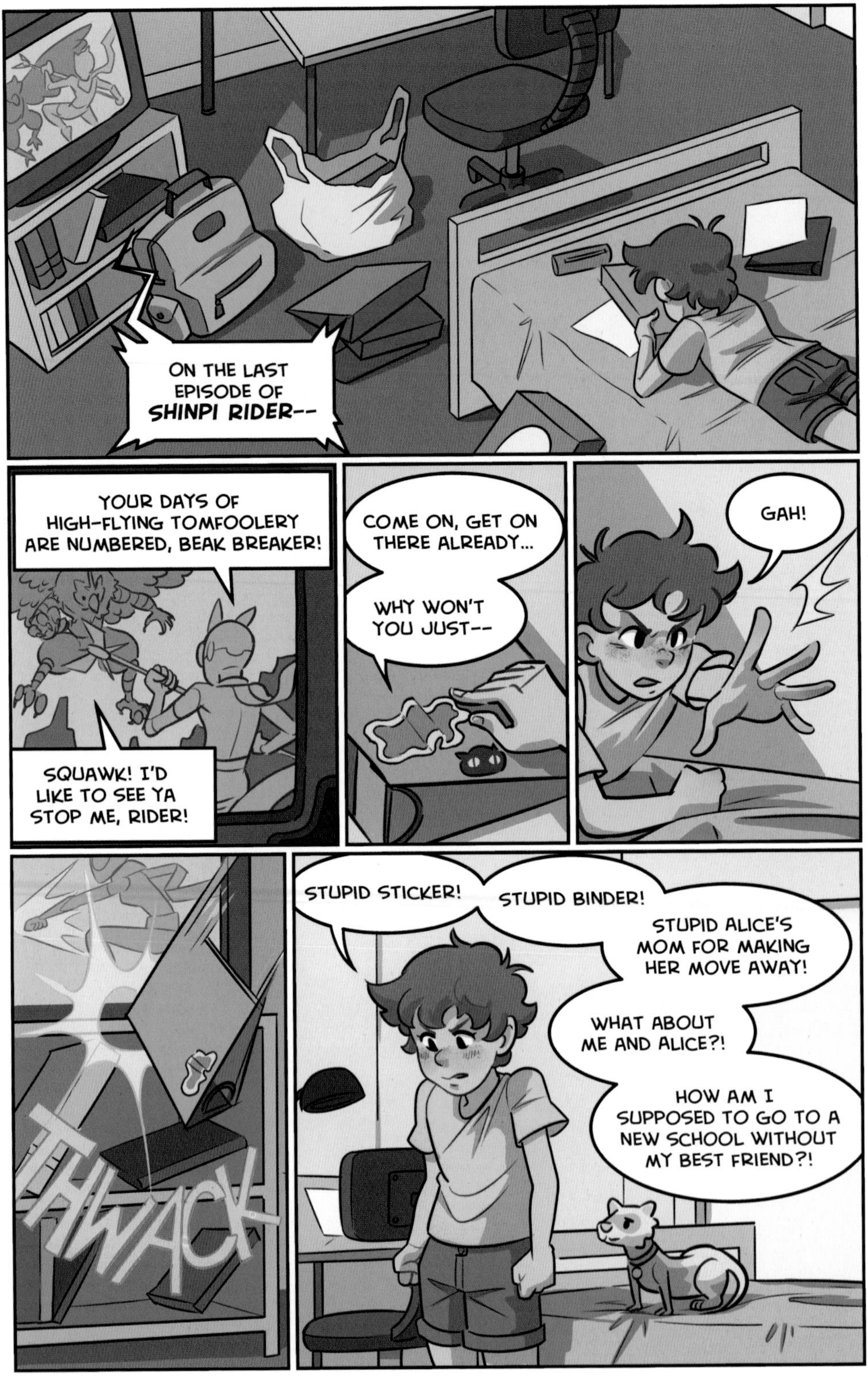
ON THE LAST EPISODE OF SHINPI RIDER--
YOUR DAYS OF HIGH-FLYING TOMFOOLERY ARE NUMBERED, BEAK BREAKER!
SQUAWK! I'D LIKE TO SEE YA STOP ME, RIDER!
COME ON, GET ON THERE ALREADY...
WHY WON'T YOU JUST--
GAH!
THWACK
STUPID STICKER!
STUPID BINDER!
STUPID ALICE'S MOM FOR MAKING HER MOVE AWAY!
WHAT ABOUT ME AND ALICE?!
HOW AM I SUPPOSED TO GO TO A NEW SCHOOL WITHOUT MY BEST FRIEND?!

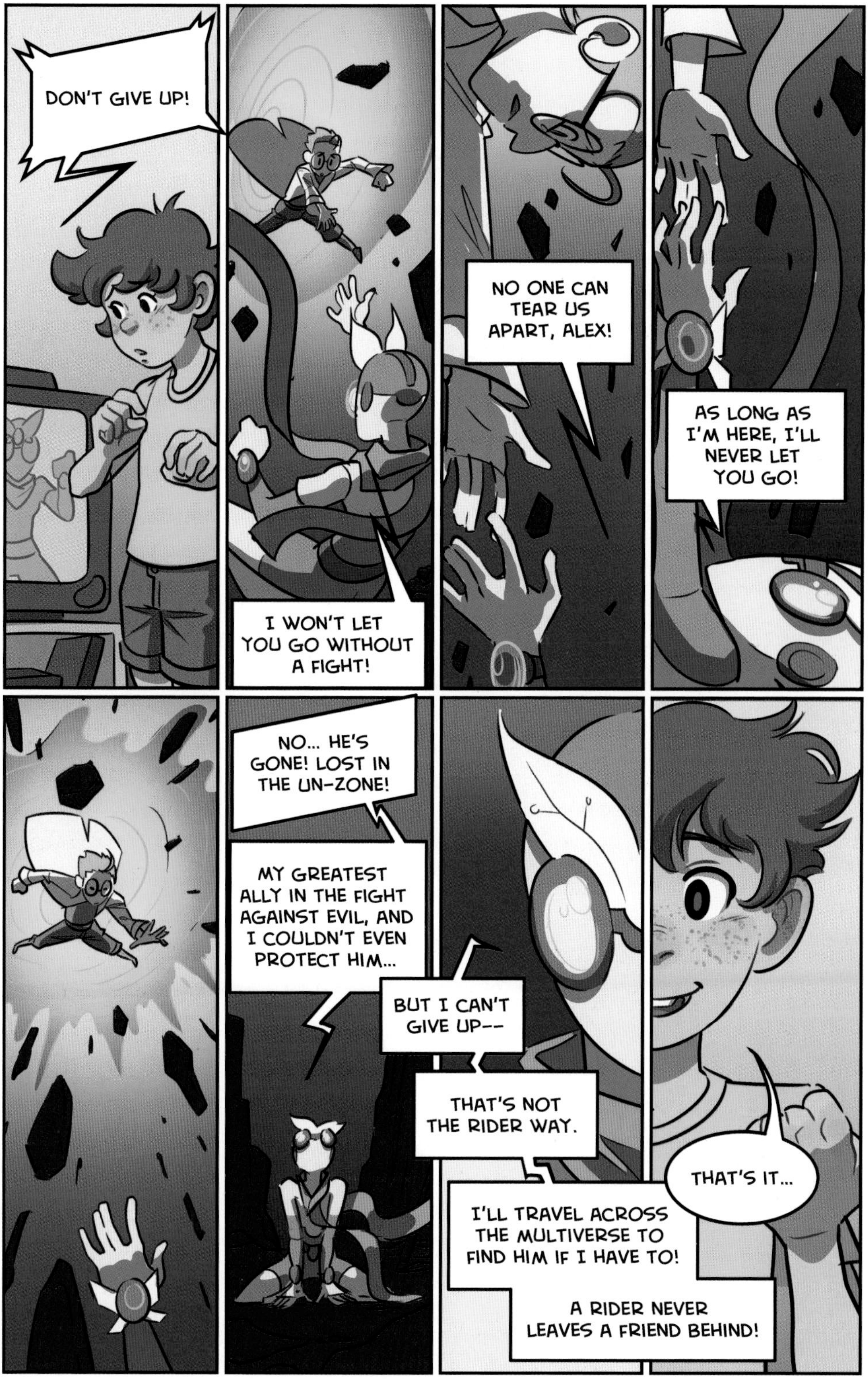
DON'T GIVE UP!
I WON'T LET YOU GO WITHOUT A FIGHT!
NO ONE CAN TEAR US APART, ALEX!
AS LONG AS I'M HERE, I'LL NEVER LET YOU GO!
NO... HE'S GONE! LOST IN THE UN-ZONE!
MY GREATEST ALLY IN THE FIGHT AGAINST EVIL, AND I COULDN'T EVEN PROTECT HIM...
BUT I CAN'T GIVE UP--
THAT'S NOT THE RIDER WAY.
I'LL TRAVEL ACROSS THE MULTIVERSE TO FIND HIM IF I HAVE TO!
A RIDER NEVER LEAVES A FRIEND BEHIND!
THAT'S IT...

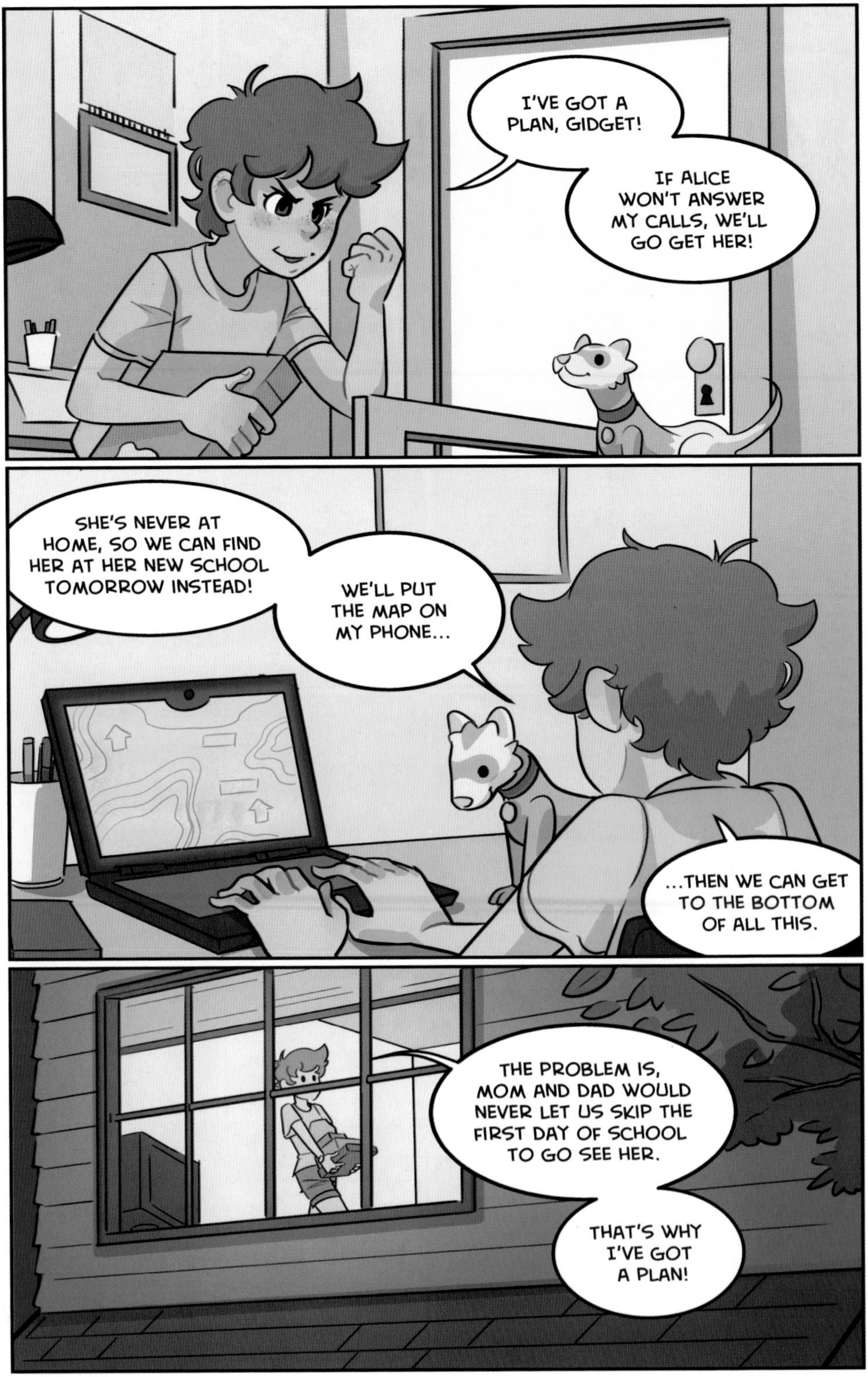
I'VE GOT A PLAN, GIDGET!
IF ALICE WON'T ANSWER MY CALLS, WE'LL GO GET HER!
SHE'S NEVER AT HOME, SO WE CAN FIND HER AT HER NEW SCHOOL TOMORROW INSTEAD!
WE'LL PUT THE MAP ON MY PHONE...
...THEN WE CAN GET TO THE BOTTOM OF ALL THIS.
THE PROBLEM IS, MOM AND DAD WOULD NEVER LET US SKIP THE FIRST DAY OF SCHOOL TO GO SEE HER.
THAT'S WHY I'VE GOT A PLAN!

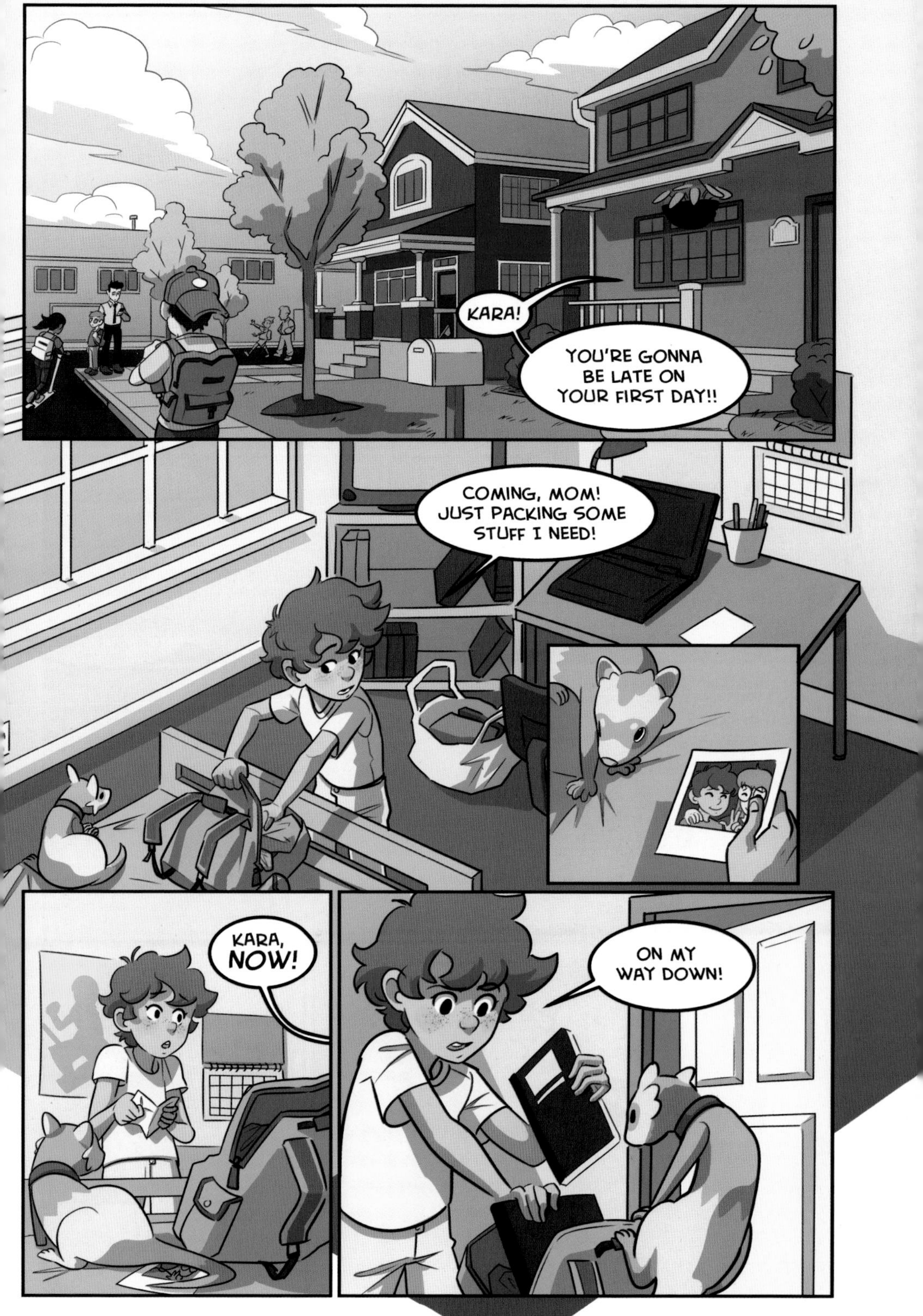
KARA!
YOU'RE GONNA BE LATE ON YOUR FIRST DAY!!
COMING, MOM! JUST PACKING SOME STUFF I NEED!
KARA, NOW!
ON MY WAY DOWN!

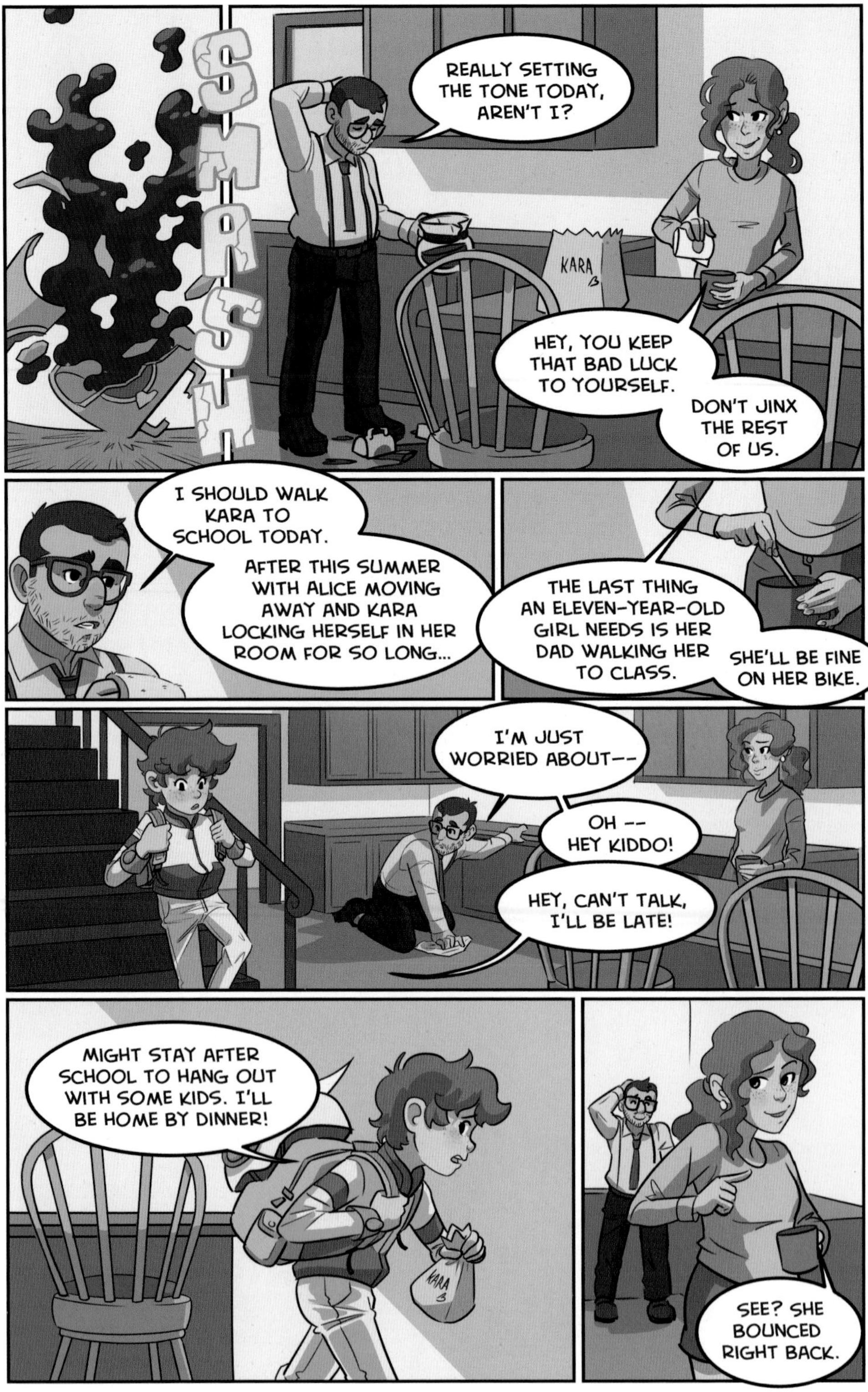
SMASH
REALLY SETTING THE TONE TODAY, AREN'T I?
KARA
HEY, YOU KEEP THAT BAD LUCK TO YOURSELF.
DON'T JINX THE REST OF US.
I SHOULD WALK KARA TO SCHOOL TODAY.
AFTER THIS SUMMER WITH ALICE MOVING AWAY AND KARA LOCKING HERSELF IN HER ROOM FOR SO LONG...
THE LAST THING AN ELEVEN-YEAR-OLD GIRL NEEDS IS HER DAD WALKING HER TO CLASS.
SHE'LL BE FINE ON HER BIKE.
I'M JUST WORRIED ABOUT--
OH -- HEY KIDDO!
HEY, CAN'T TALK, I'LL BE LATE!
MIGHT STAY AFTER SCHOOL TO HANG OUT WITH SOME KIDS. I'LL BE HOME BY DINNER!
KARA
SEE? SHE BOUNCED RIGHT BACK.

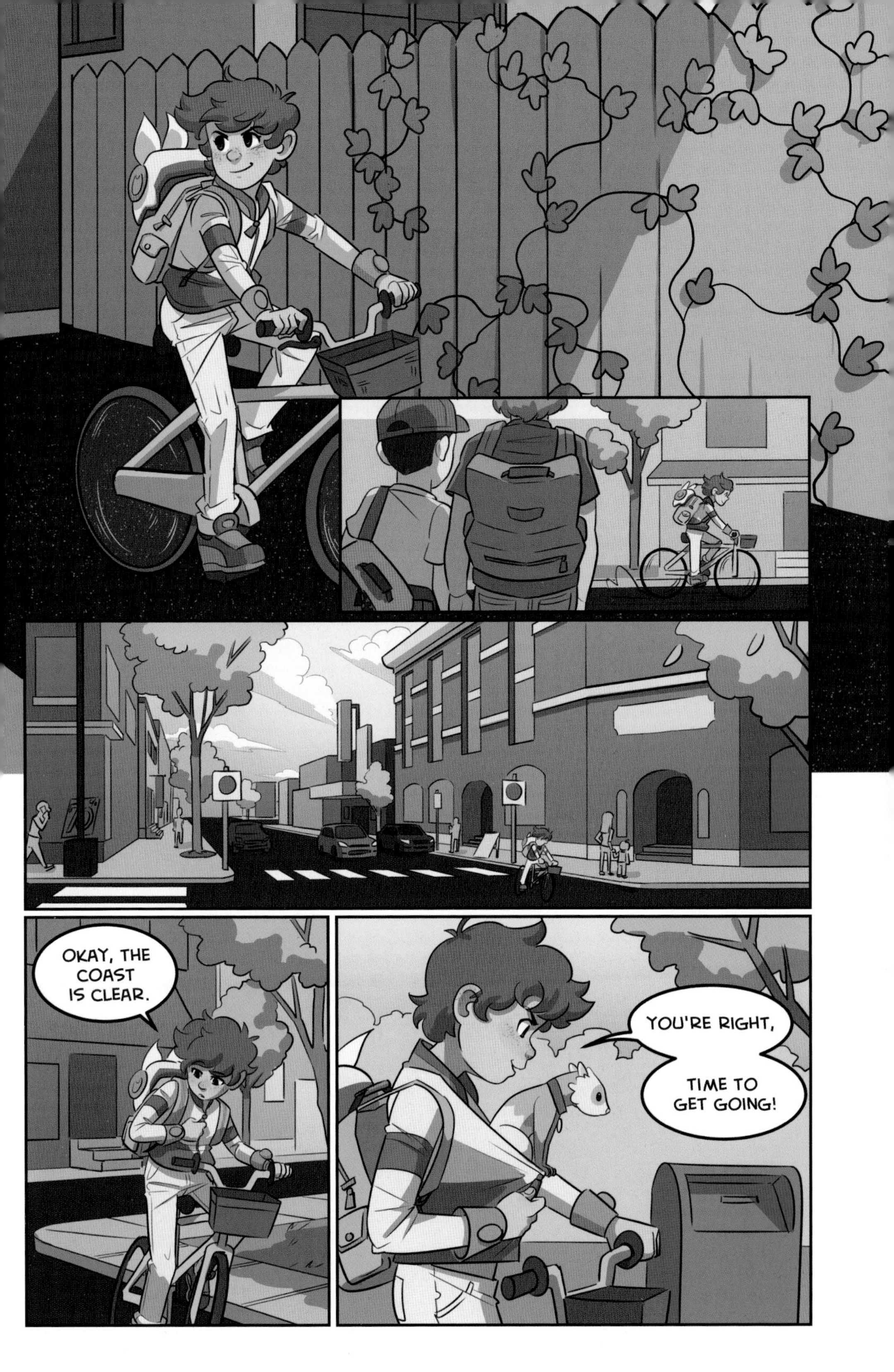
OKAY, THE COAST IS CLEAR.
YOU'RE RIGHT,
TIME TO GET GOING!

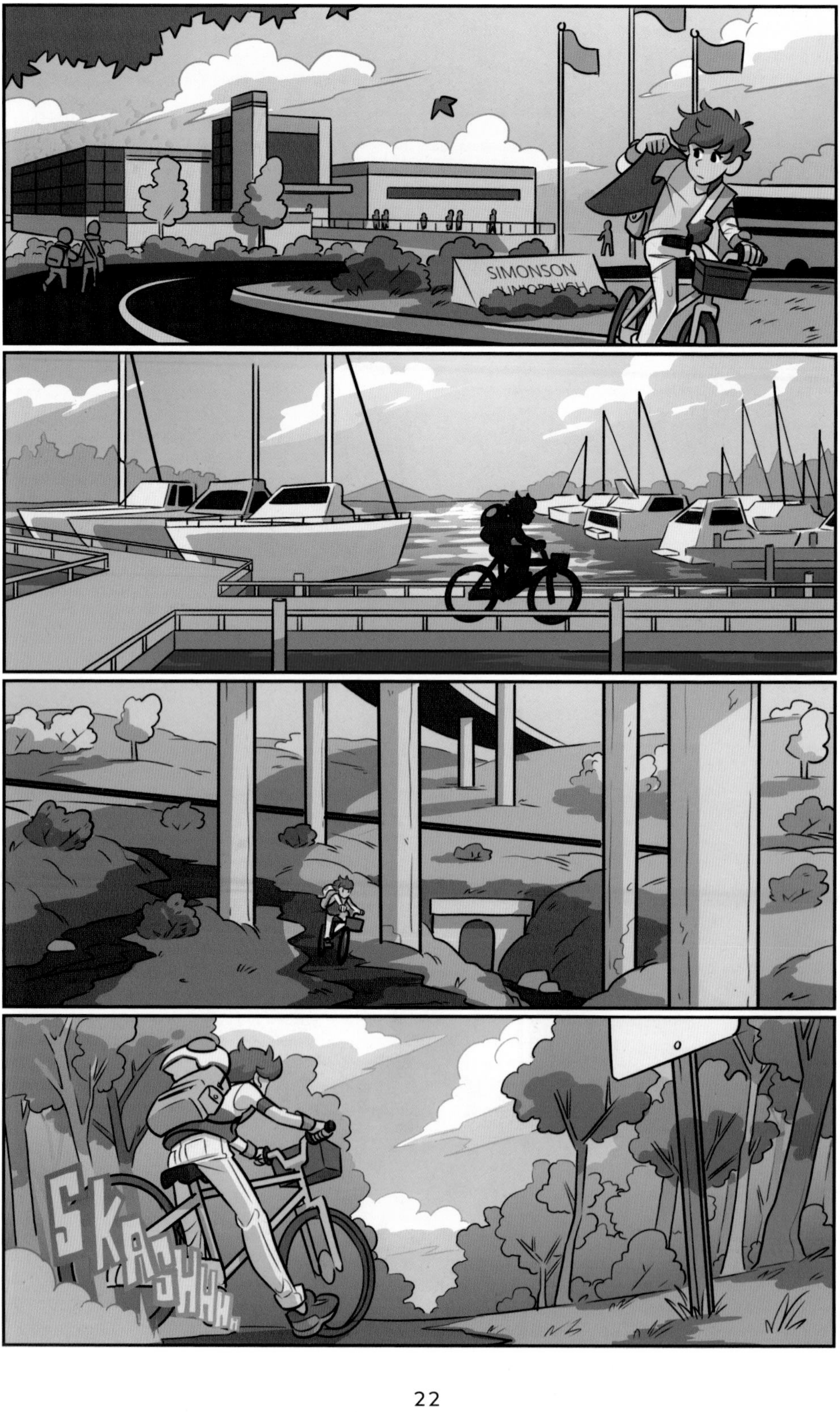
SIMONSON
SKASHHHH

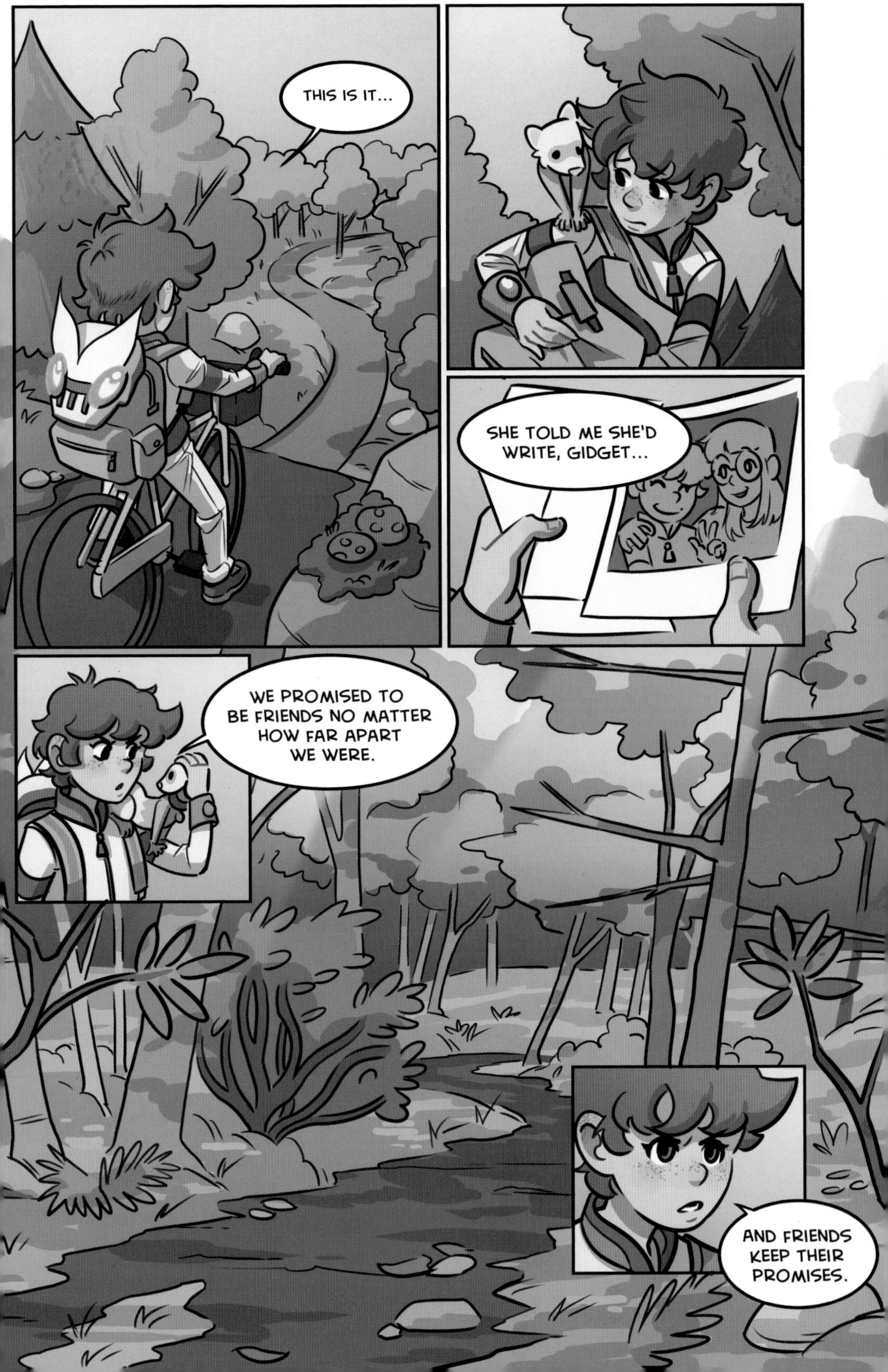
THIS IS IT...
SHE TOLD ME SHE'D WRITE, GIDGET...
WE PROMISED TO BE FRIENDS NO MATTER HOW FAR APART WE WERE.
AND FRIENDS KEEP THEIR PROMISES.

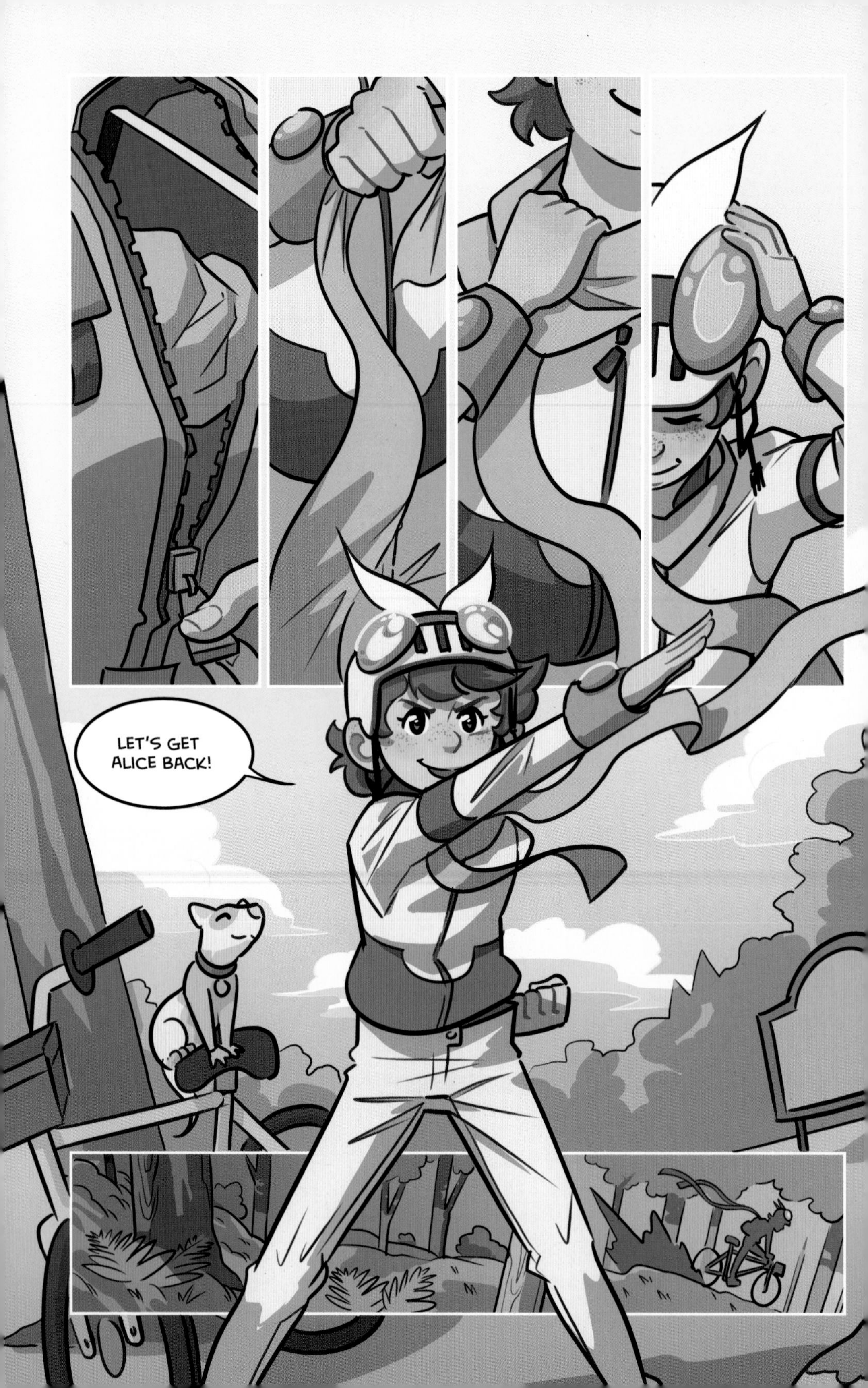
LET'S GET ALICE BACK!

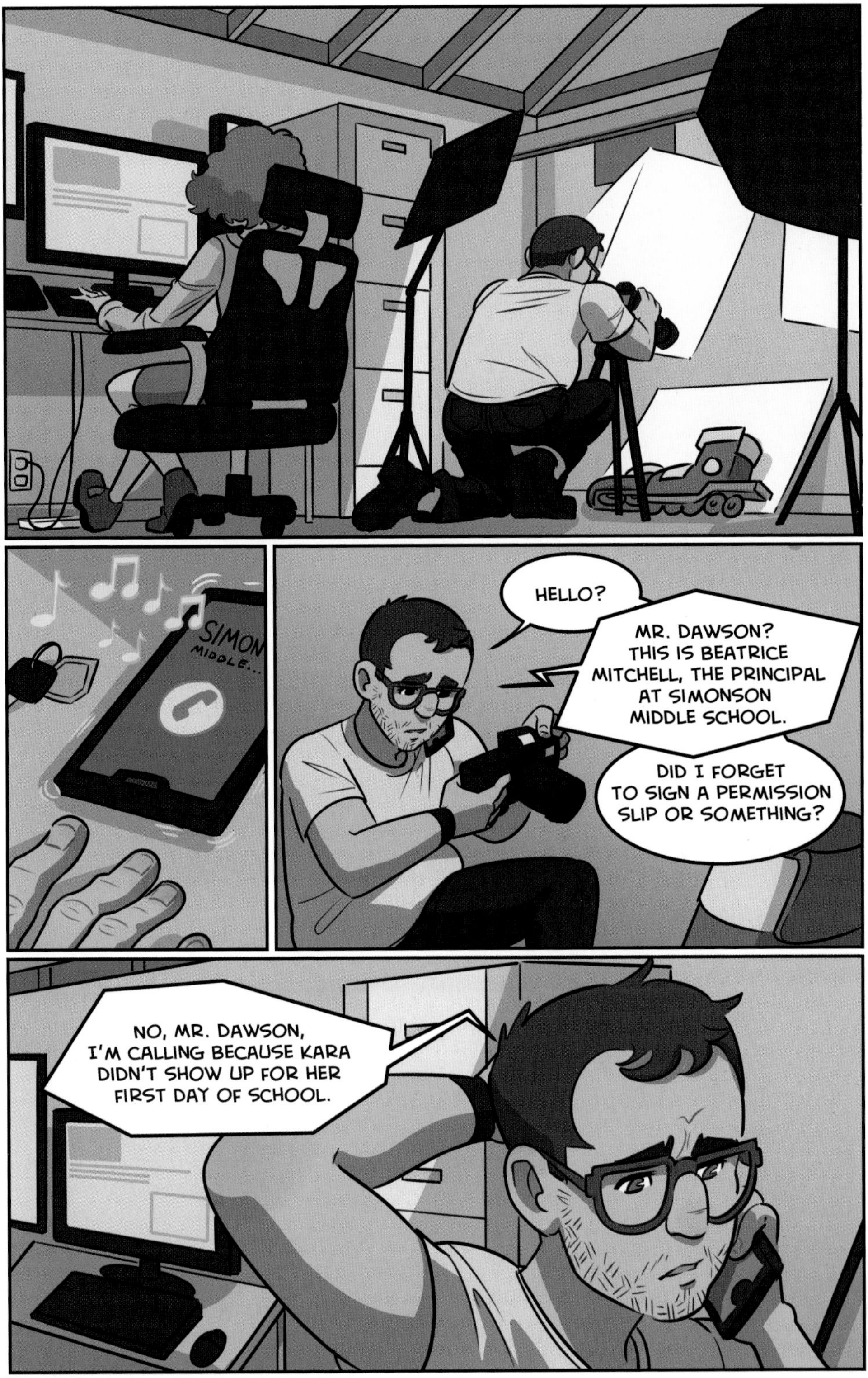
SIMON
MIDDLE...
HELLO?
MR. DAWSON? THIS IS BEATRICE MITCHELL, THE PRINCIPAL AT SIMONSON MIDDLE SCHOOL.
DID I FORGET TO SIGN A PERMISSION SLIP OR SOMETHING?
NO, MR. DAWSON, I'M CALLING BECAUSE KARA DIDN'T SHOW UP FOR HER FIRST DAY OF SCHOOL.

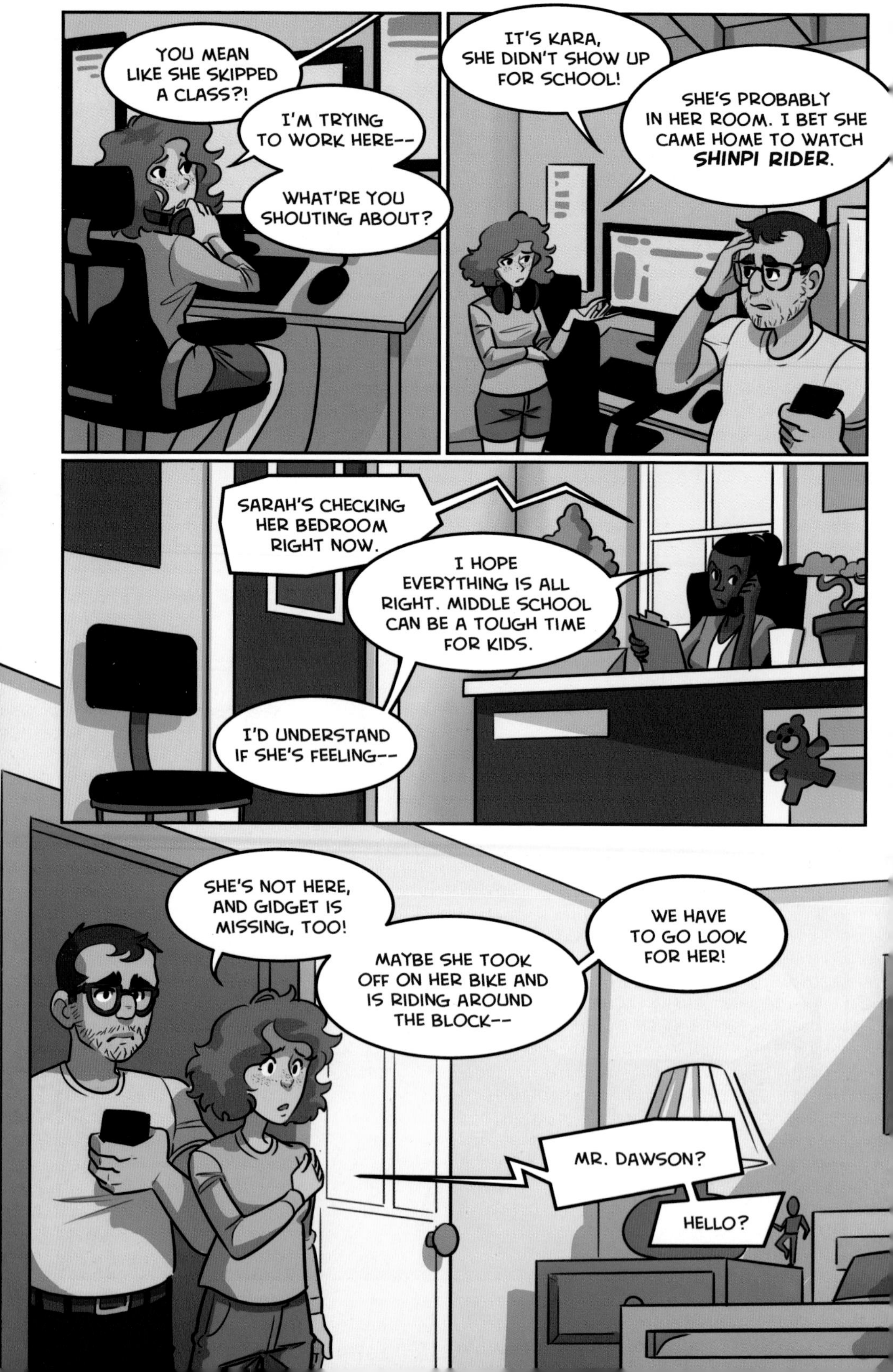
YOU MEAN LIKE SHE SKIPPED A CLASS?!
I'M TRYING TO WORK HERE--
WHAT'RE YOU SHOUTING ABOUT?
IT'S KARA, SHE DIDN'T SHOW UP FOR SCHOOL!
SHE'S PROBABLY IN HER ROOM. I BET SHE CAME HOME TO WATCH SHINPI RIDER.
SARAH'S CHECKING HER BEDROOM RIGHT NOW.
I HOPE EVERYTHING IS ALL RIGHT. MIDDLE SCHOOL CAN BE A TOUGH TIME FOR KIDS.
I'D UNDERSTAND IF SHE'S FEELING--
SHE'S NOT HERE, AND GIDGET IS MISSING, TOO!
MAYBE SHE TOOK OFF ON HER BIKE AND IS RIDING AROUND THE BLOCK--
WE HAVE TO GO LOOK FOR HER!
MR. DAWSON?
HELLO?

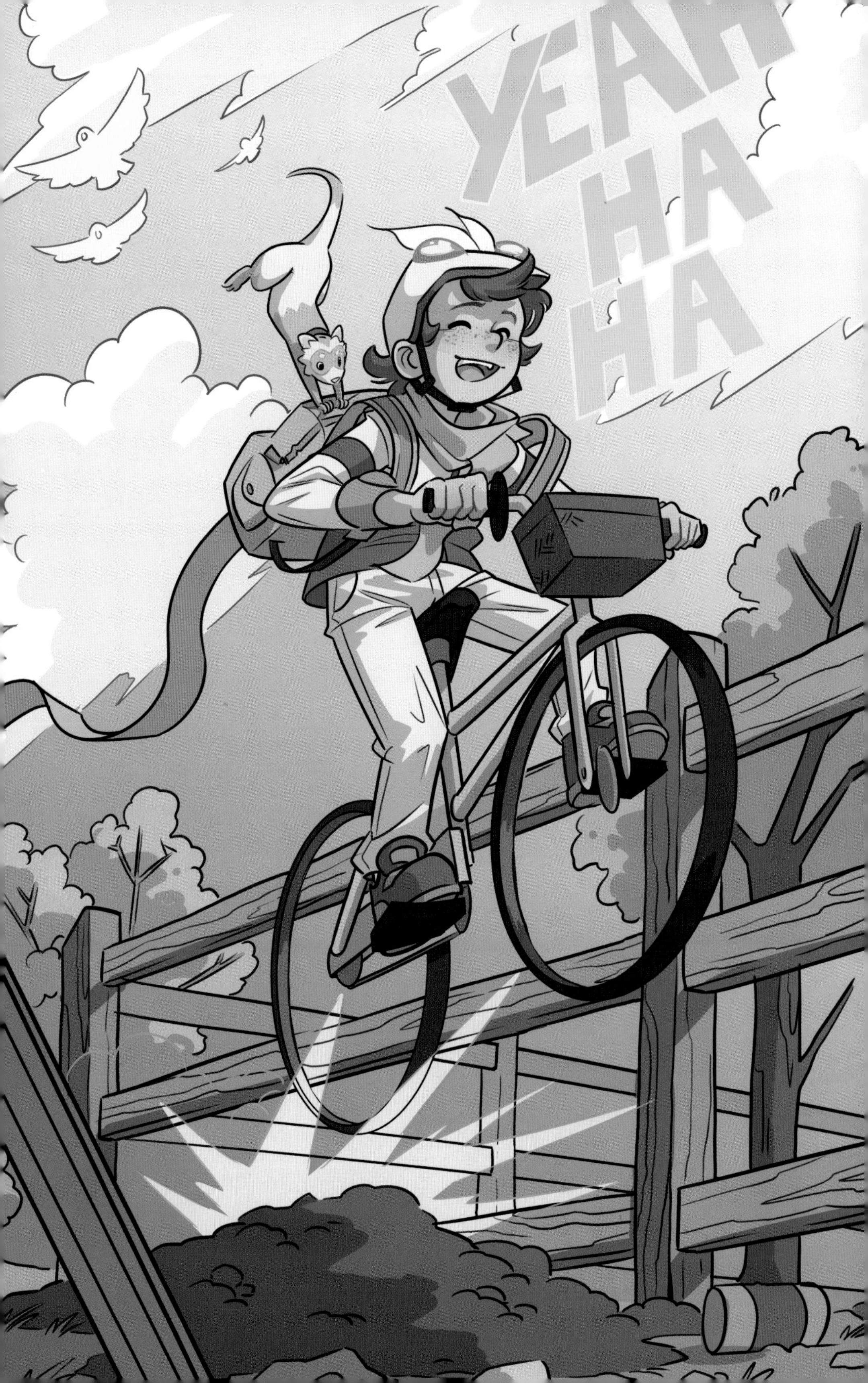
YEAH HA HA

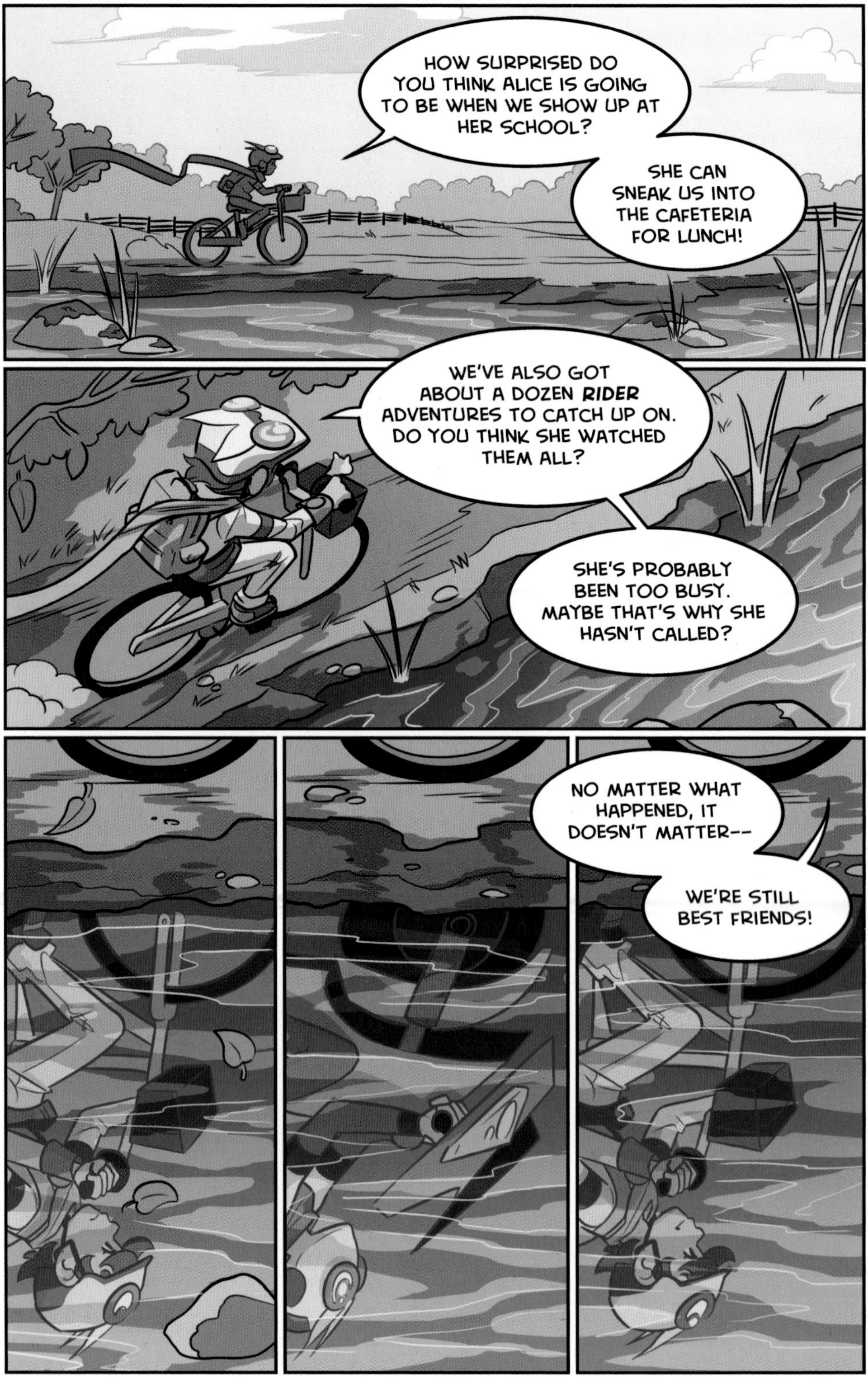
HOW SURPRISED DO YOU THINK ALICE IS GOING TO BE WHEN WE SHOW UP AT HER SCHOOL?
SHE CAN SNEAK US INTO THE CAFETERIA FOR LUNCH!
WE'VE ALSO GOT ABOUT A DOZEN RIDER ADVENTURES TO CATCH UP ON. DO YOU THINK SHE WATCHED THEM ALL?
SHE'S PROBABLY BEEN TOO BUSY. MAYBE THAT'S WHY SHE HASN'T CALLED?
NO MATTER WHAT HAPPENED, IT DOESN'T MATTER--
WE'RE STILL BEST FRIENDS!

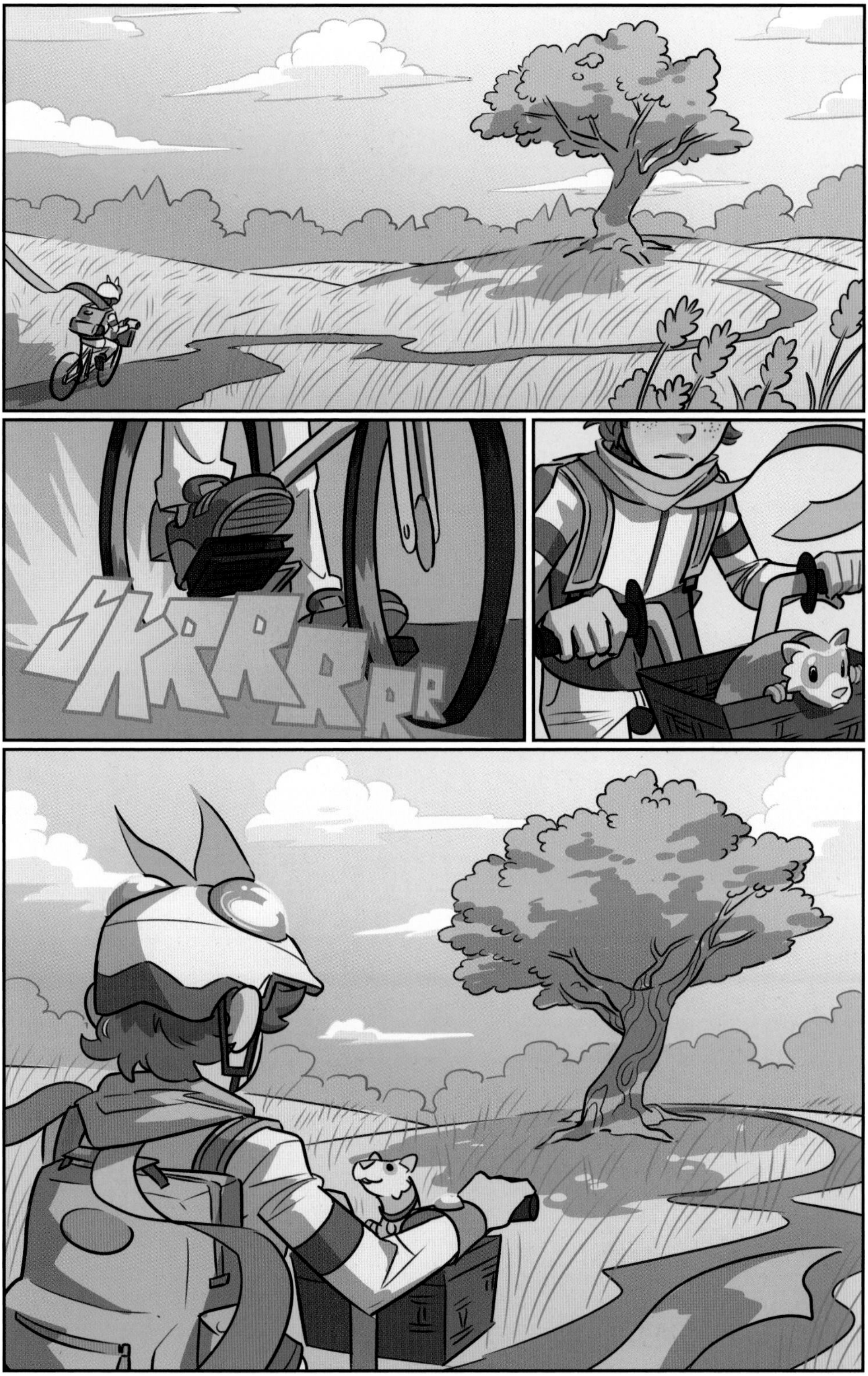
SKRRRRR

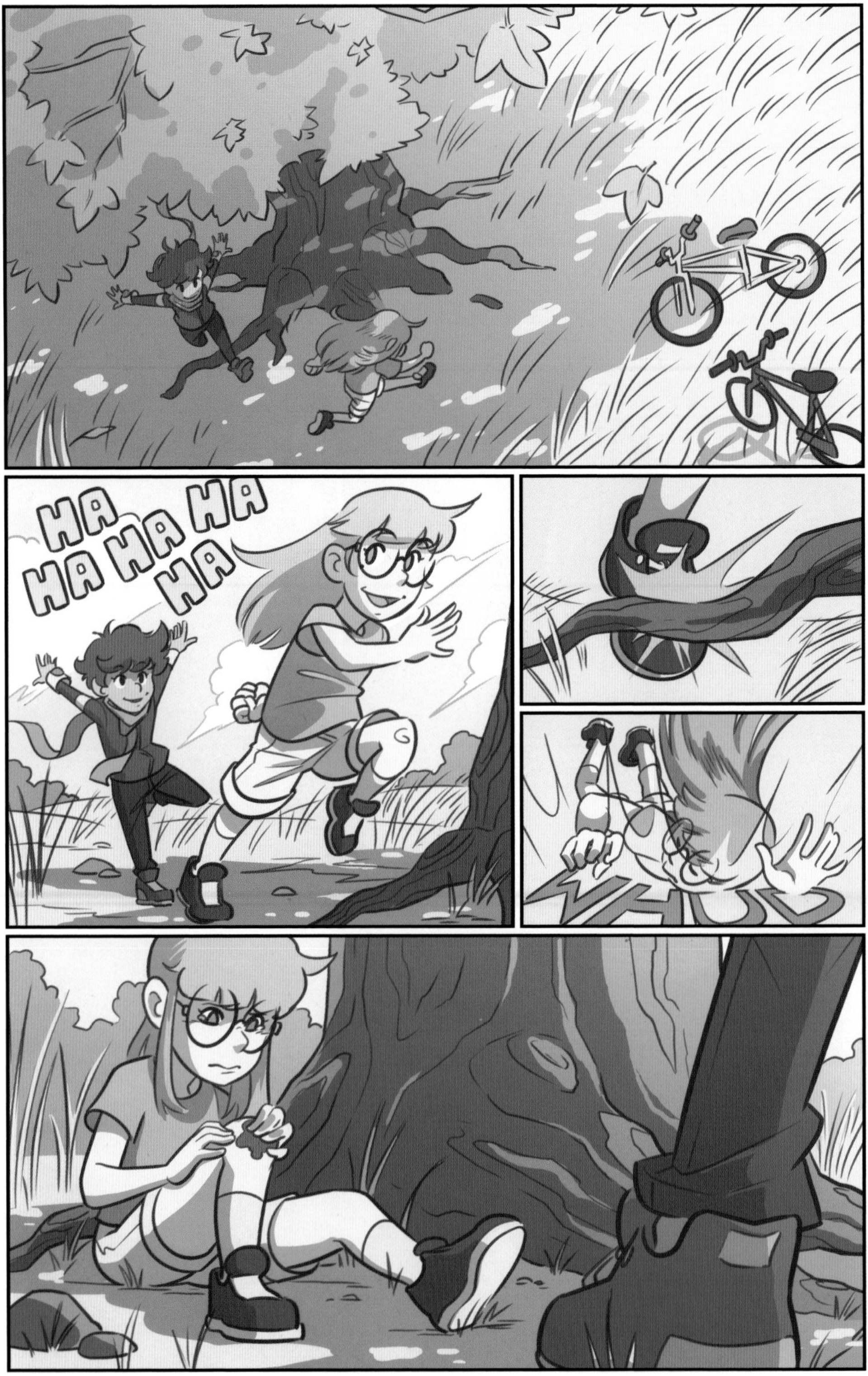
HA HA HA HA HA HA

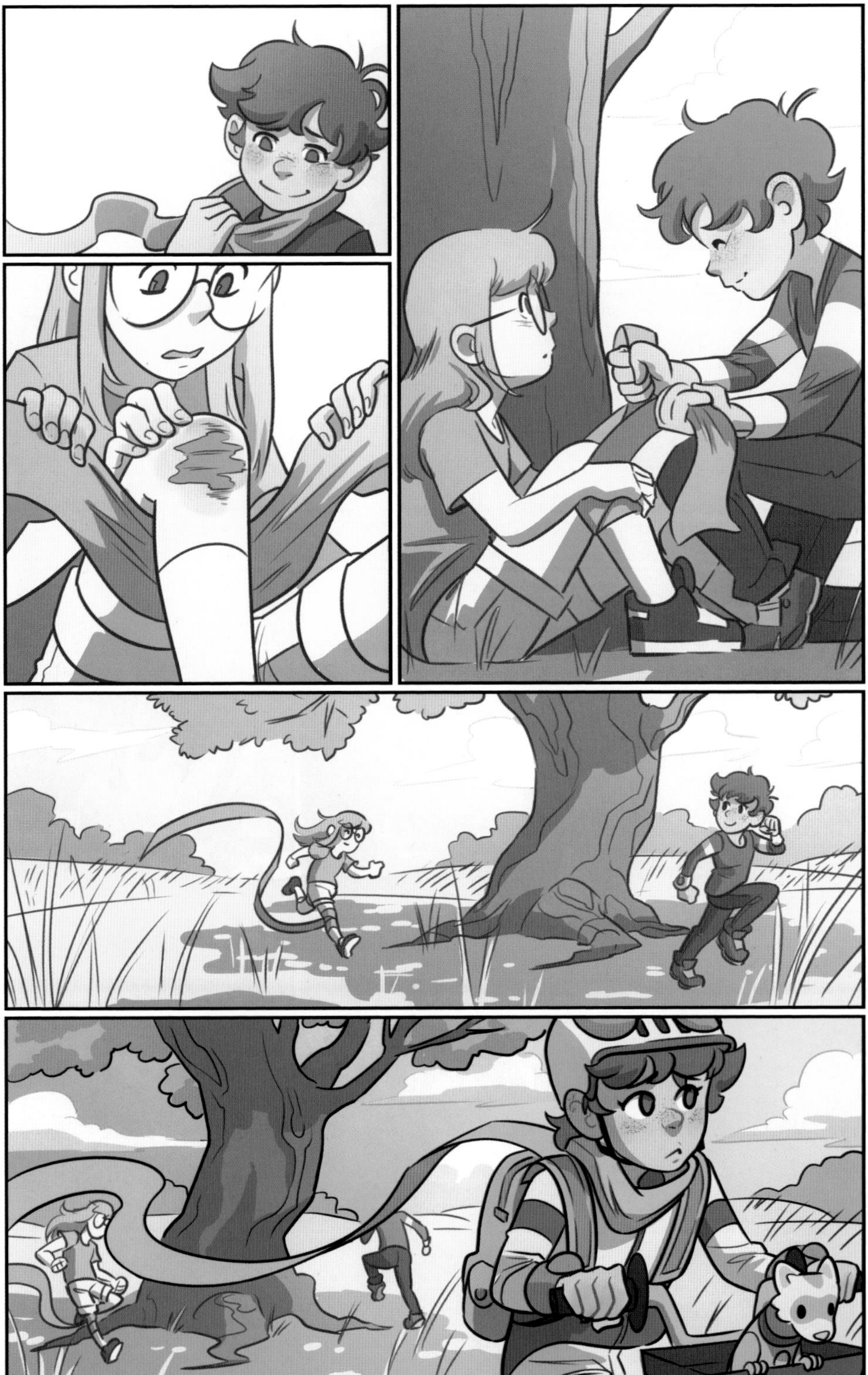

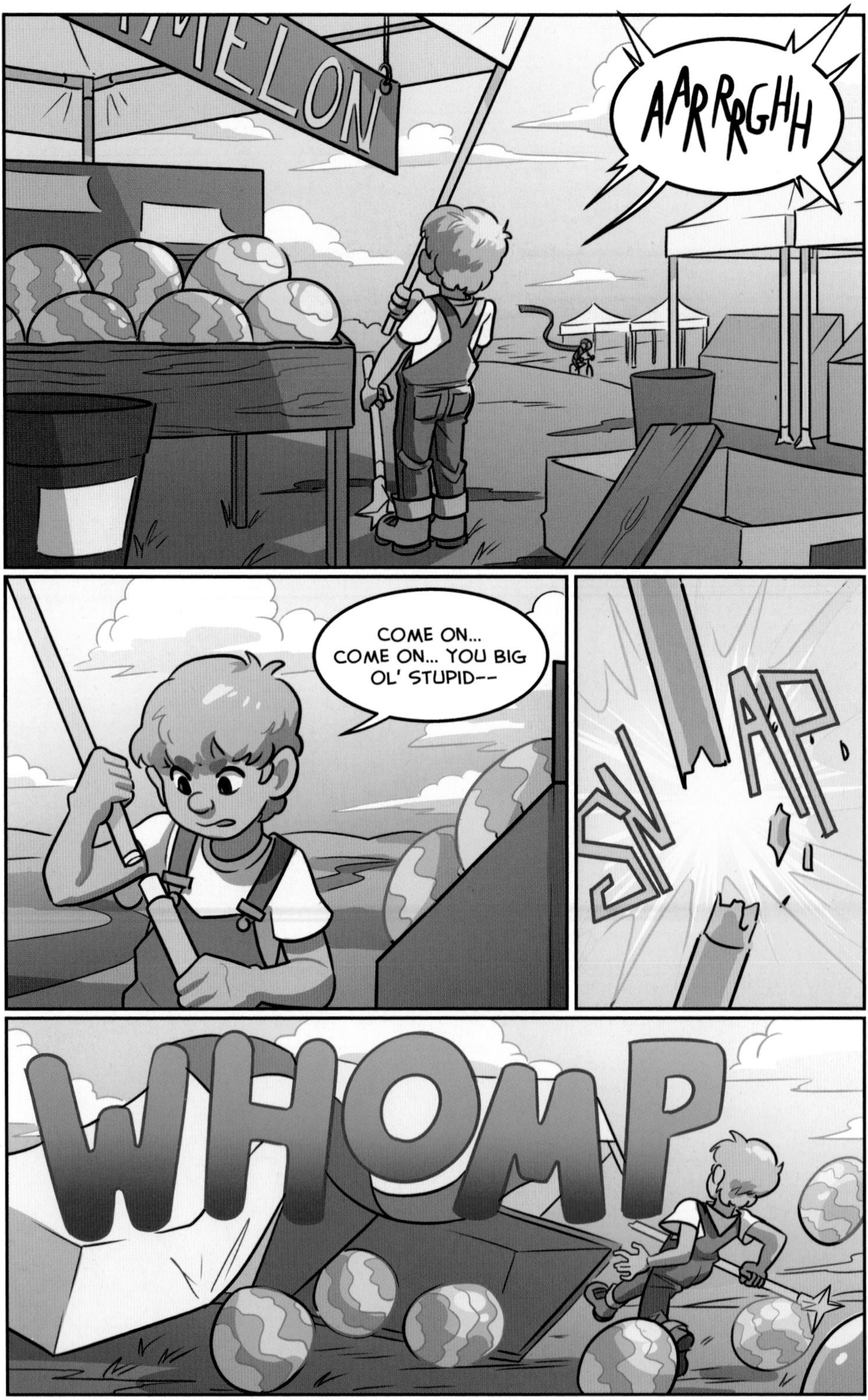
MELON
AARRRGHH
COME ON... COME ON... YOU BIG OL' STUPID--
SNAP
WHOMP

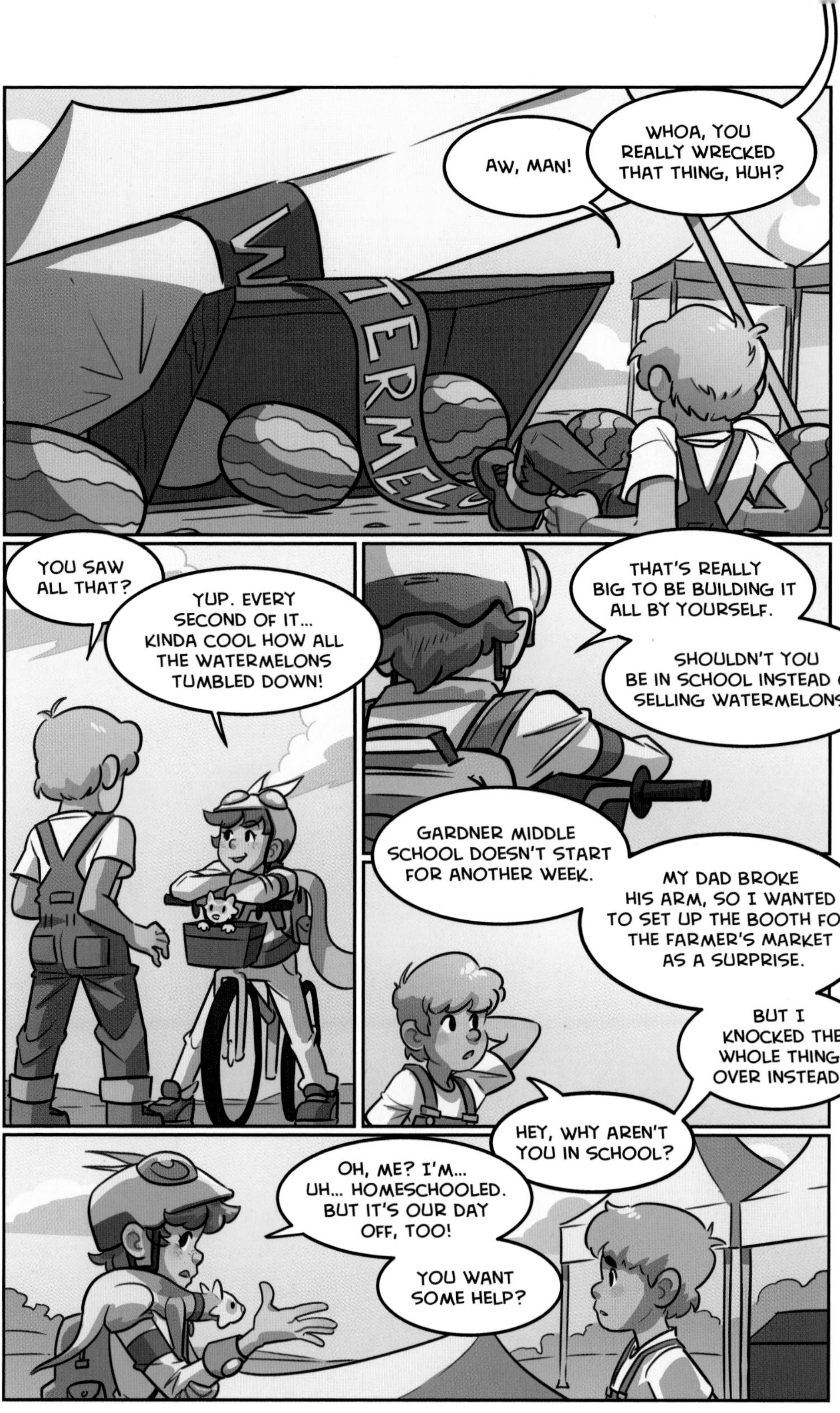
AW, MAN!
WHOA, YOU REALLY WRECKED THAT THING, HUH?
YOU SAW ALL THAT?
YUP. EVERY SECOND OF IT... KINDA COOL HOW ALL THE WATERMELONS TUMBLED DOWN!
THAT'S REALLY BIG TO BE BUILDING IT ALL BY YOURSELF.
SHOULDN'T YOU BE IN SCHOOL INSTEAD OF SELLING WATERMELONS?
GARDNER MIDDLE SCHOOL DOESN'T START FOR ANOTHER WEEK.
MY DAD BROKE HIS ARM, SO I WANTED TO SET UP THE BOOTH FOR THE FARMER'S MARKET AS A SURPRISE.
BUT I KNOCKED THE WHOLE THING OVER INSTEAD.
HEY, WHY AREN'T YOU IN SCHOOL?
OH, ME? I'M... UH... HOMESCHOOLED. BUT IT'S OUR DAY OFF, TOO!
YOU WANT SOME HELP?

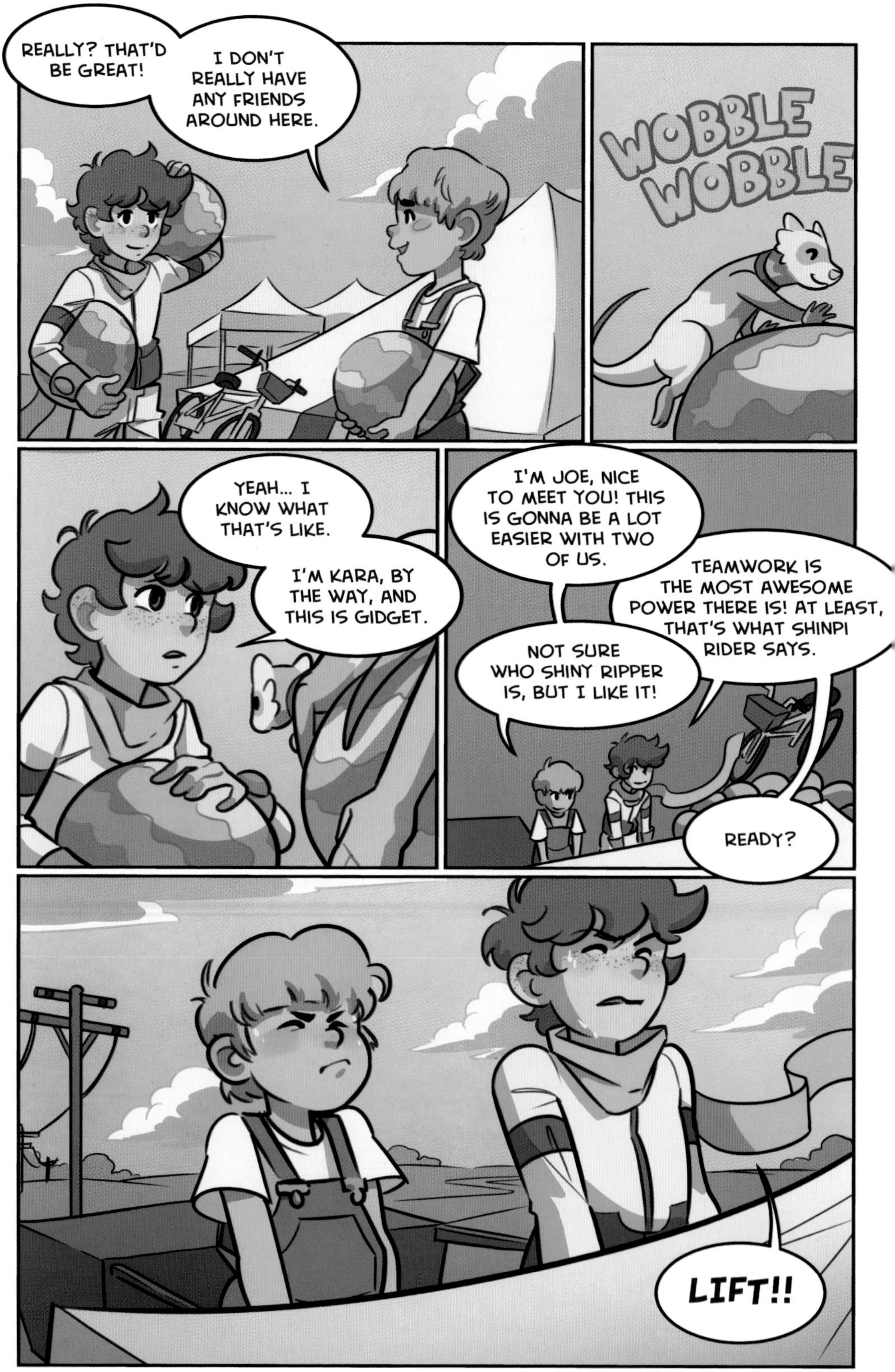
REALLY? THAT'D BE GREAT!
I DON'T REALLY HAVE ANY FRIENDS AROUND HERE.
WOBBLE WOBBLE
YEAH... I KNOW WHAT THAT'S LIKE.
I'M KARA, BY THE WAY, AND THIS IS GIDGET.
I'M JOE, NICE TO MEET YOU! THIS IS GONNA BE A LOT EASIER WITH TWO OF US.
TEAMWORK IS THE MOST AWESOME POWER THERE IS! AT LEAST, THAT'S WHAT SHINPI RIDER SAYS.
NOT SURE WHO SHINY RIPPER IS, BUT I LIKE IT!
READY?
LIFT!!

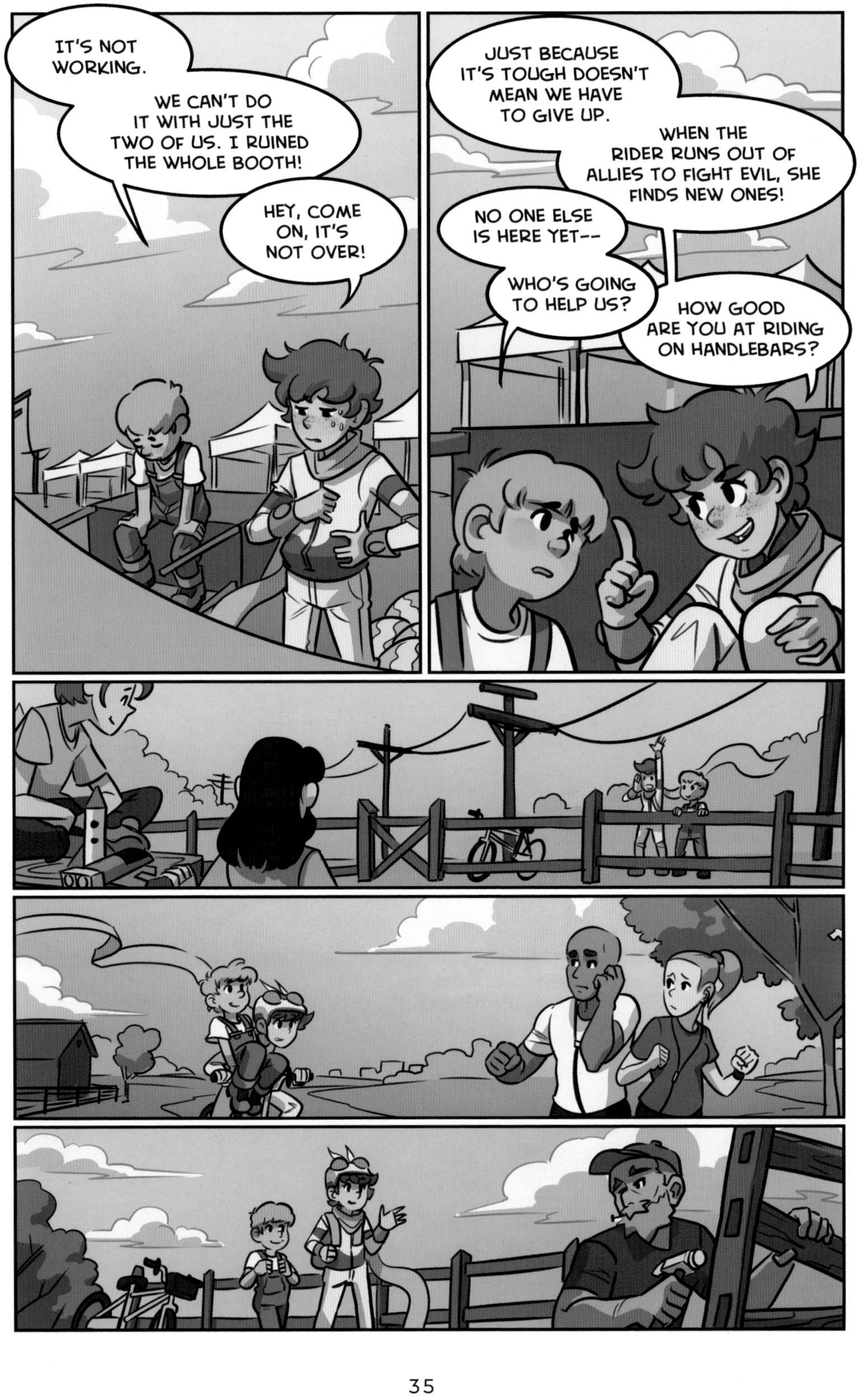
IT'S NOT WORKING.
WE CAN'T DO IT WITH JUST THE TWO OF US. I RUINED THE WHOLE BOOTH!
HEY, COME ON, IT'S NOT OVER!
JUST BECAUSE IT'S TOUGH DOESN'T MEAN WE HAVE TO GIVE UP.
WHEN THE RIDER RUNS OUT OF ALLIES TO FIGHT EVIL, SHE FINDS NEW ONES!
NO ONE ELSE IS HERE YET--
WHO'S GOING TO HELP US?
HOW GOOD ARE YOU AT RIDING ON HANDLEBARS?

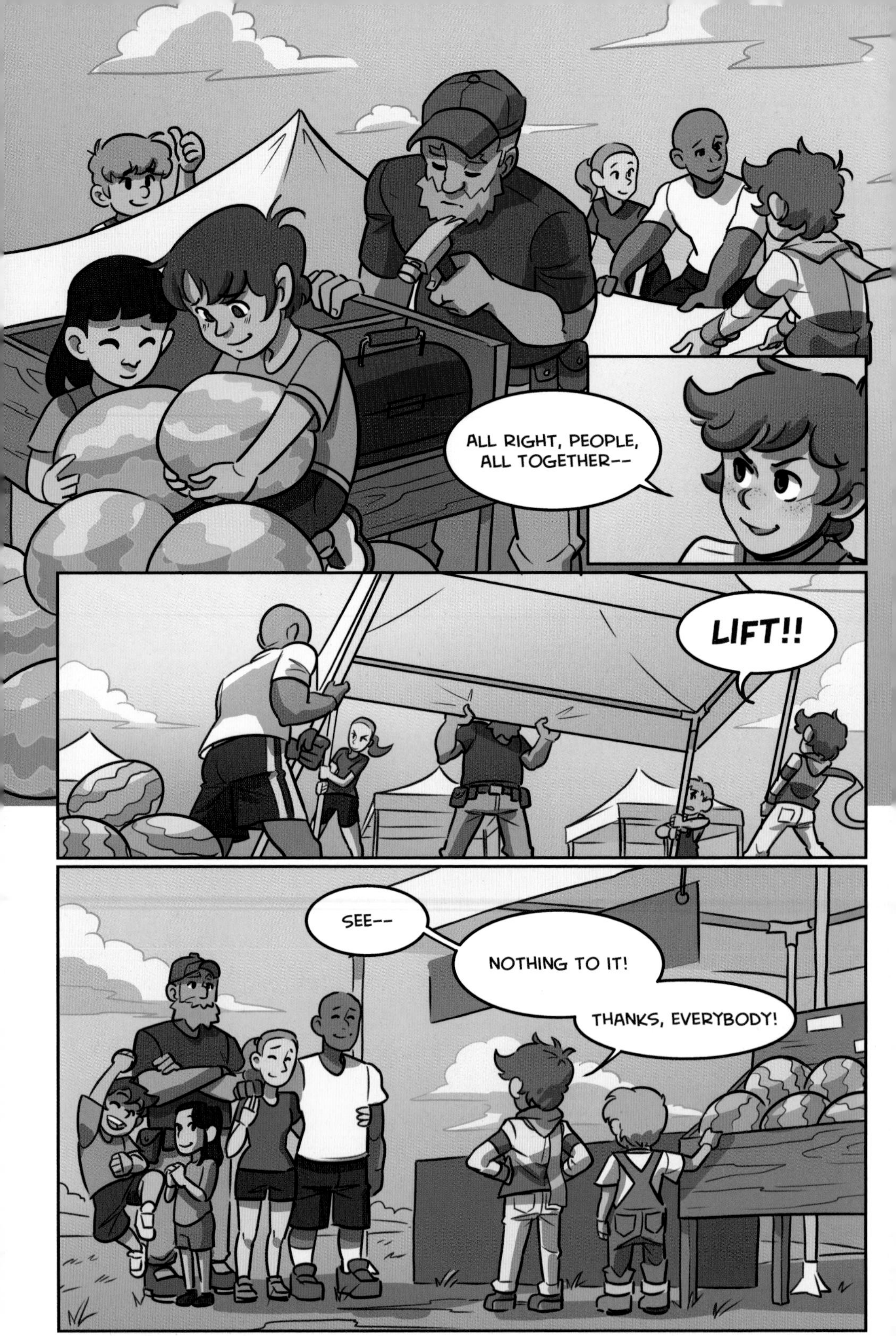
ALL RIGHT, PEOPLE, ALL TOGETHER--
LIFT!!
SEE--
NOTHING TO IT!
THANKS, EVERYBODY!

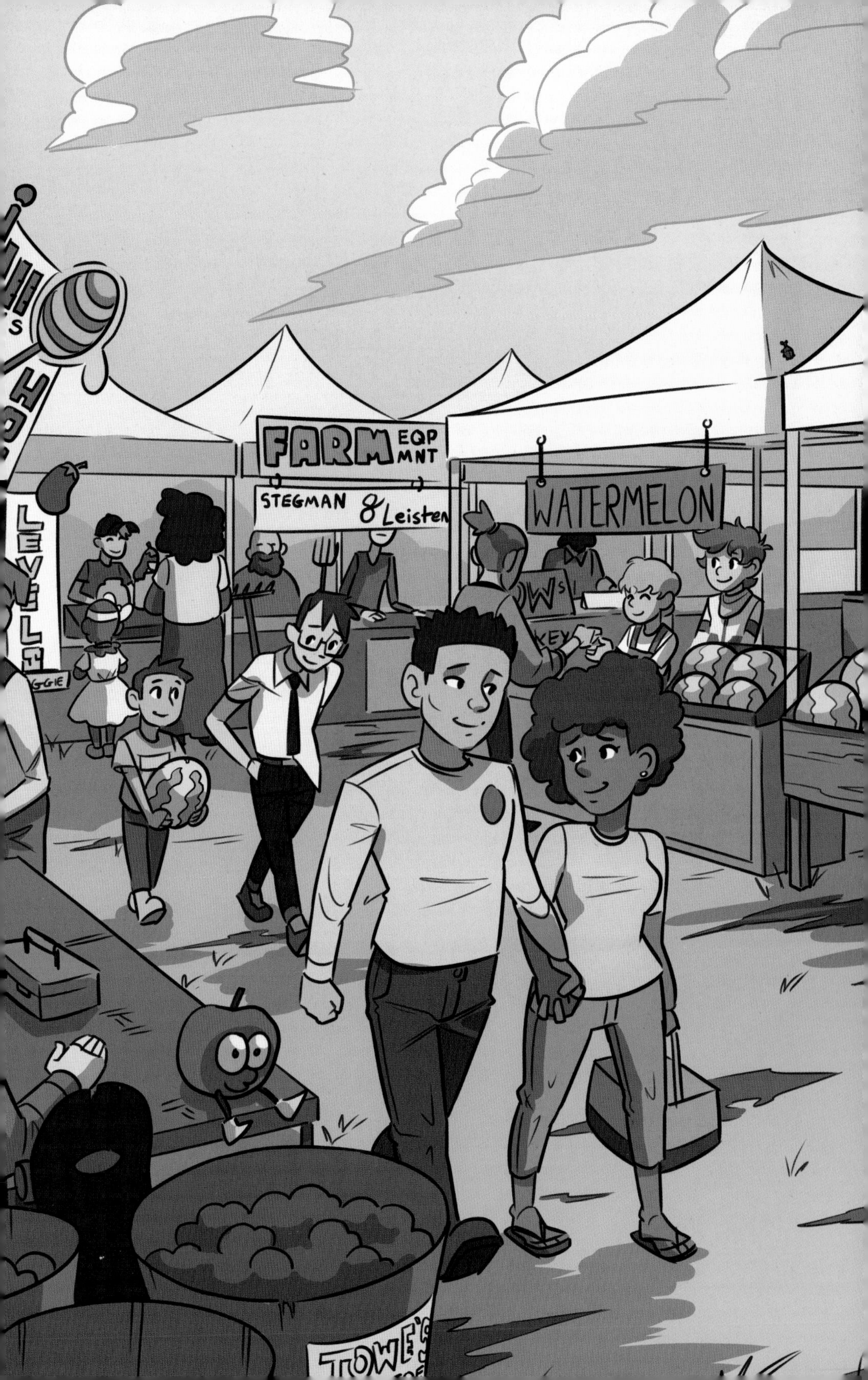
FARM EQP MNT
STEGMAN & Leisten
WATERMELON

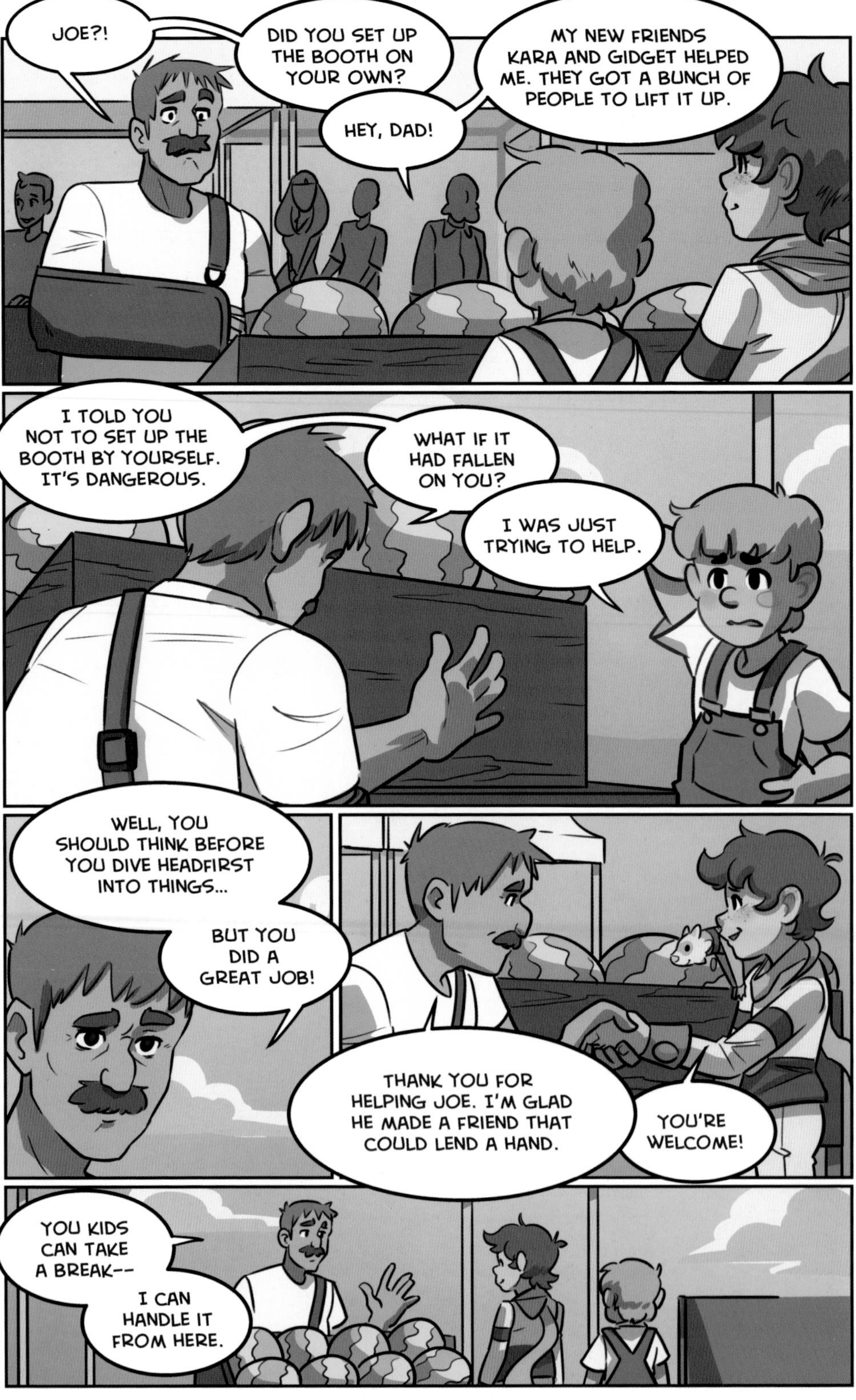
JOE?!
DID YOU SET UP THE BOOTH ON YOUR OWN?
HEY, DAD!
MY NEW FRIENDS KARA AND GIDGET HELPED ME. THEY GOT A BUNCH OF PEOPLE TO LIFT IT UP.
I TOLD YOU NOT TO SET UP THE BOOTH BY YOURSELF. IT'S DANGEROUS.
WHAT IF IT HAD FALLEN ON YOU?
I WAS JUST TRYING TO HELP.
WELL, YOU SHOULD THINK BEFORE YOU DIVE HEADFIRST INTO THINGS...
BUT YOU DID A GREAT JOB!
THANK YOU FOR HELPING JOE. I'M GLAD HE MADE A FRIEND THAT COULD LEND A HAND.
YOU'RE WELCOME!
YOU KIDS CAN TAKE A BREAK--
I CAN HANDLE IT FROM HERE.

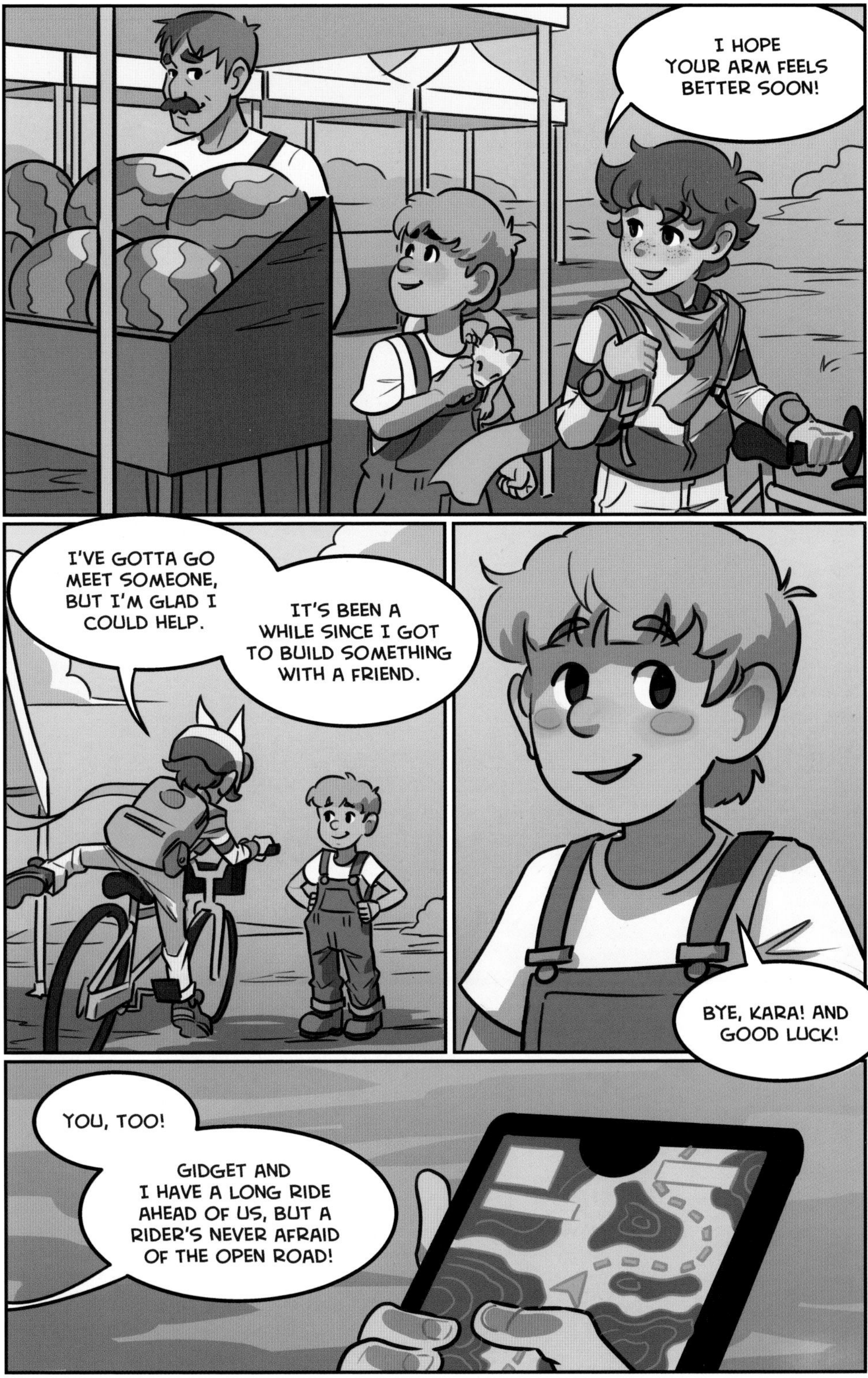
I HOPE YOUR ARM FEELS BETTER SOON!
I'VE GOTTA GO MEET SOMEONE, BUT I'M GLAD I COULD HELP.
IT'S BEEN A WHILE SINCE I GOT TO BUILD SOMETHING WITH A FRIEND.
BYE, KARA! AND GOOD LUCK!
YOU, TOO!
GIDGET AND I HAVE A LONG RIDE AHEAD OF US, BUT A RIDER'S NEVER AFRAID OF THE OPEN ROAD!

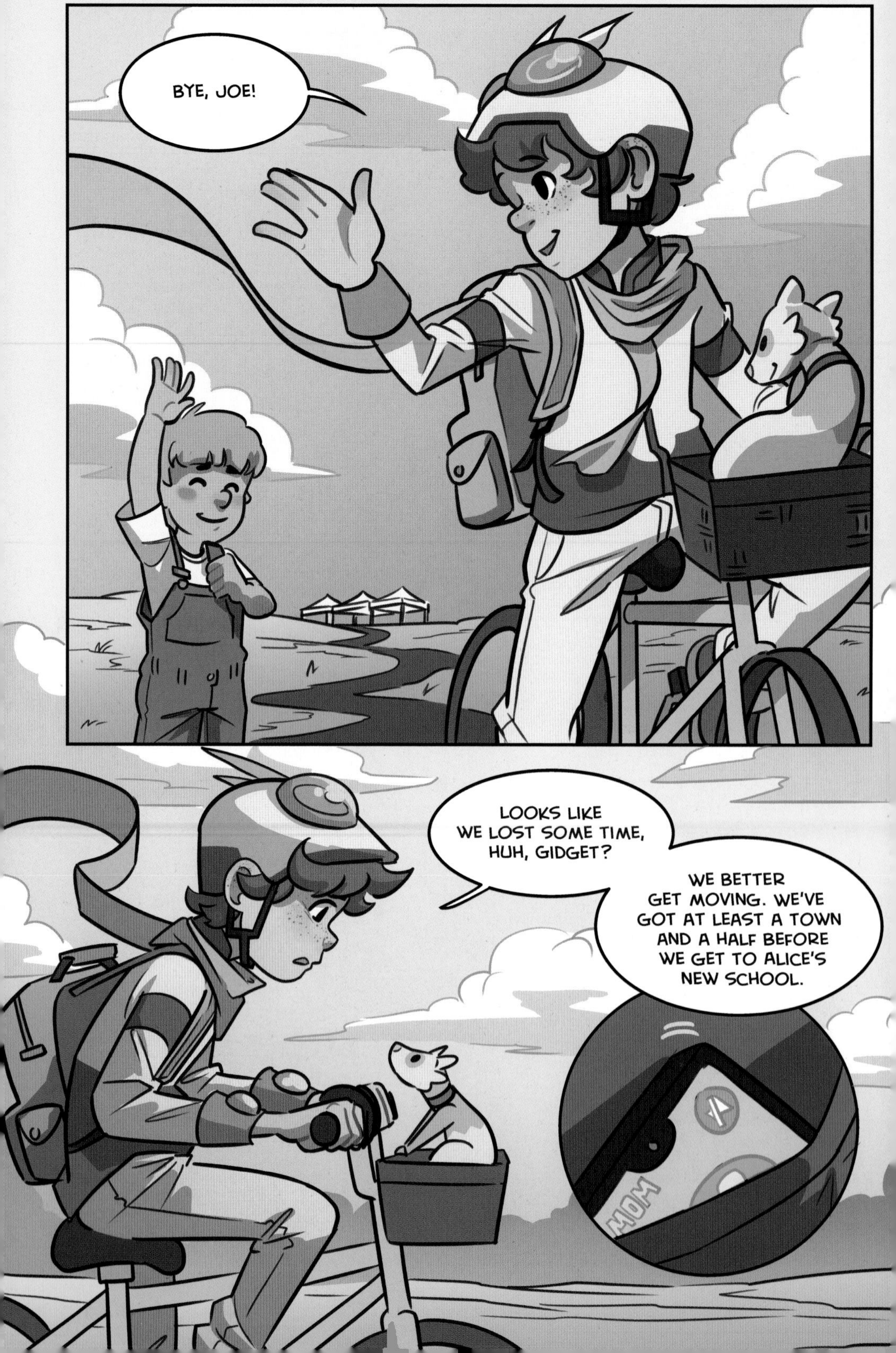
BYE, JOE!
LOOKS LIKE WE LOST SOME TIME, HUH, GIDGET?
WE BETTER GET MOVING. WE'VE GOT AT LEAST A TOWN AND A HALF BEFORE WE GET TO ALICE'S NEW SCHOOL.
MOM

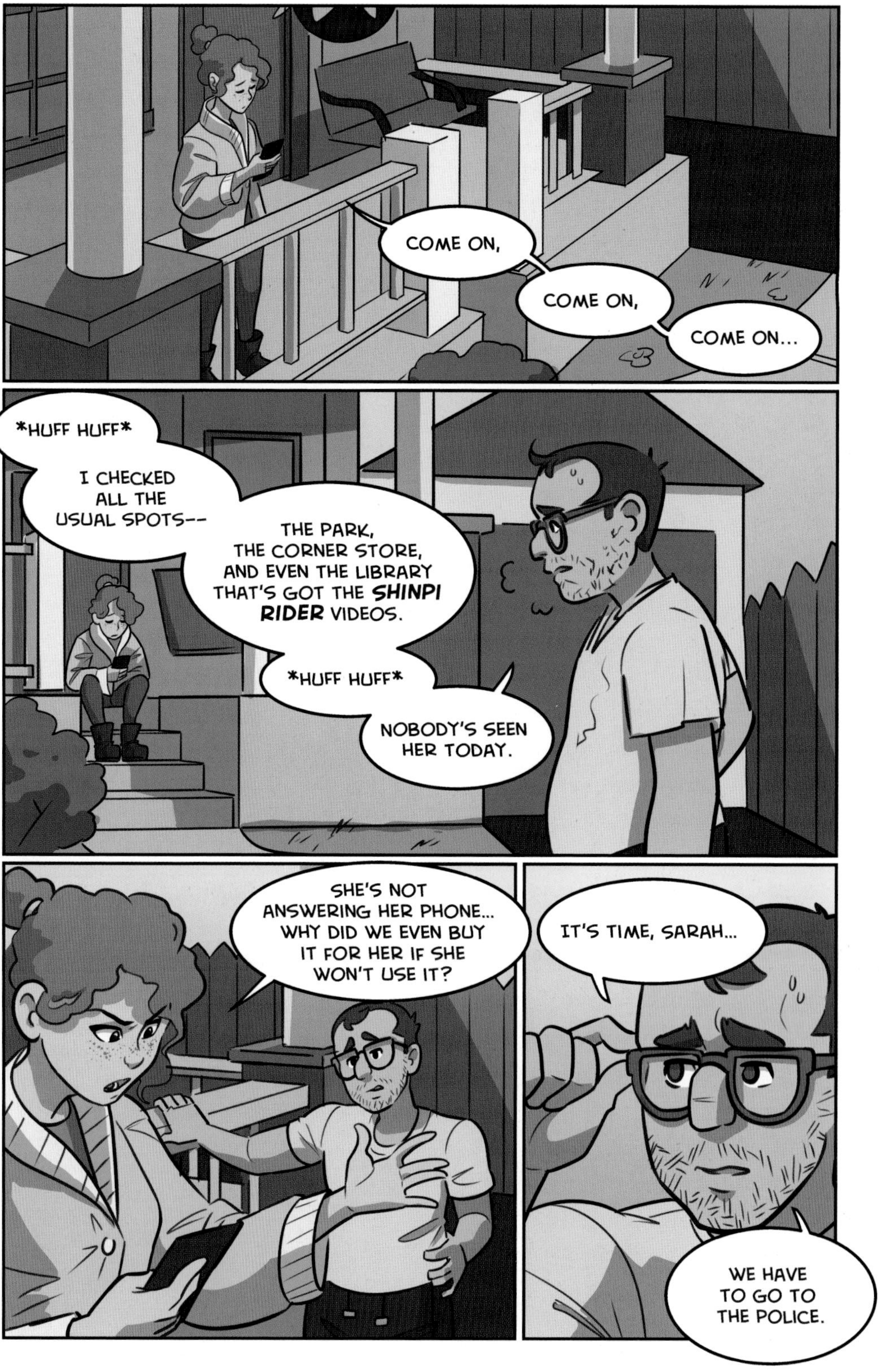
COME ON,
COME ON,
COME ON...
HUFF HUFF
I CHECKED ALL THE USUAL SPOTS--
THE PARK, THE CORNER STORE, AND EVEN THE LIBRARY THAT'S GOT THE **SHINPI RIDER** VIDEOS.
HUFF HUFF
NOBODY'S SEEN HER TODAY.
SHE'S NOT ANSWERING HER PHONE... WHY DID WE EVEN BUY IT FOR HER IF SHE WON'T USE IT?
IT'S TIME, SARAH...
WE HAVE TO GO TO THE POLICE.

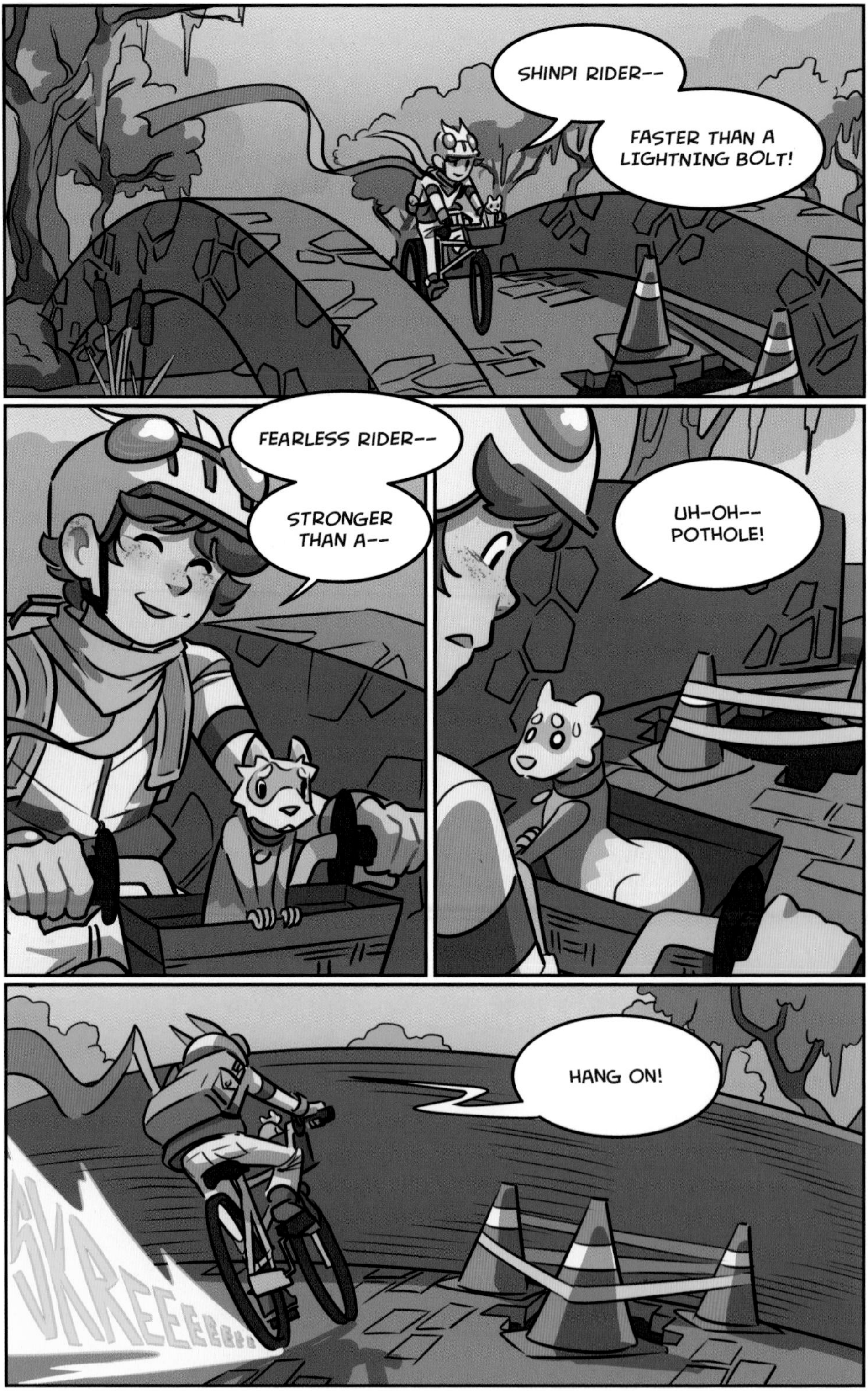
SHINPI RIDER--
FASTER THAN A LIGHTNING BOLT!
FEARLESS RIDER--
STRONGER THAN A--
UH-OH-- POTHOLE!
HANG ON!
SKREEEEEEE

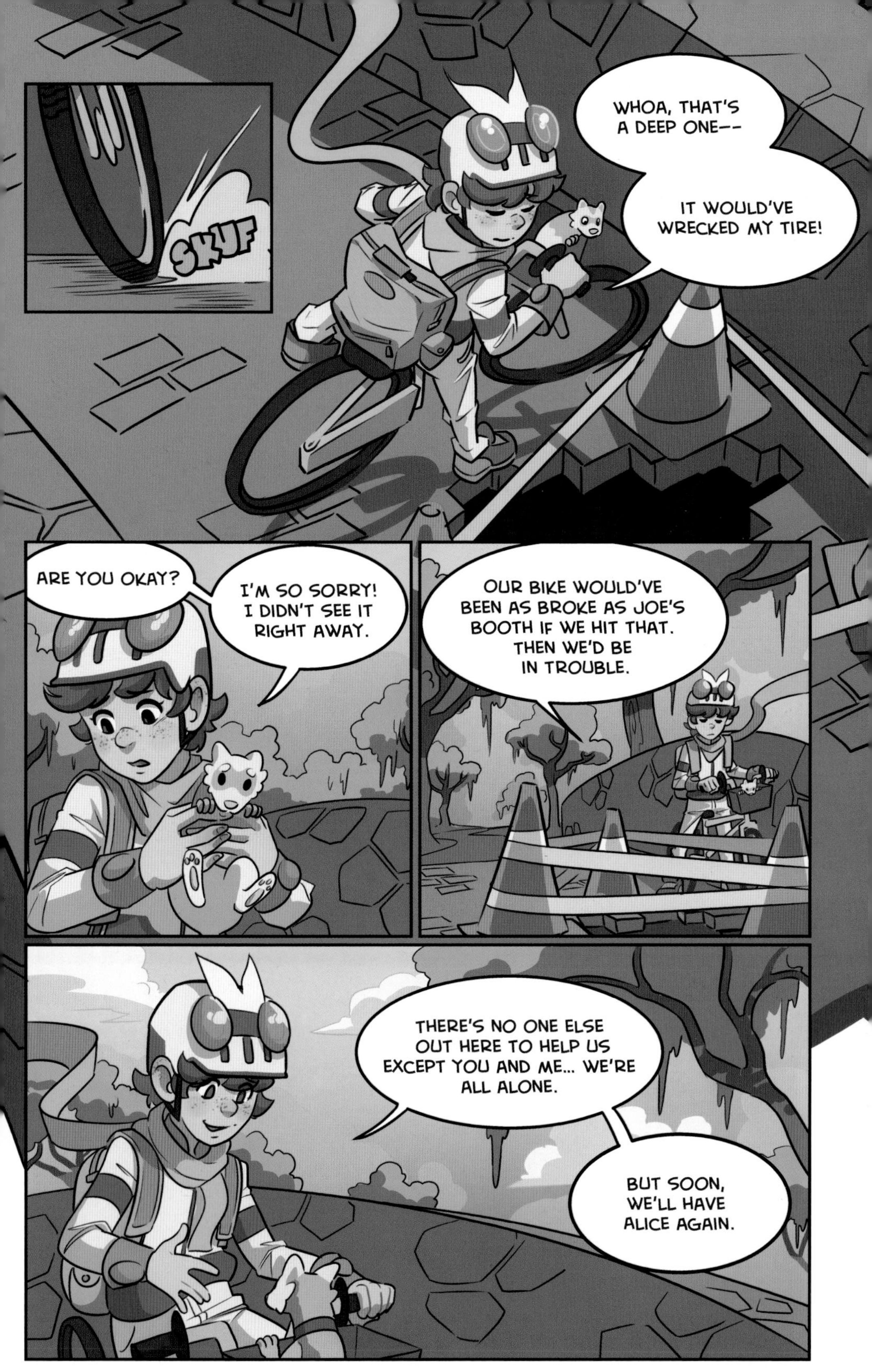
SKUF
WHOA, THAT'S A DEEP ONE--
IT WOULD'VE WRECKED MY TIRE!
ARE YOU OKAY?
I'M SO SORRY! I DIDN'T SEE IT RIGHT AWAY.
OUR BIKE WOULD'VE BEEN AS BROKE AS JOE'S BOOTH IF WE HIT THAT. THEN WE'D BE IN TROUBLE.
THERE'S NO ONE ELSE OUT HERE TO HELP US EXCEPT YOU AND ME... WE'RE ALL ALONE.
BUT SOON, WE'LL HAVE ALICE AGAIN.

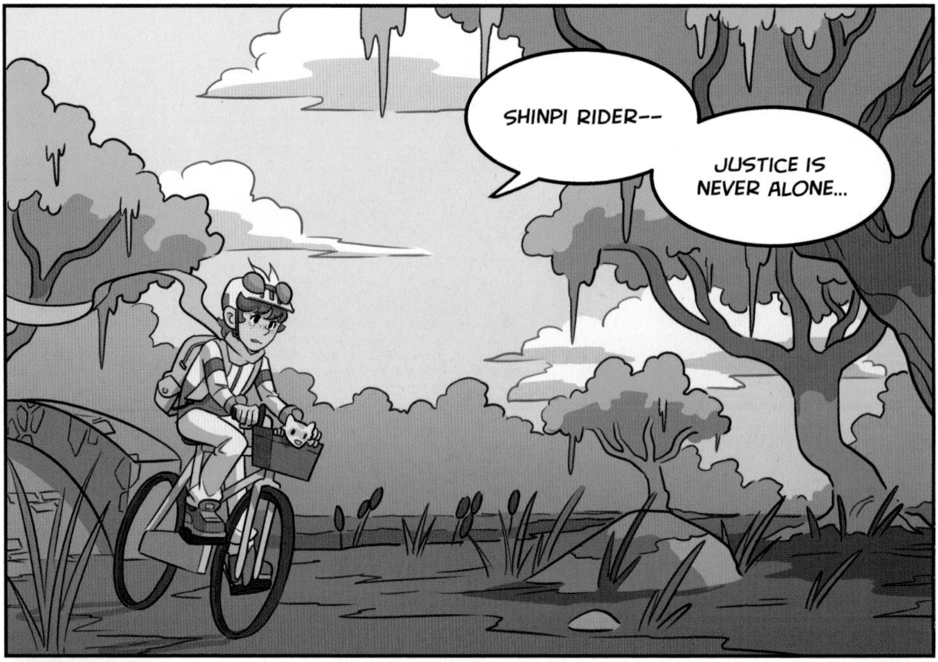
SHINPI RIDER--
JUSTICE IS NEVER ALONE...

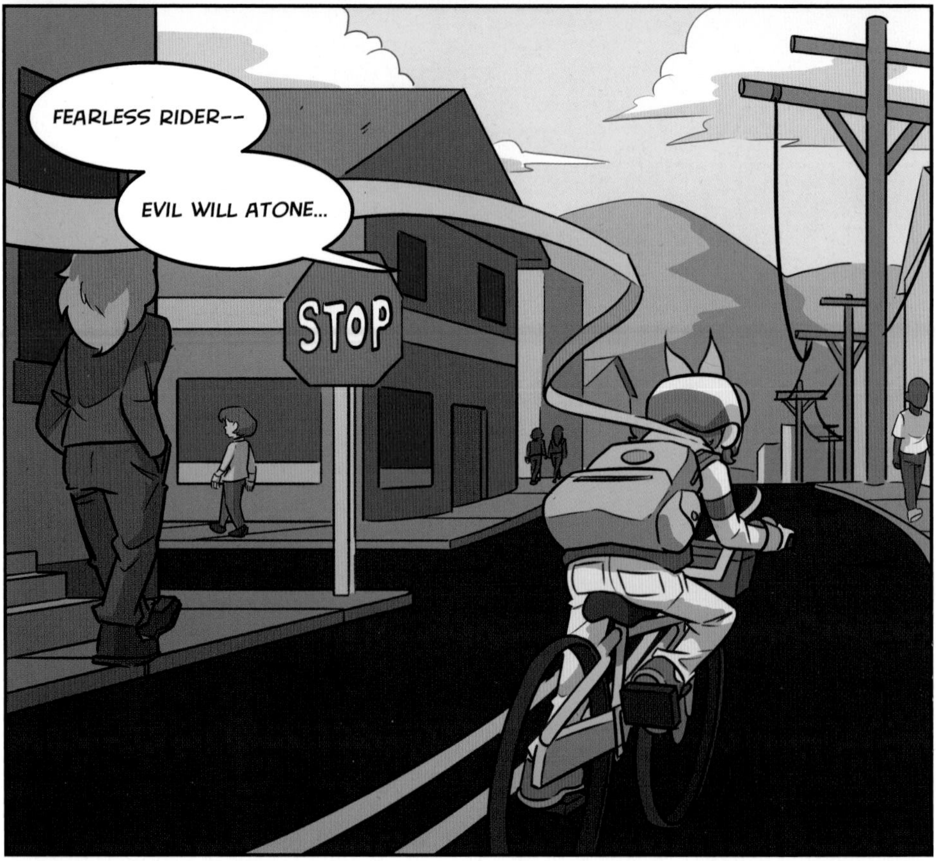
FEARLESS RIDER--
EVIL WILL ATONE...
STOP

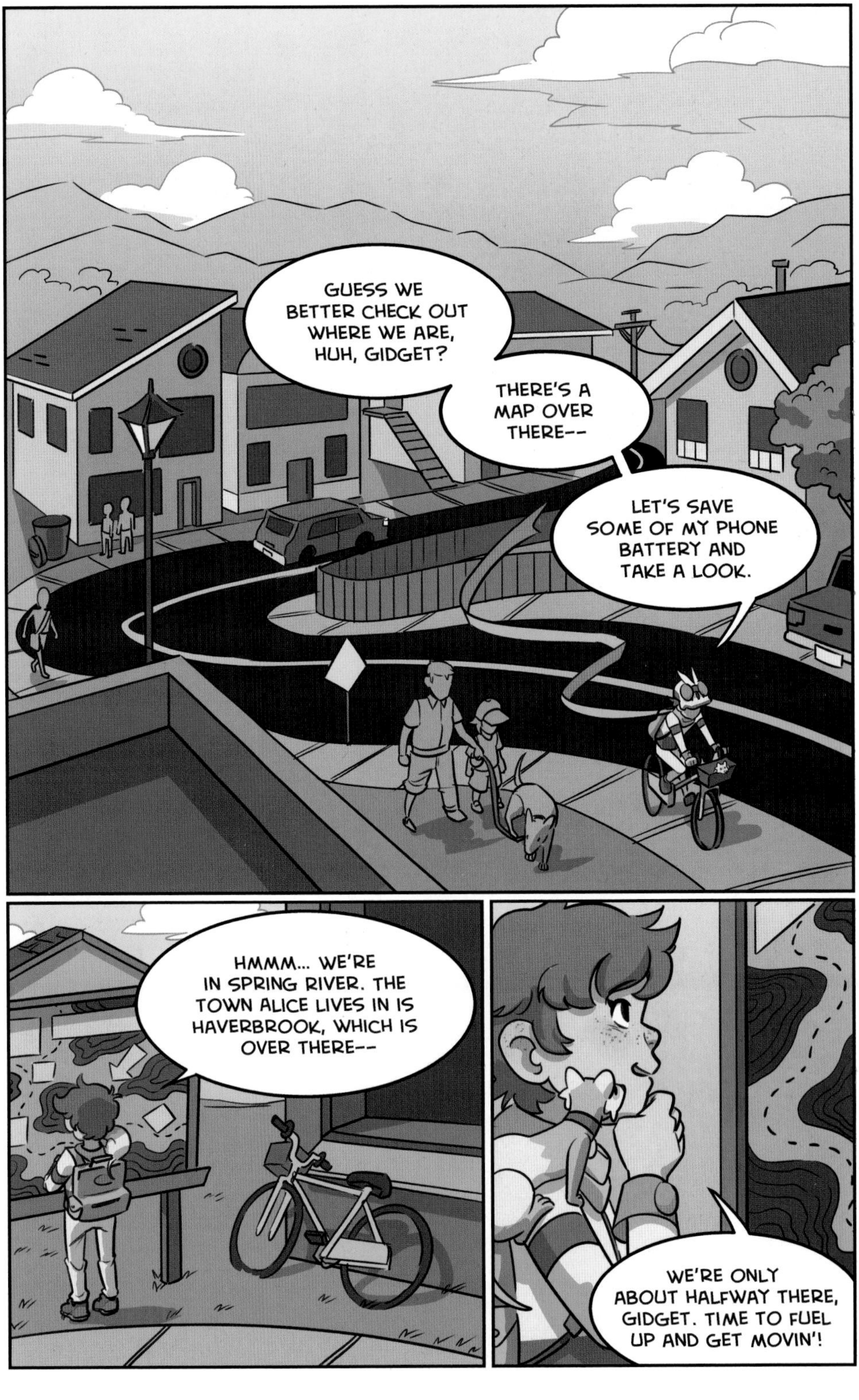
GUESS WE BETTER CHECK OUT WHERE WE ARE, HUH, GIDGET?
THERE'S A MAP OVER THERE--
LET'S SAVE SOME OF MY PHONE BATTERY AND TAKE A LOOK.
HMMM... WE'RE IN SPRING RIVER. THE TOWN ALICE LIVES IN IS HAVERBROOK, WHICH IS OVER THERE--
WE'RE ONLY ABOUT HALFWAY THERE, GIDGET. TIME TO FUEL UP AND GET MOVIN'!

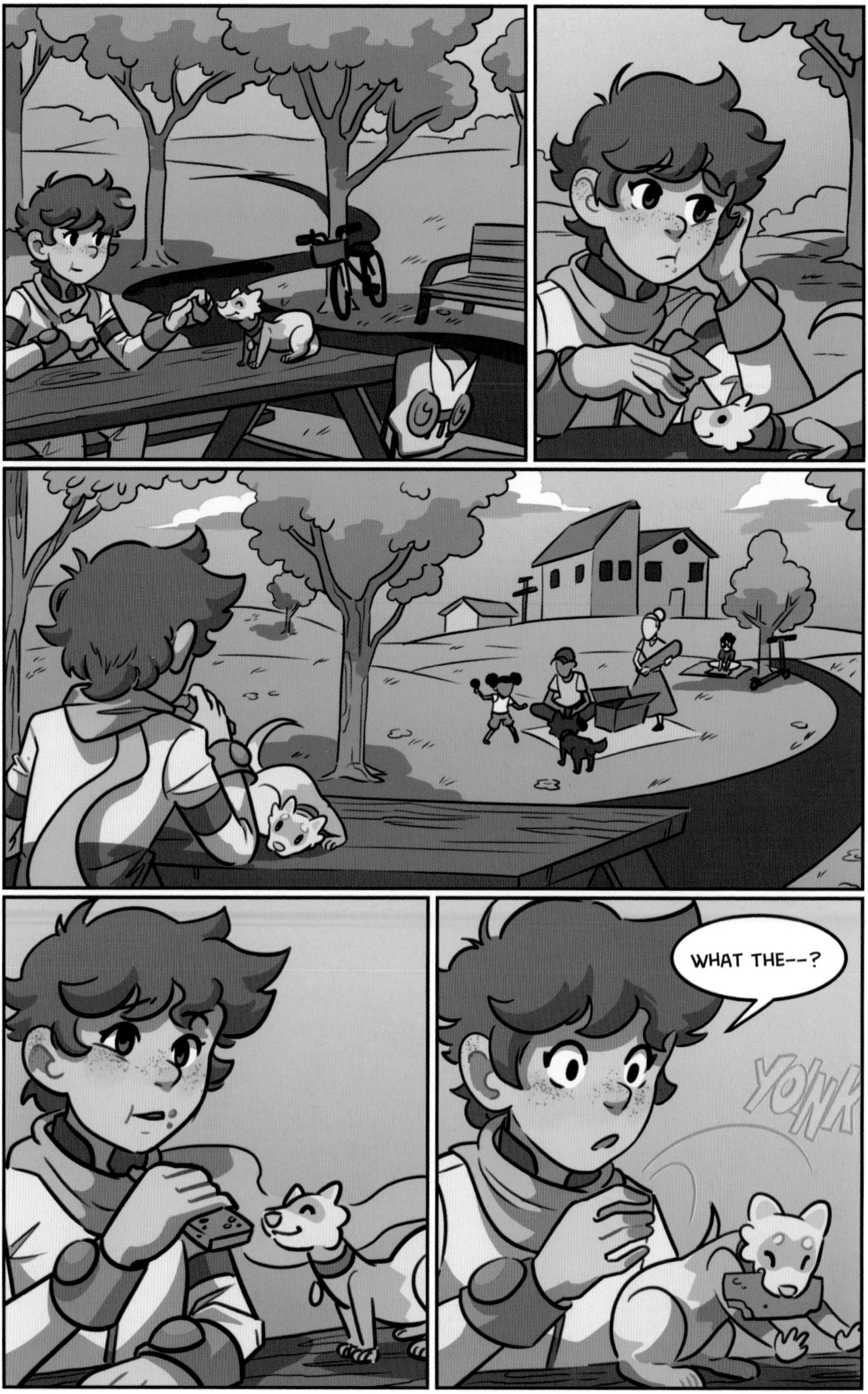
WHAT THE--?
YONK

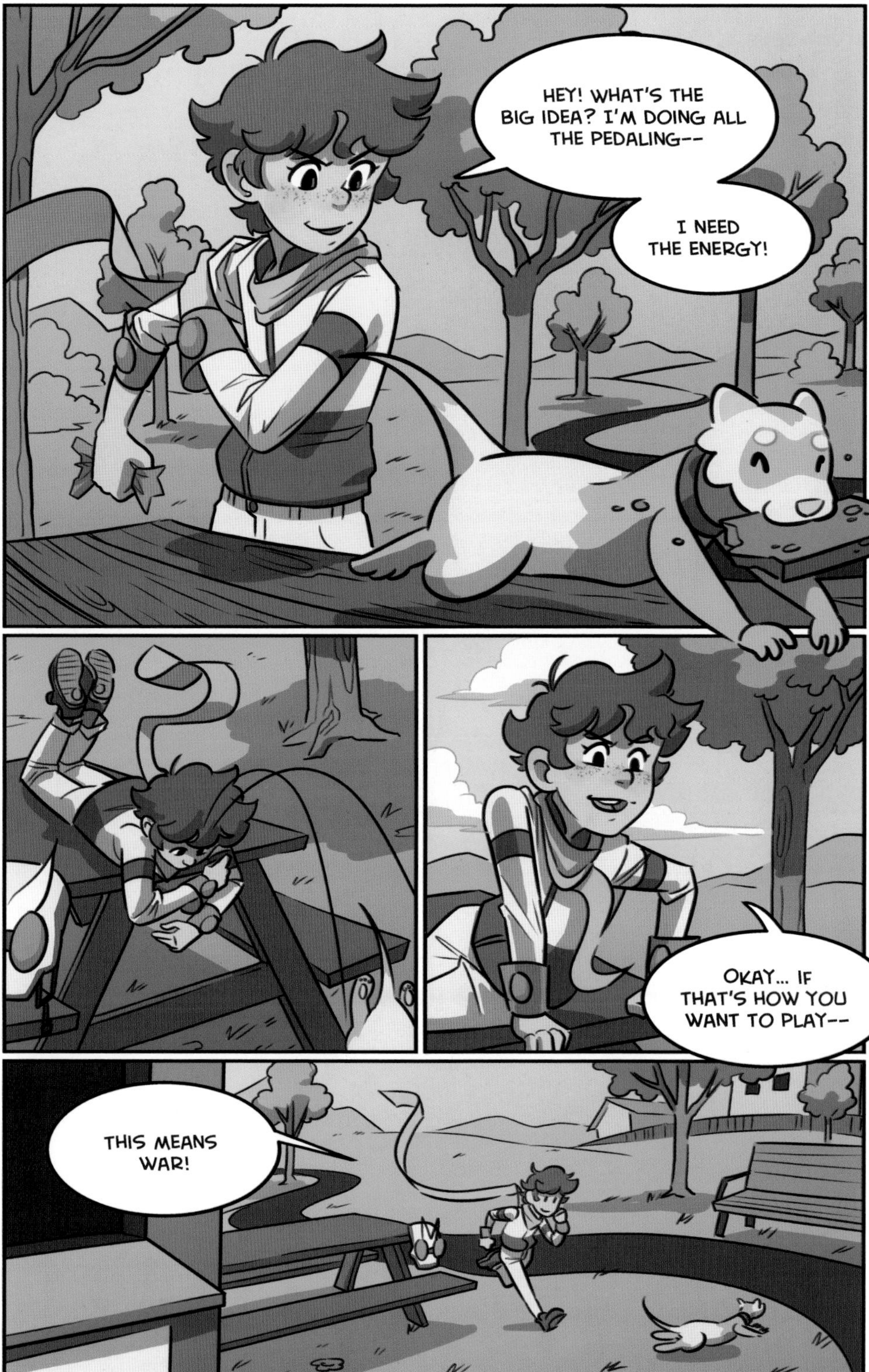
HEY! WHAT'S THE BIG IDEA? I'M DOING ALL THE PEDALING--
I NEED THE ENERGY!
OKAY... IF THAT'S HOW YOU WANT TO PLAY--
THIS MEANS WAR!

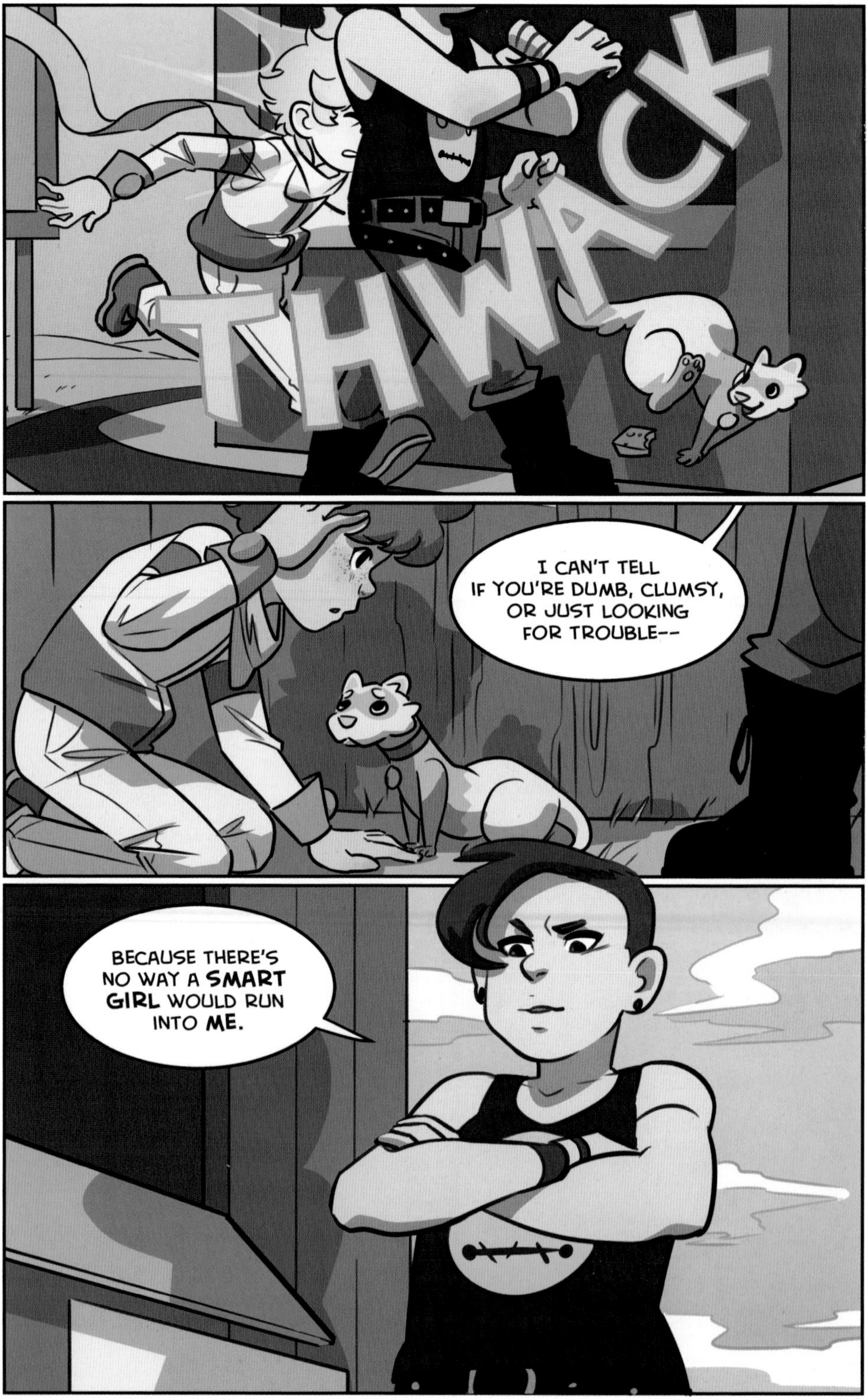
THWACK
I CAN'T TELL IF YOU'RE DUMB, CLUMSY, OR JUST LOOKING FOR TROUBLE--
BECAUSE THERE'S NO WAY A SMART GIRL WOULD RUN INTO ME.

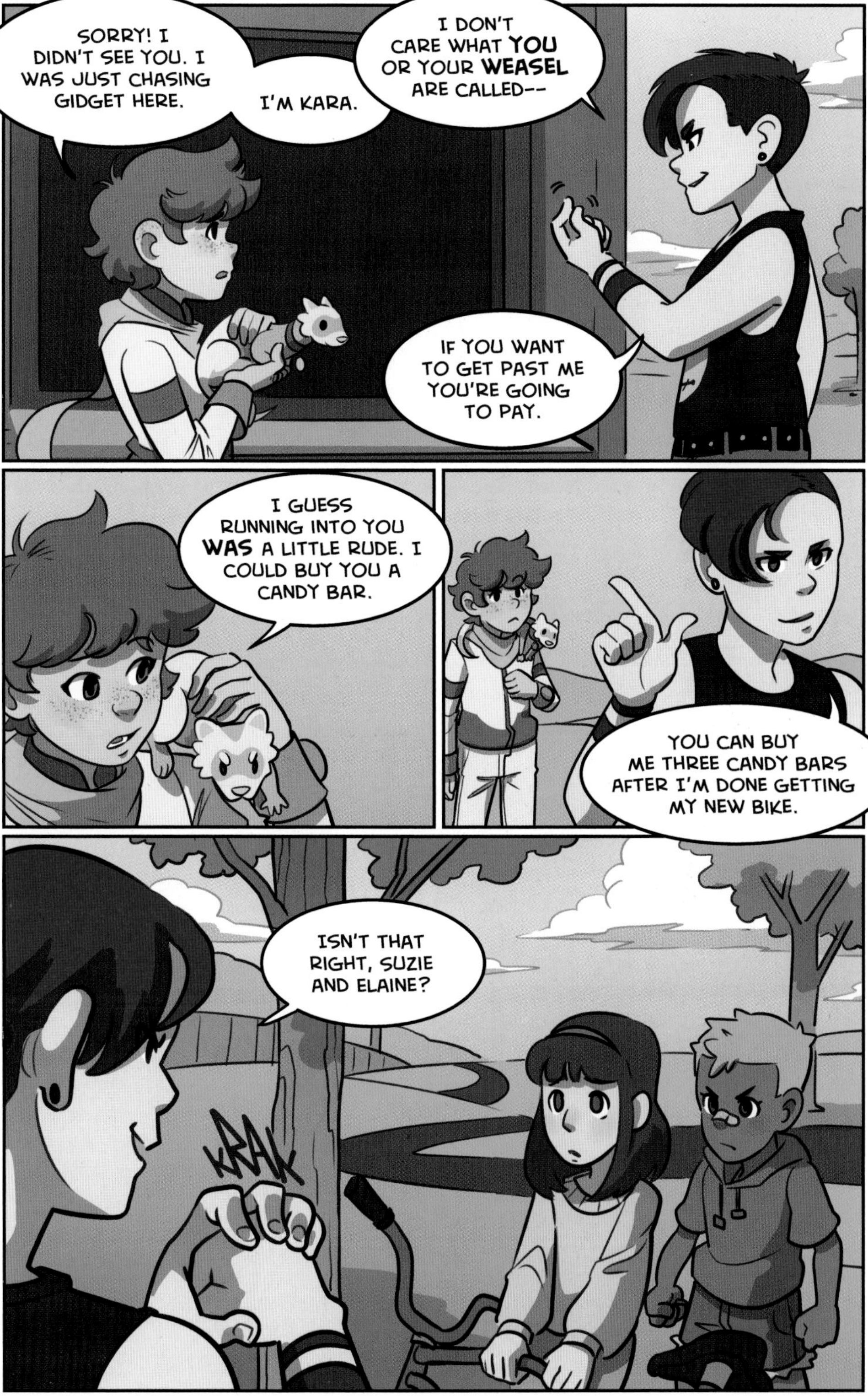
SORRY! I DIDN'T SEE YOU. I WAS JUST CHASING GIDGET HERE.
I'M KARA.
I DON'T CARE WHAT YOU OR YOUR WEASEL ARE CALLED--
IF YOU WANT TO GET PAST ME YOU'RE GOING TO PAY.
I GUESS RUNNING INTO YOU WAS A LITTLE RUDE. I COULD BUY YOU A CANDY BAR.
YOU CAN BUY ME THREE CANDY BARS AFTER I'M DONE GETTING MY NEW BIKE.
ISN'T THAT RIGHT, SUZIE AND ELAINE?
KRAK

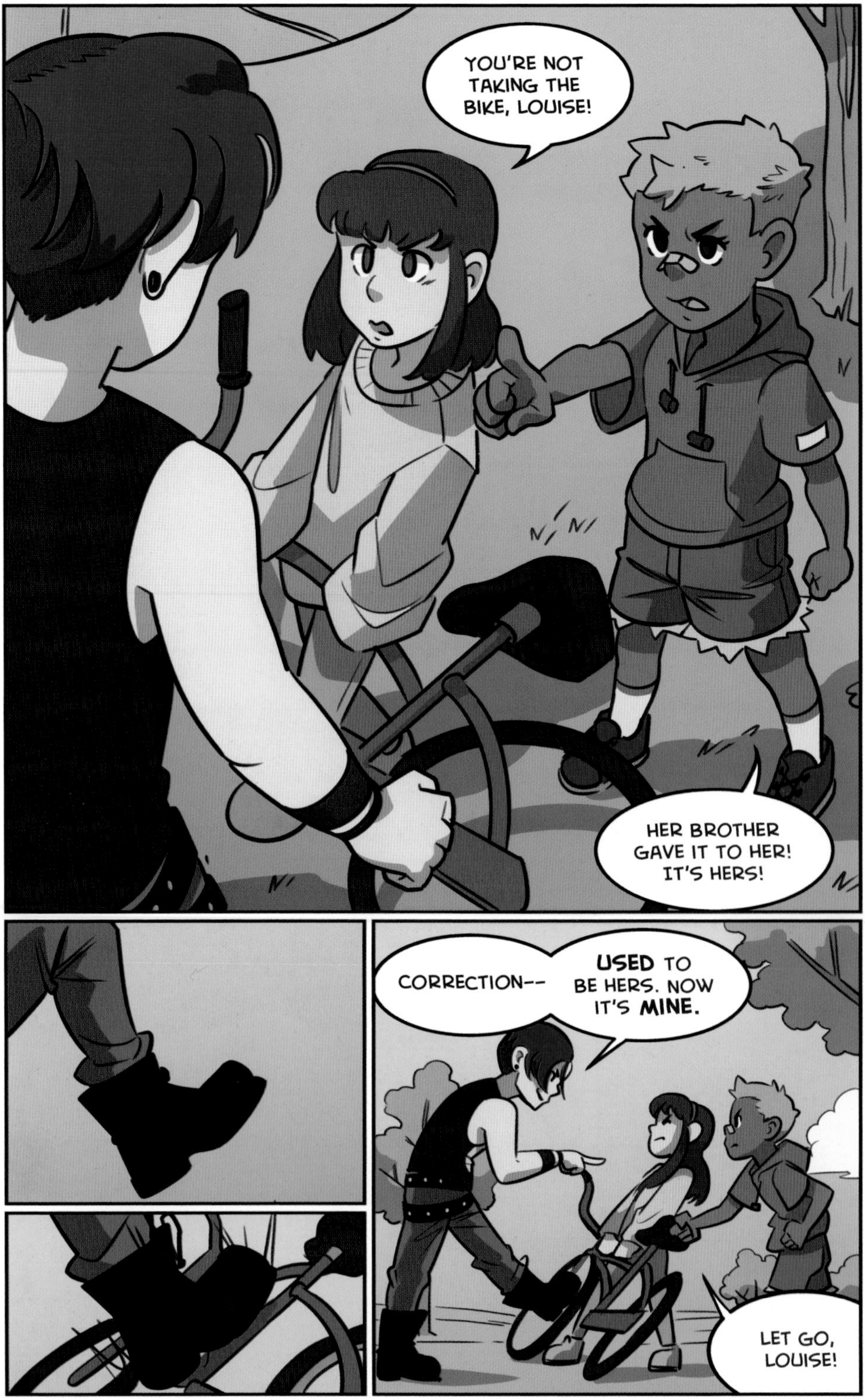
YOU'RE NOT TAKING THE BIKE, LOUISE!
HER BROTHER GAVE IT TO HER! IT'S HERS!
CORRECTION--
USED TO BE HERS. NOW IT'S MINE.
LET GO, LOUISE!

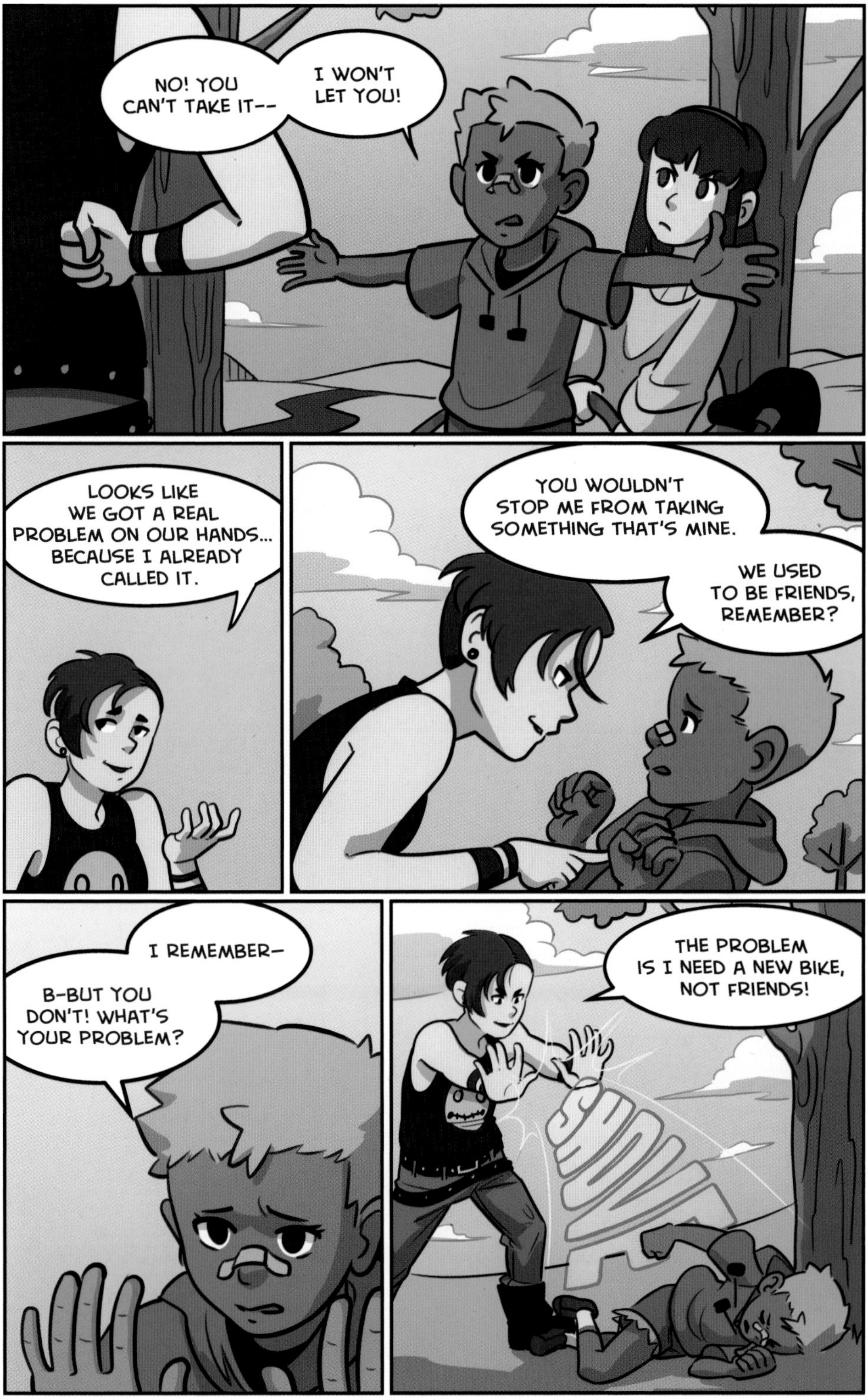
NO! YOU CAN'T TAKE IT--
I WON'T LET YOU!
LOOKS LIKE WE GOT A REAL PROBLEM ON OUR HANDS... BECAUSE I ALREADY CALLED IT.
YOU WOULDN'T STOP ME FROM TAKING SOMETHING THAT'S MINE.
WE USED TO BE FRIENDS, REMEMBER?
I REMEMBER–
B–BUT YOU DON'T! WHAT'S YOUR PROBLEM?
THE PROBLEM IS I NEED A NEW BIKE, NOT FRIENDS!
SHOVE

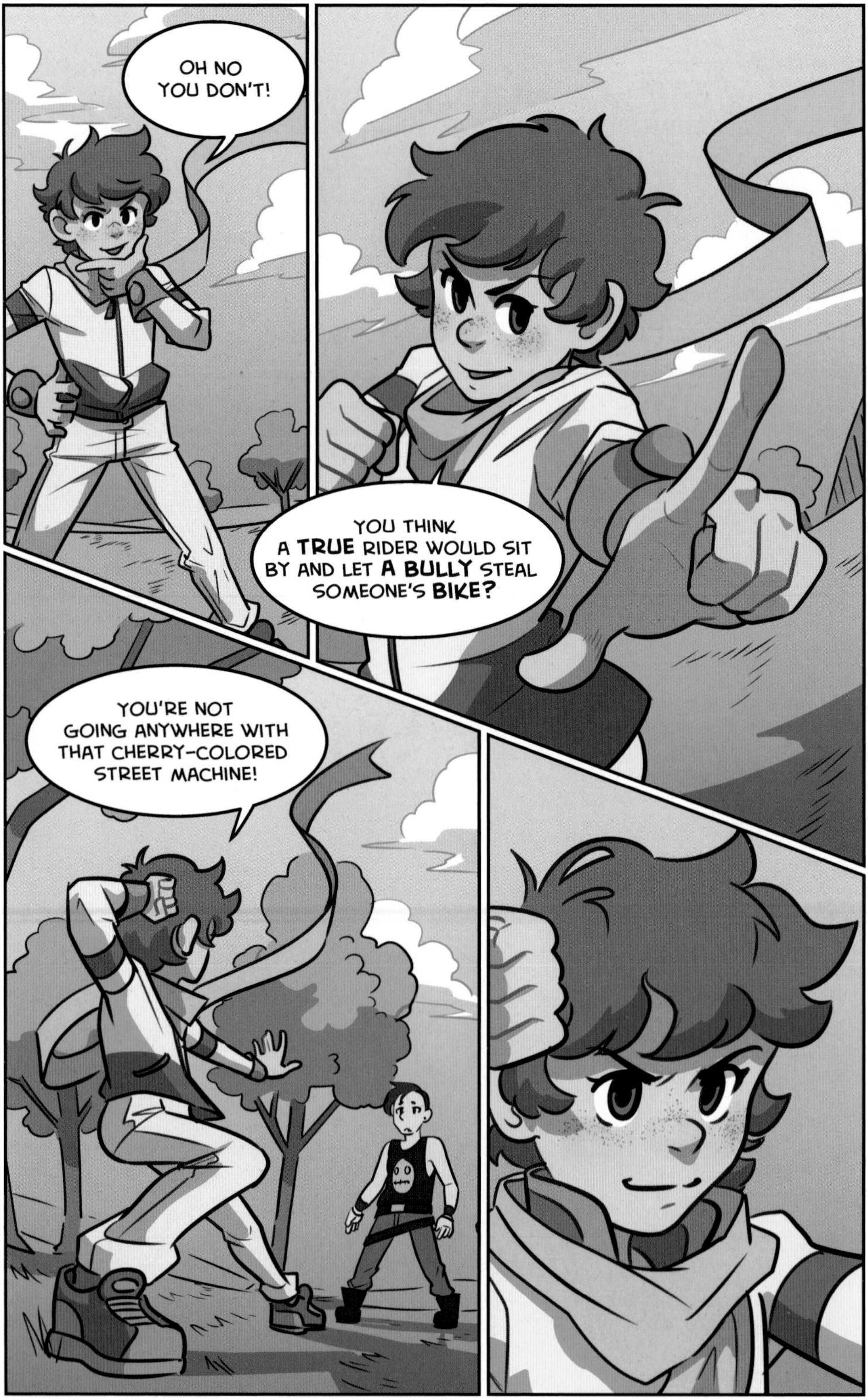
OH NO YOU DON'T!
YOU THINK A **TRUE** RIDER WOULD SIT BY AND LET **A BULLY** STEAL SOMEONE'S **BIKE?**
YOU'RE NOT GOING ANYWHERE WITH THAT CHERRY-COLORED STREET MACHINE!

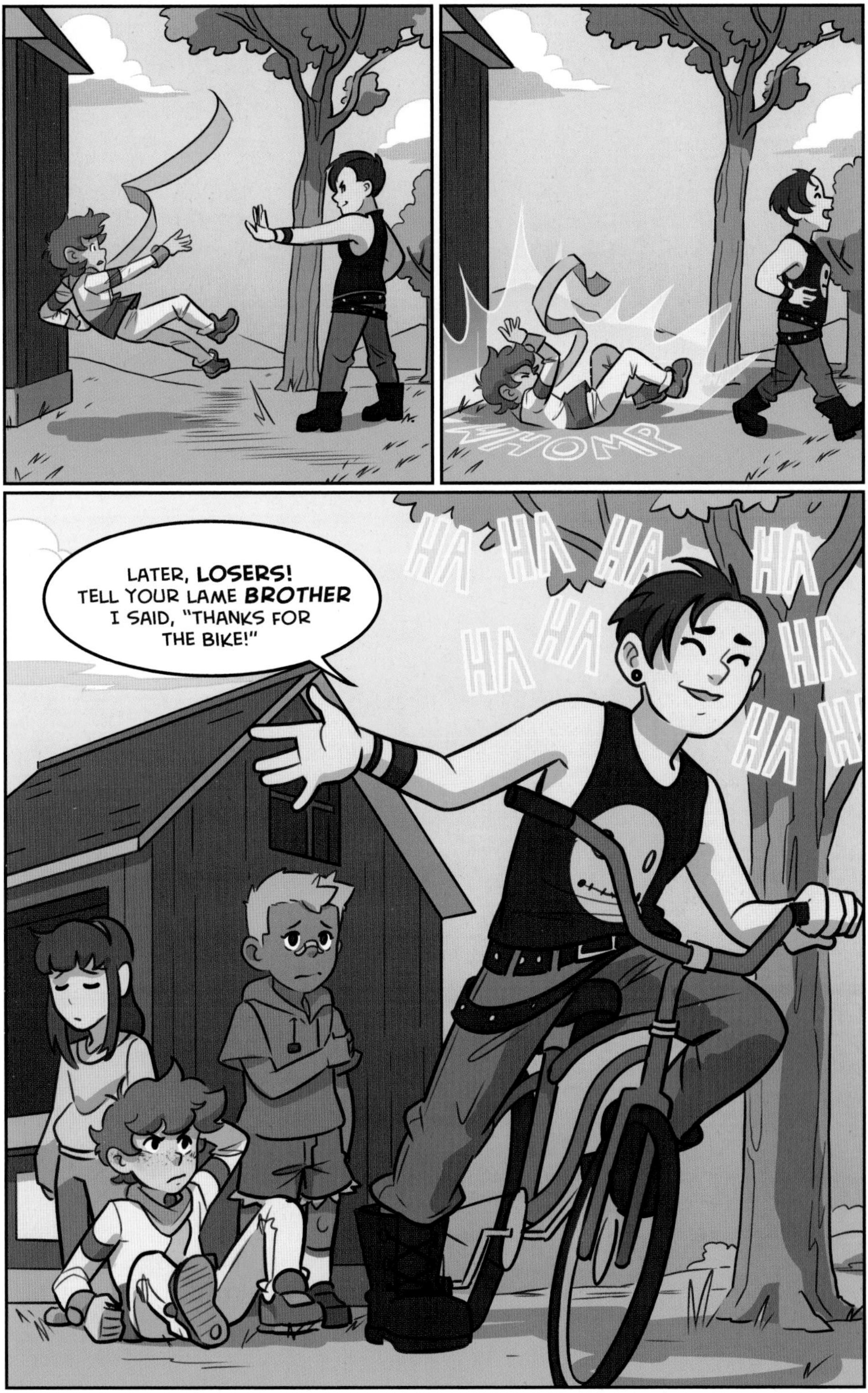
WHOMP
LATER, **LOSERS!** TELL YOUR LAME **BROTHER** I SAID, "THANKS FOR THE BIKE!"
HA HA HA HA HA HA HA HA HA HA

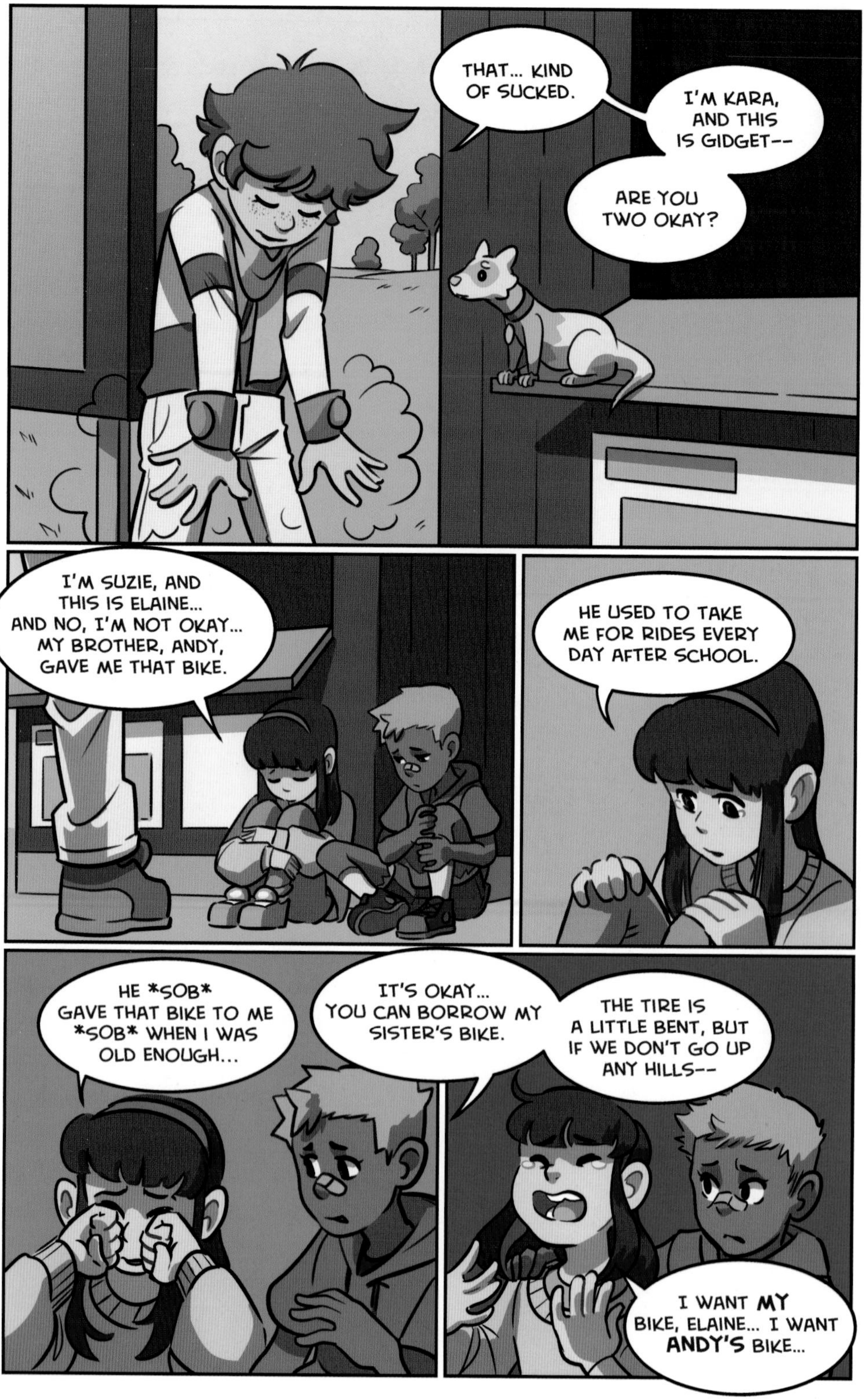
THAT... KIND OF SUCKED.
I'M KARA, AND THIS IS GIDGET--
ARE YOU TWO OKAY?
I'M SUZIE, AND THIS IS ELAINE... AND NO, I'M NOT OKAY... MY BROTHER, ANDY, GAVE ME THAT BIKE.
HE USED TO TAKE ME FOR RIDES EVERY DAY AFTER SCHOOL.
HE *SOB* GAVE THAT BIKE TO ME *SOB* WHEN I WAS OLD ENOUGH...
IT'S OKAY... YOU CAN BORROW MY SISTER'S BIKE.
THE TIRE IS A LITTLE BENT, BUT IF WE DON'T GO UP ANY HILLS--
I WANT **MY** BIKE, ELAINE... I WANT **ANDY'S** BIKE...

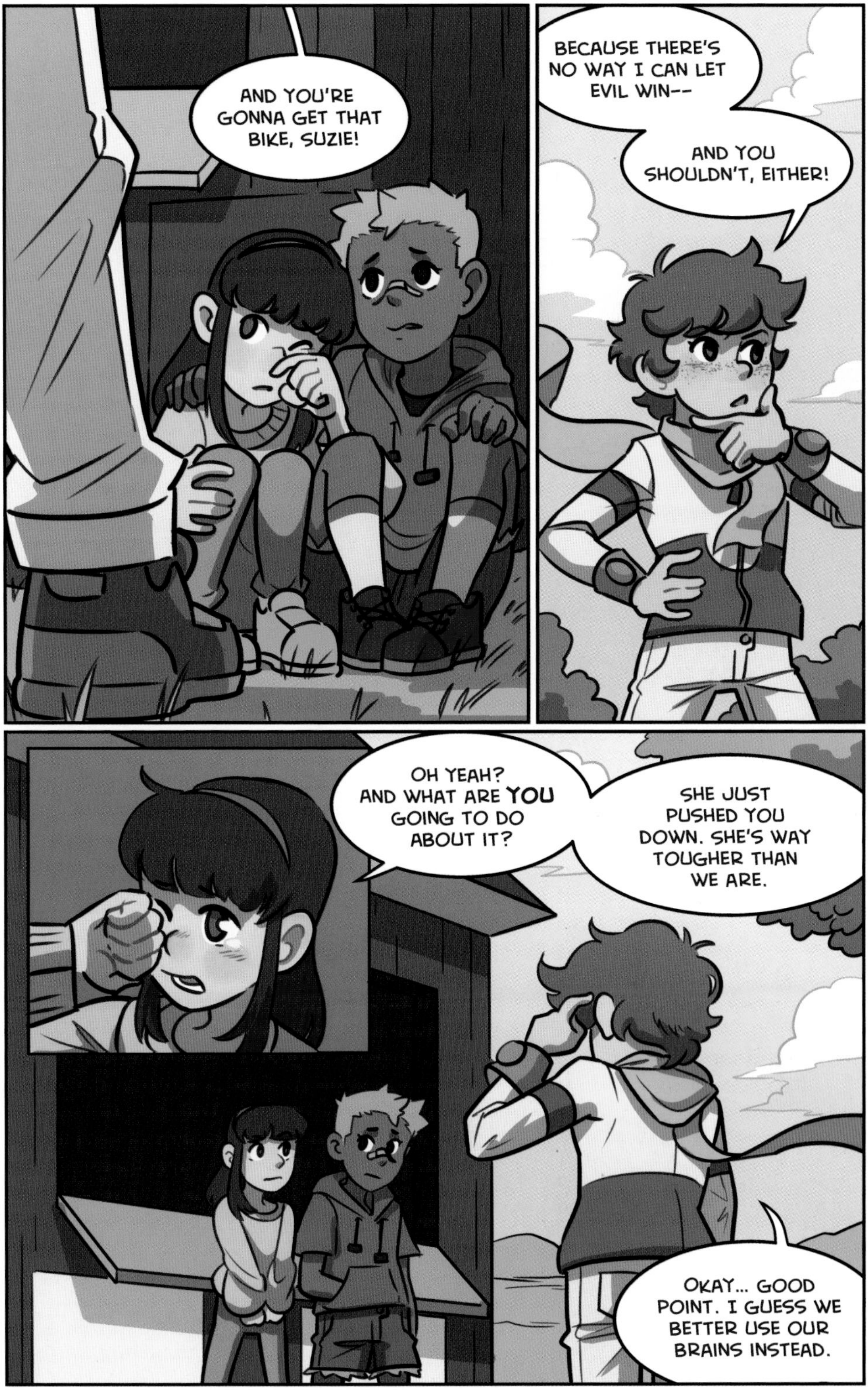
AND YOU'RE GONNA GET THAT BIKE, SUZIE!
BECAUSE THERE'S NO WAY I CAN LET EVIL WIN--
AND YOU SHOULDN'T, EITHER!
OH YEAH? AND WHAT ARE **YOU** GOING TO DO ABOUT IT?
SHE JUST PUSHED YOU DOWN. SHE'S WAY TOUGHER THAN WE ARE.
OKAY... GOOD POINT. I GUESS WE BETTER USE OUR BRAINS INSTEAD.

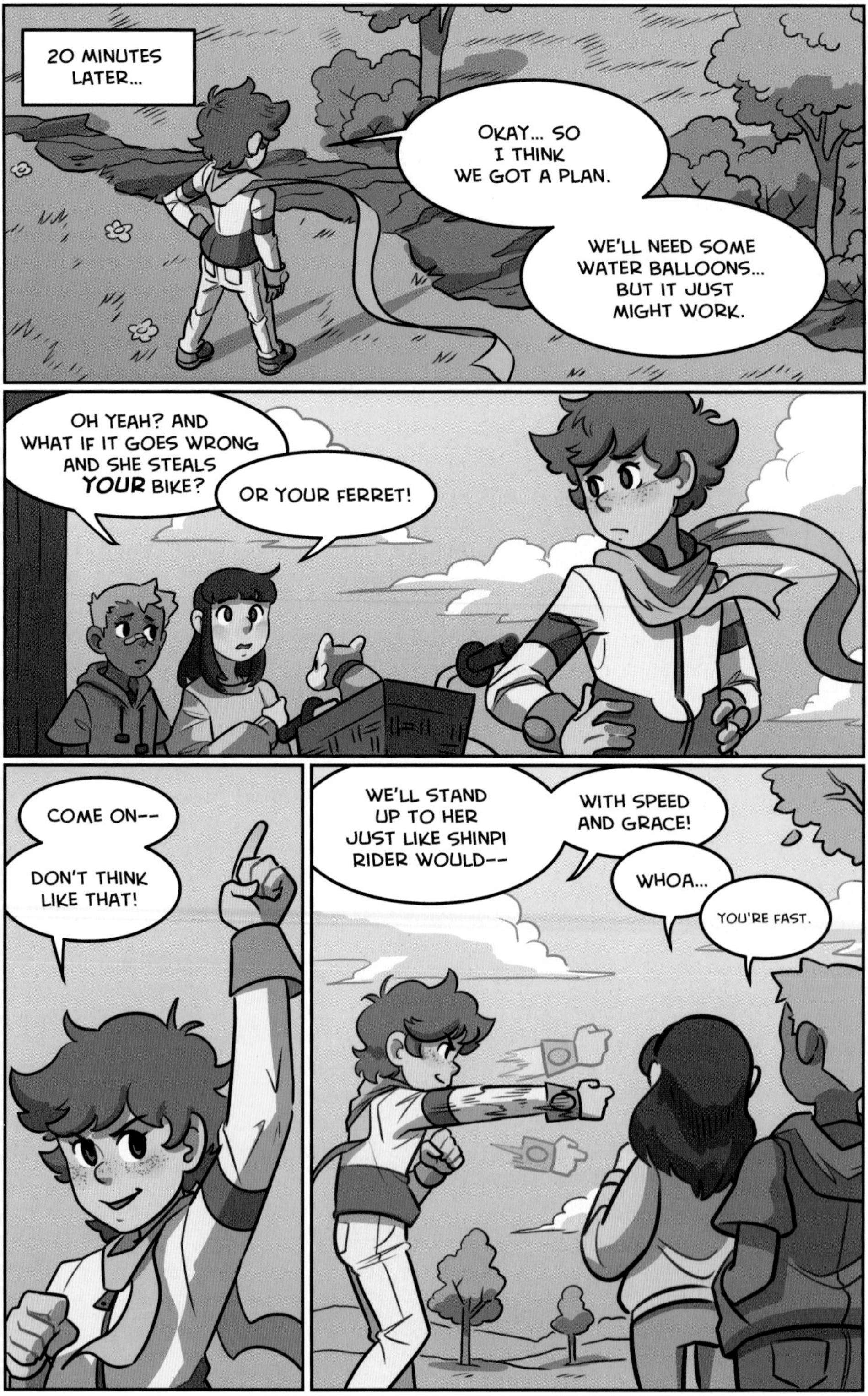
20 MINUTES LATER...
OKAY... SO I THINK WE GOT A PLAN.
WE'LL NEED SOME WATER BALLOONS... BUT IT JUST MIGHT WORK.
OH YEAH? AND WHAT IF IT GOES WRONG AND SHE STEALS **YOUR** BIKE?
OR YOUR FERRET!
COME ON--
DON'T THINK LIKE THAT!
WE'LL STAND UP TO HER JUST LIKE SHINPI RIDER WOULD--
WITH SPEED AND GRACE!
WHOA...
YOU'RE FAST.

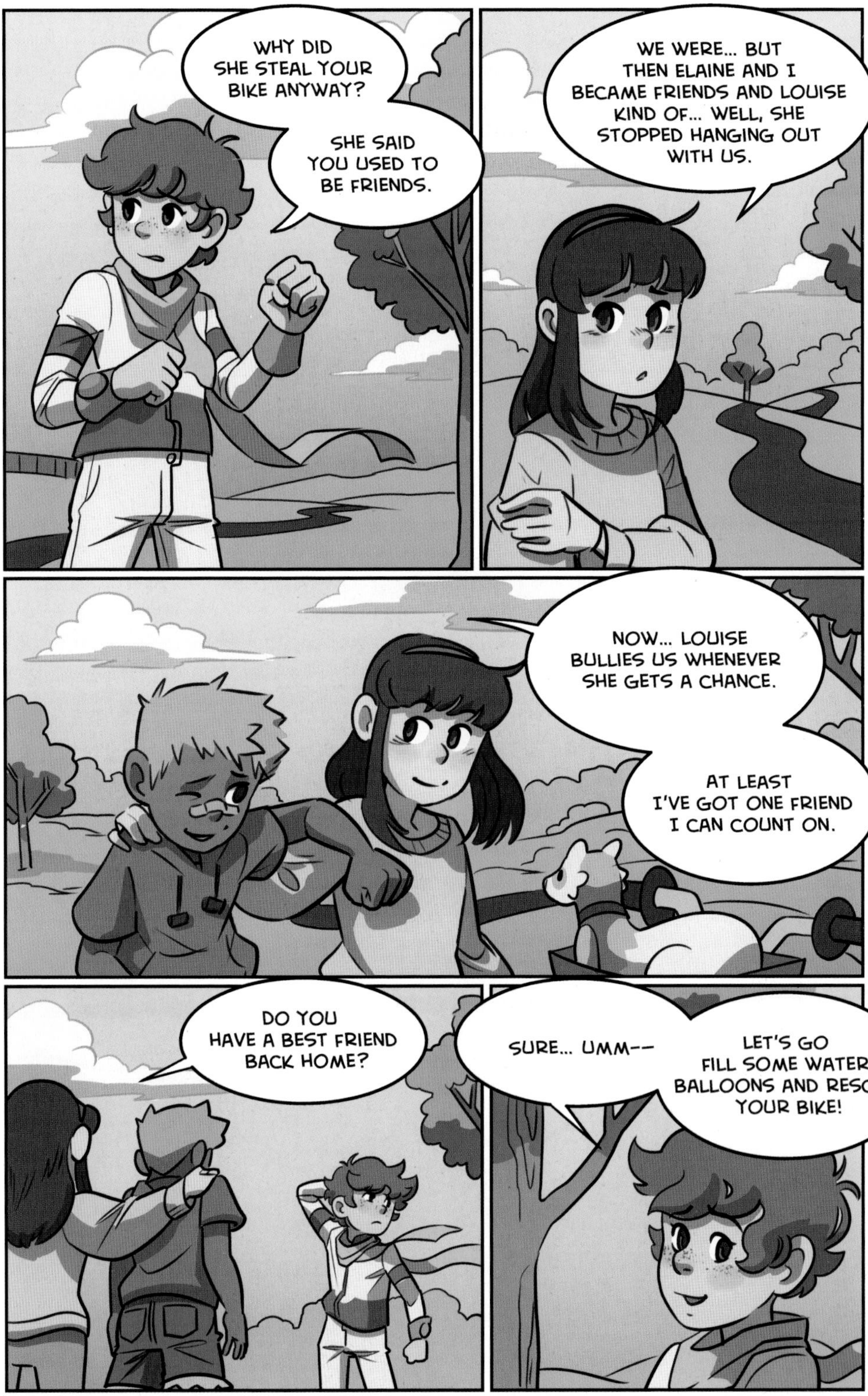
WHY DID SHE STEAL YOUR BIKE ANYWAY?
SHE SAID YOU USED TO BE FRIENDS.
WE WERE... BUT THEN ELAINE AND I BECAME FRIENDS AND LOUISE KIND OF... WELL, SHE STOPPED HANGING OUT WITH US.
NOW... LOUISE BULLIES US WHENEVER SHE GETS A CHANCE.
AT LEAST I'VE GOT ONE FRIEND I CAN COUNT ON.
DO YOU HAVE A BEST FRIEND BACK HOME?
SURE... UMM--
LET'S GO FILL SOME WATER BALLOONS AND RESCUE YOUR BIKE!

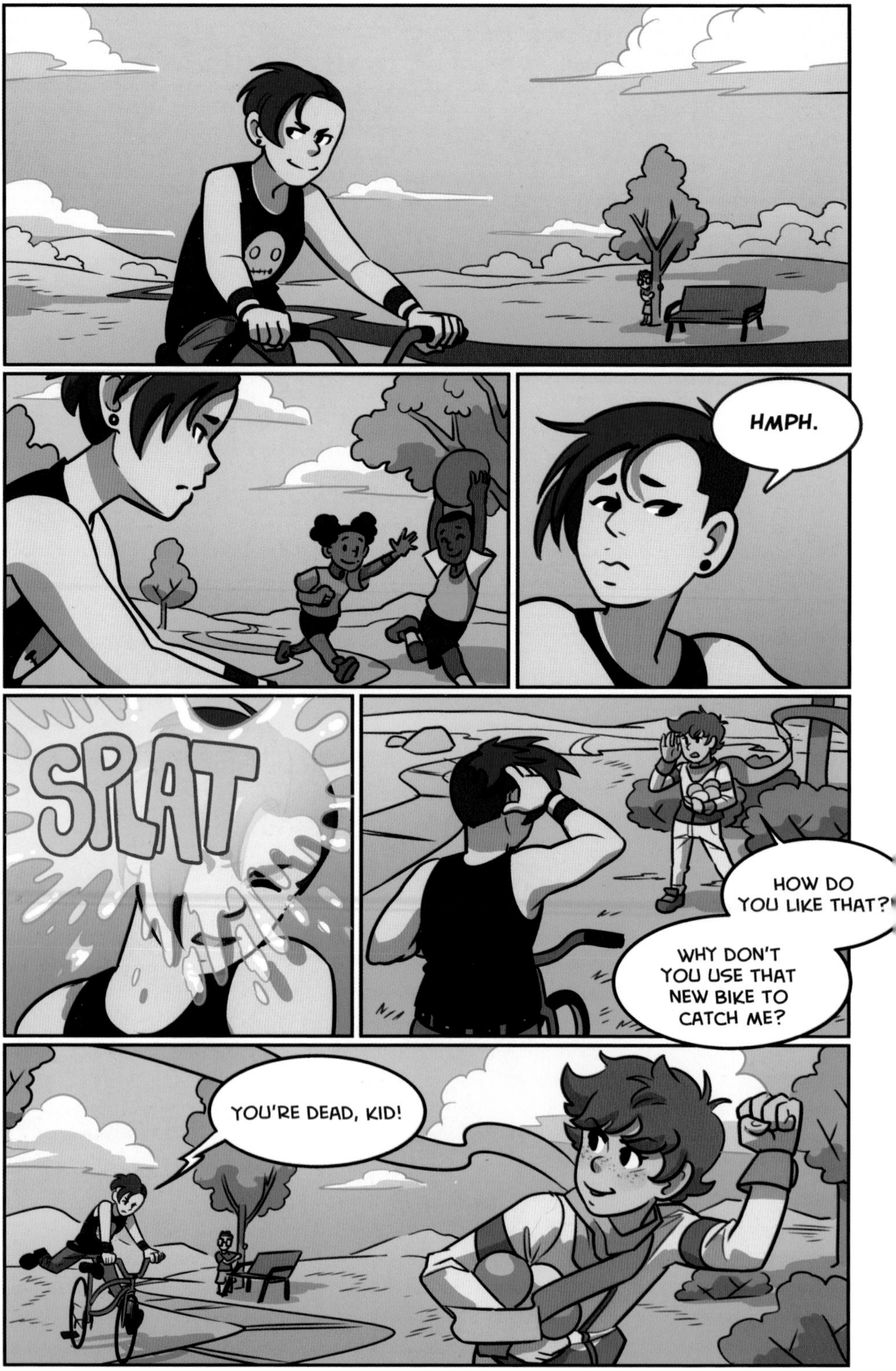
HMPH.
SPLAT
HOW DO YOU LIKE THAT?
WHY DON'T YOU USE THAT NEW BIKE TO CATCH ME?
YOU'RE DEAD, KID!

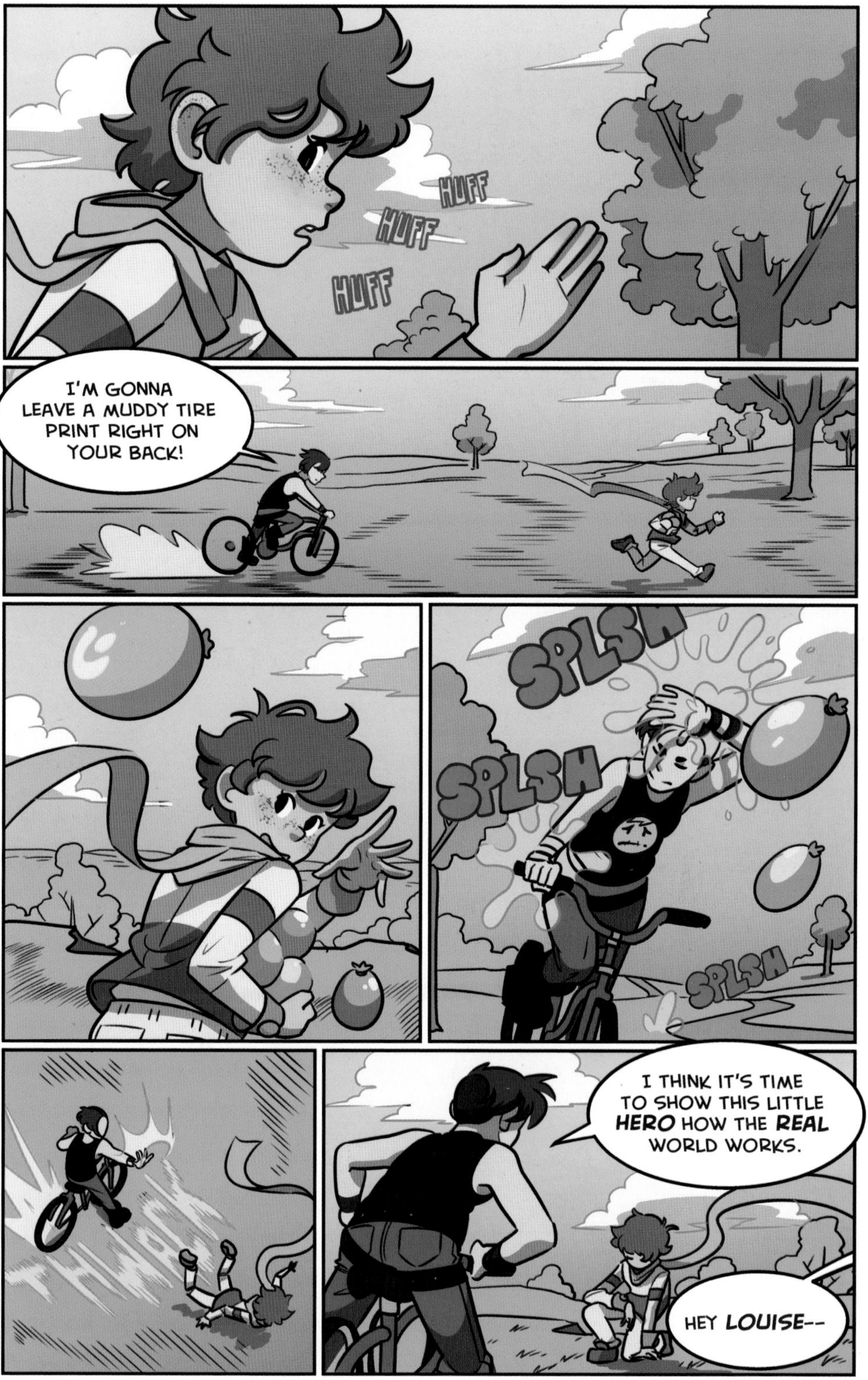
HUFF
HUFF
HUFF
I'M GONNA LEAVE A MUDDY TIRE PRINT RIGHT ON YOUR BACK!
SPLSH
SPLSH
SPLSH
I THINK IT'S TIME TO SHOW THIS LITTLE **HERO** HOW THE **REAL** WORLD WORKS.
HEY **LOUISE**--

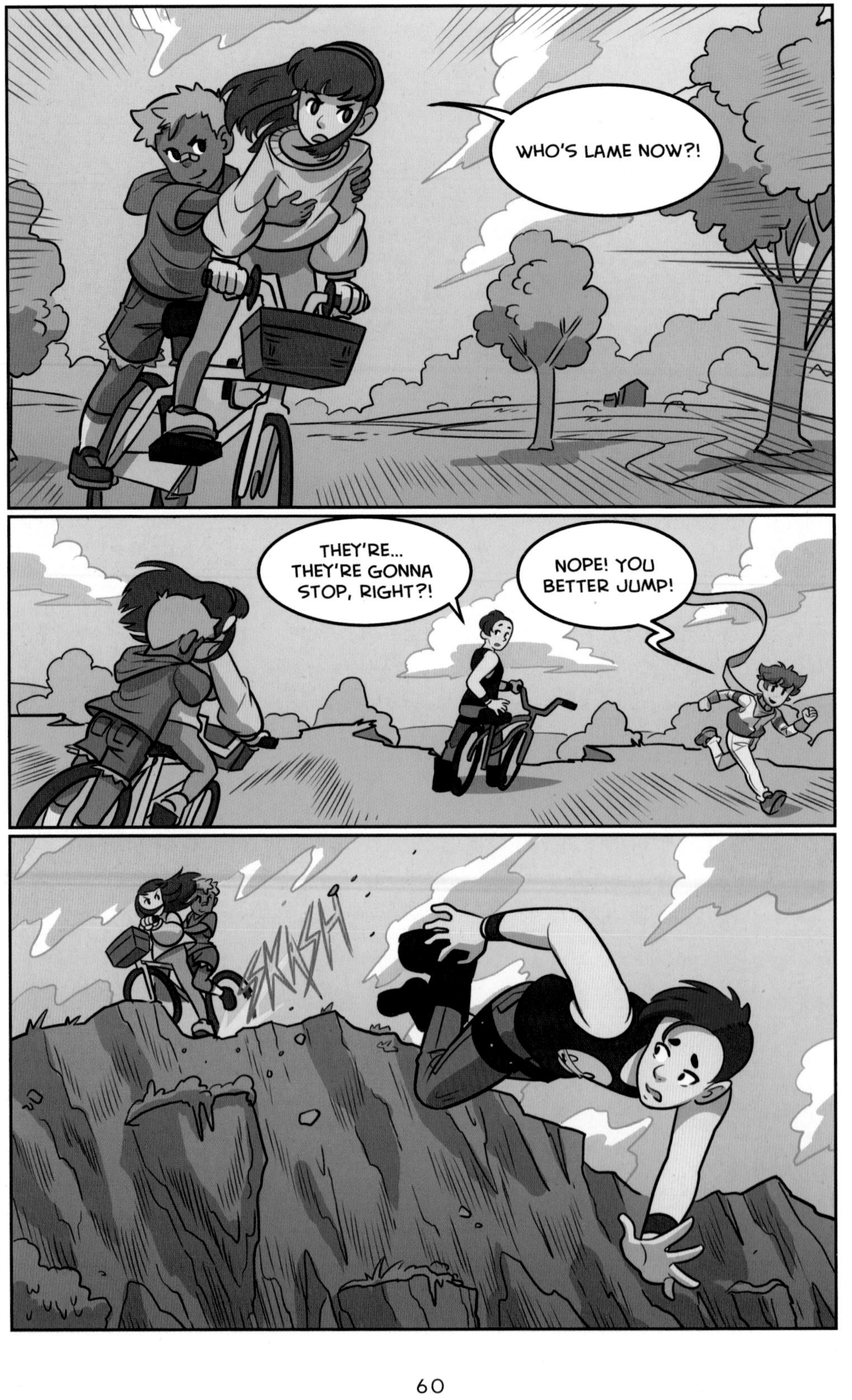
WHO'S LAME NOW?!
THEY'RE... THEY'RE GONNA STOP, RIGHT?!
NOPE! YOU BETTER JUMP!

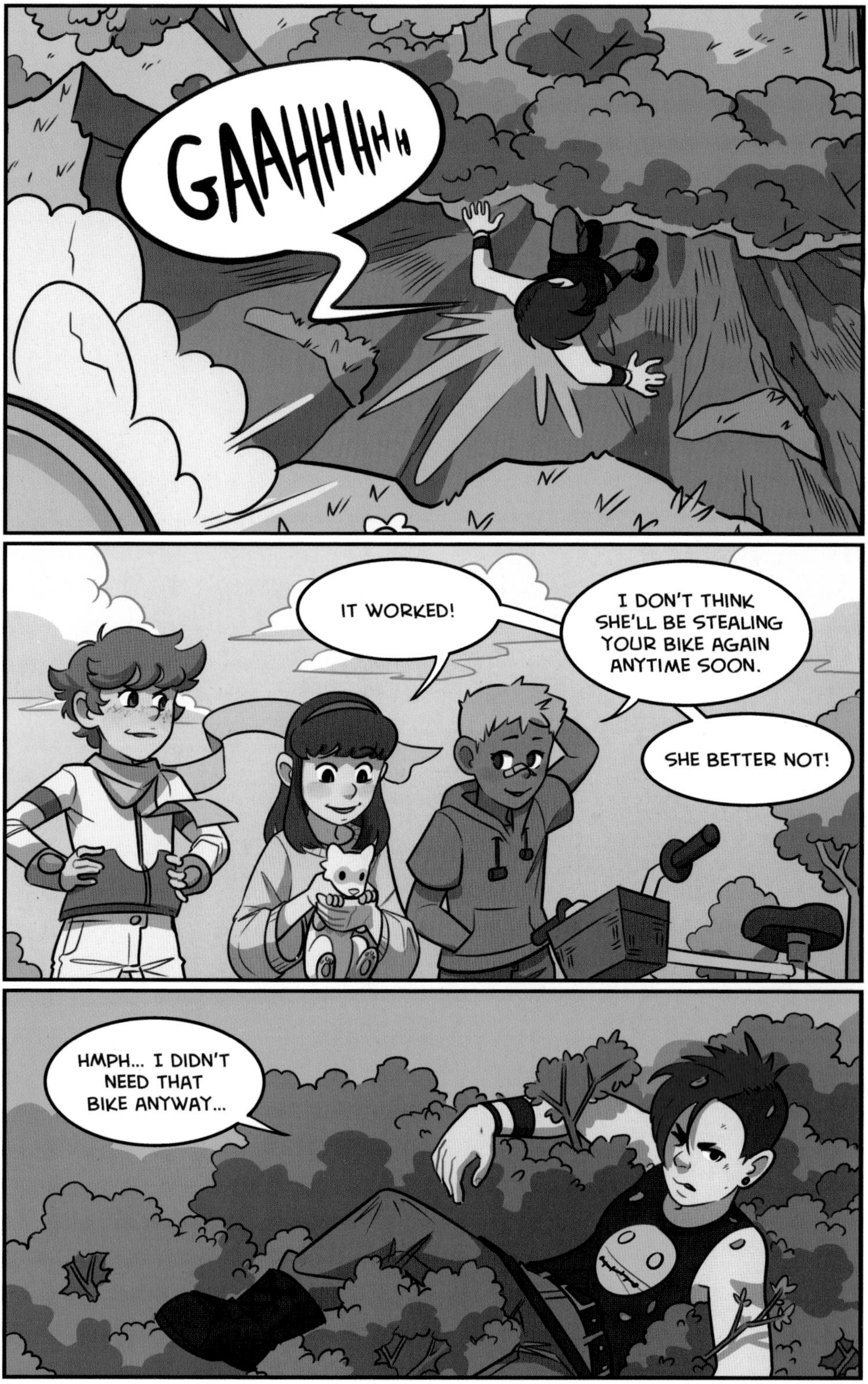
GAAHHHHH
IT WORKED!
I DON'T THINK SHE'LL BE STEALING YOUR BIKE AGAIN ANYTIME SOON.
SHE BETTER NOT!
HMPH... I DIDN'T NEED THAT BIKE ANYWAY...

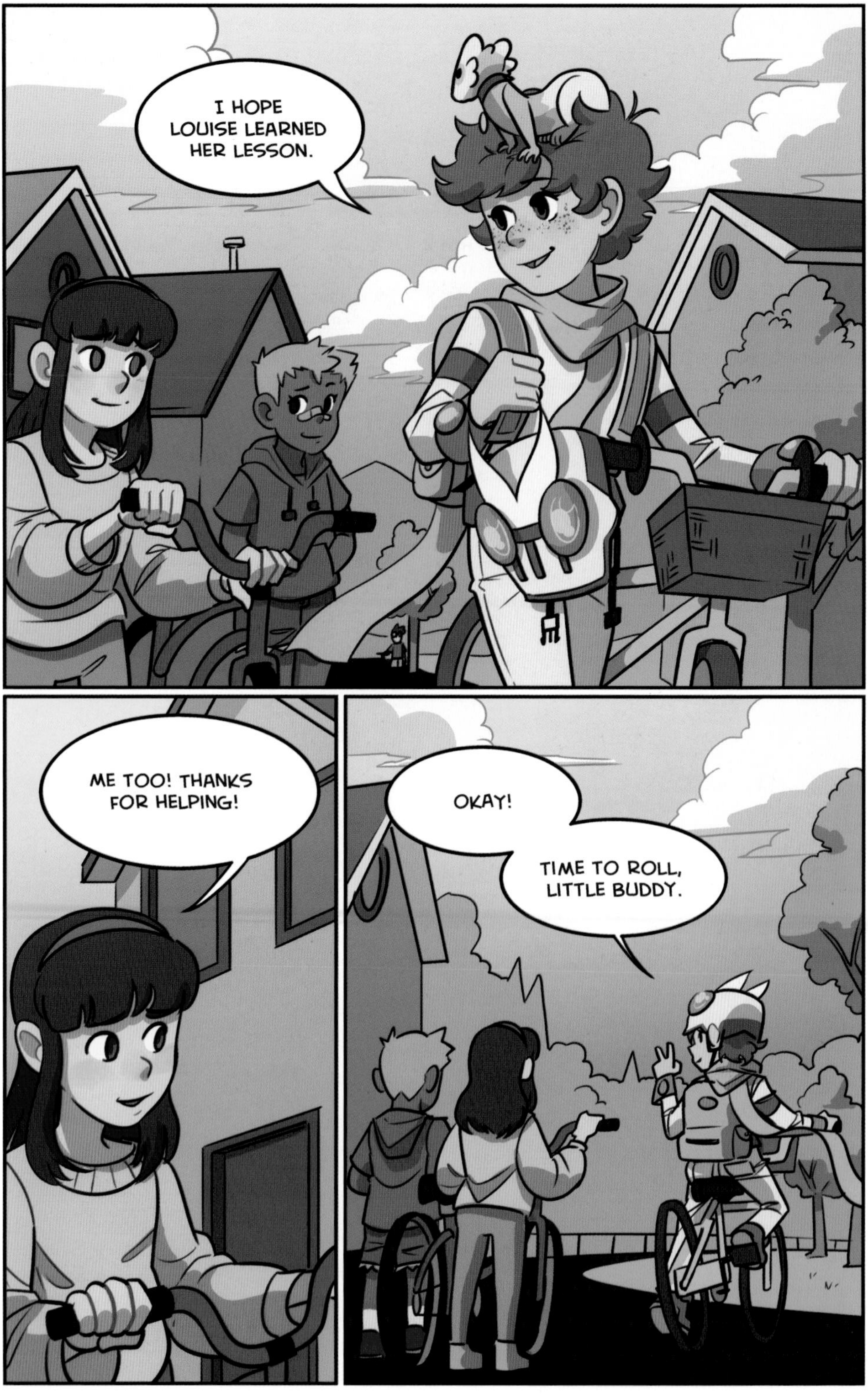
I HOPE LOUISE LEARNED HER LESSON.
ME TOO! THANKS FOR HELPING!
OKAY!
TIME TO ROLL, LITTLE BUDDY.

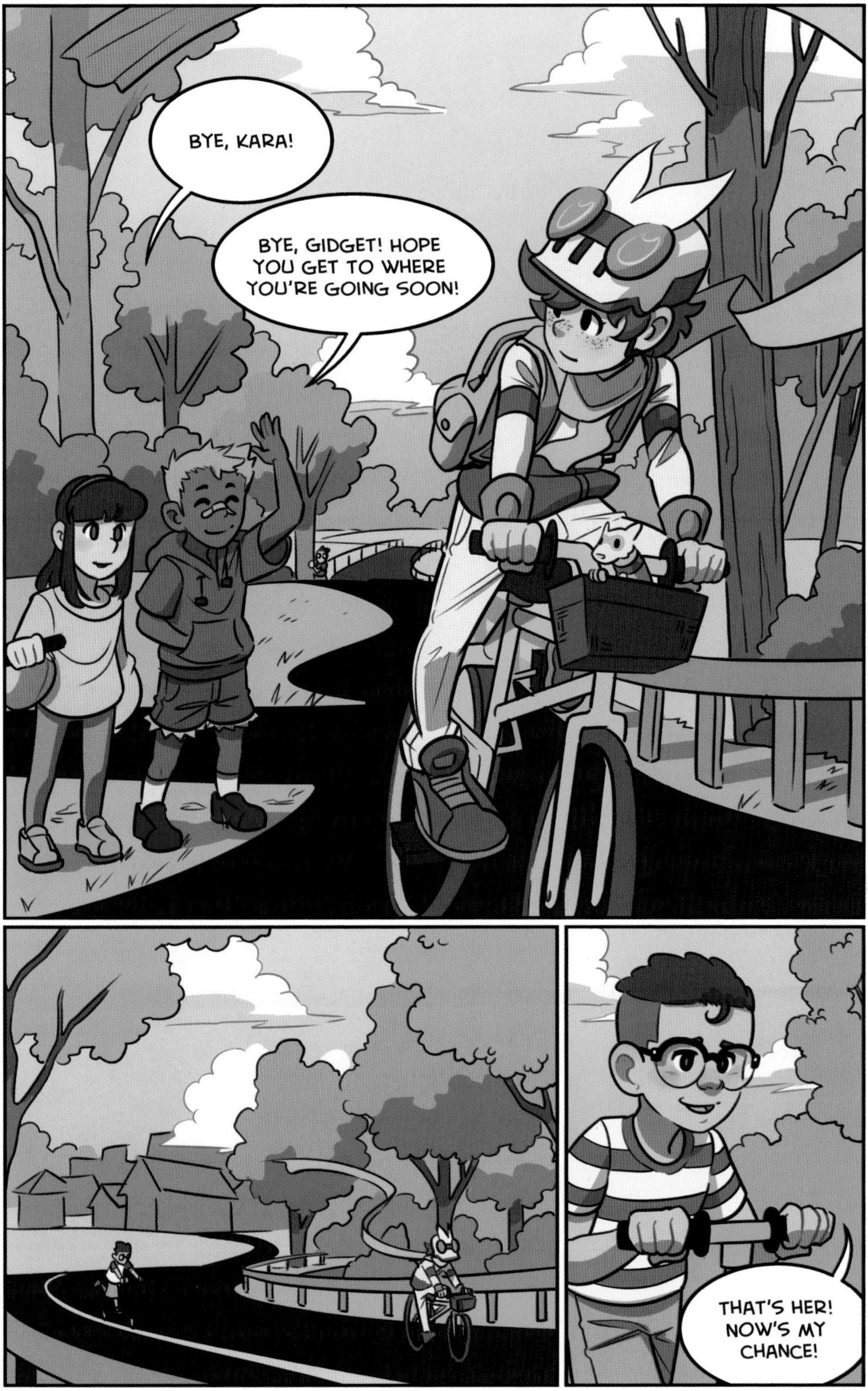
BYE, KARA!
BYE, GIDGET! HOPE YOU GET TO WHERE YOU'RE GOING SOON!
THAT'S HER! NOW'S MY CHANCE!

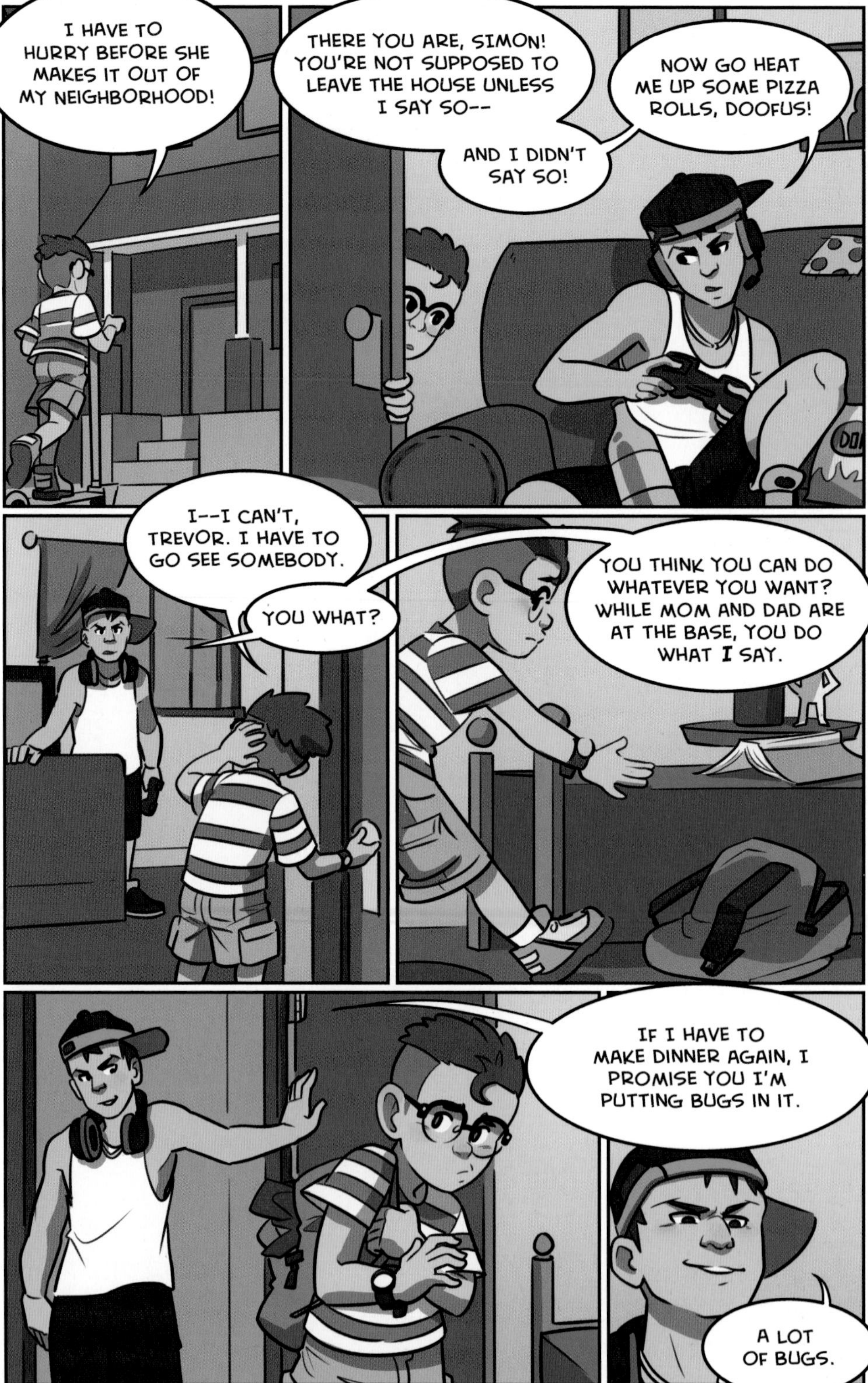
I HAVE TO HURRY BEFORE SHE MAKES IT OUT OF MY NEIGHBORHOOD!
THERE YOU ARE, SIMON! YOU'RE NOT SUPPOSED TO LEAVE THE HOUSE UNLESS I SAY SO--
AND I DIDN'T SAY SO!
NOW GO HEAT ME UP SOME PIZZA ROLLS, DOOFUS!
I--I CAN'T, TREVOR. I HAVE TO GO SEE SOMEBODY.
YOU WHAT?
YOU THINK YOU CAN DO WHATEVER YOU WANT? WHILE MOM AND DAD ARE AT THE BASE, YOU DO WHAT **I** SAY.
IF I HAVE TO MAKE DINNER AGAIN, I PROMISE YOU I'M PUTTING BUGS IN IT.
A LOT OF BUGS.

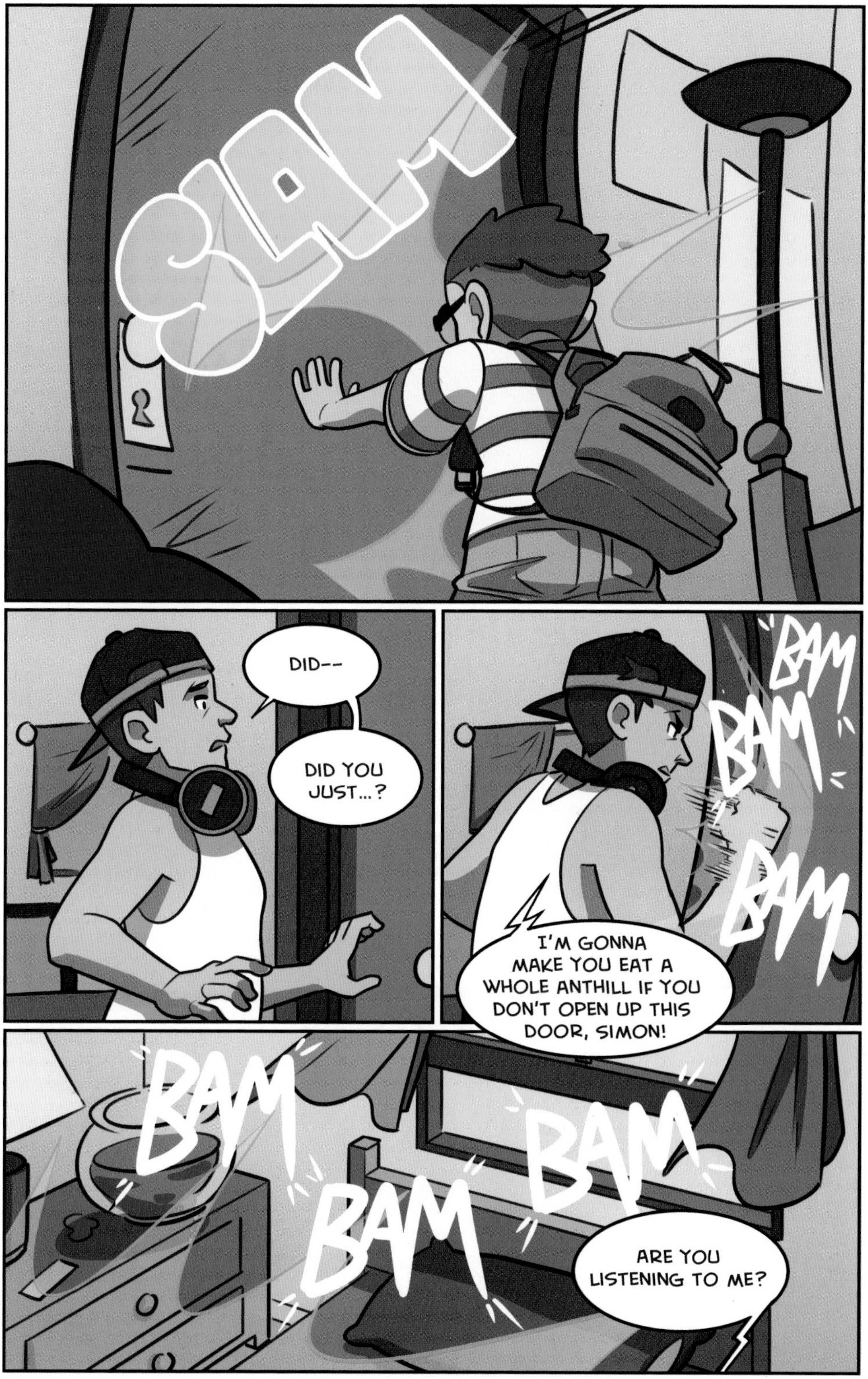
SLAM
DID--
DID YOU JUST...?
BAM
BAM
BAM
I'M GONNA MAKE YOU EAT A WHOLE ANTHILL IF YOU DON'T OPEN UP THIS DOOR, SIMON!
BAM
BAM
BAM
ARE YOU LISTENING TO ME?

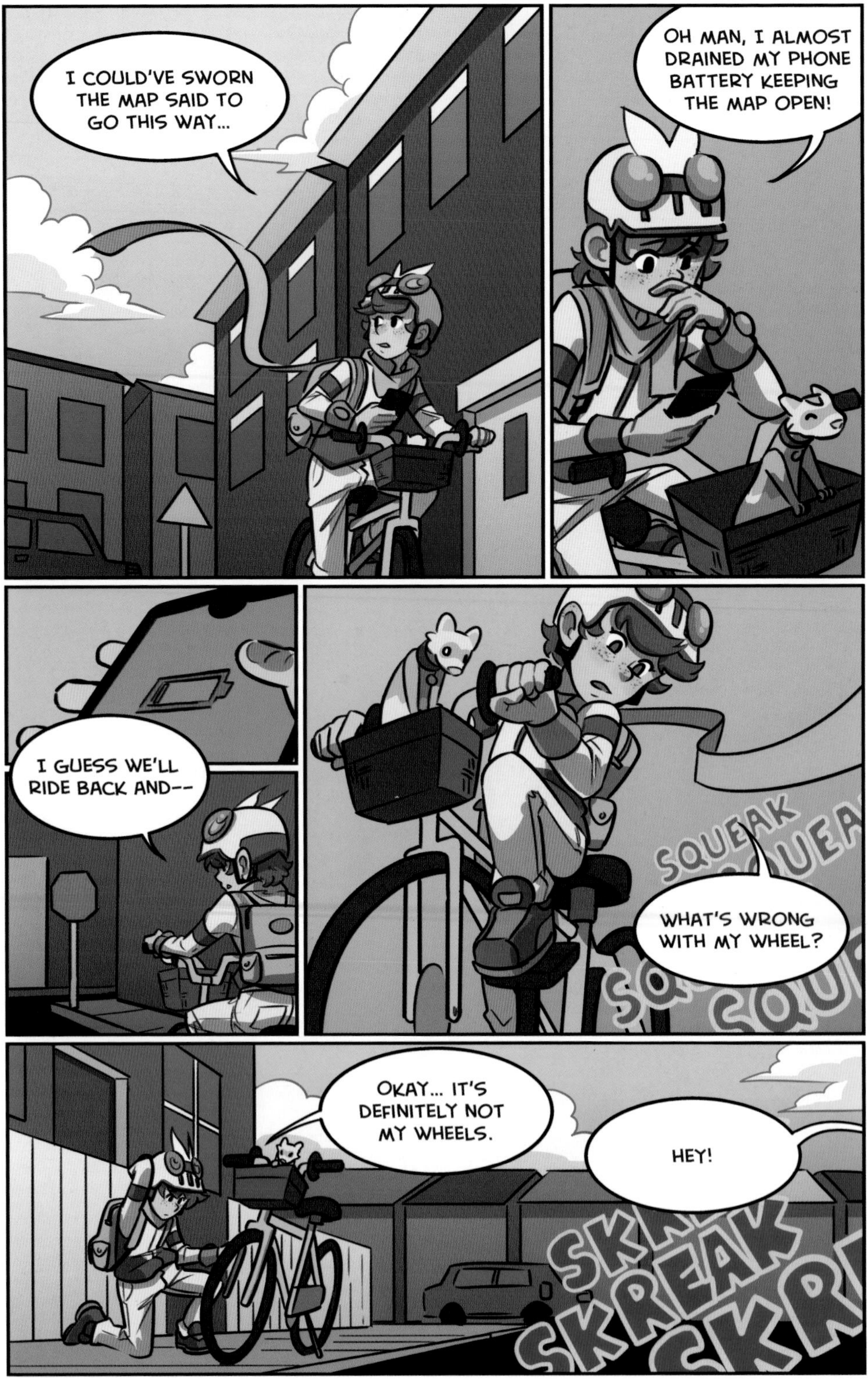

I COULD'VE SWORN THE MAP SAID TO GO THIS WAY...
OH MAN, I ALMOST DRAINED MY PHONE BATTERY KEEPING THE MAP OPEN!
I GUESS WE'LL RIDE BACK AND--
SQUEAK
WHAT'S WRONG WITH MY WHEEL?
OKAY... IT'S DEFINITELY NOT MY WHEELS.
HEY!
SKREAK

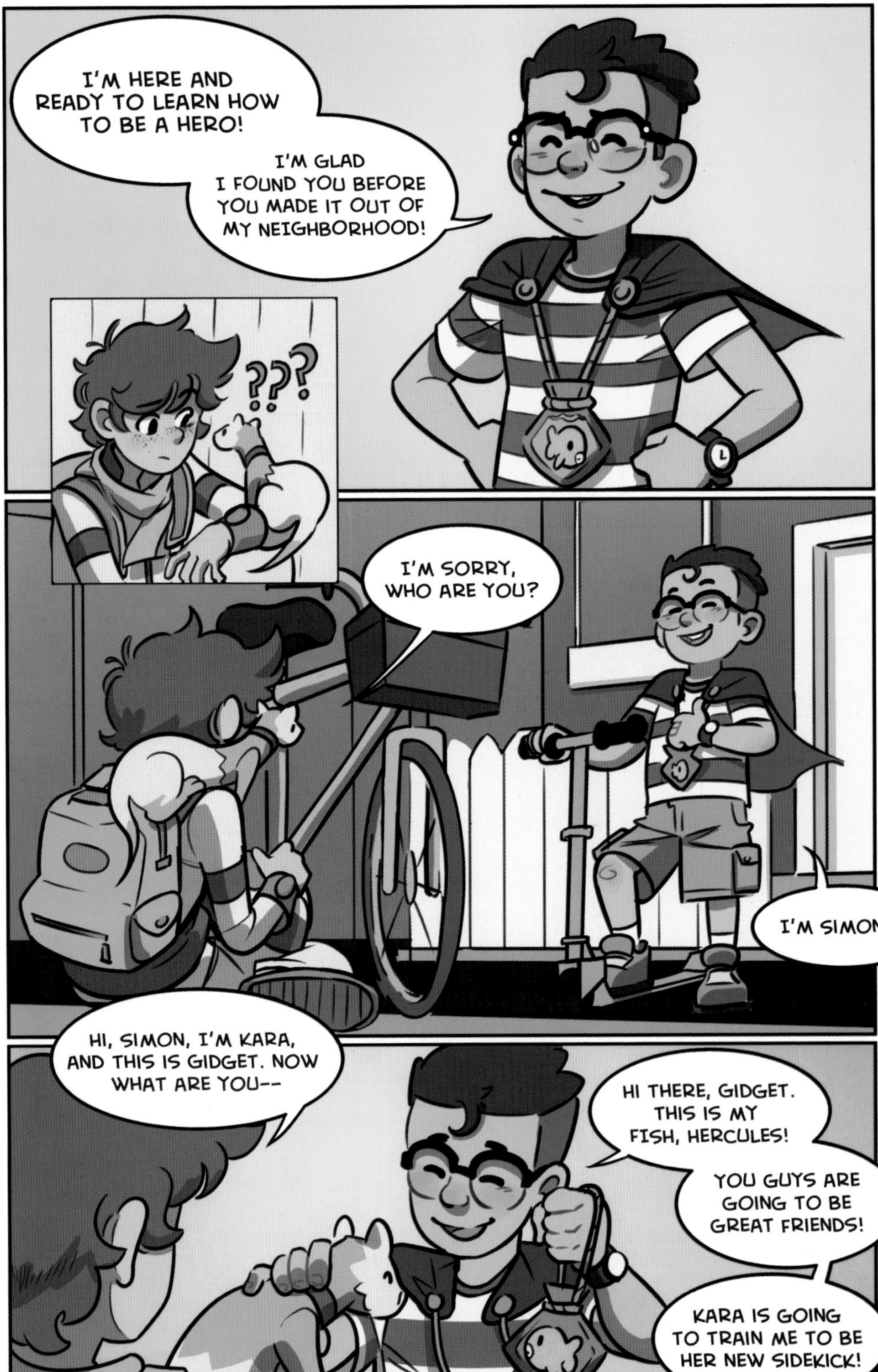
I'M HERE AND READY TO LEARN HOW TO BE A HERO!
I'M GLAD I FOUND YOU BEFORE YOU MADE IT OUT OF MY NEIGHBORHOOD!
???
I'M SORRY, WHO ARE YOU?
I'M SIMON--
HI, SIMON, I'M KARA, AND THIS IS GIDGET. NOW WHAT ARE YOU--
HI THERE, GIDGET. THIS IS MY FISH, HERCULES!
YOU GUYS ARE GOING TO BE GREAT FRIENDS!
KARA IS GOING TO TRAIN ME TO BE HER NEW SIDEKICK!

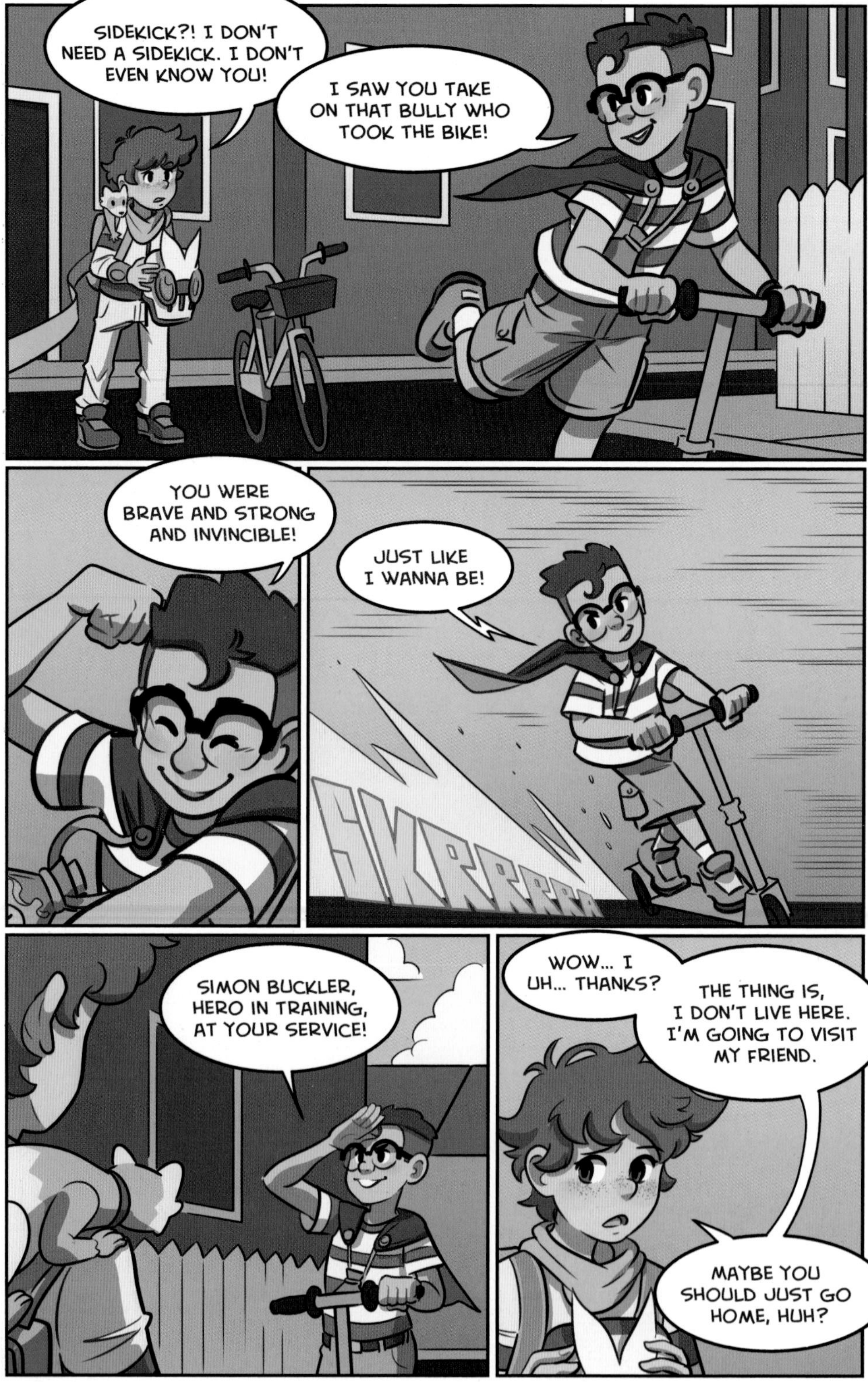
SIDEKICK?! I DON'T NEED A SIDEKICK. I DON'T EVEN KNOW YOU!
I SAW YOU TAKE ON THAT BULLY WHO TOOK THE BIKE!
YOU WERE BRAVE AND STRONG AND INVINCIBLE!
JUST LIKE I WANNA BE!
SKRRRRR
SIMON BUCKLER, HERO IN TRAINING, AT YOUR SERVICE!
WOW... I UH... THANKS?
THE THING IS, I DON'T LIVE HERE. I'M GOING TO VISIT MY FRIEND.
MAYBE YOU SHOULD JUST GO HOME, HUH?

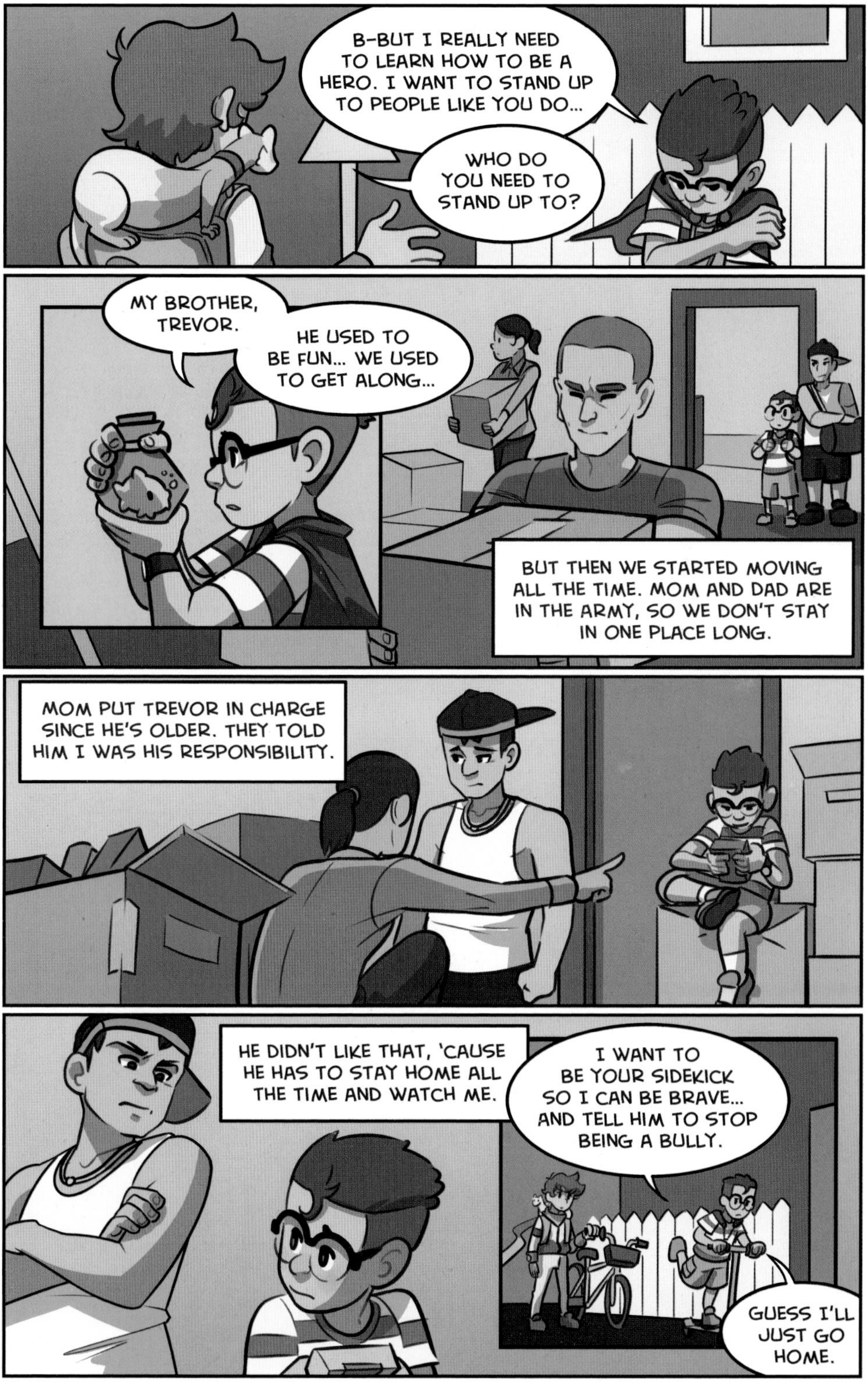

B-BUT I REALLY NEED TO LEARN HOW TO BE A HERO. I WANT TO STAND UP TO PEOPLE LIKE YOU DO...
WHO DO YOU NEED TO STAND UP TO?
MY BROTHER, TREVOR.
HE USED TO BE FUN... WE USED TO GET ALONG...
BUT THEN WE STARTED MOVING ALL THE TIME. MOM AND DAD ARE IN THE ARMY, SO WE DON'T STAY IN ONE PLACE LONG.
MOM PUT TREVOR IN CHARGE SINCE HE'S OLDER. THEY TOLD HIM I WAS HIS RESPONSIBILITY.
HE DIDN'T LIKE THAT, 'CAUSE HE HAS TO STAY HOME ALL THE TIME AND WATCH ME.
I WANT TO BE YOUR SIDEKICK SO I CAN BE BRAVE... AND TELL HIM TO STOP BEING A BULLY.
GUESS I'LL JUST GO HOME.

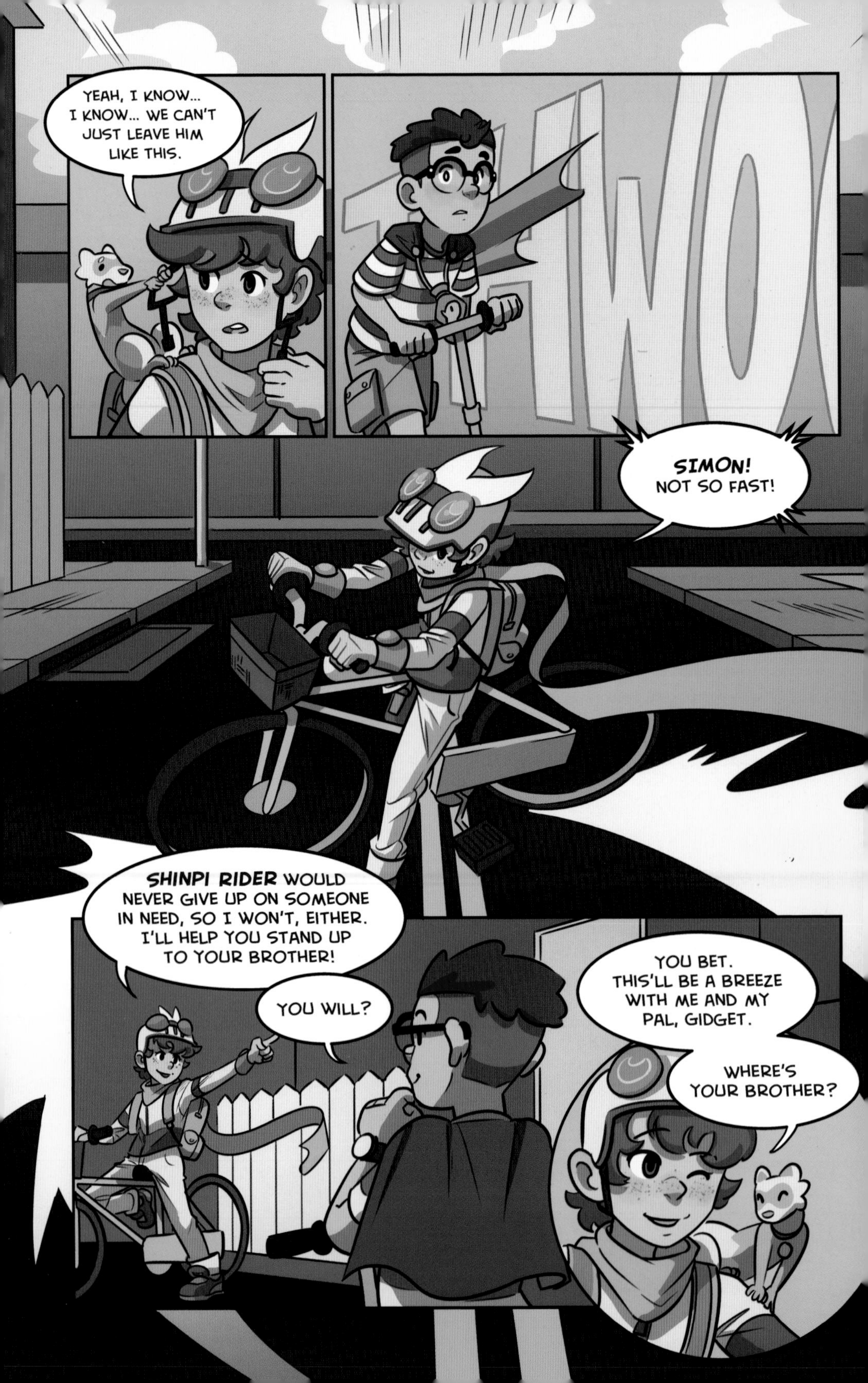
YEAH, I KNOW... I KNOW... WE CAN'T JUST LEAVE HIM LIKE THIS.
SIMON! NOT SO FAST!
SHINPI RIDER WOULD NEVER GIVE UP ON SOMEONE IN NEED, SO I WON'T, EITHER. I'LL HELP YOU STAND UP TO YOUR BROTHER!
YOU WILL?
YOU BET. THIS'LL BE A BREEZE WITH ME AND MY PAL, GIDGET.
WHERE'S YOUR BROTHER?

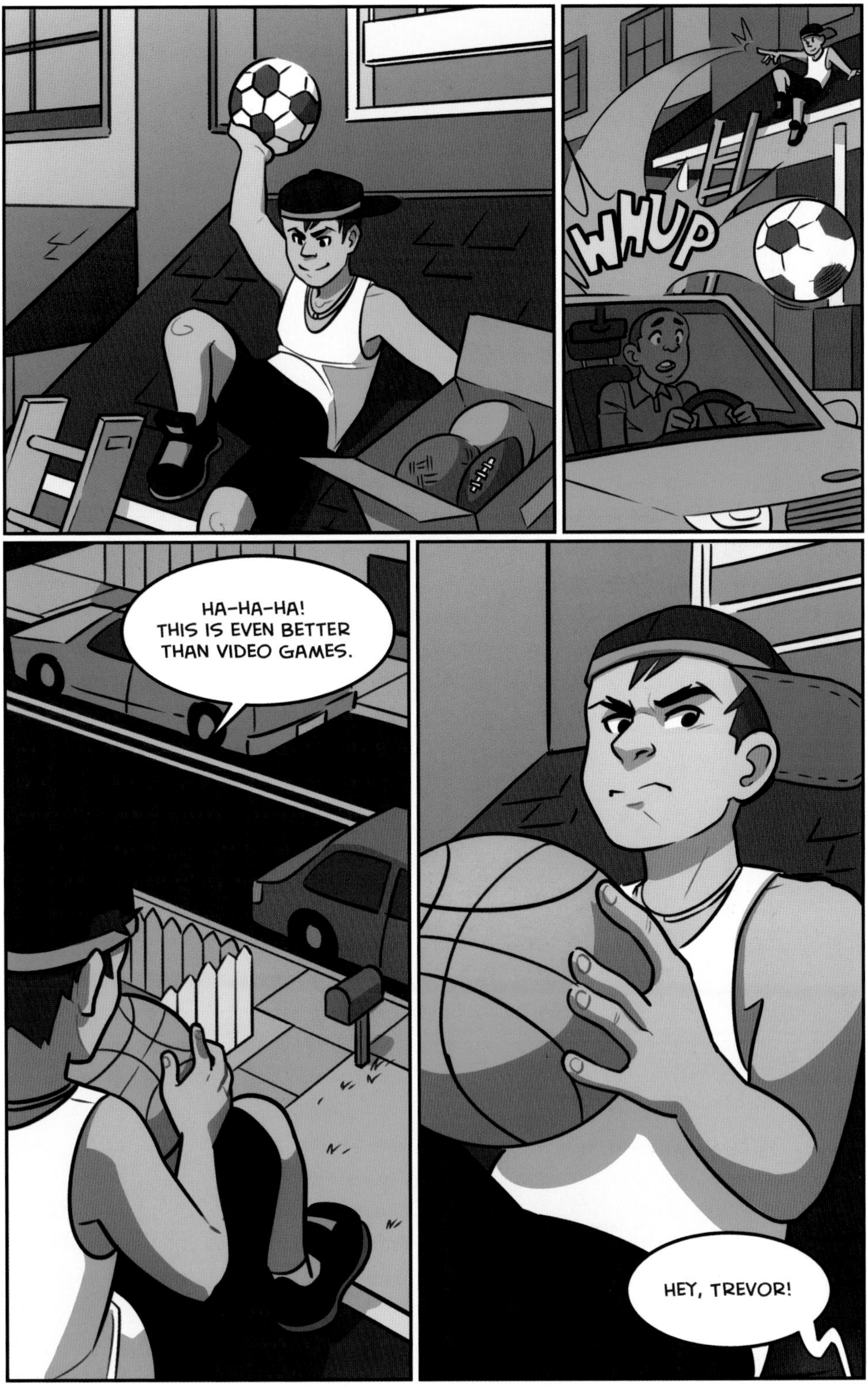
WHUP
HA-HA-HA! THIS IS EVEN BETTER THAN VIDEO GAMES.
HEY, TREVOR!

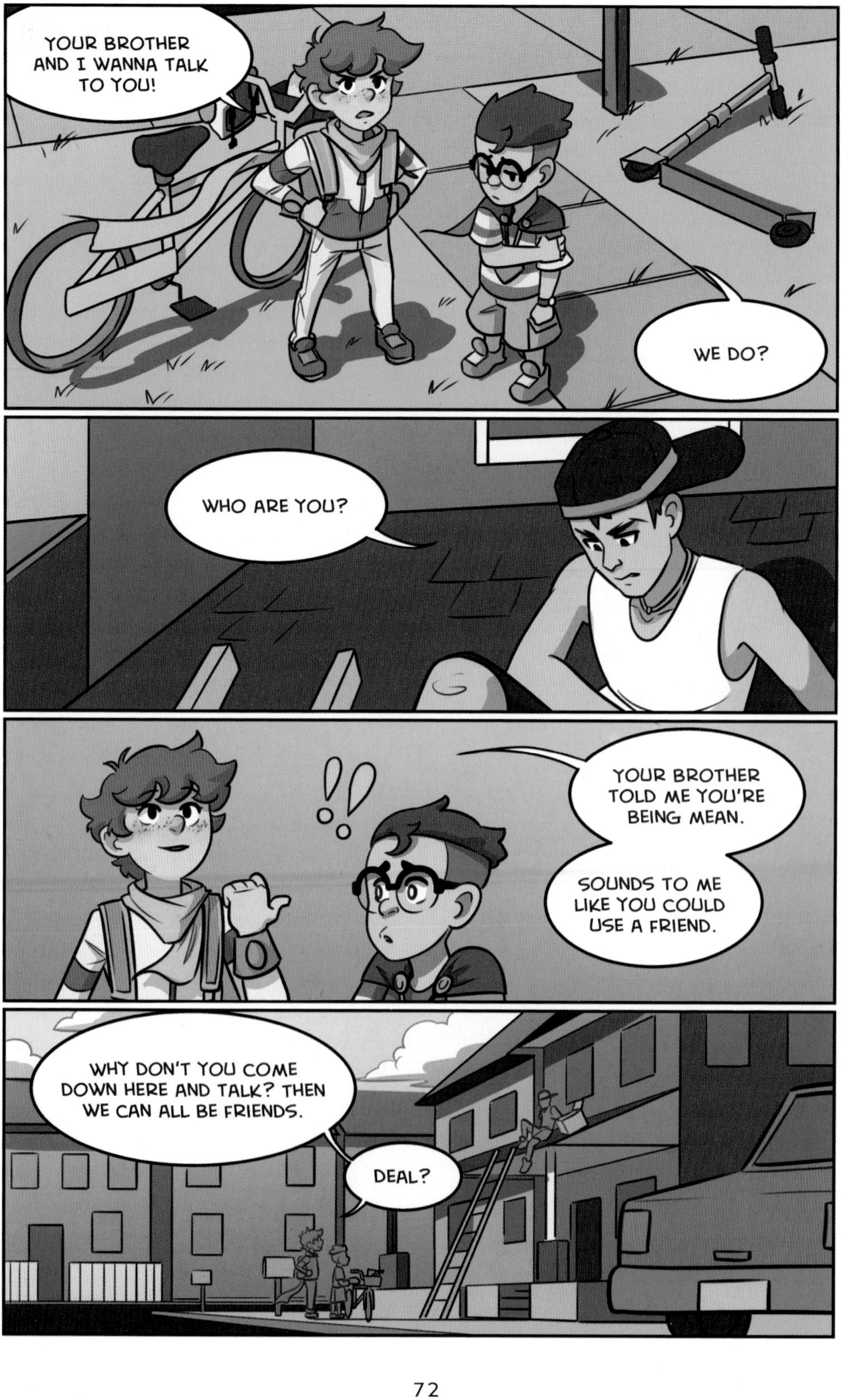
YOUR BROTHER AND I WANNA TALK TO YOU!
WE DO?
WHO ARE YOU?
YOUR BROTHER TOLD ME YOU'RE BEING MEAN.
SOUNDS TO ME LIKE YOU COULD USE A FRIEND.
WHY DON'T YOU COME DOWN HERE AND TALK? THEN WE CAN ALL BE FRIENDS.
DEAL?

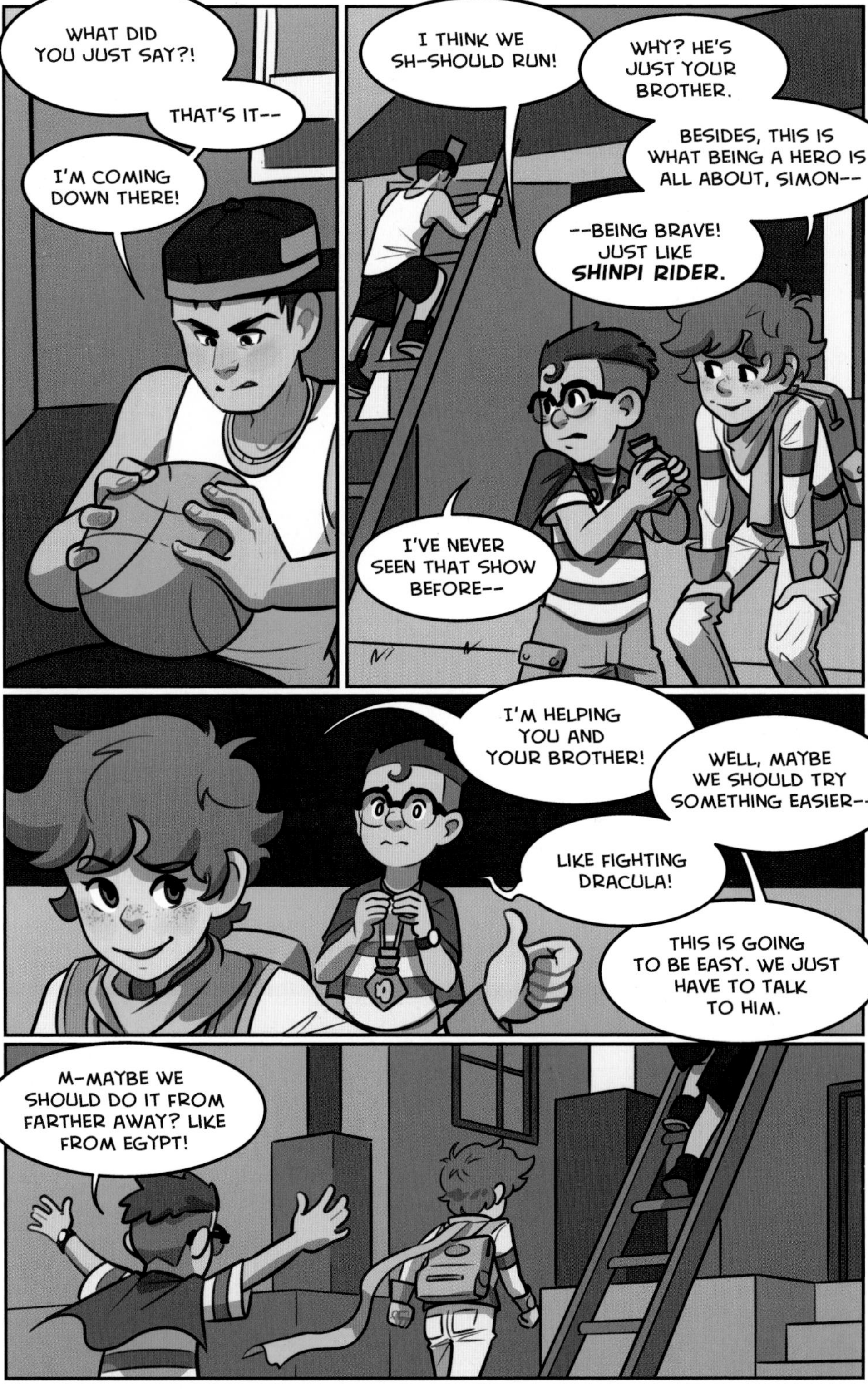
WHAT DID YOU JUST SAY?!
THAT'S IT--
I'M COMING DOWN THERE!
I THINK WE SH-SHOULD RUN!
WHY? HE'S JUST YOUR BROTHER.
BESIDES, THIS IS WHAT BEING A HERO IS ALL ABOUT, SIMON--
--BEING BRAVE! JUST LIKE **SHINPI RIDER.**
I'VE NEVER SEEN THAT SHOW BEFORE--
I'M HELPING YOU AND YOUR BROTHER!
WELL, MAYBE WE SHOULD TRY SOMETHING EASIER--
LIKE FIGHTING DRACULA!
THIS IS GOING TO BE EASY. WE JUST HAVE TO TALK TO HIM.
M-MAYBE WE SHOULD DO IT FROM FARTHER AWAY? LIKE FROM EGYPT!

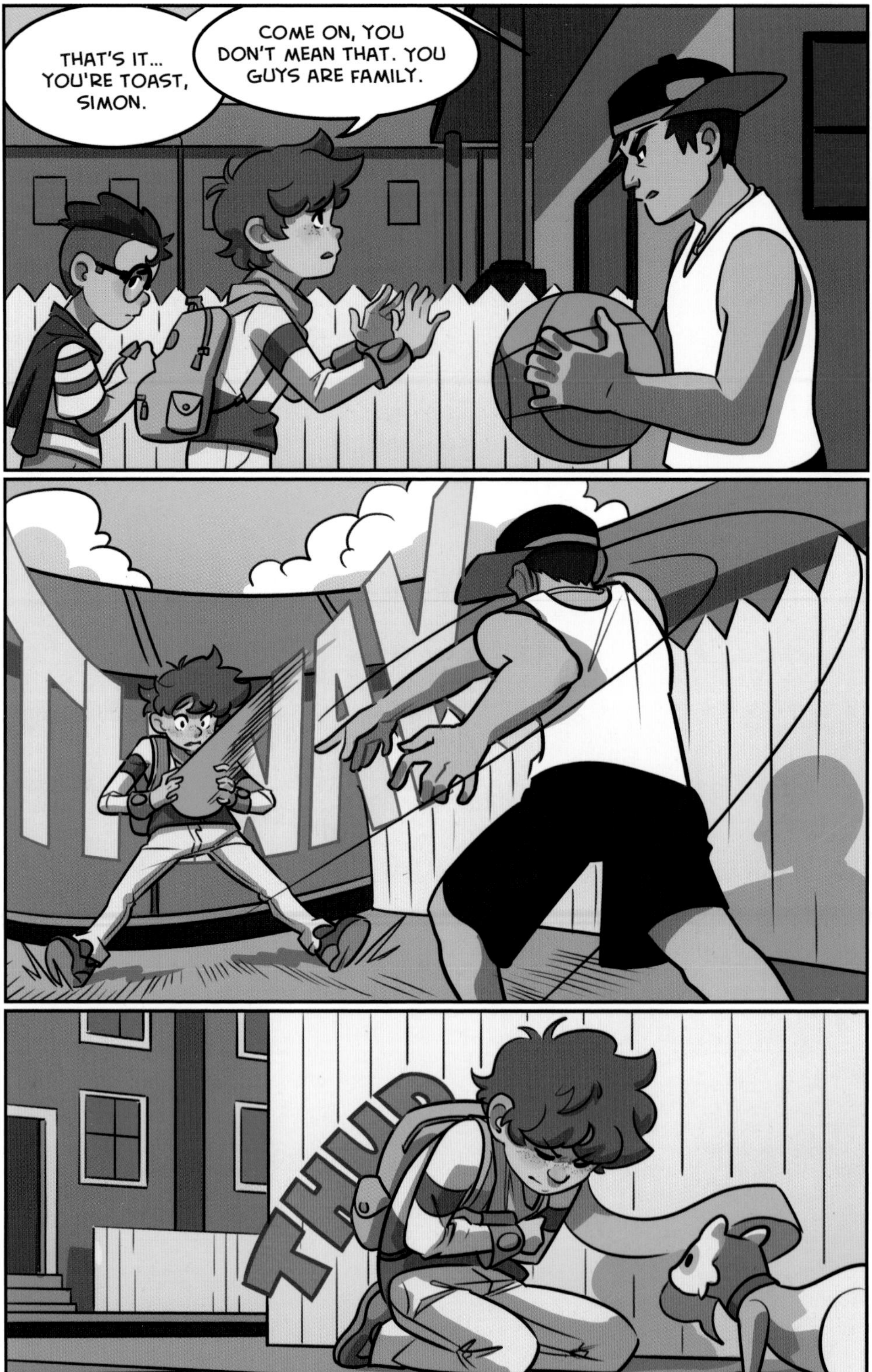
THAT'S IT... YOU'RE TOAST, SIMON.
COME ON, YOU DON'T MEAN THAT. YOU GUYS ARE FAMILY.
THWAK
THUD

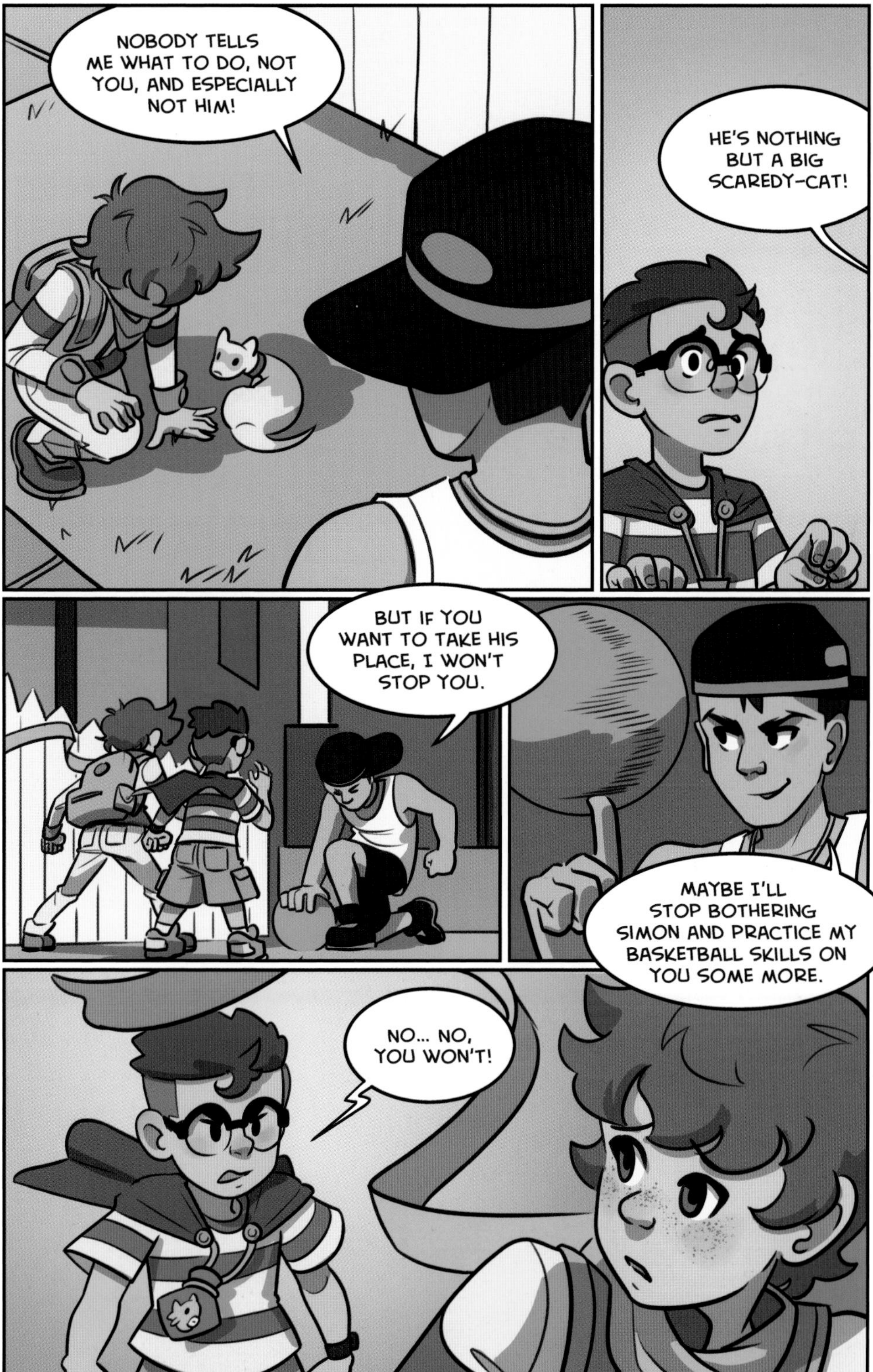
NOBODY TELLS ME WHAT TO DO, NOT YOU, AND ESPECIALLY NOT HIM!
HE'S NOTHING BUT A BIG SCAREDY-CAT!
BUT IF YOU WANT TO TAKE HIS PLACE, I WON'T STOP YOU.
MAYBE I'LL STOP BOTHERING SIMON AND PRACTICE MY BASKETBALL SKILLS ON YOU SOME MORE.
NO... NO, YOU WON'T!

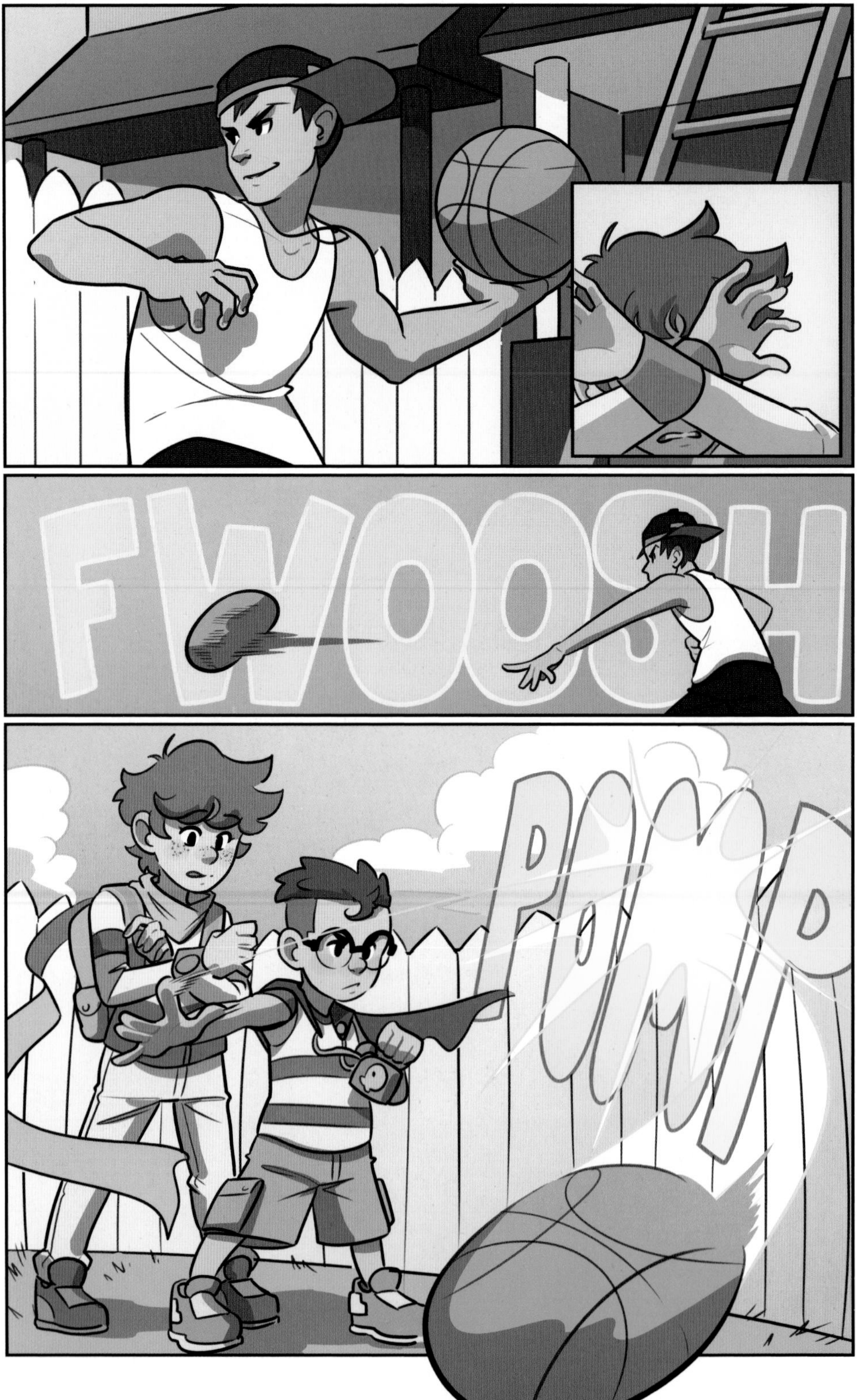
FWOOSH
POMP

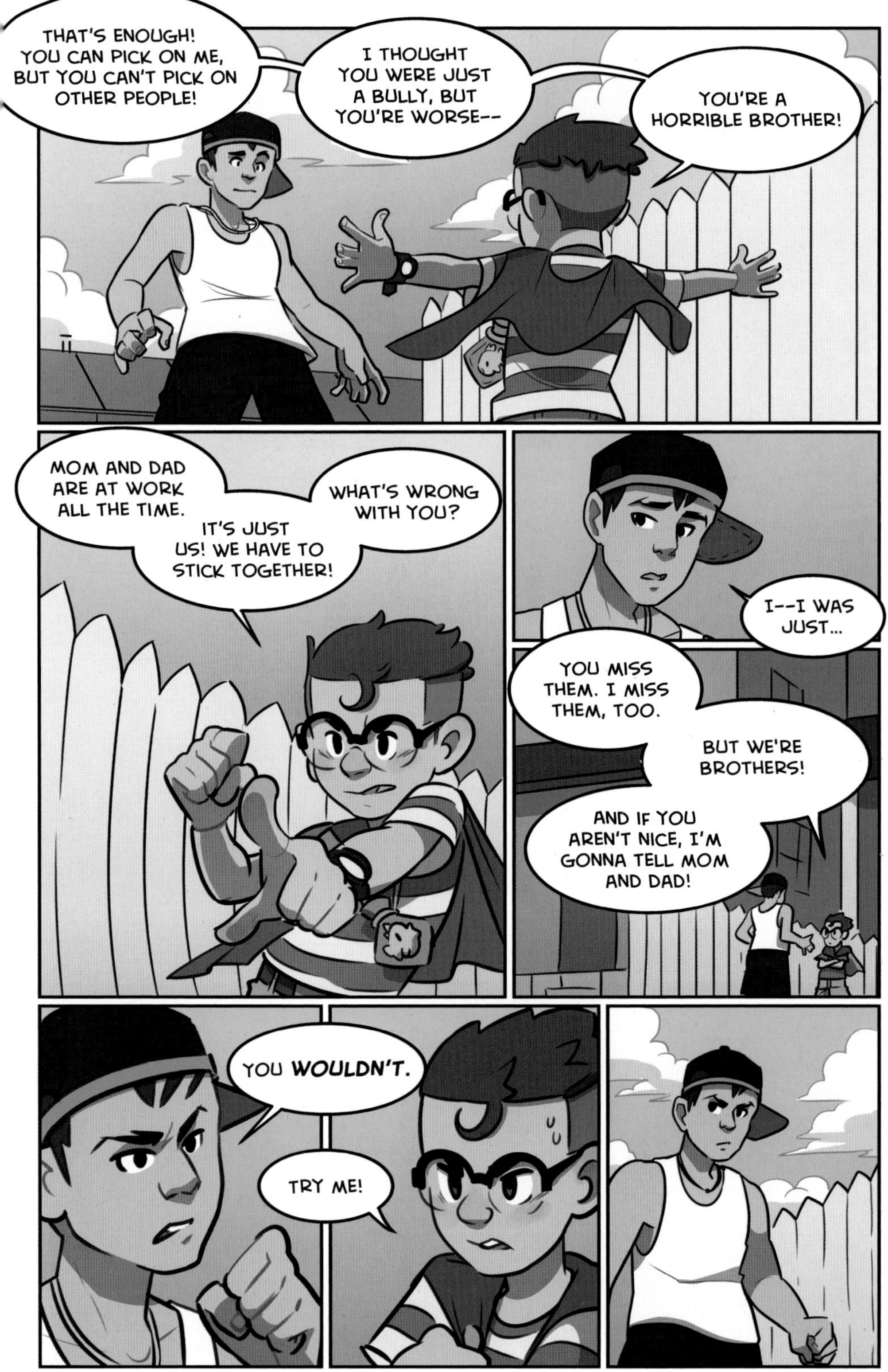
THAT'S ENOUGH! YOU CAN PICK ON ME, BUT YOU CAN'T PICK ON OTHER PEOPLE!
I THOUGHT YOU WERE JUST A BULLY, BUT YOU'RE WORSE--
YOU'RE A HORRIBLE BROTHER!
MOM AND DAD ARE AT WORK ALL THE TIME.
WHAT'S WRONG WITH YOU?
IT'S JUST US! WE HAVE TO STICK TOGETHER!
I--I WAS JUST...
YOU MISS THEM. I MISS THEM, TOO.
BUT WE'RE BROTHERS!
AND IF YOU AREN'T NICE, I'M GONNA TELL MOM AND DAD!
YOU **WOULDN'T.**
TRY ME!

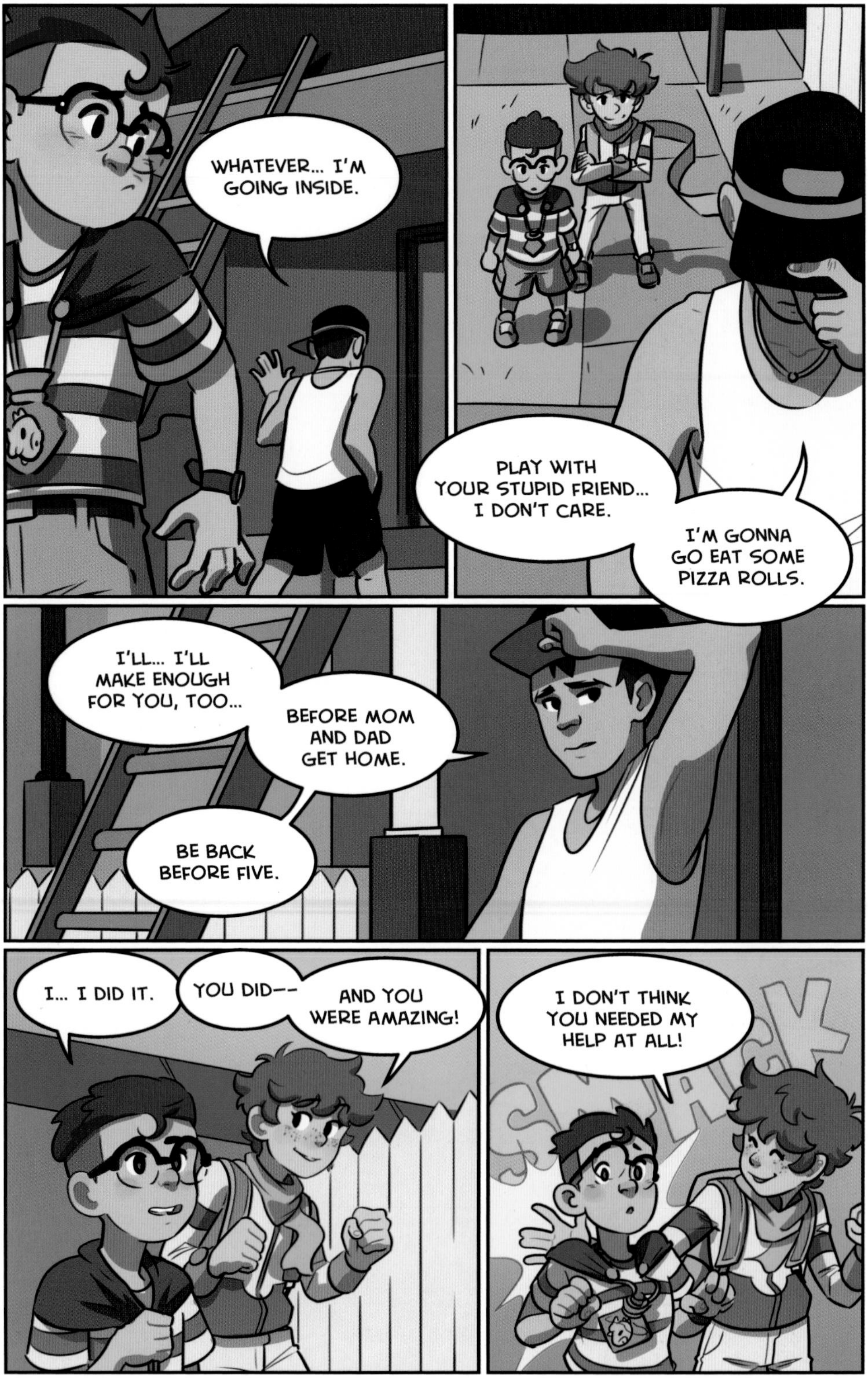
WHATEVER... I'M GOING INSIDE.
PLAY WITH YOUR STUPID FRIEND... I DON'T CARE.
I'M GONNA GO EAT SOME PIZZA ROLLS.
I'LL... I'LL MAKE ENOUGH FOR YOU, TOO...
BEFORE MOM AND DAD GET HOME.
BE BACK BEFORE FIVE.
I... I DID IT.
YOU DID--
AND YOU WERE AMAZING!
I DON'T THINK YOU NEEDED MY HELP AT ALL!
SMACK

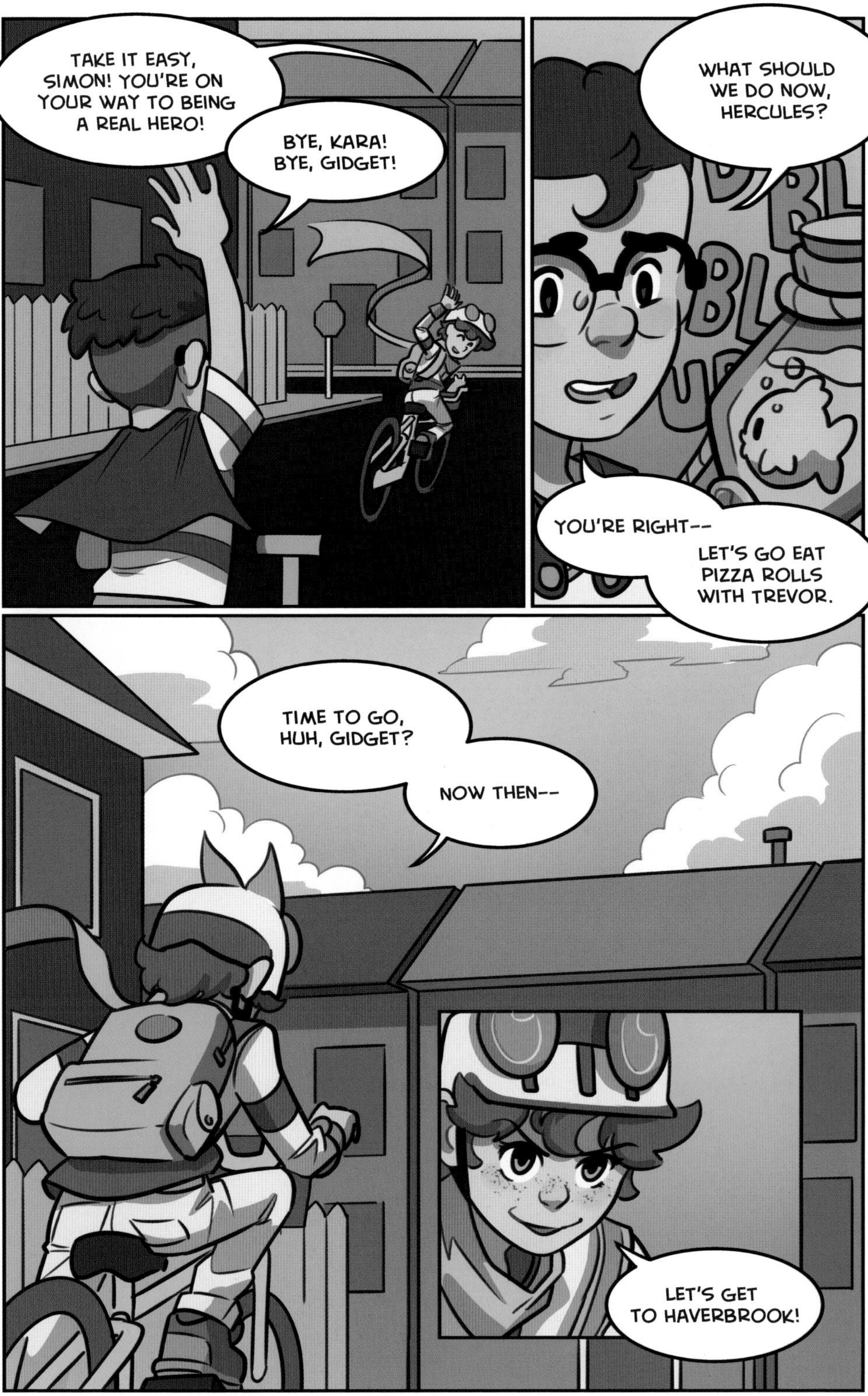
TAKE IT EASY, SIMON! YOU'RE ON YOUR WAY TO BEING A REAL HERO!
BYE, KARA! BYE, GIDGET!
WHAT SHOULD WE DO NOW, HERCULES?
YOU'RE RIGHT-- LET'S GO EAT PIZZA ROLLS WITH TREVOR.
TIME TO GO, HUH, GIDGET?
NOW THEN--
LET'S GET TO HAVERBROOK!

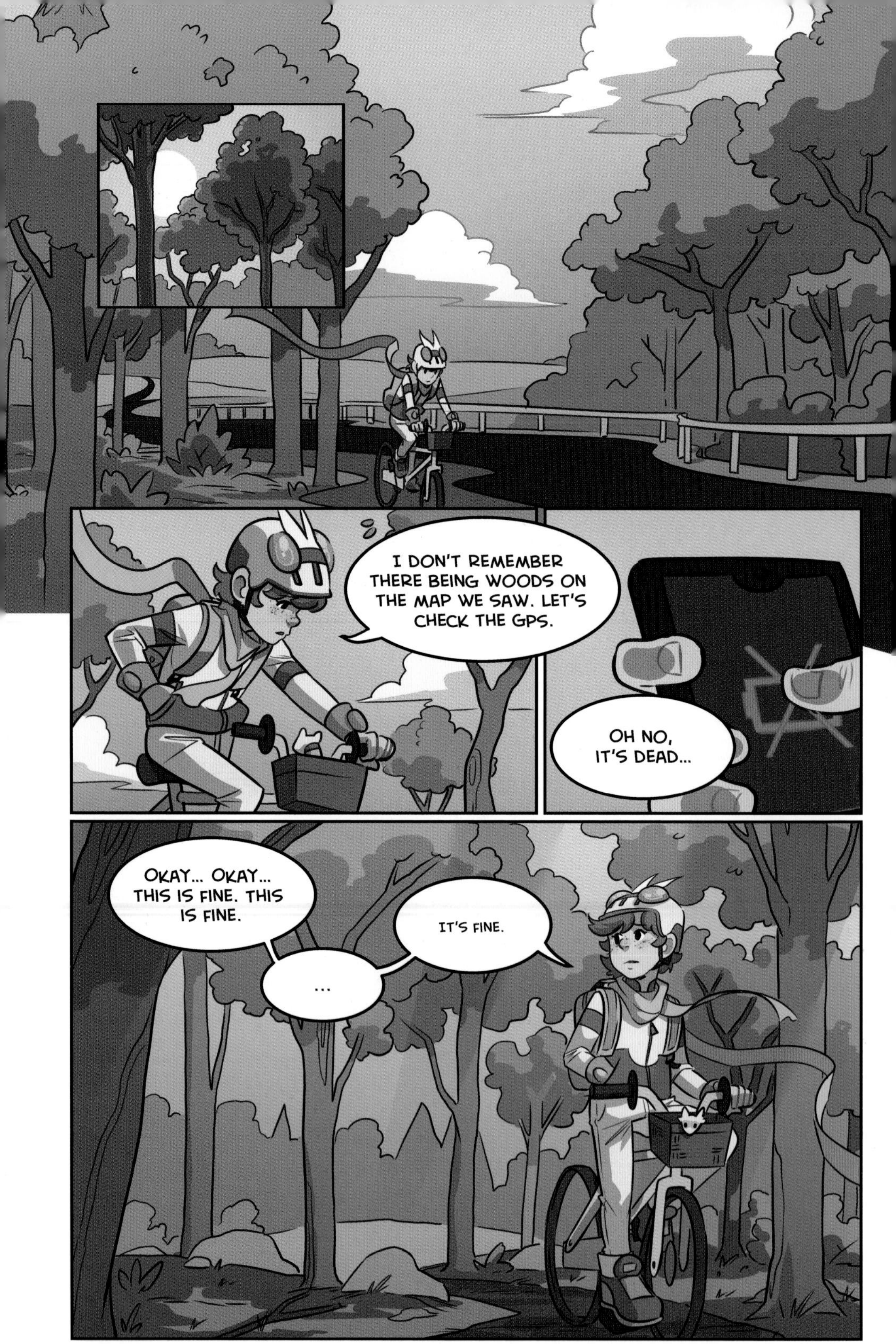
I DON'T REMEMBER THERE BEING WOODS ON THE MAP WE SAW. LET'S CHECK THE GPS.
OH NO, IT'S DEAD...
OKAY... OKAY... THIS IS FINE. THIS IS FINE.
...
IT'S FINE.

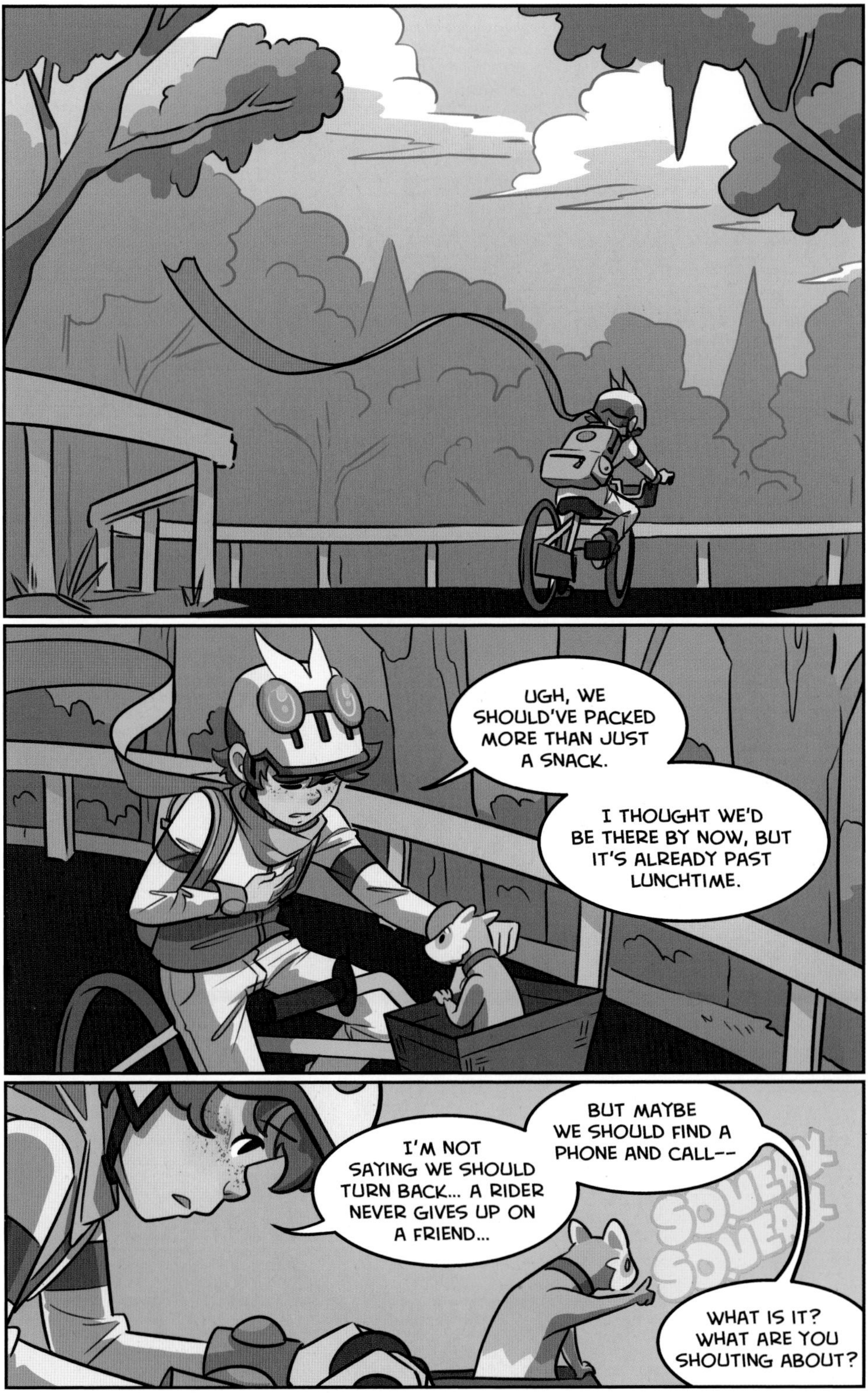
UGH, WE SHOULD'VE PACKED MORE THAN JUST A SNACK.
I THOUGHT WE'D BE THERE BY NOW, BUT IT'S ALREADY PAST LUNCHTIME.
I'M NOT SAYING WE SHOULD TURN BACK... A RIDER NEVER GIVES UP ON A FRIEND...
BUT MAYBE WE SHOULD FIND A PHONE AND CALL--
SQUEAK SQUEAK
WHAT IS IT? WHAT ARE YOU SHOUTING ABOUT?

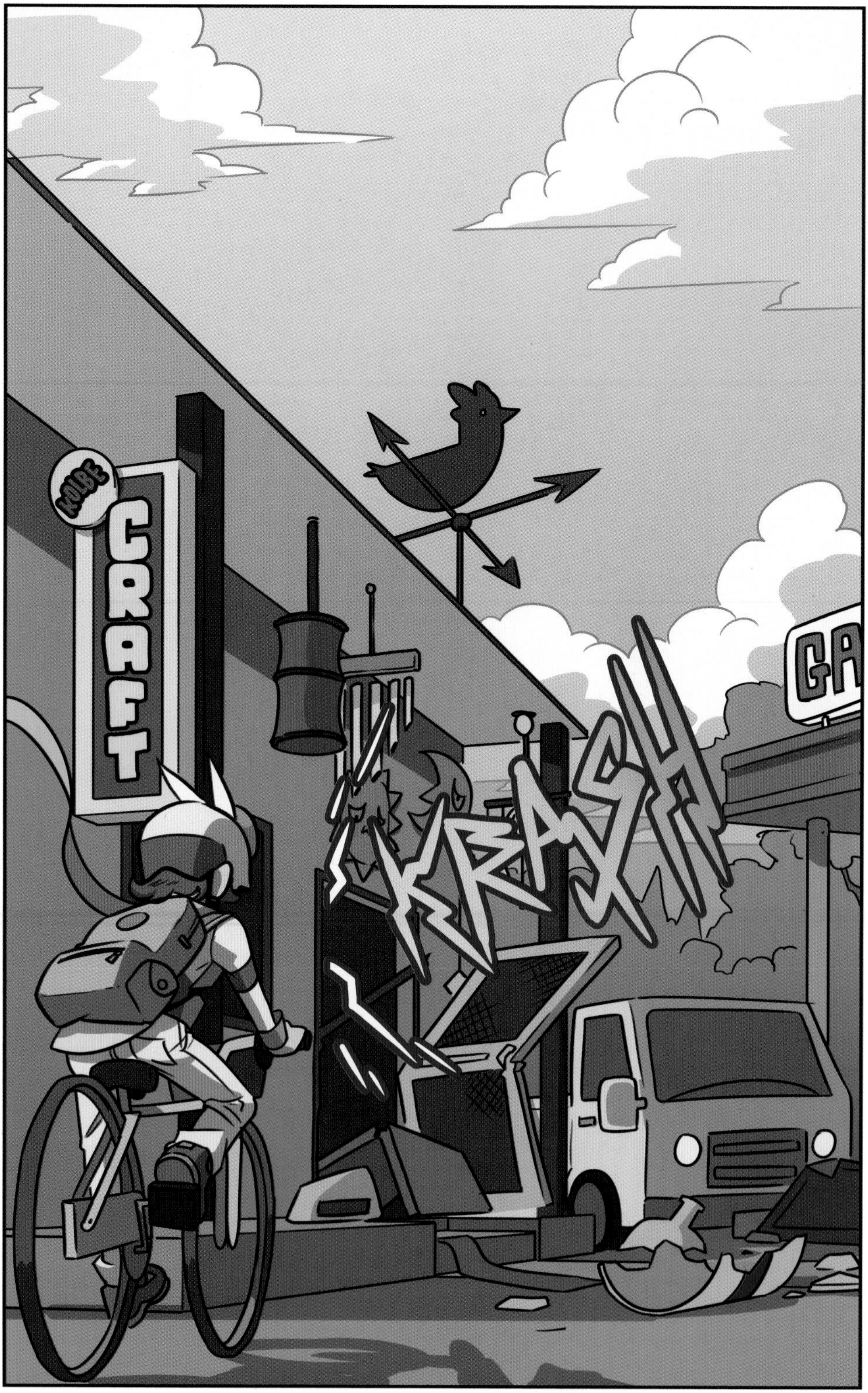
KOLBE
CRAFT
KRASH

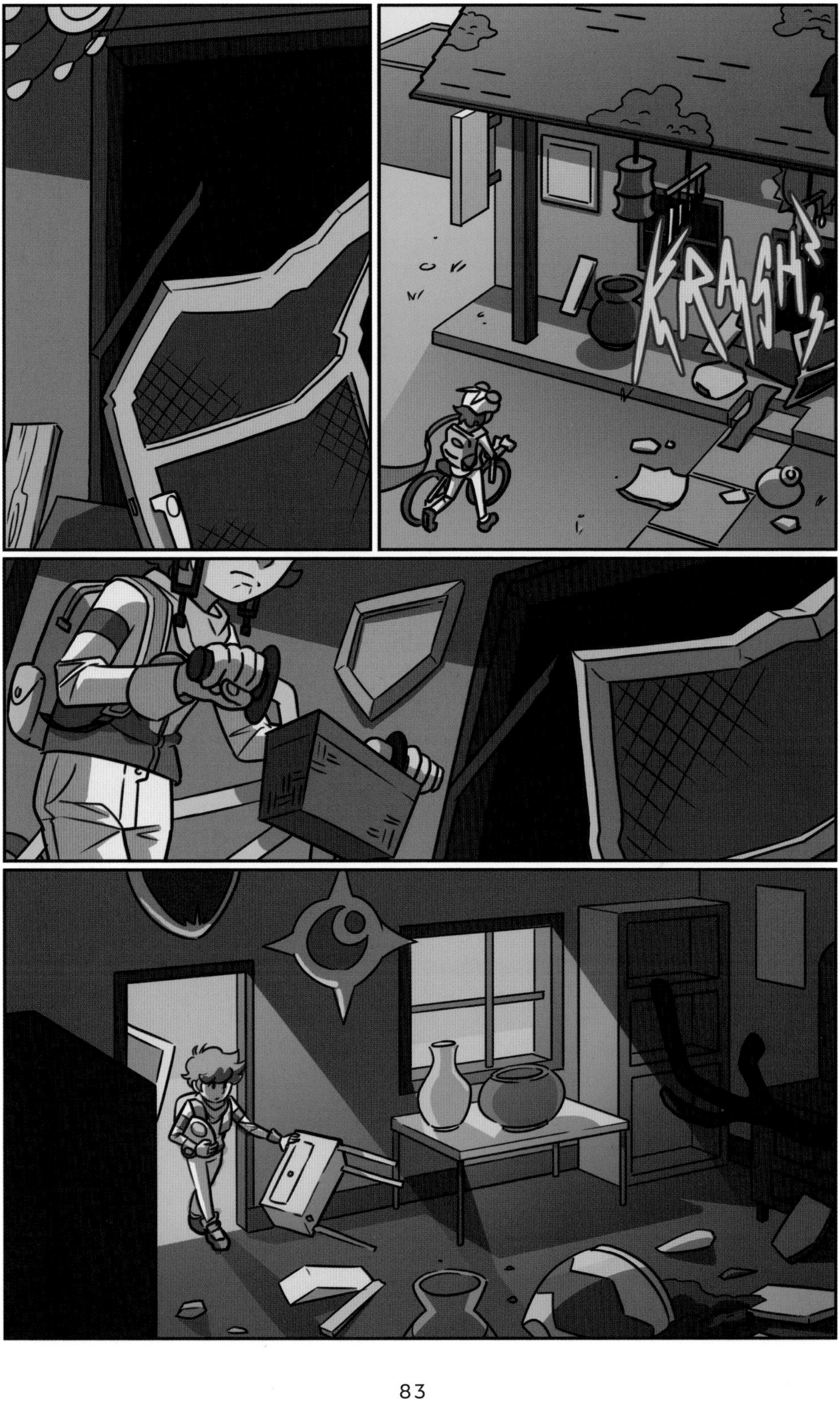
KRASH

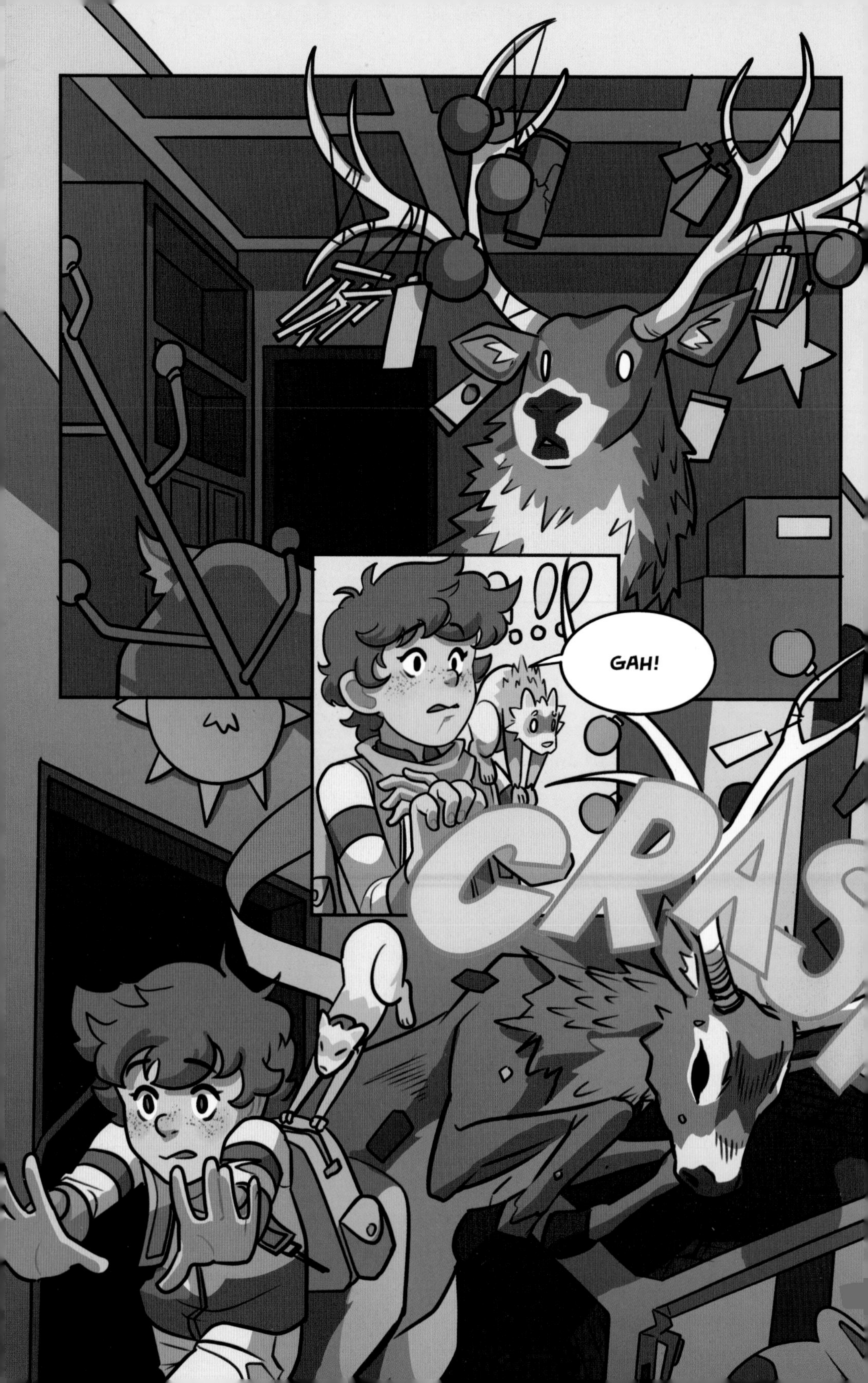
GAH!
CRAS

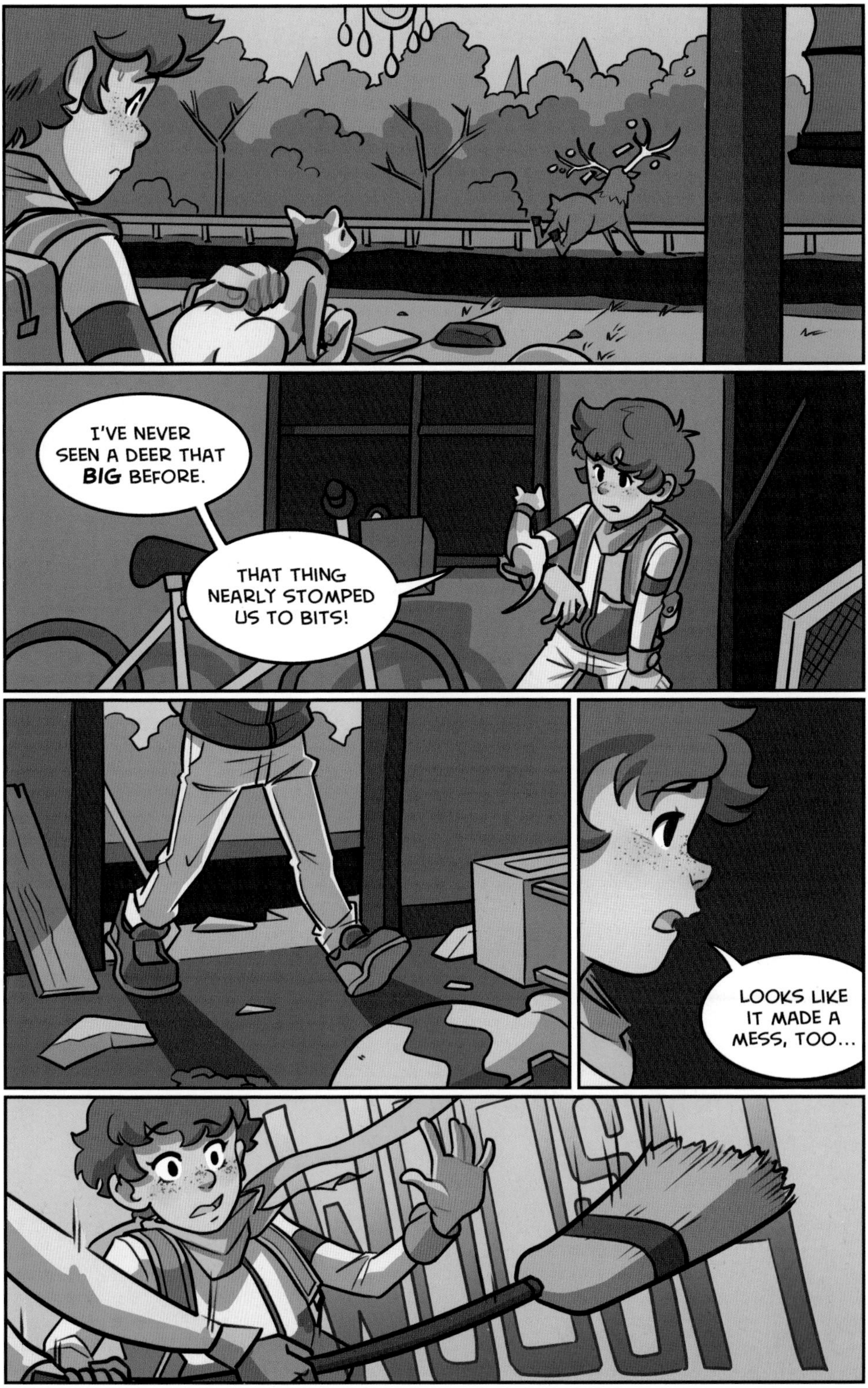
I'VE NEVER SEEN A DEER THAT BIG BEFORE.
THAT THING NEARLY STOMPED US TO BITS!
LOOKS LIKE IT MADE A MESS, TOO...

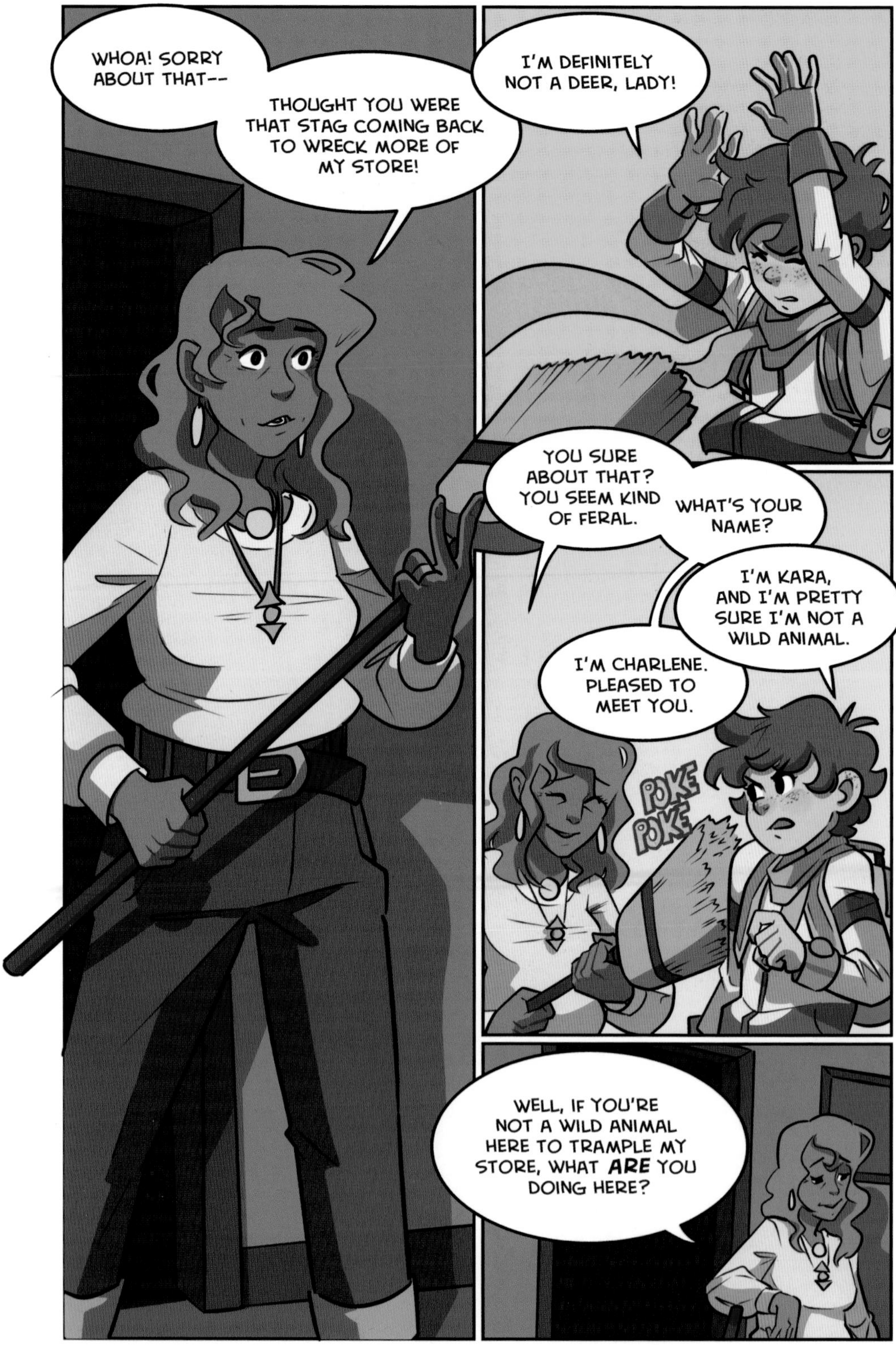
WHOA! SORRY ABOUT THAT--
THOUGHT YOU WERE THAT STAG COMING BACK TO WRECK MORE OF MY STORE!
I'M DEFINITELY NOT A DEER, LADY!
YOU SURE ABOUT THAT? YOU SEEM KIND OF FERAL.
WHAT'S YOUR NAME?
I'M KARA, AND I'M PRETTY SURE I'M NOT A WILD ANIMAL.
I'M CHARLENE. PLEASED TO MEET YOU.
POKE POKE
WELL, IF YOU'RE NOT A WILD ANIMAL HERE TO TRAMPLE MY STORE, WHAT **ARE** YOU DOING HERE?

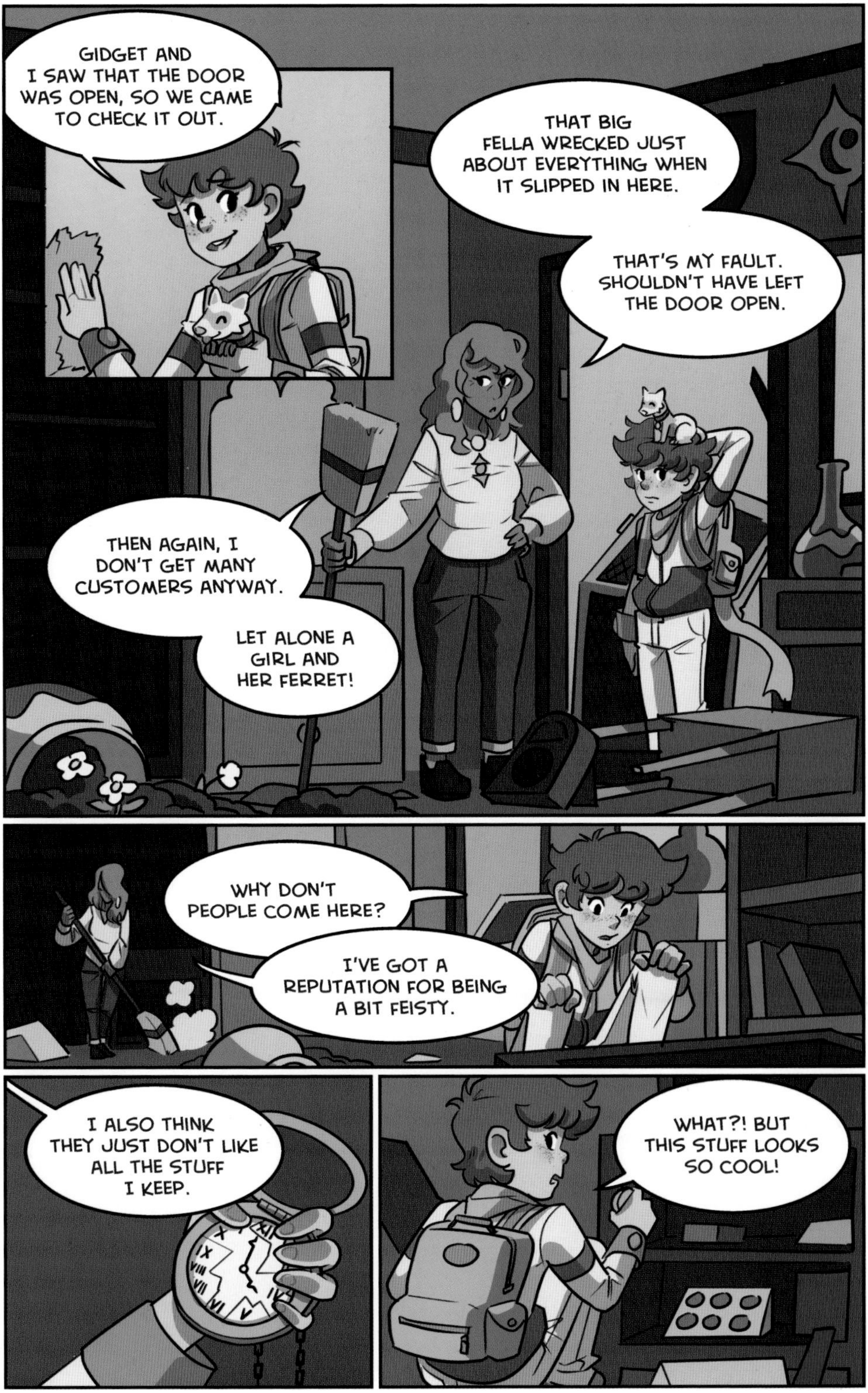
GIDGET AND I SAW THAT THE DOOR WAS OPEN, SO WE CAME TO CHECK IT OUT.
THAT BIG FELLA WRECKED JUST ABOUT EVERYTHING WHEN IT SLIPPED IN HERE.
THAT'S MY FAULT. SHOULDN'T HAVE LEFT THE DOOR OPEN.
THEN AGAIN, I DON'T GET MANY CUSTOMERS ANYWAY.
LET ALONE A GIRL AND HER FERRET!
WHY DON'T PEOPLE COME HERE?
I'VE GOT A REPUTATION FOR BEING A BIT FEISTY.
I ALSO THINK THEY JUST DON'T LIKE ALL THE STUFF I KEEP.
WHAT?! BUT THIS STUFF LOOKS SO COOL!

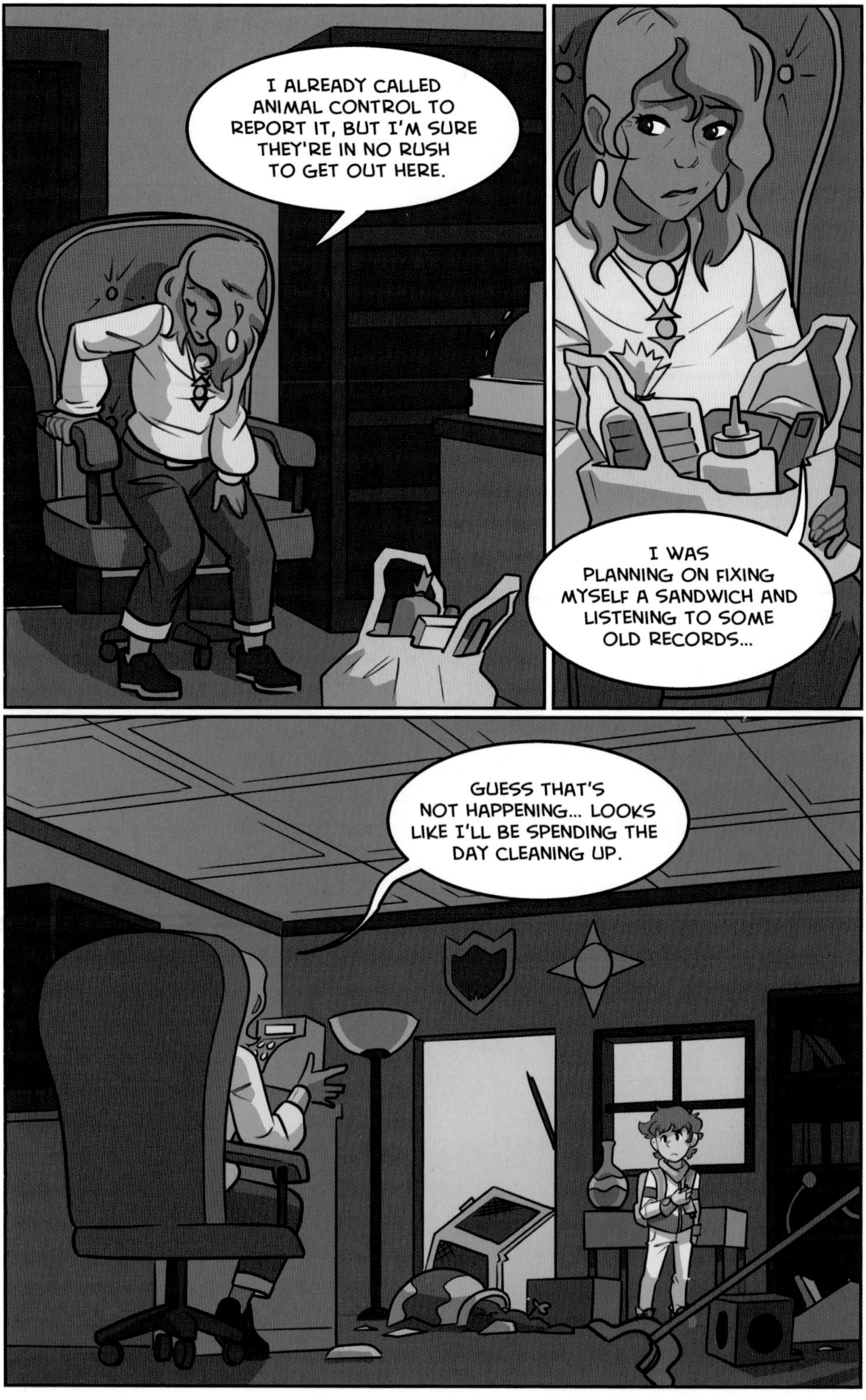
I ALREADY CALLED ANIMAL CONTROL TO REPORT IT, BUT I'M SURE THEY'RE IN NO RUSH TO GET OUT HERE.
I WAS PLANNING ON FIXING MYSELF A SANDWICH AND LISTENING TO SOME OLD RECORDS...
GUESS THAT'S NOT HAPPENING... LOOKS LIKE I'LL BE SPENDING THE DAY CLEANING UP.

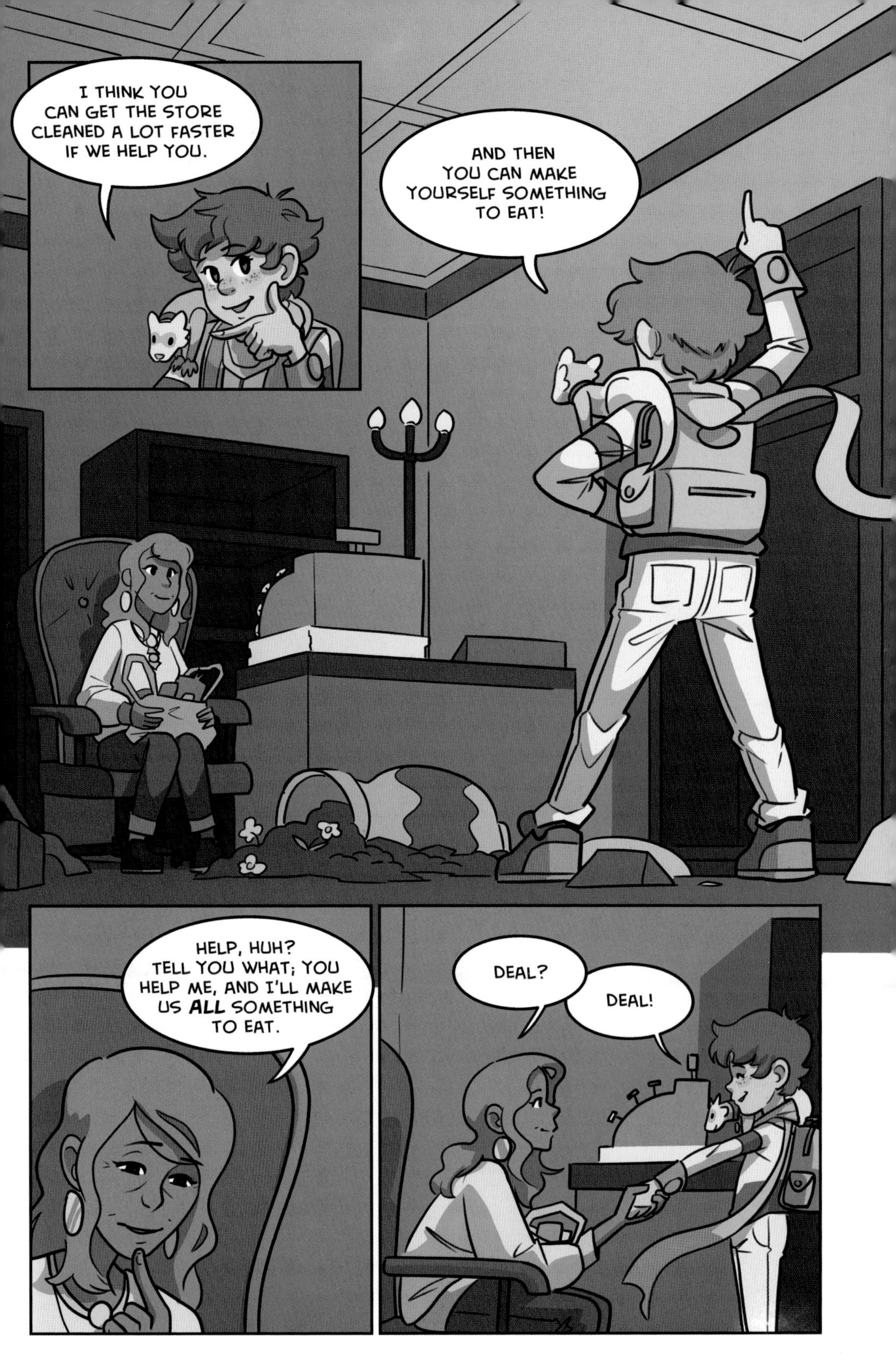
I THINK YOU CAN GET THE STORE CLEANED A LOT FASTER IF WE HELP YOU.
AND THEN YOU CAN MAKE YOURSELF SOMETHING TO EAT!
HELP, HUH? TELL YOU WHAT; YOU HELP ME, AND I'LL MAKE US **ALL** SOMETHING TO EAT.
DEAL?
DEAL!

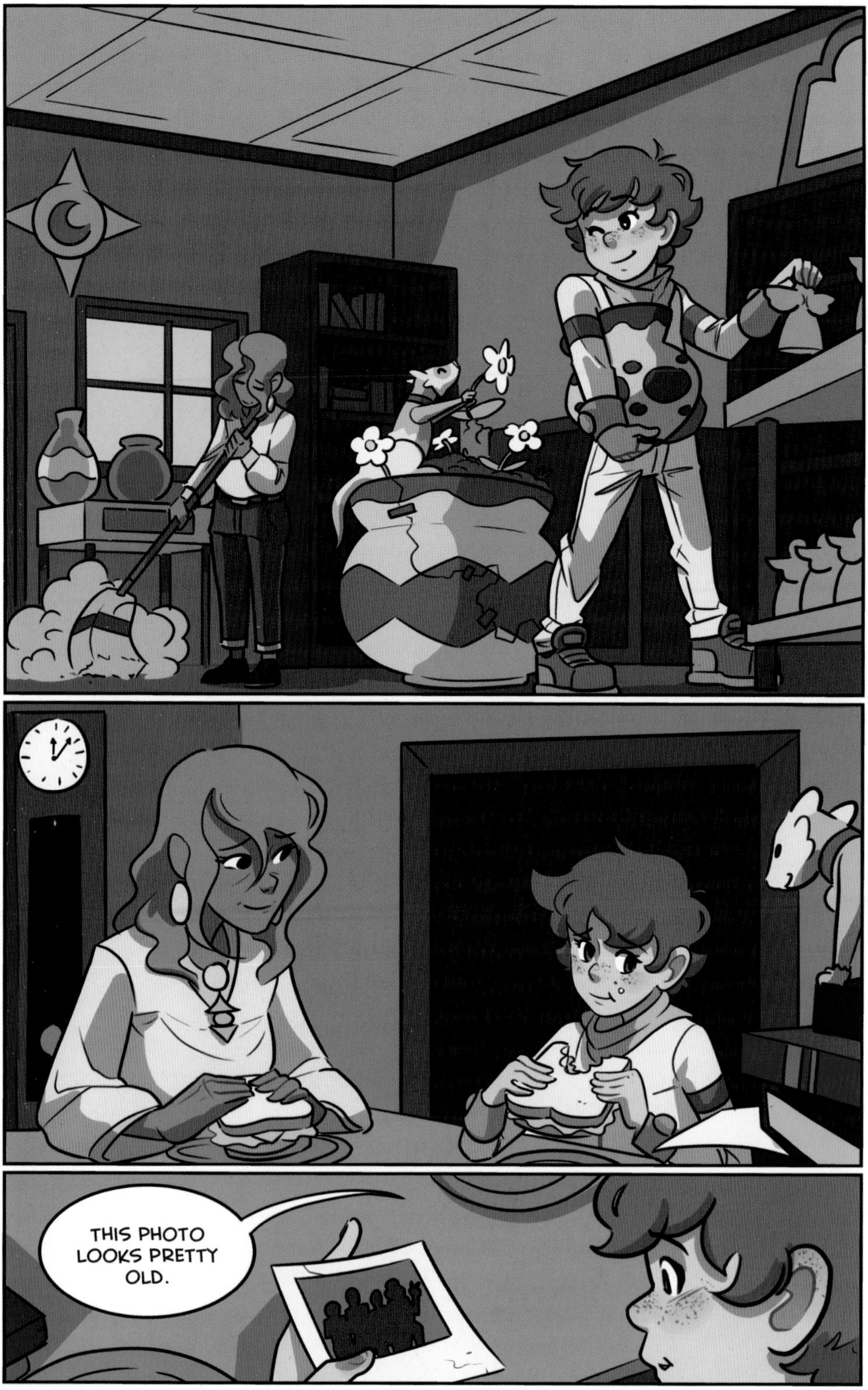
THIS PHOTO LOOKS PRETTY OLD.

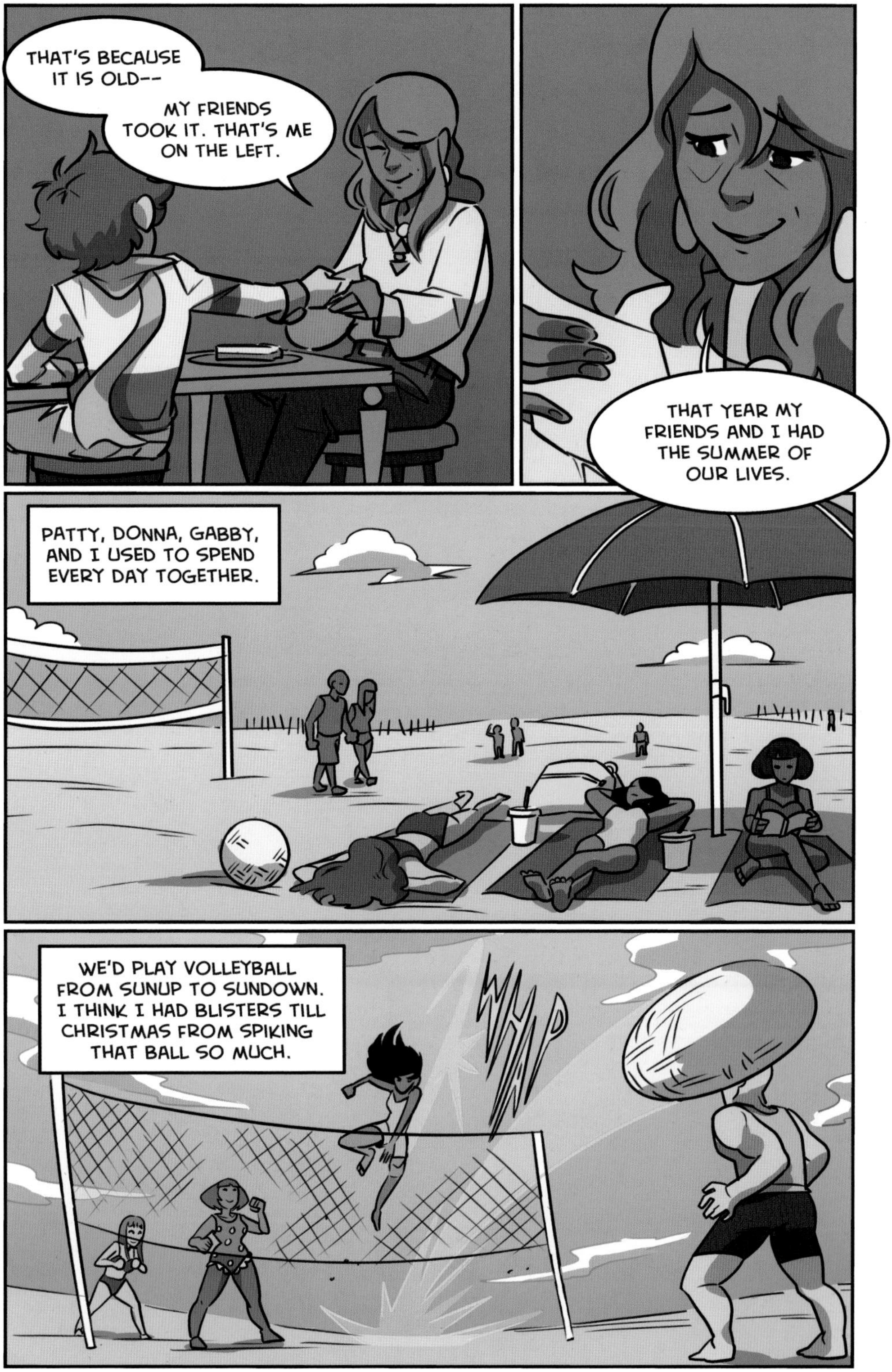
THAT'S BECAUSE IT IS OLD--
MY FRIENDS TOOK IT. THAT'S ME ON THE LEFT.
THAT YEAR MY FRIENDS AND I HAD THE SUMMER OF OUR LIVES.
PATTY, DONNA, GABBY, AND I USED TO SPEND EVERY DAY TOGETHER.
WE'D PLAY VOLLEYBALL FROM SUNUP TO SUNDOWN. I THINK I HAD BLISTERS TILL CHRISTMAS FROM SPIKING THAT BALL SO MUCH.
WHAP

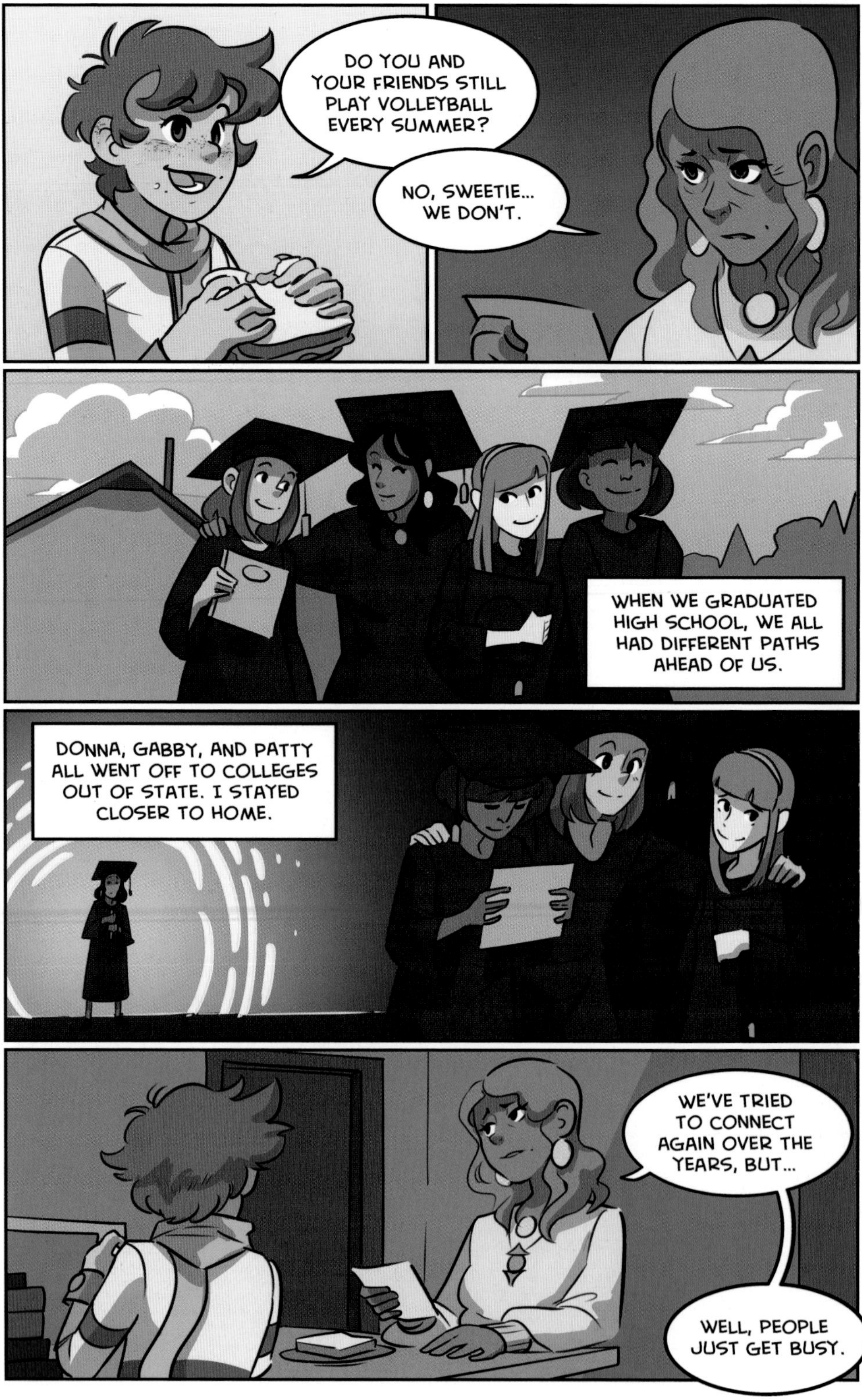
DO YOU AND YOUR FRIENDS STILL PLAY VOLLEYBALL EVERY SUMMER?
NO, SWEETIE... WE DON'T.
WHEN WE GRADUATED HIGH SCHOOL, WE ALL HAD DIFFERENT PATHS AHEAD OF US.
DONNA, GABBY, AND PATTY ALL WENT OFF TO COLLEGES OUT OF STATE. I STAYED CLOSER TO HOME.
WE'VE TRIED TO CONNECT AGAIN OVER THE YEARS, BUT...
WELL, PEOPLE JUST GET BUSY.

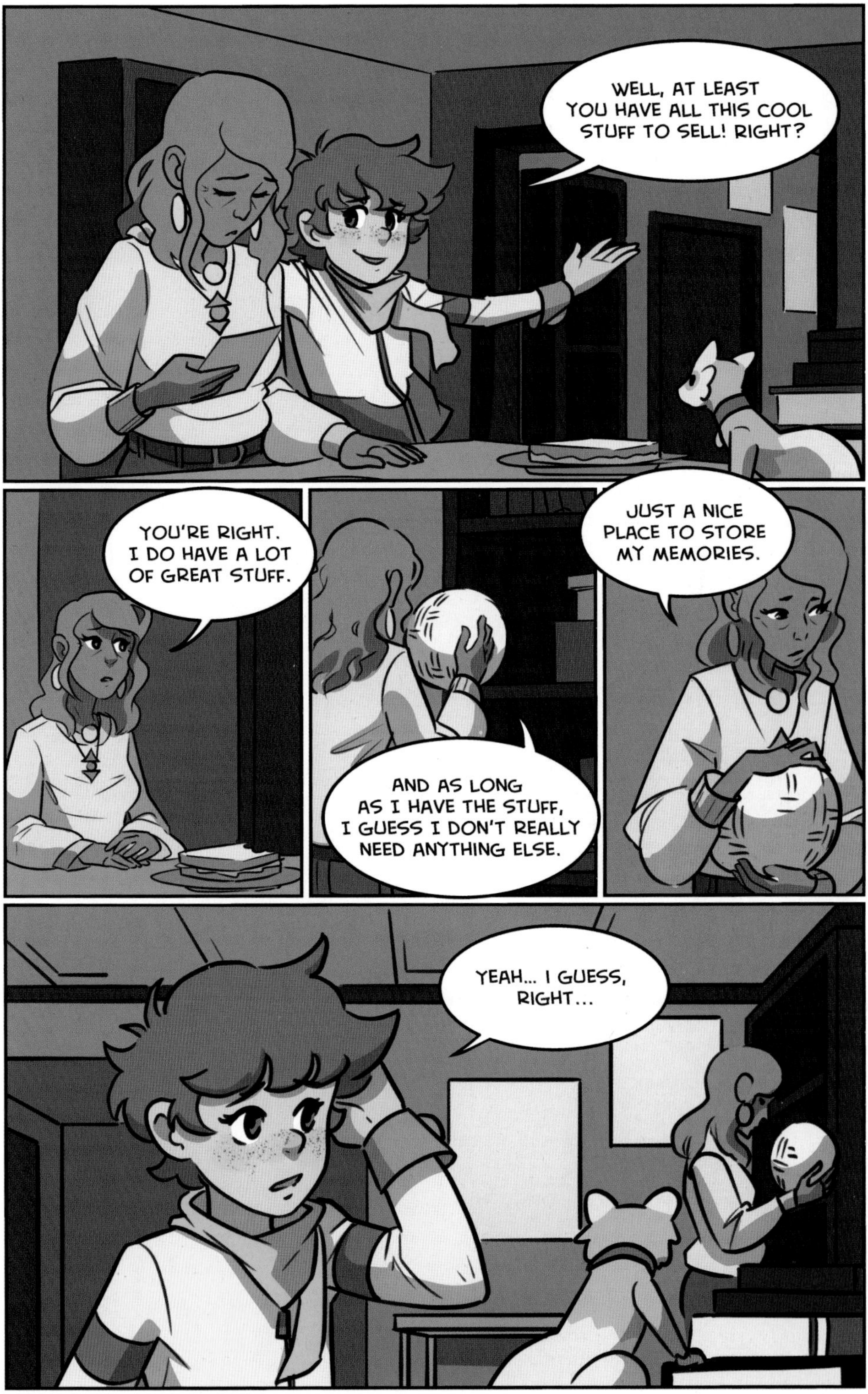
WELL, AT LEAST YOU HAVE ALL THIS COOL STUFF TO SELL! RIGHT?
YOU'RE RIGHT. I DO HAVE A LOT OF GREAT STUFF.
AND AS LONG AS I HAVE THE STUFF, I GUESS I DON'T REALLY NEED ANYTHING ELSE.
JUST A NICE PLACE TO STORE MY MEMORIES.
YEAH... I GUESS, RIGHT...

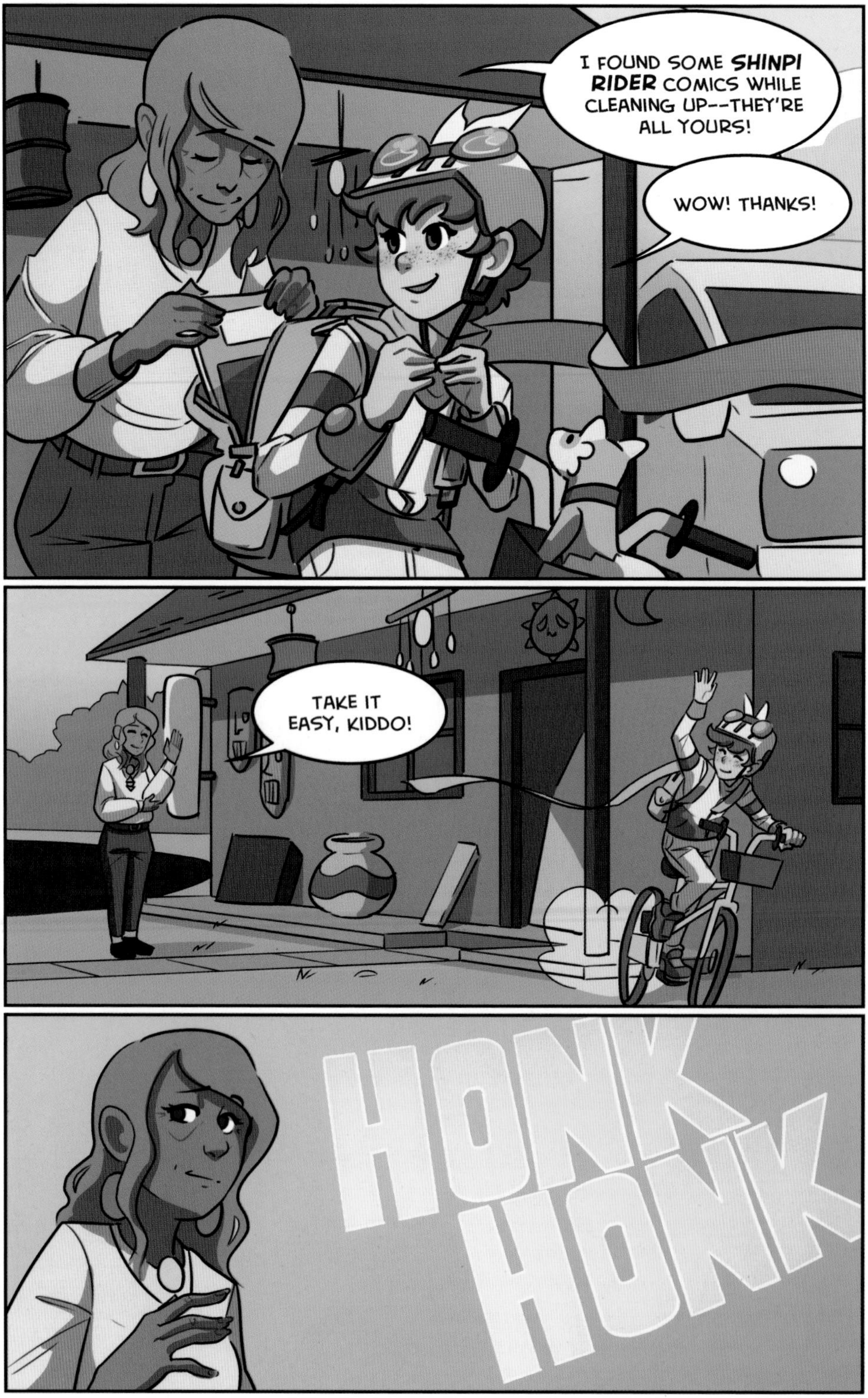
I FOUND SOME SHINPI RIDER COMICS WHILE CLEANING UP--THEY'RE ALL YOURS!
WOW! THANKS!
TAKE IT EASY, KIDDO!
HONK HONK

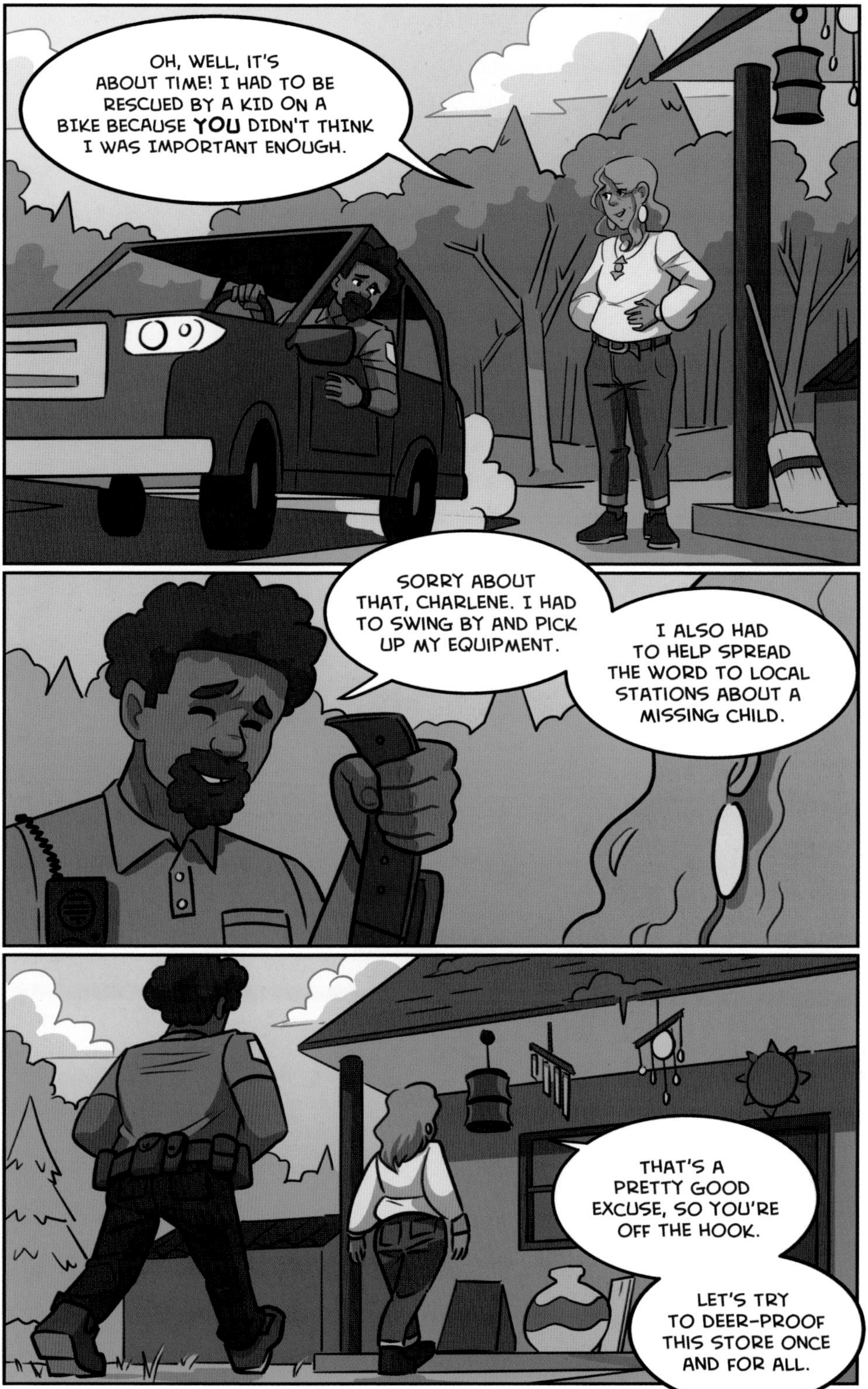
OH, WELL, IT'S ABOUT TIME! I HAD TO BE RESCUED BY A KID ON A BIKE BECAUSE YOU DIDN'T THINK I WAS IMPORTANT ENOUGH.
SORRY ABOUT THAT, CHARLENE. I HAD TO SWING BY AND PICK UP MY EQUIPMENT.
I ALSO HAD TO HELP SPREAD THE WORD TO LOCAL STATIONS ABOUT A MISSING CHILD.
THAT'S A PRETTY GOOD EXCUSE, SO YOU'RE OFF THE HOOK.
LET'S TRY TO DEER-PROOF THIS STORE ONCE AND FOR ALL.

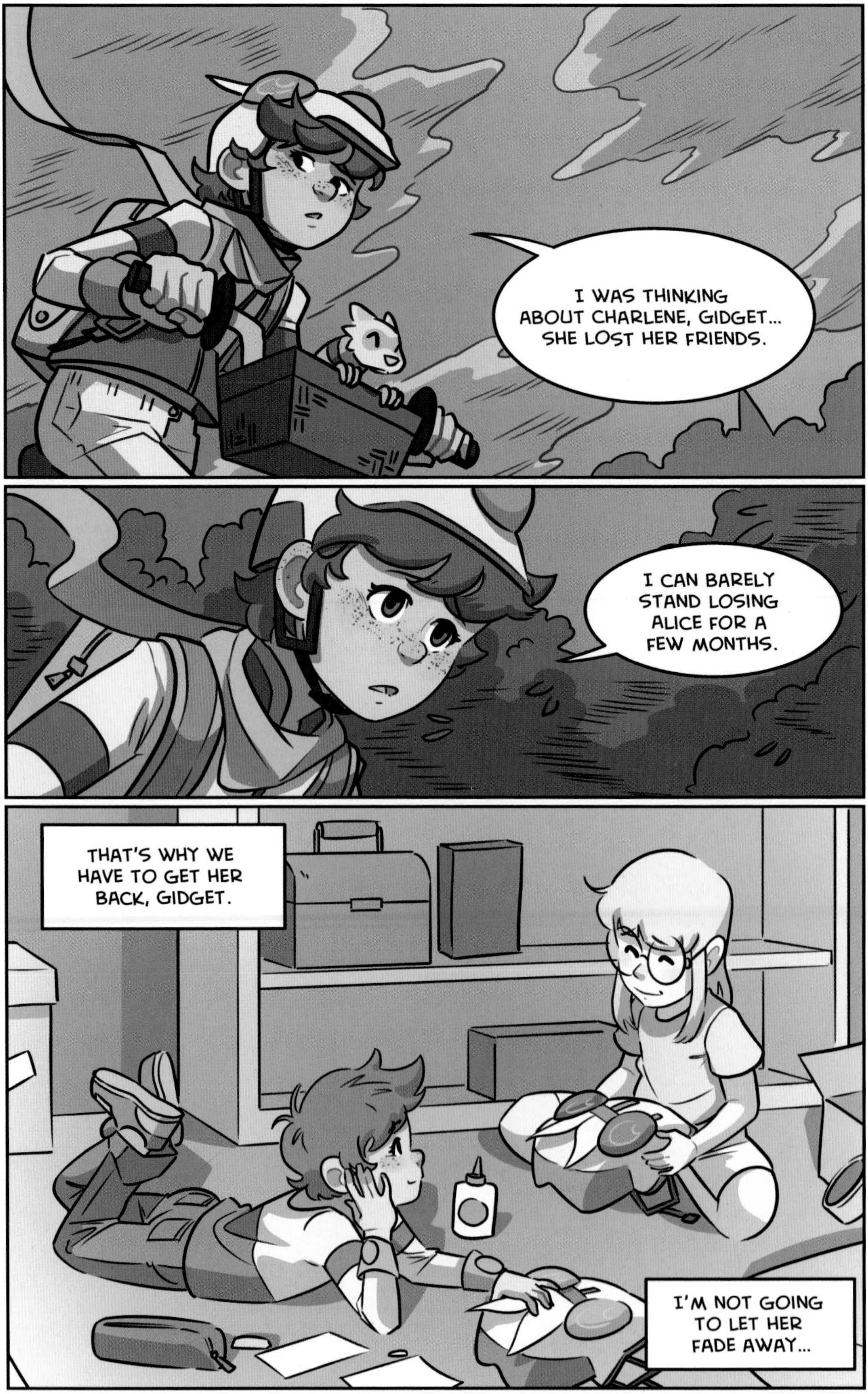
I WAS THINKING ABOUT CHARLENE, GIDGET... SHE LOST HER FRIENDS.
I CAN BARELY STAND LOSING ALICE FOR A FEW MONTHS.
THAT'S WHY WE HAVE TO GET HER BACK, GIDGET.
I'M NOT GOING TO LET HER FADE AWAY...

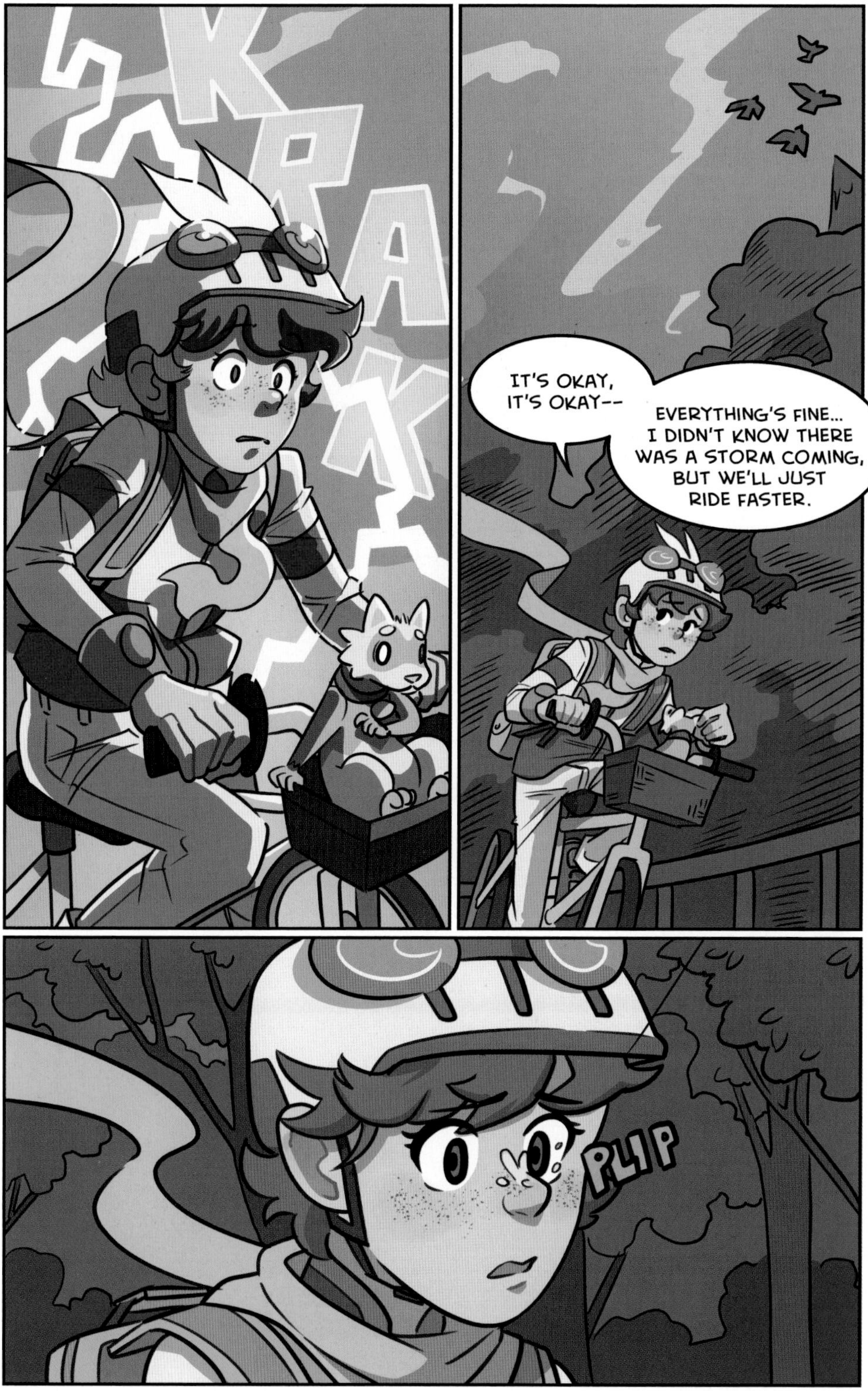
KRAKK
IT'S OKAY, IT'S OKAY--
EVERYTHING'S FINE... I DIDN'T KNOW THERE WAS A STORM COMING, BUT WE'LL JUST RIDE FASTER.
PLIP

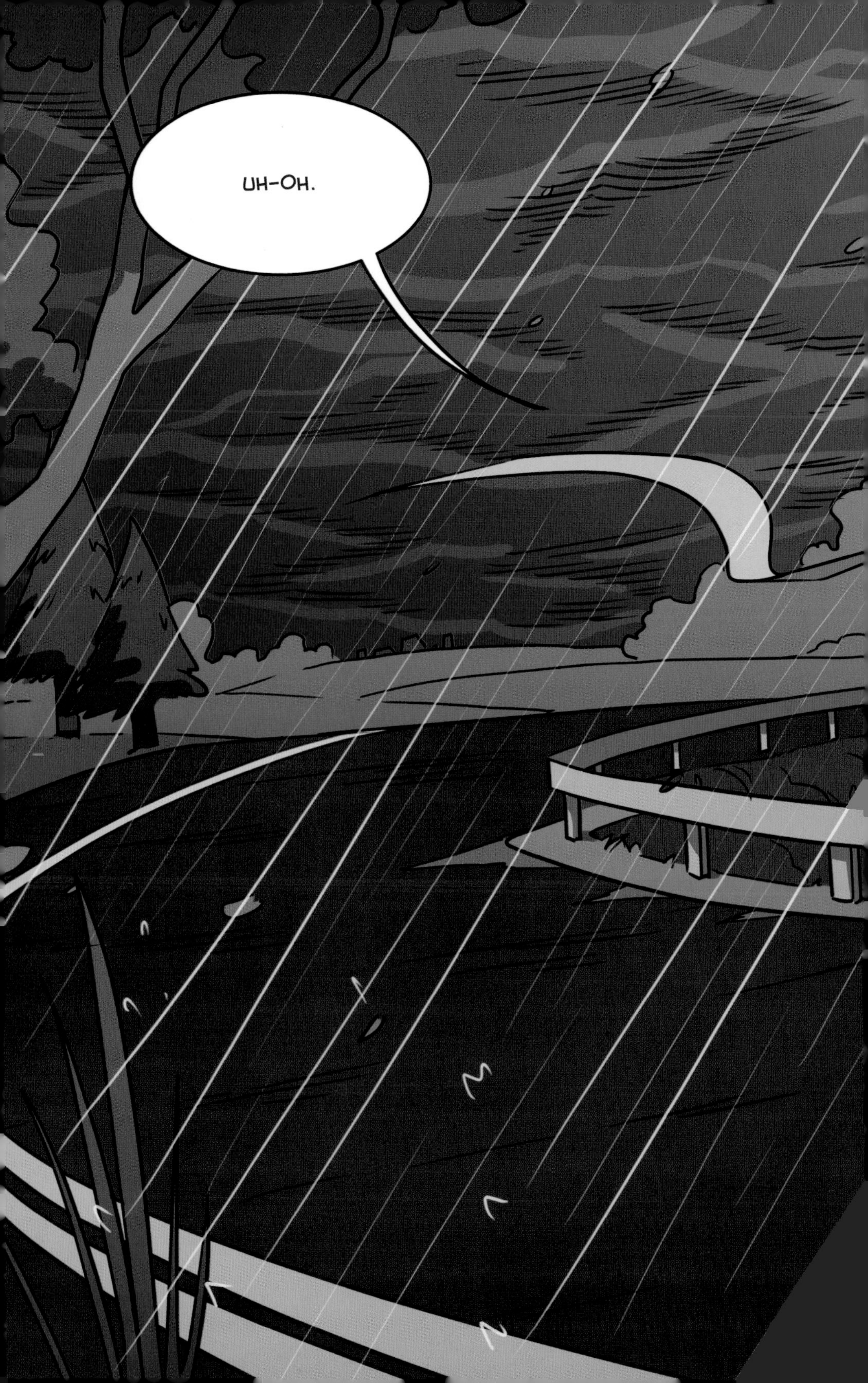
UH-OH.

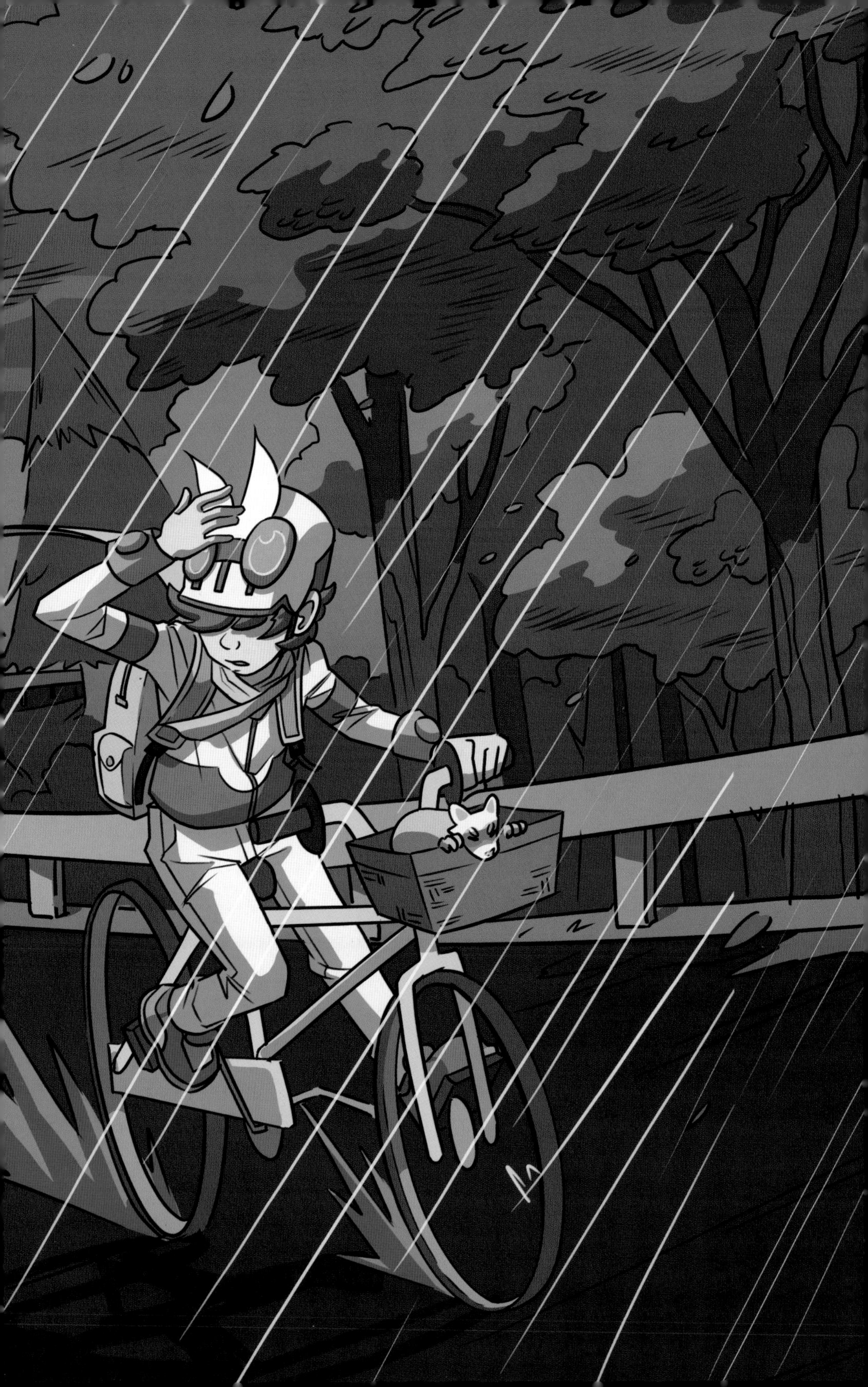

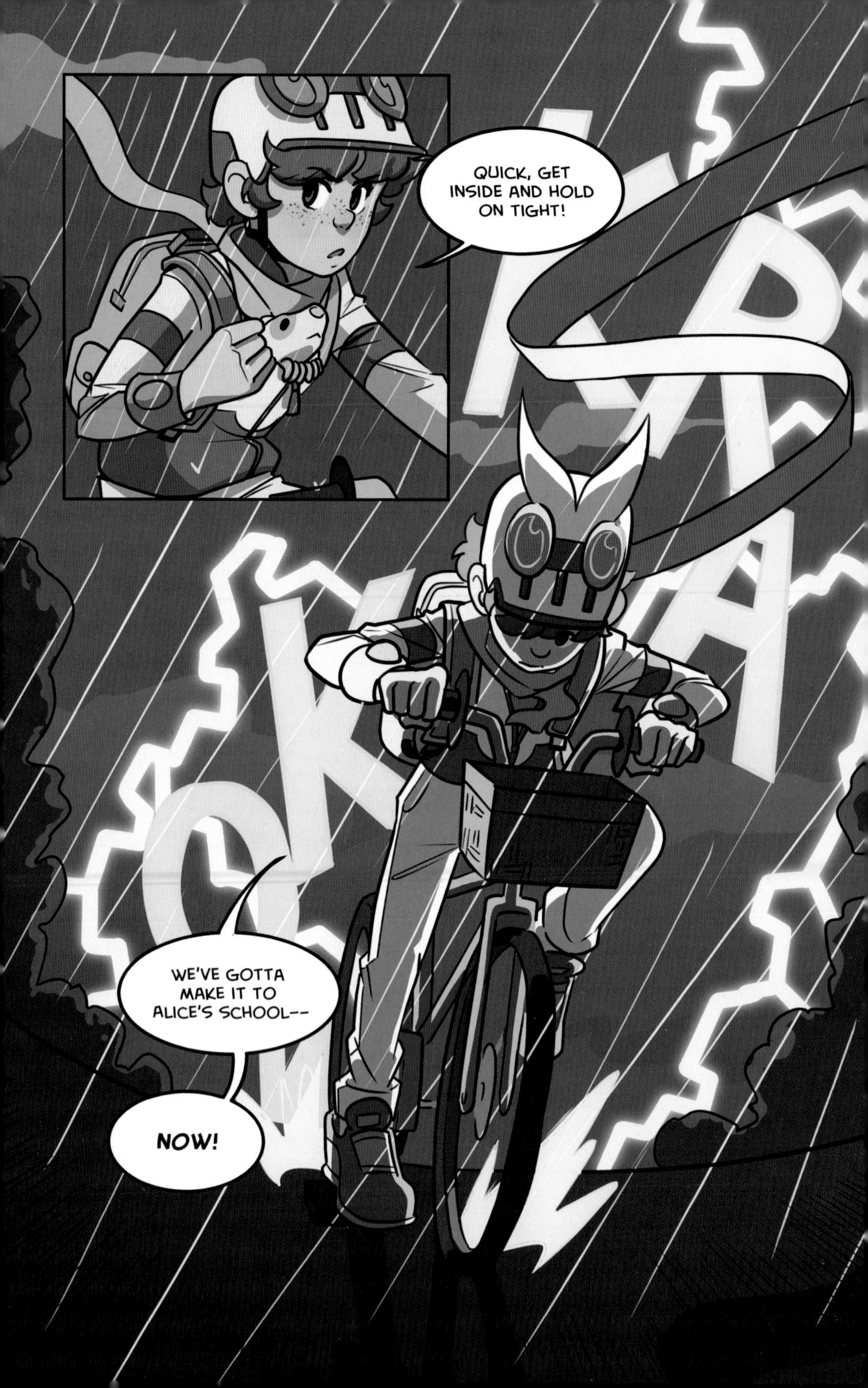
QUICK, GET INSIDE AND HOLD ON TIGHT!
WE'VE GOTTA MAKE IT TO ALICE'S SCHOOL--
NOW!

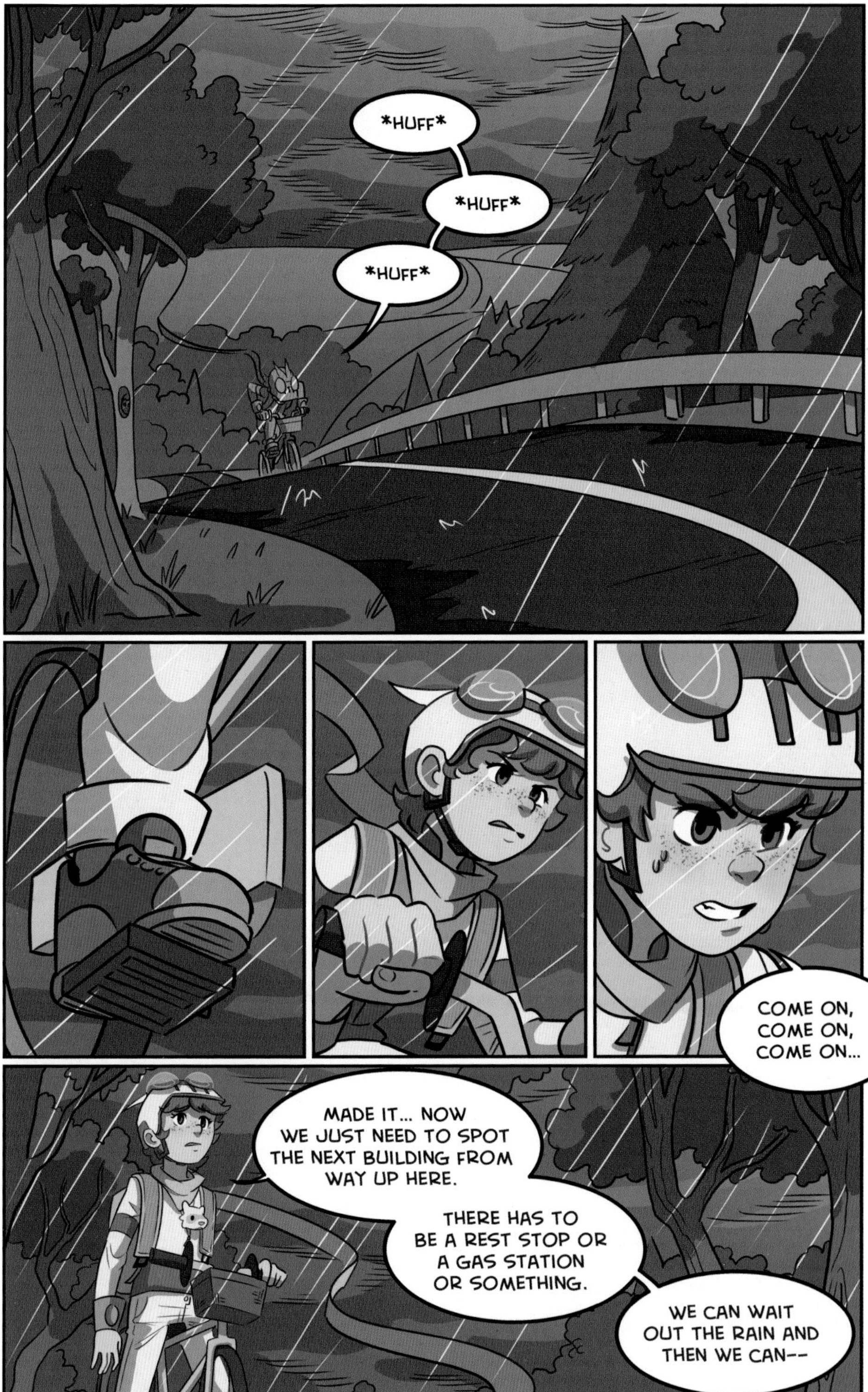
HUFF
HUFF
HUFF
COME ON, COME ON, COME ON...
MADE IT... NOW WE JUST NEED TO SPOT THE NEXT BUILDING FROM WAY UP HERE.
THERE HAS TO BE A REST STOP OR A GAS STATION OR SOMETHING.
WE CAN WAIT OUT THE RAIN AND THEN WE CAN--

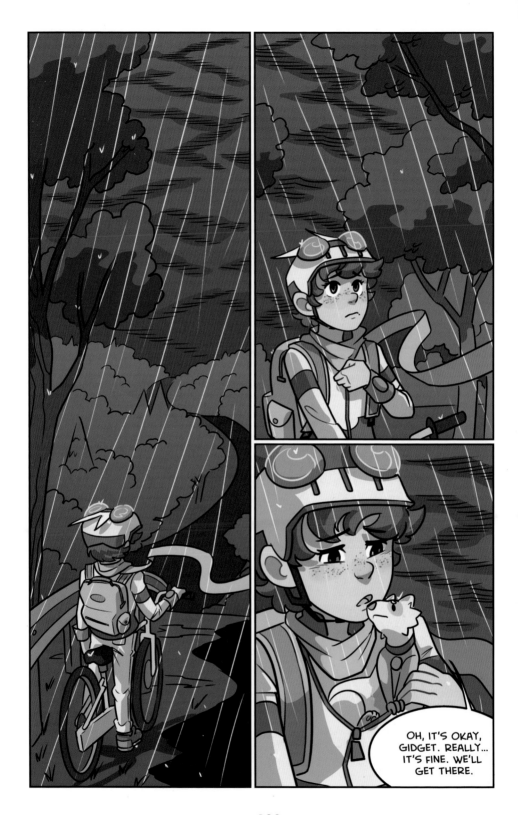

OH, IT'S OKAY, GIDGET. REALLY... IT'S FINE. WE'LL GET THERE.

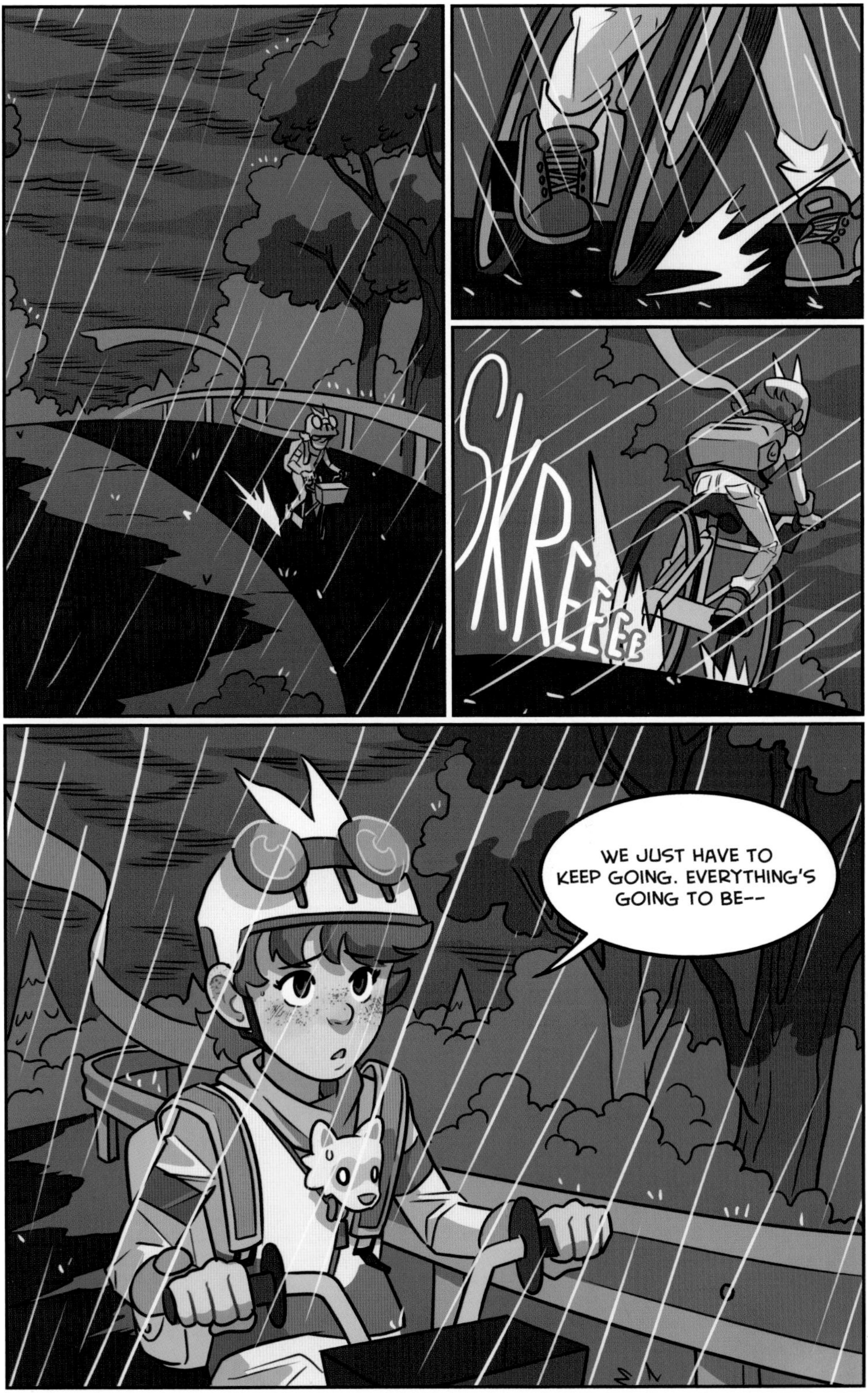
SKREEEE
WE JUST HAVE TO KEEP GOING. EVERYTHING'S GOING TO BE--

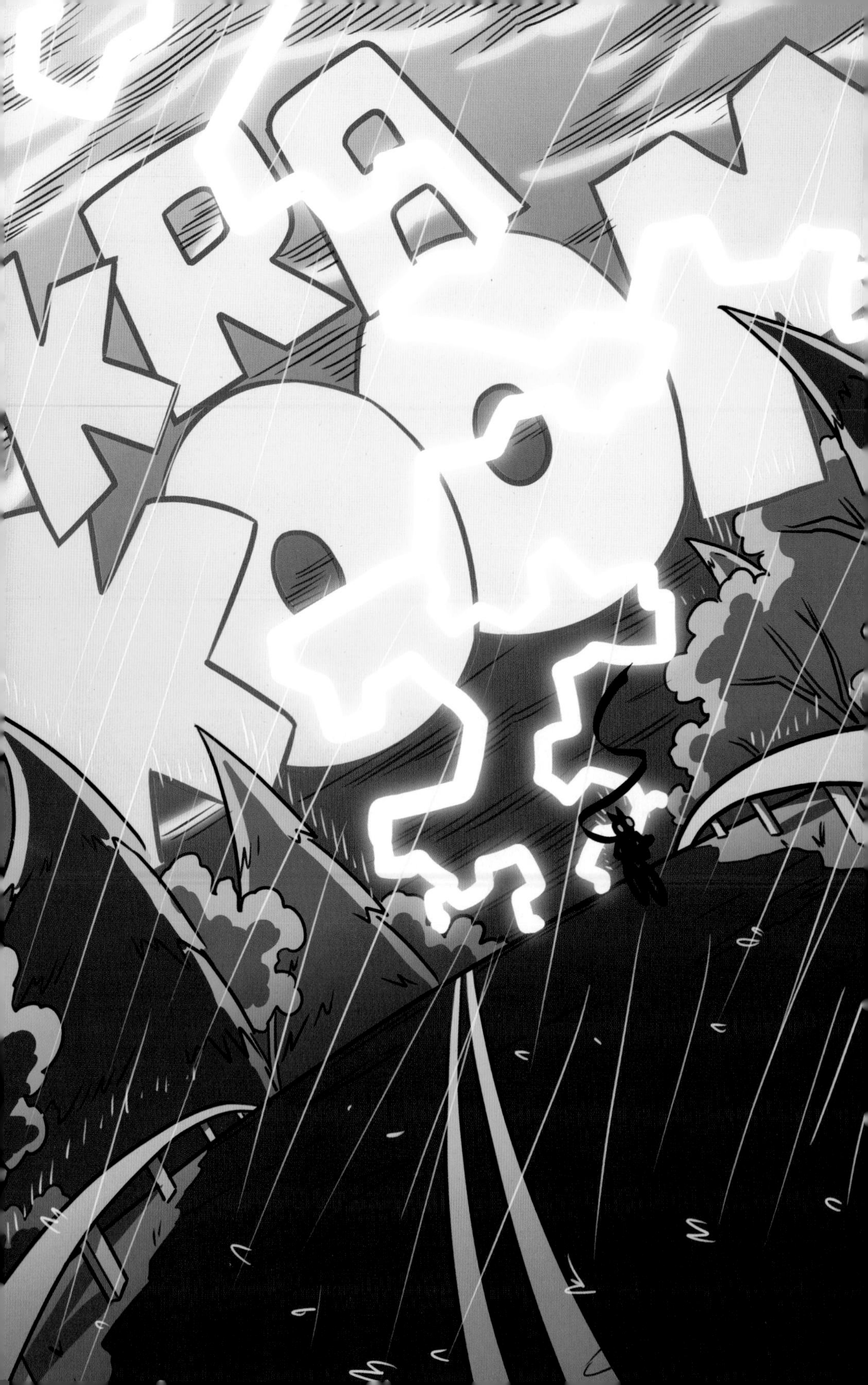

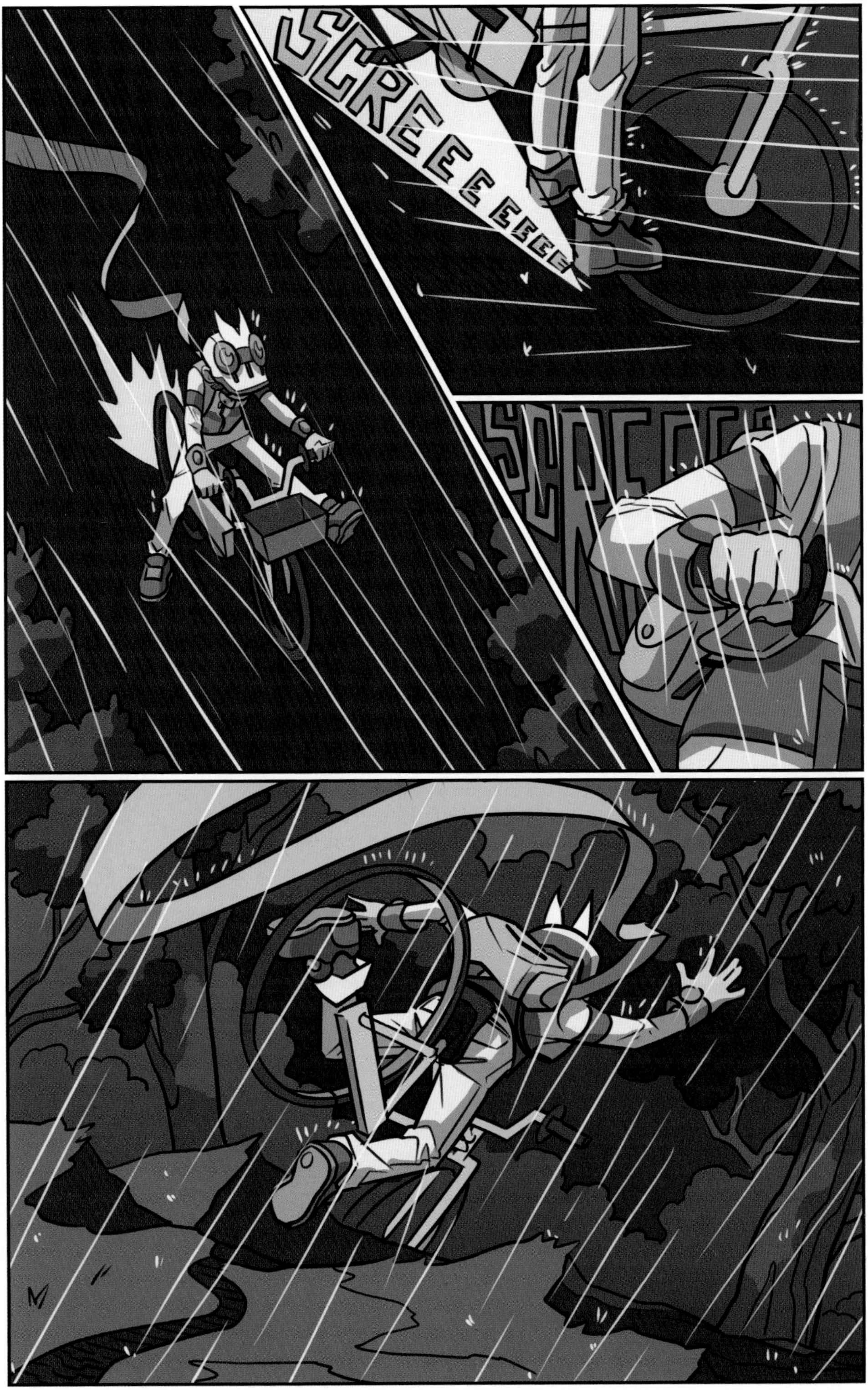
SCREEEEEEEE

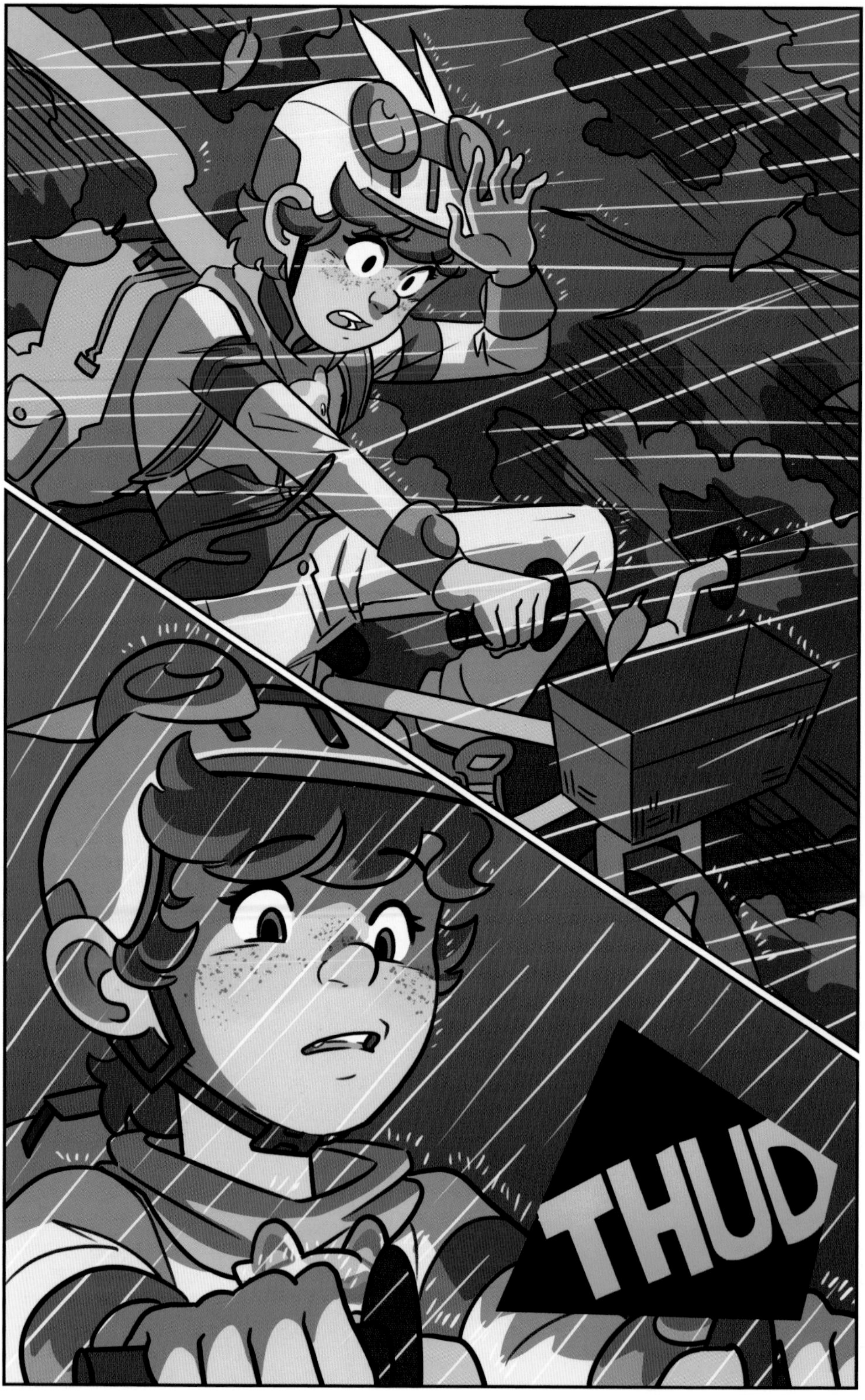
THUD

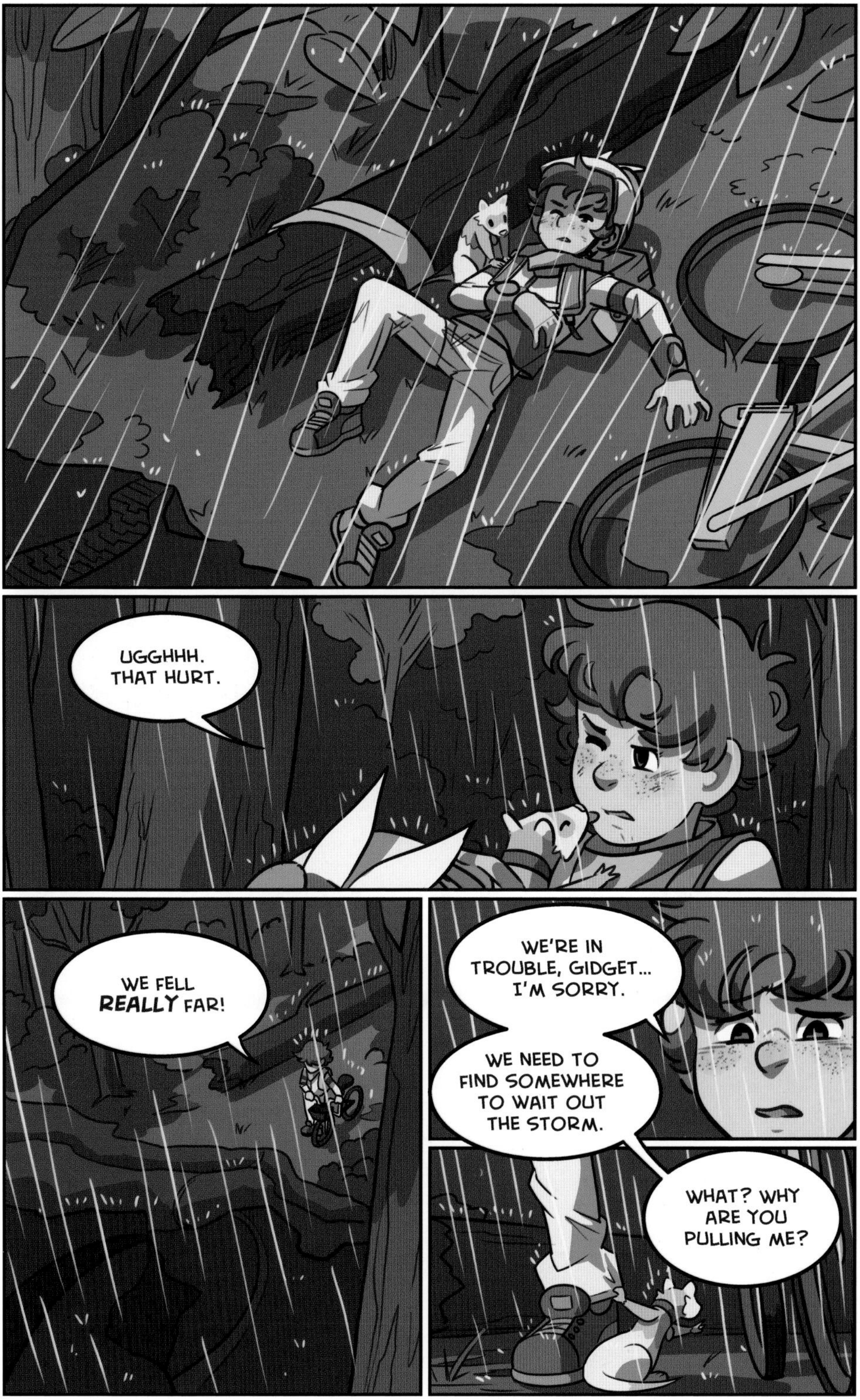
UGGHHH. THAT HURT.
WE FELL **REALLY** FAR!
WE'RE IN TROUBLE, GIDGET... I'M SORRY.
WE NEED TO FIND SOMEWHERE TO WAIT OUT THE STORM.
WHAT? WHY ARE YOU PULLING ME?

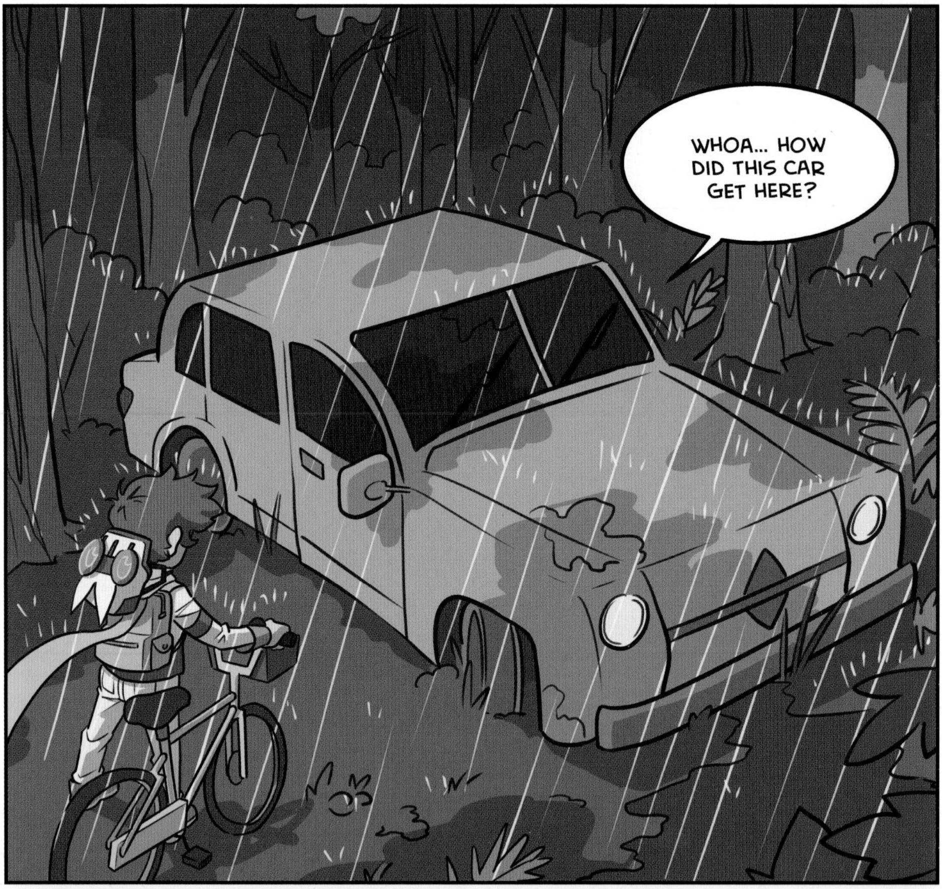
WHOA... HOW DID THIS CAR GET HERE?

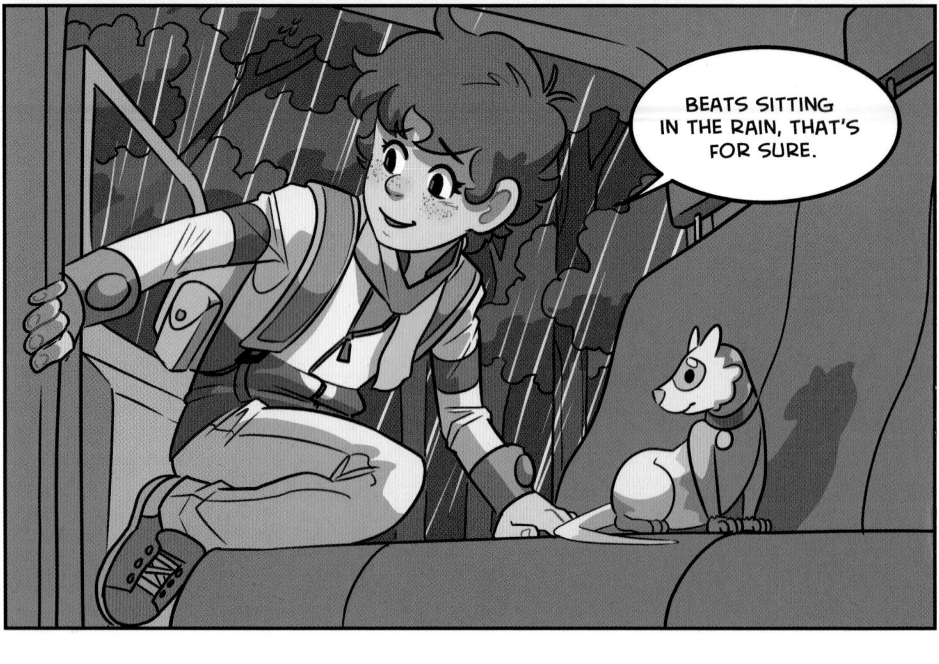
BEATS SITTING IN THE RAIN, THAT'S FOR SURE.

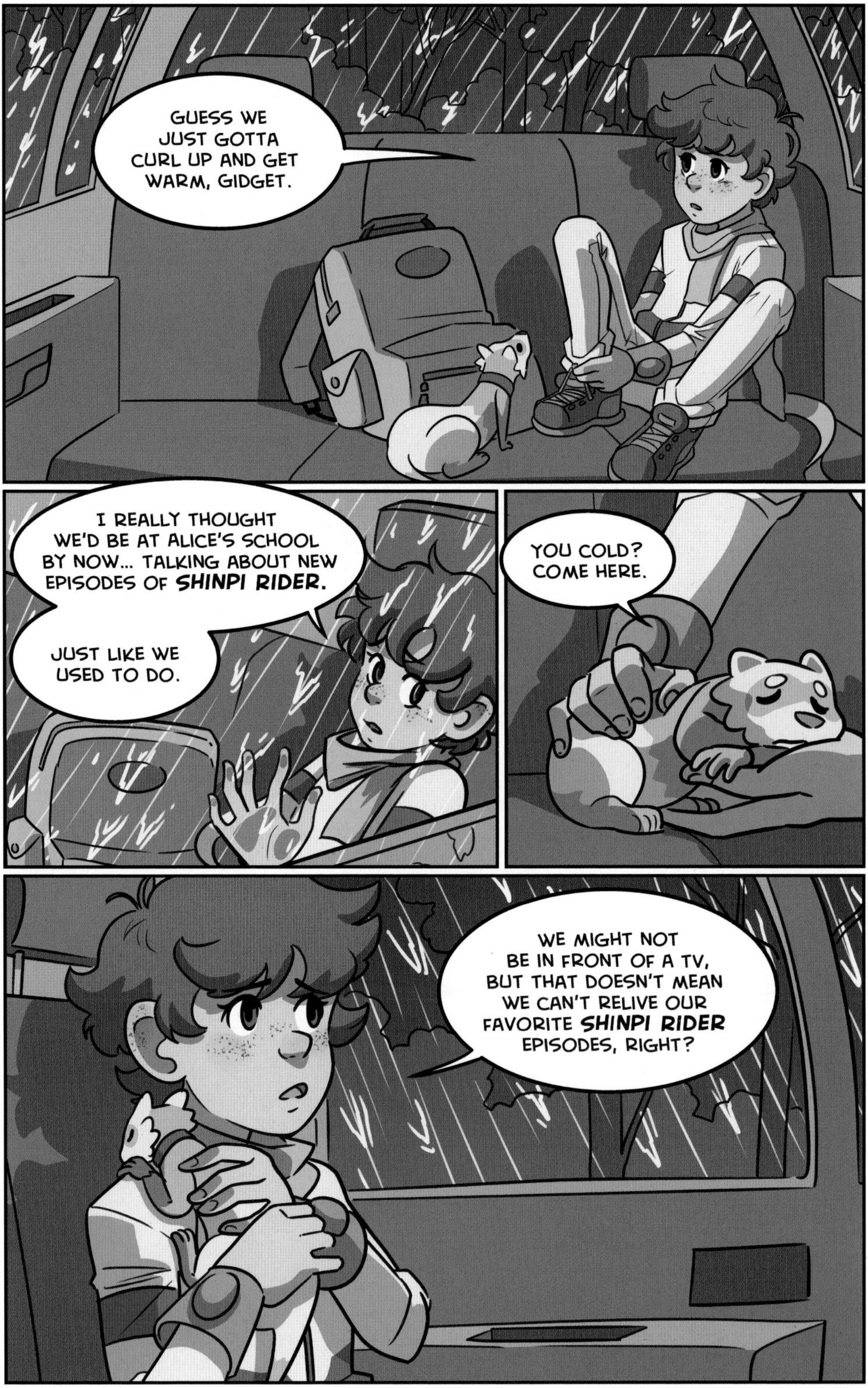
GUESS WE JUST GOTTA CURL UP AND GET WARM, GIDGET.
I REALLY THOUGHT WE'D BE AT ALICE'S SCHOOL BY NOW... TALKING ABOUT NEW EPISODES OF SHINPI RIDER.
JUST LIKE WE USED TO DO.
YOU COLD? COME HERE.
WE MIGHT NOT BE IN FRONT OF A TV, BUT THAT DOESN'T MEAN WE CAN'T RELIVE OUR FAVORITE SHINPI RIDER EPISODES, RIGHT?

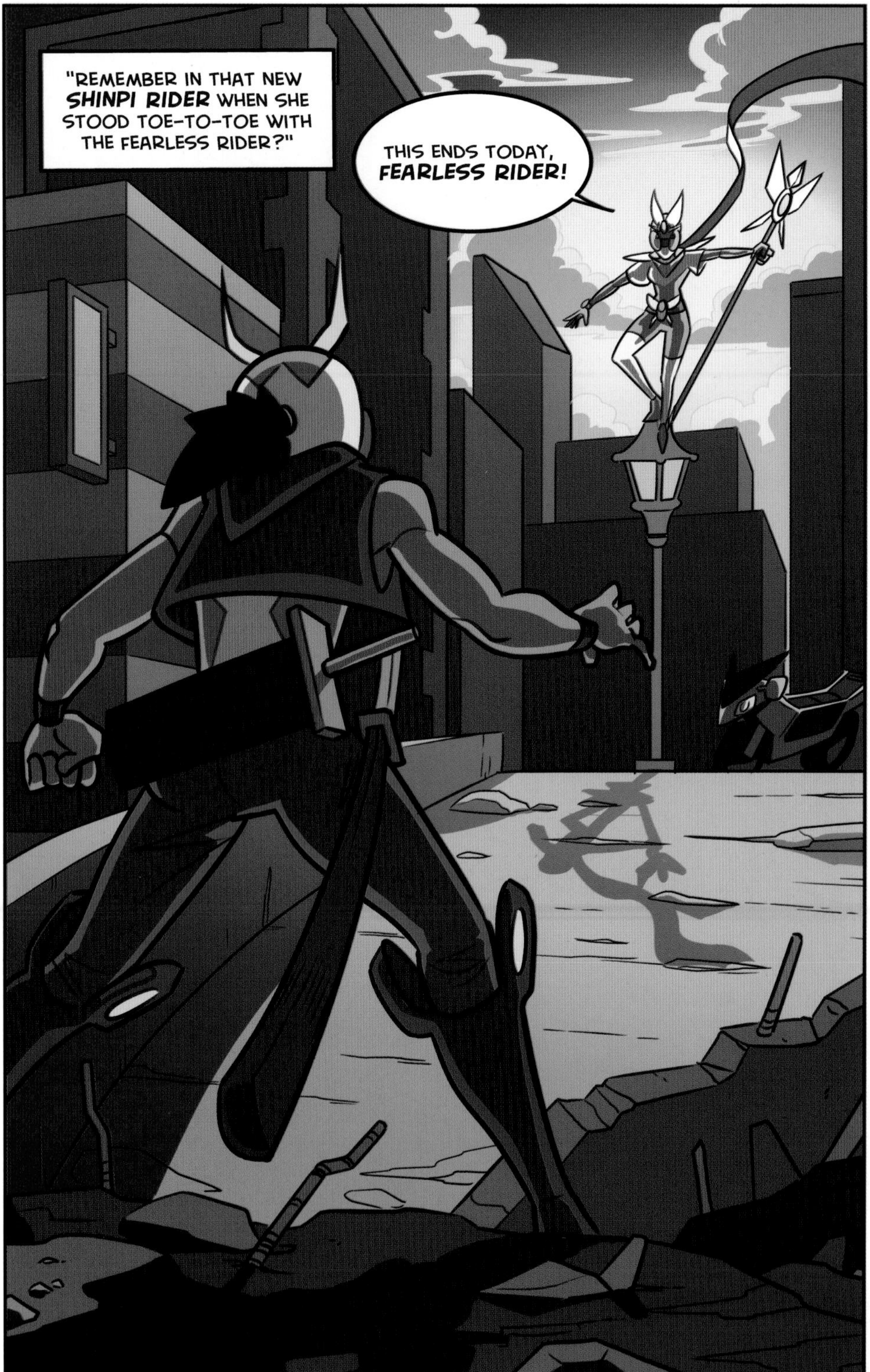
"REMEMBER IN THAT NEW SHINPI RIDER WHEN SHE STOOD TOE-TO-TOE WITH THE FEARLESS RIDER?"
THIS ENDS TODAY, FEARLESS RIDER!

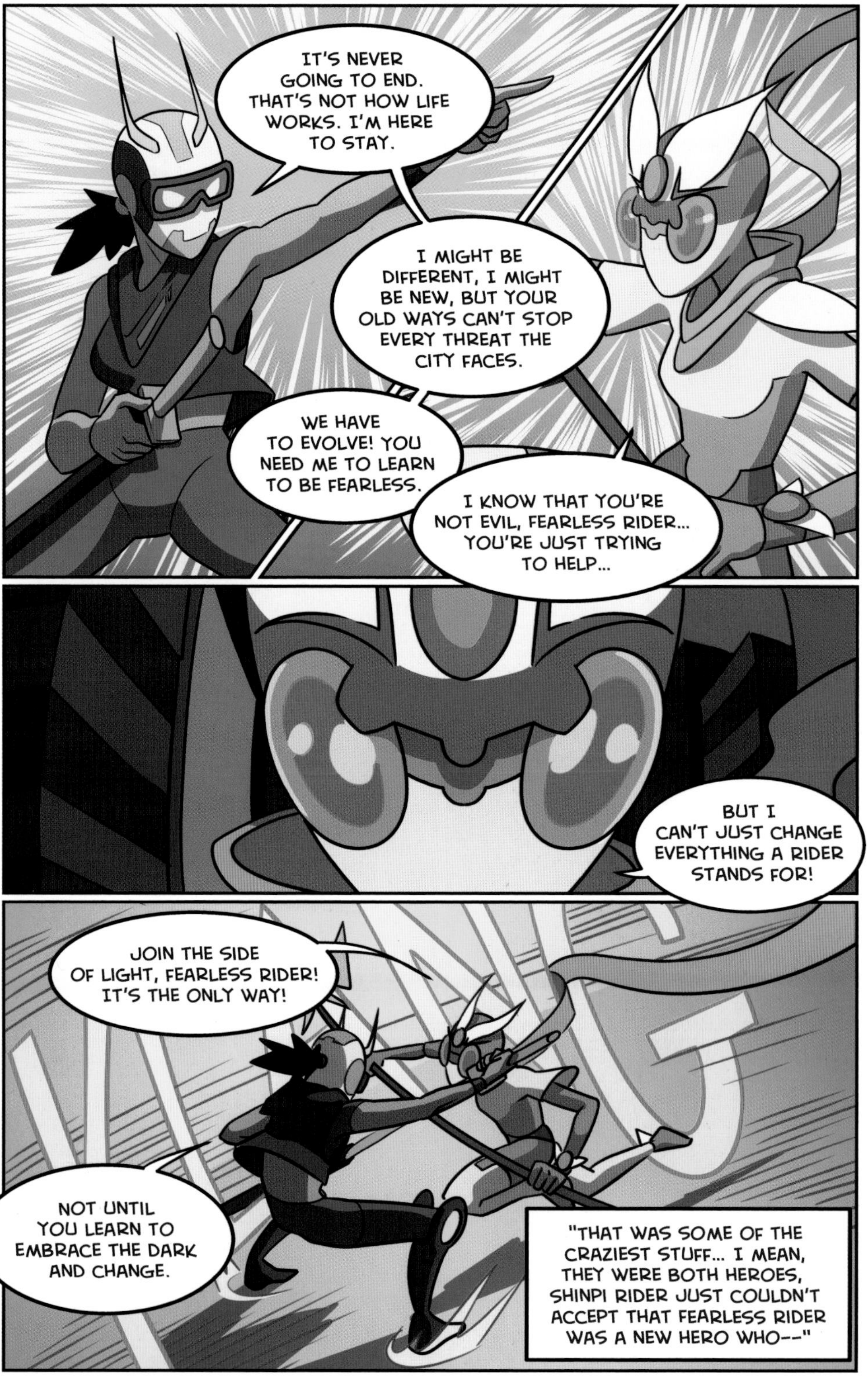
IT'S NEVER GOING TO END. THAT'S NOT HOW LIFE WORKS. I'M HERE TO STAY.
I MIGHT BE DIFFERENT, I MIGHT BE NEW, BUT YOUR OLD WAYS CAN'T STOP EVERY THREAT THE CITY FACES.
WE HAVE TO EVOLVE! YOU NEED ME TO LEARN TO BE FEARLESS.
I KNOW THAT YOU'RE NOT EVIL, FEARLESS RIDER... YOU'RE JUST TRYING TO HELP...
BUT I CAN'T JUST CHANGE EVERYTHING A RIDER STANDS FOR!
JOIN THE SIDE OF LIGHT, FEARLESS RIDER! IT'S THE ONLY WAY!
NOT UNTIL YOU LEARN TO EMBRACE THE DARK AND CHANGE.
"THAT WAS SOME OF THE CRAZIEST STUFF... I MEAN, THEY WERE BOTH HEROES, SHINPI RIDER JUST COULDN'T ACCEPT THAT FEARLESS RIDER WAS A NEW HERO WHO--"

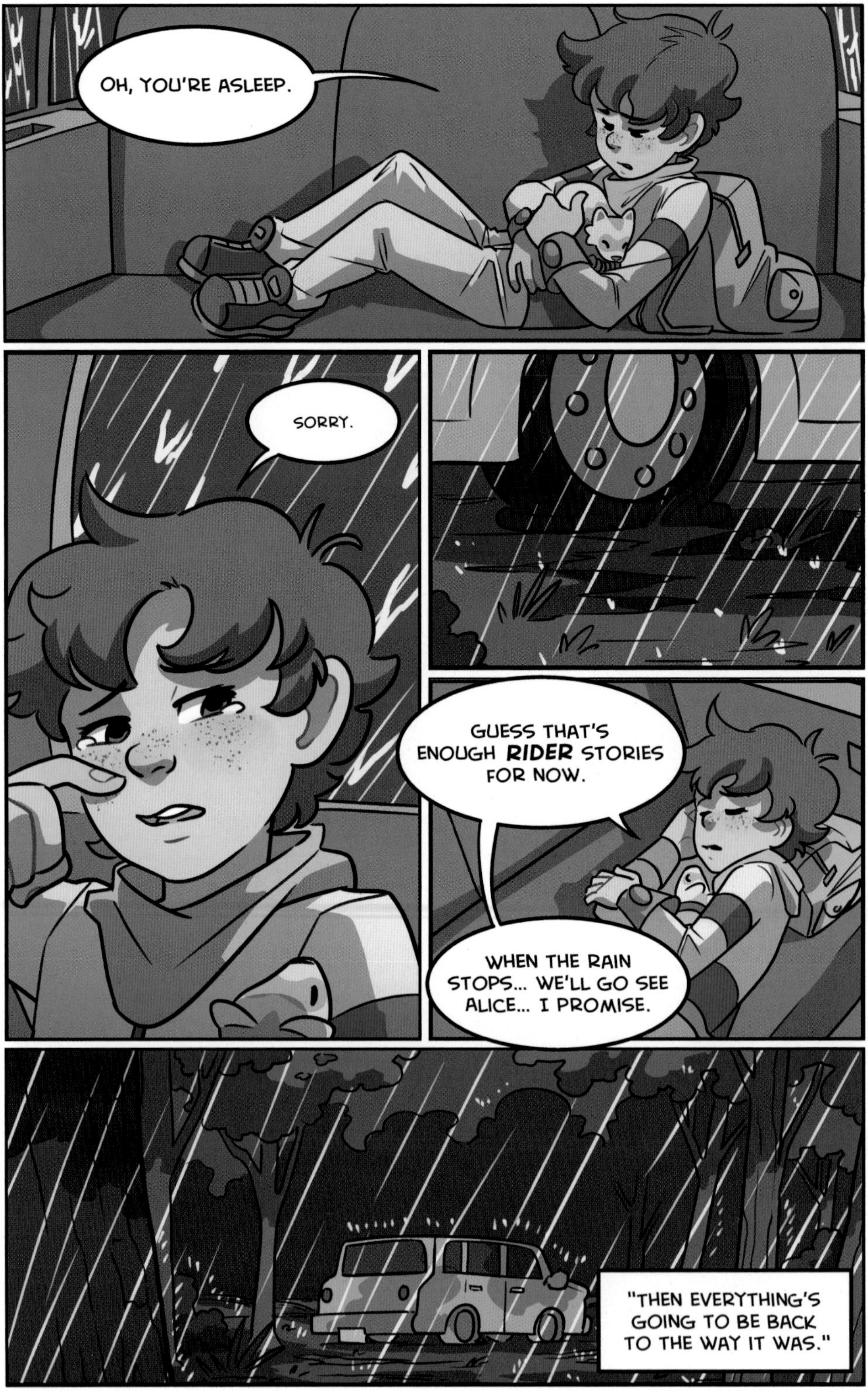
OH, YOU'RE ASLEEP.
SORRY.
GUESS THAT'S ENOUGH RIDER STORIES FOR NOW.
WHEN THE RAIN STOPS... WE'LL GO SEE ALICE... I PROMISE.
"THEN EVERYTHING'S GOING TO BE BACK TO THE WAY IT WAS."

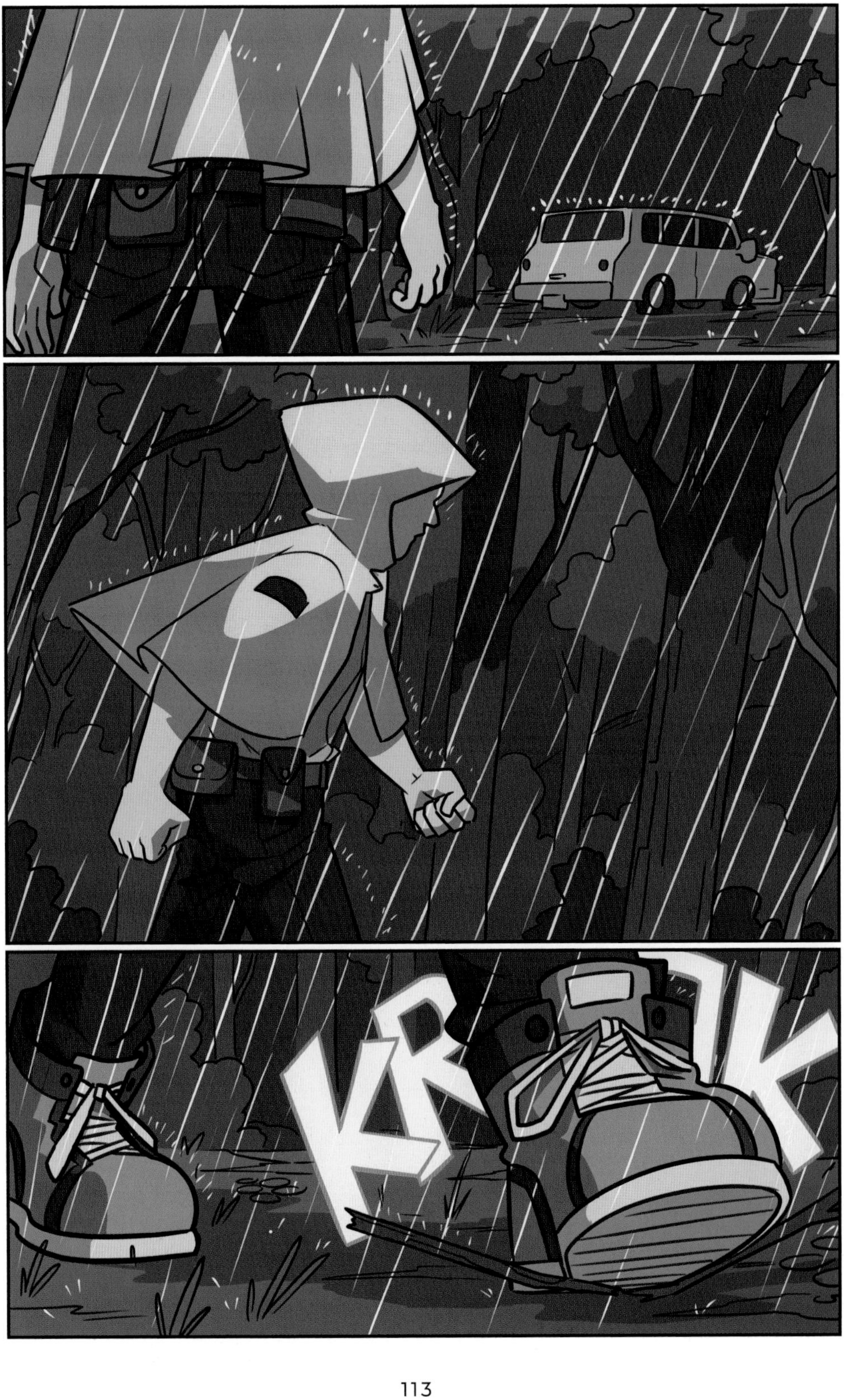

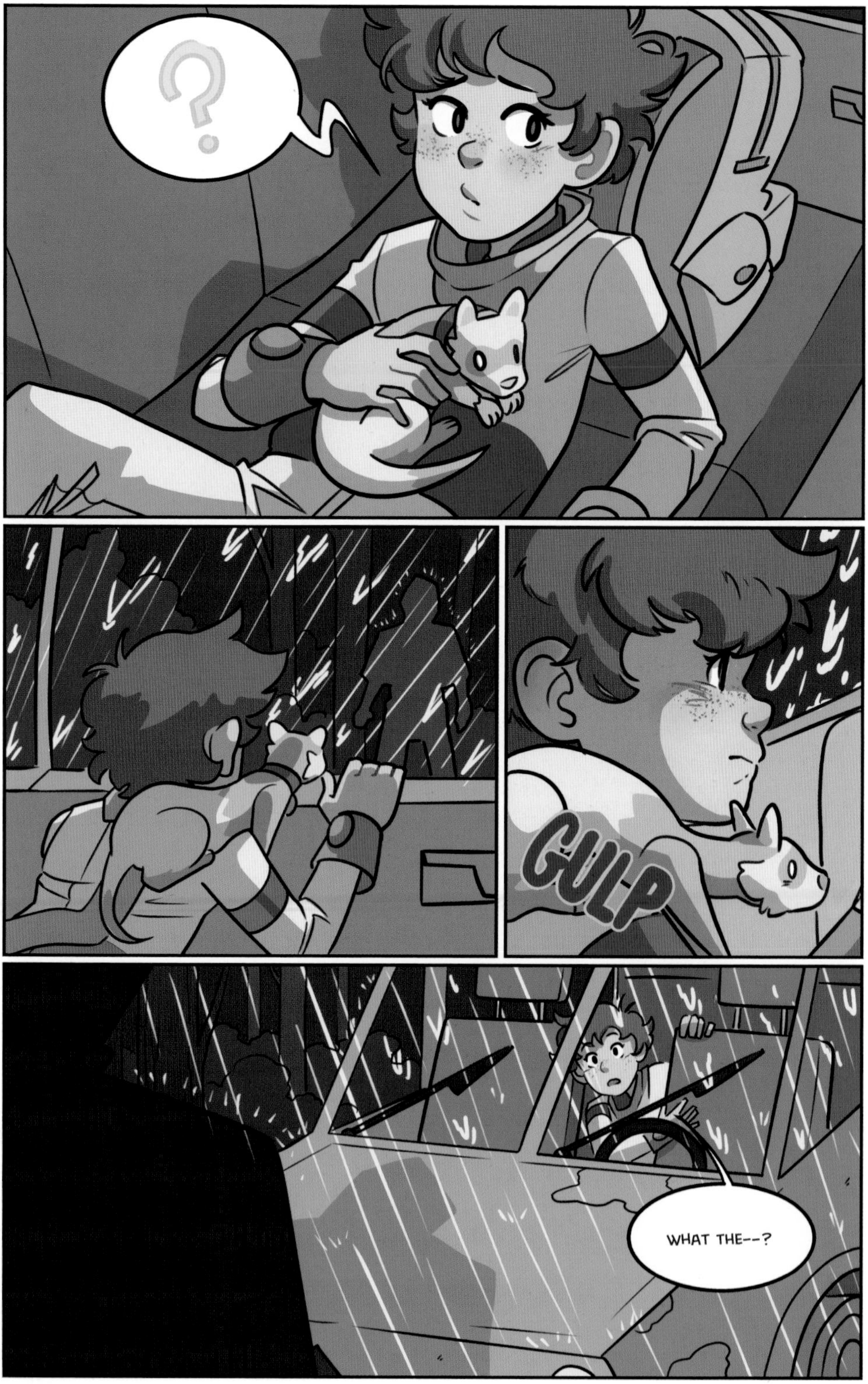
?
GULP
WHAT THE--?

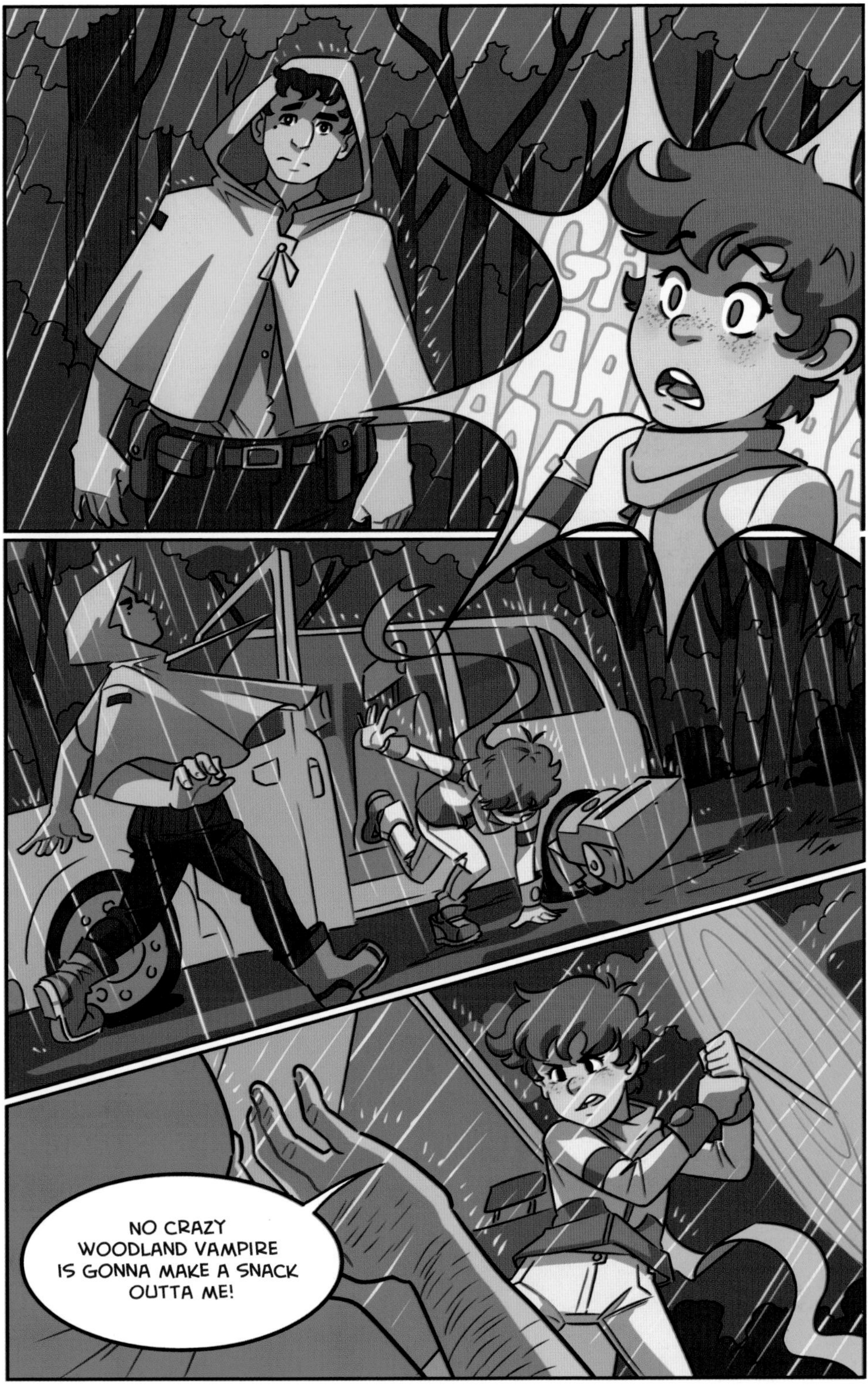
NO CRAZY WOODLAND VAMPIRE IS GONNA MAKE A SNACK OUTTA ME!

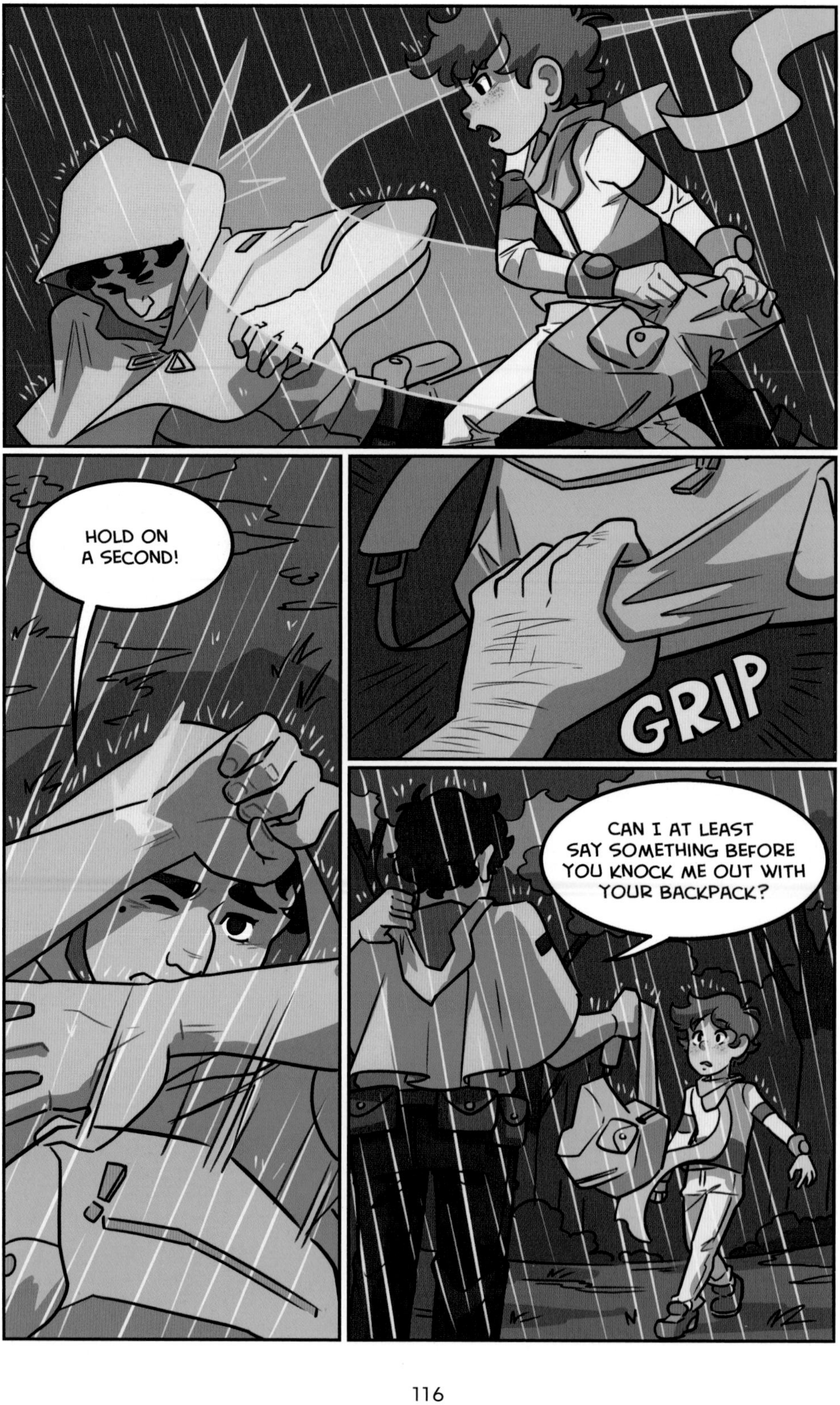
HOLD ON A SECOND!
GRIP
CAN I AT LEAST SAY SOMETHING BEFORE YOU KNOCK ME OUT WITH YOUR BACKPACK?

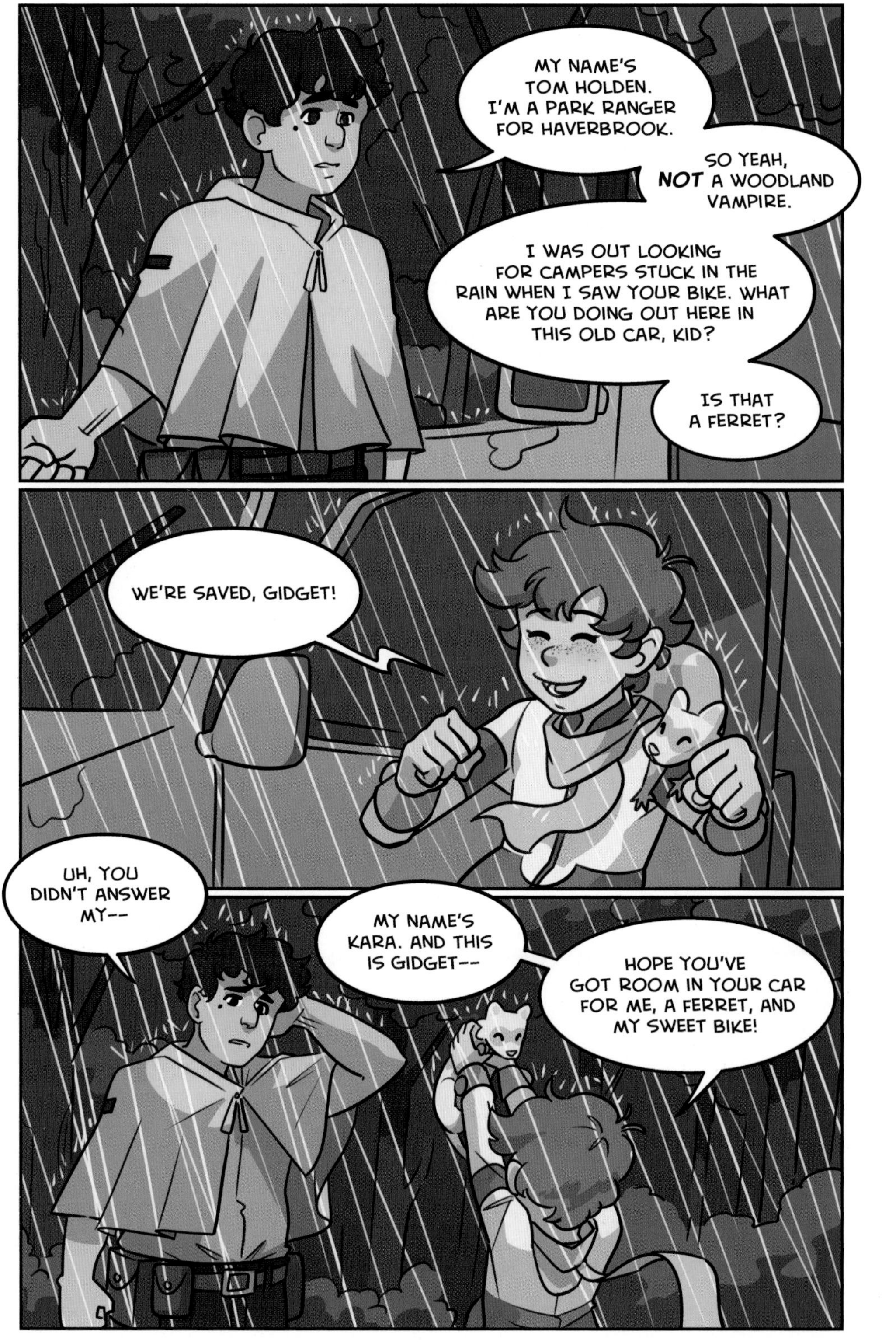
MY NAME'S TOM HOLDEN. I'M A PARK RANGER FOR HAVERBROOK.
SO YEAH, NOT A WOODLAND VAMPIRE.
I WAS OUT LOOKING FOR CAMPERS STUCK IN THE RAIN WHEN I SAW YOUR BIKE. WHAT ARE YOU DOING OUT HERE IN THIS OLD CAR, KID?
IS THAT A FERRET?
WE'RE SAVED, GIDGET!
UH, YOU DIDN'T ANSWER MY--
MY NAME'S KARA. AND THIS IS GIDGET--
HOPE YOU'VE GOT ROOM IN YOUR CAR FOR ME, A FERRET, AND MY SWEET BIKE!

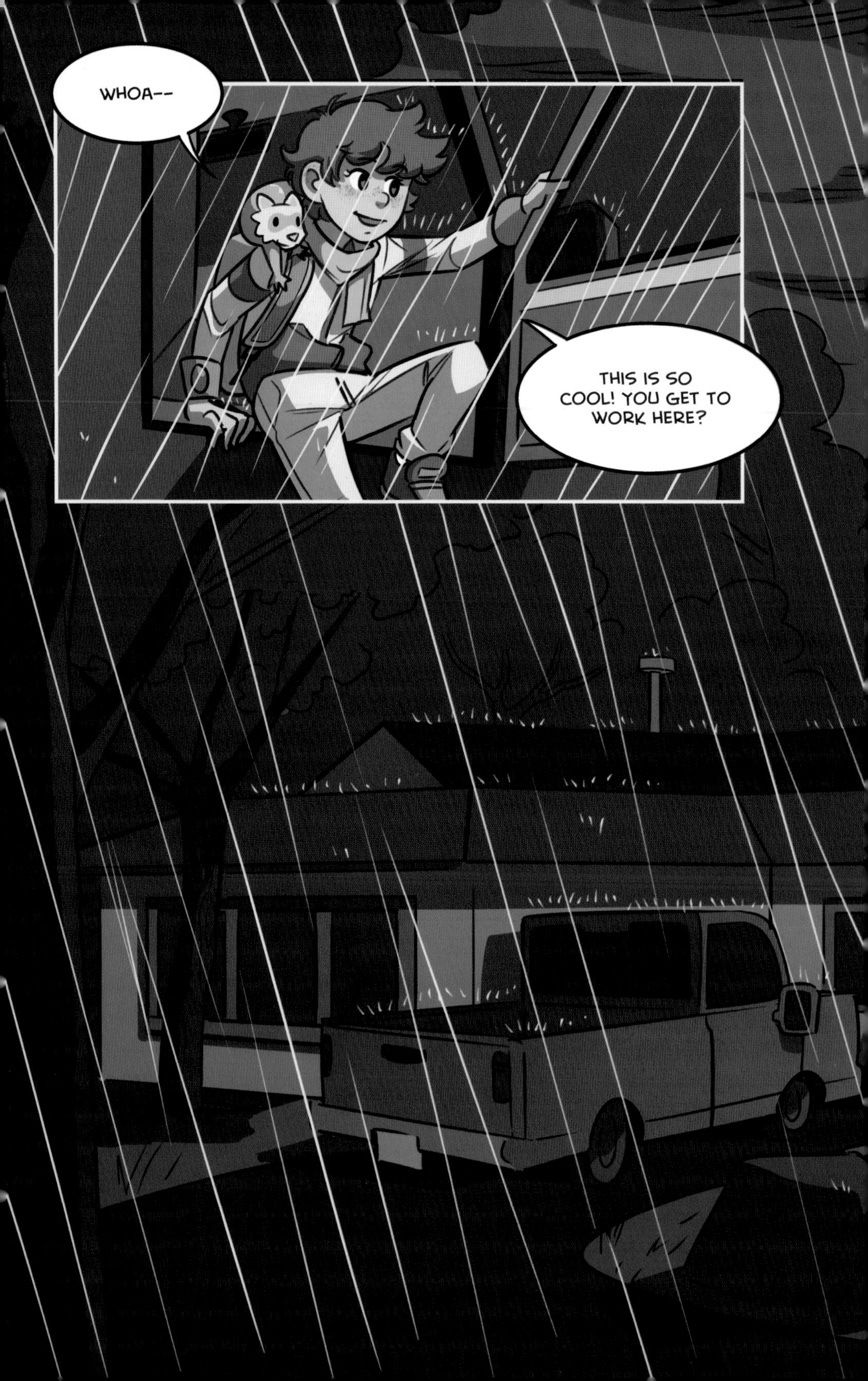
WHOA--
THIS IS SO COOL! YOU GET TO WORK HERE?

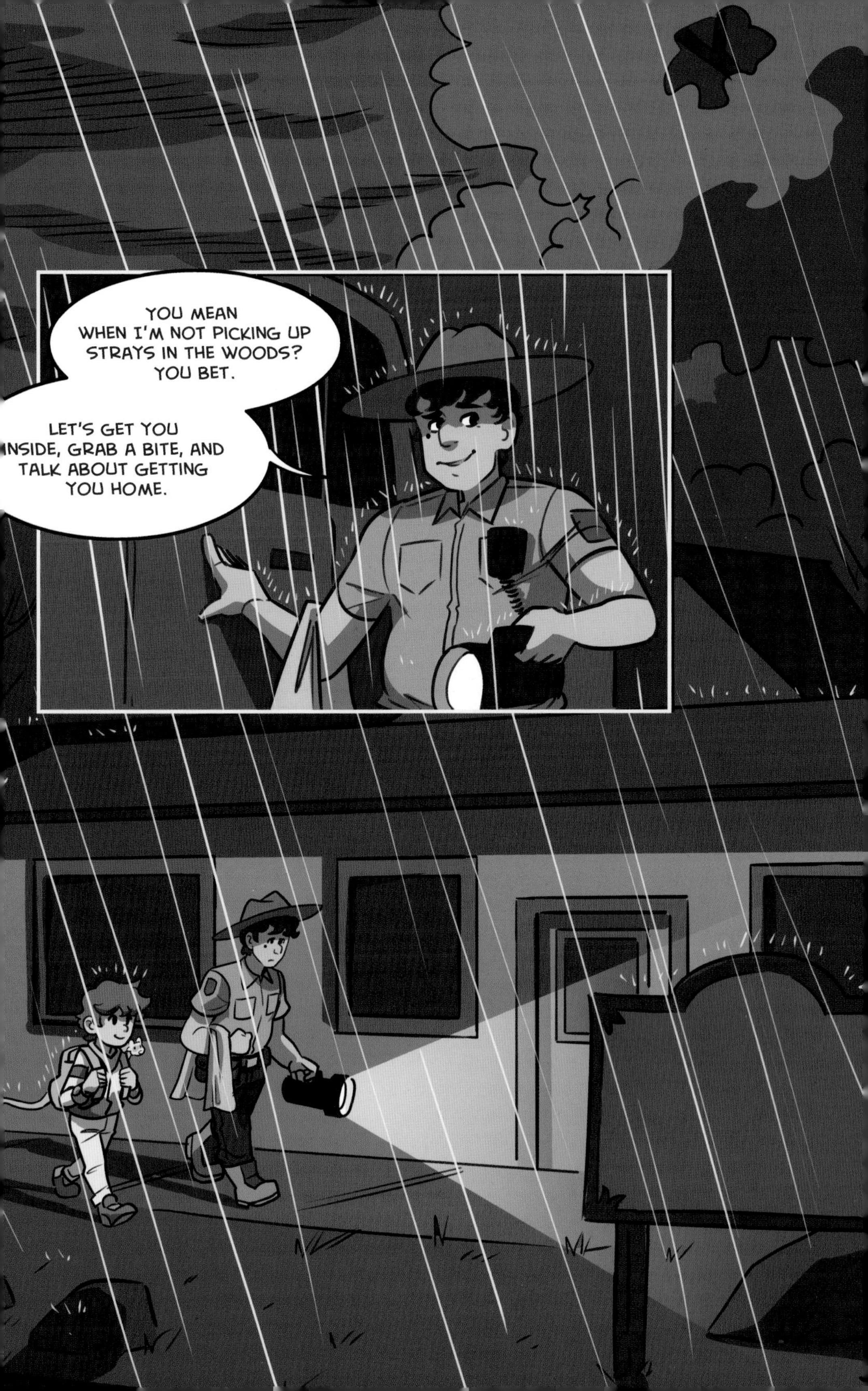
YOU MEAN WHEN I'M NOT PICKING UP STRAYS IN THE WOODS? YOU BET.
LET'S GET YOU INSIDE, GRAB A BITE, AND TALK ABOUT GETTING YOU HOME.

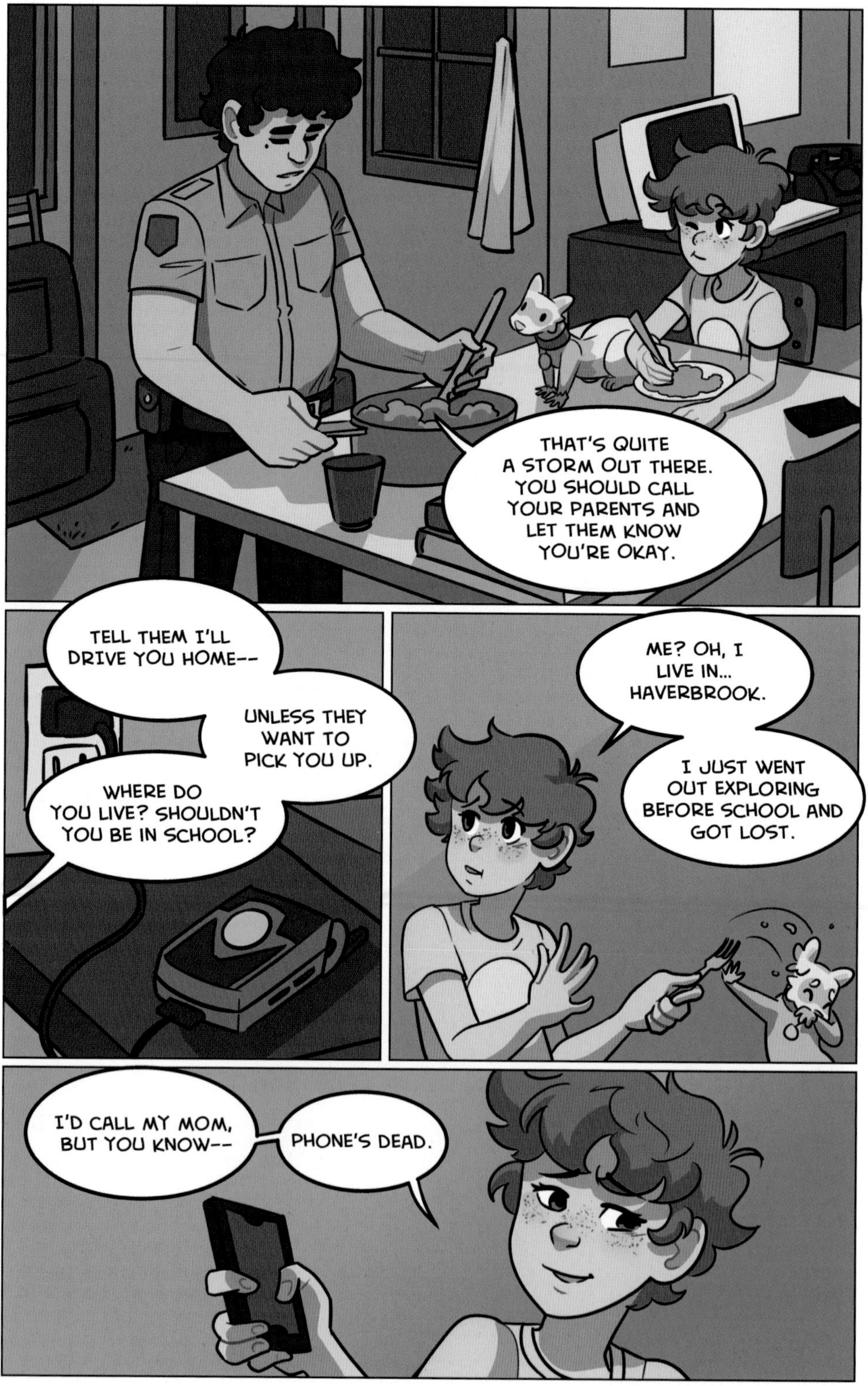
THAT'S QUITE A STORM OUT THERE. YOU SHOULD CALL YOUR PARENTS AND LET THEM KNOW YOU'RE OKAY.
TELL THEM I'LL DRIVE YOU HOME--
UNLESS THEY WANT TO PICK YOU UP.
WHERE DO YOU LIVE? SHOULDN'T YOU BE IN SCHOOL?
ME? OH, I LIVE IN... HAVERBROOK.
I JUST WENT OUT EXPLORING BEFORE SCHOOL AND GOT LOST.
I'D CALL MY MOM, BUT YOU KNOW--
PHONE'S DEAD.

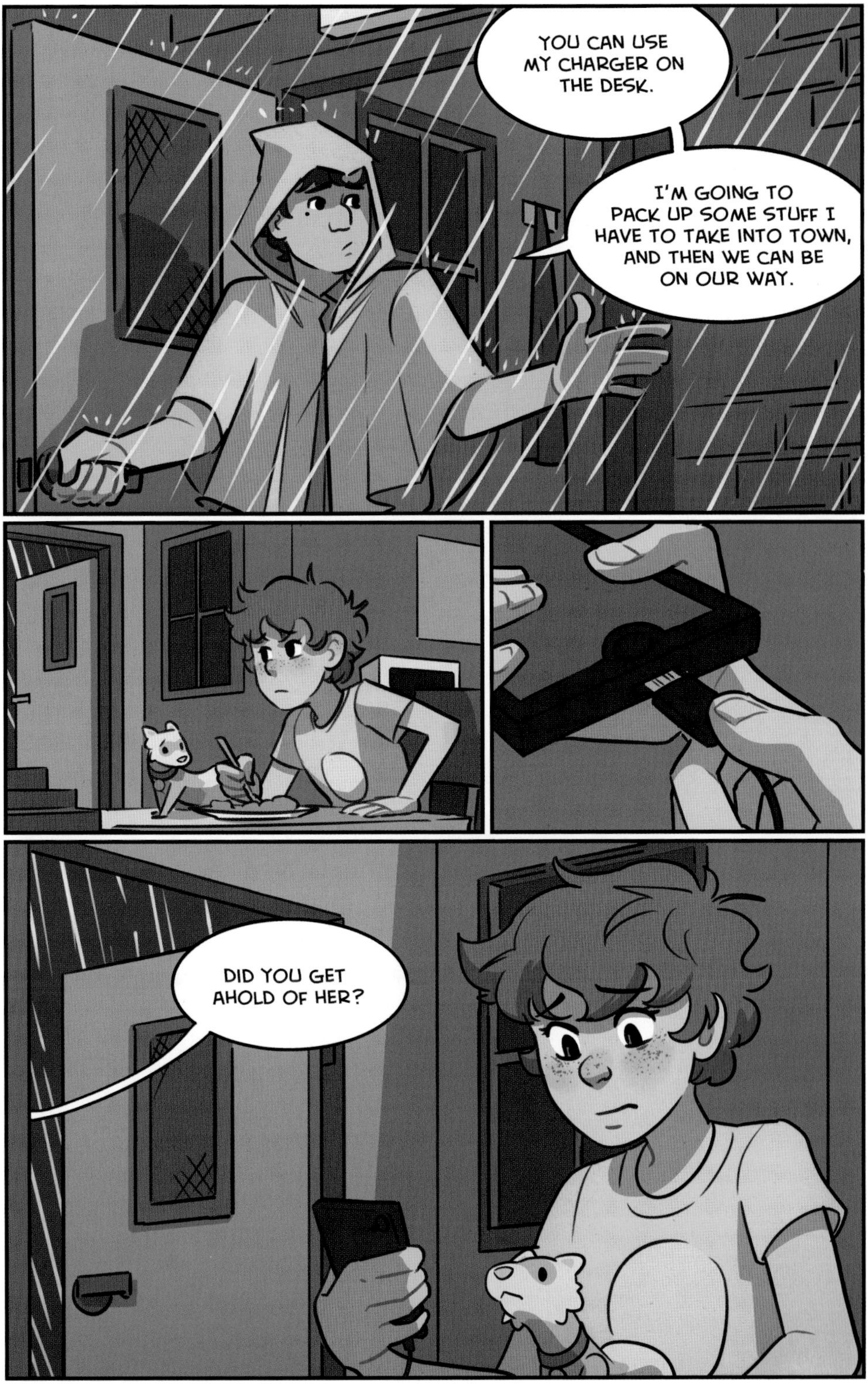
YOU CAN USE MY CHARGER ON THE DESK.
I'M GOING TO PACK UP SOME STUFF I HAVE TO TAKE INTO TOWN, AND THEN WE CAN BE ON OUR WAY.
DID YOU GET AHOLD OF HER?

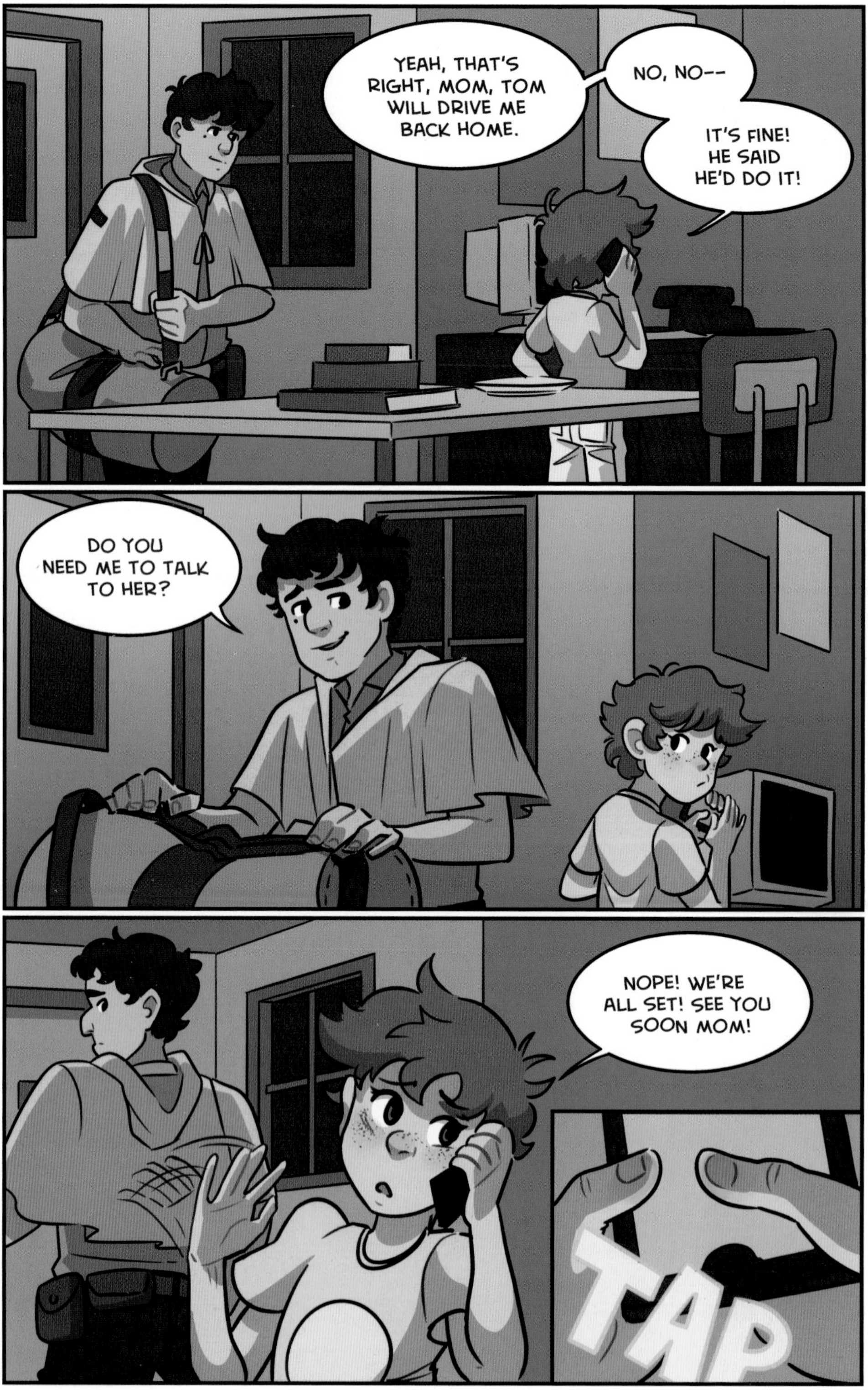
YEAH, THAT'S RIGHT, MOM, TOM WILL DRIVE ME BACK HOME.
NO, NO--
IT'S FINE! HE SAID HE'D DO IT!
DO YOU NEED ME TO TALK TO HER?
NOPE! WE'RE ALL SET! SEE YOU SOON MOM!
TAP

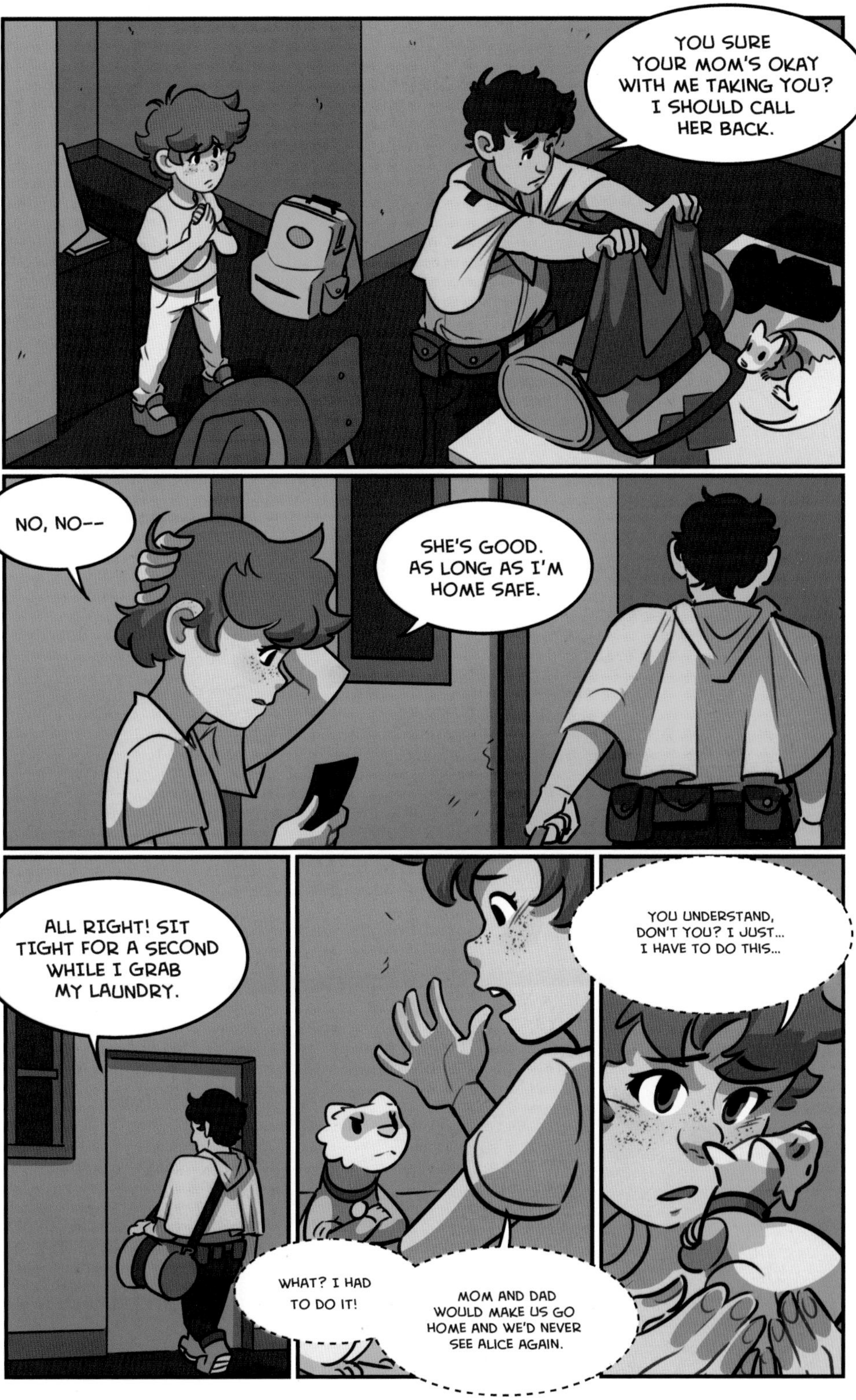
YOU SURE YOUR MOM'S OKAY WITH ME TAKING YOU? I SHOULD CALL HER BACK.
NO, NO--
SHE'S GOOD. AS LONG AS I'M HOME SAFE.
ALL RIGHT! SIT TIGHT FOR A SECOND WHILE I GRAB MY LAUNDRY.
YOU UNDERSTAND, DON'T YOU? I JUST... I HAVE TO DO THIS...
WHAT? I HAD TO DO IT!
MOM AND DAD WOULD MAKE US GO HOME AND WE'D NEVER SEE ALICE AGAIN.

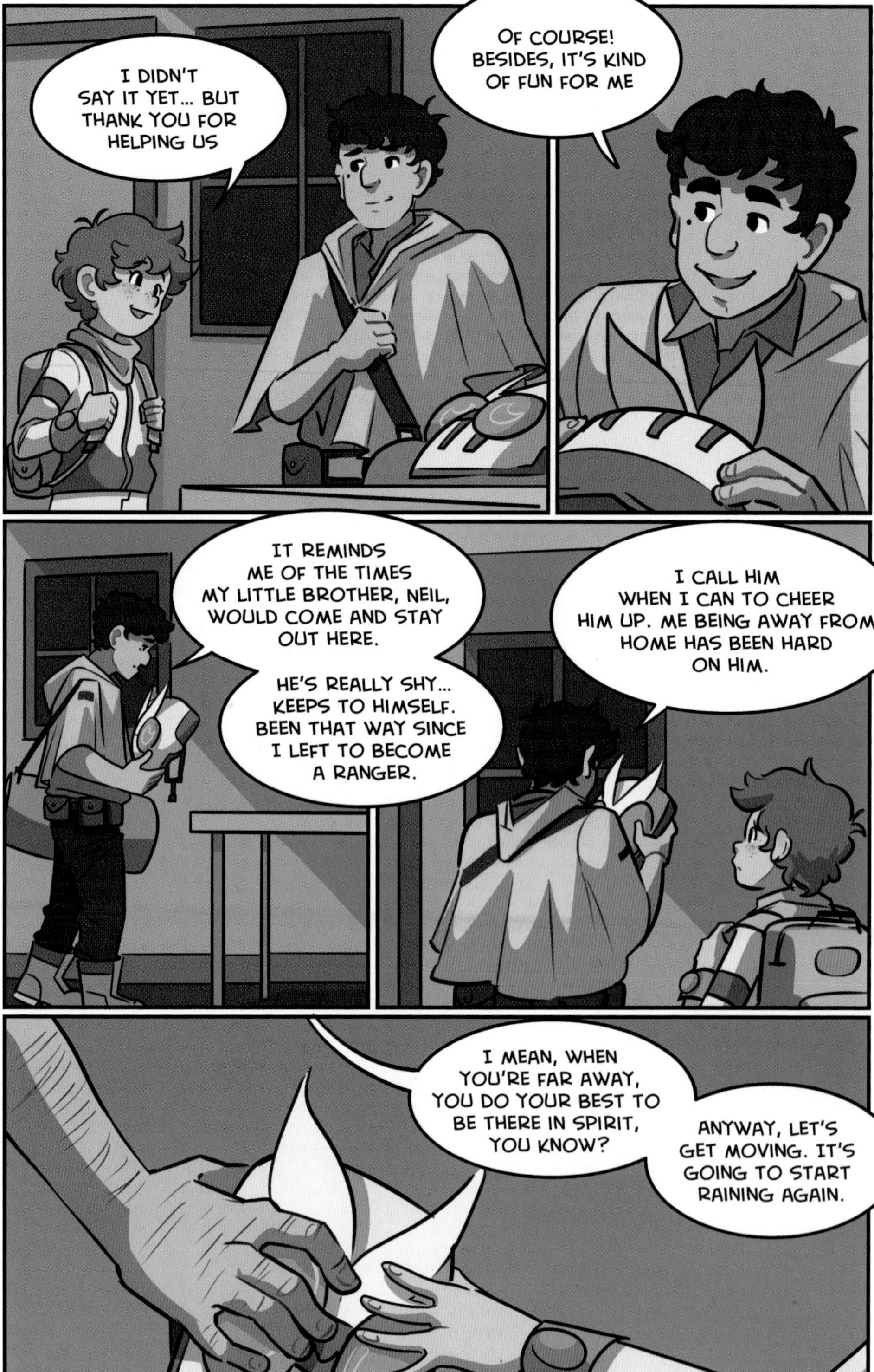
I DIDN'T SAY IT YET... BUT THANK YOU FOR HELPING US
OF COURSE! BESIDES, IT'S KIND OF FUN FOR ME
IT REMINDS ME OF THE TIMES MY LITTLE BROTHER, NEIL, WOULD COME AND STAY OUT HERE.
HE'S REALLY SHY... KEEPS TO HIMSELF. BEEN THAT WAY SINCE I LEFT TO BECOME A RANGER.
I CALL HIM WHEN I CAN TO CHEER HIM UP. ME BEING AWAY FROM HOME HAS BEEN HARD ON HIM.
I MEAN, WHEN YOU'RE FAR AWAY, YOU DO YOUR BEST TO BE THERE IN SPIRIT, YOU KNOW?
ANYWAY, LET'S GET MOVING. IT'S GOING TO START RAINING AGAIN.

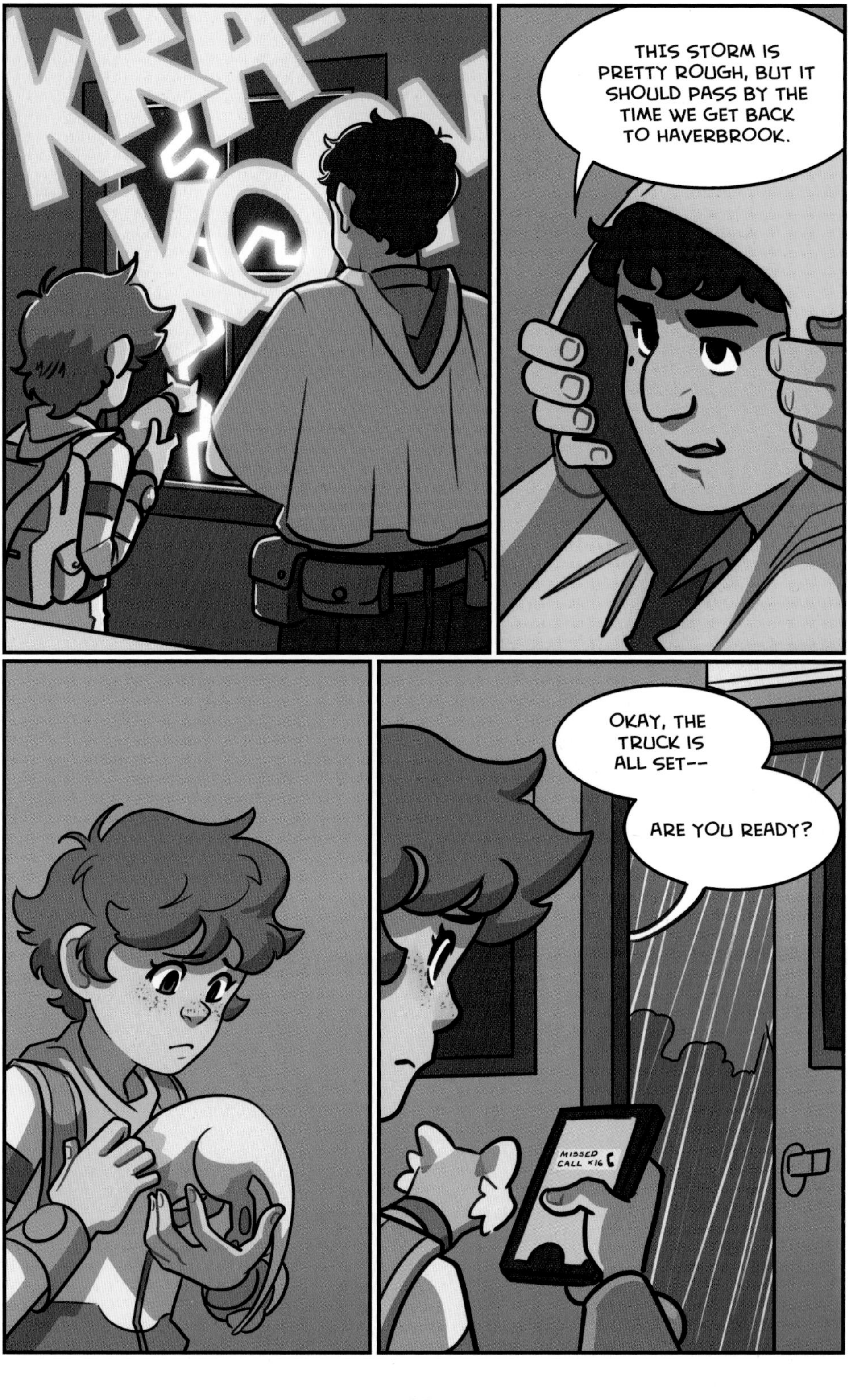
KRA-KOOOW
THIS STORM IS PRETTY ROUGH, BUT IT SHOULD PASS BY THE TIME WE GET BACK TO HAVERBROOK.
OKAY, THE TRUCK IS ALL SET--
ARE YOU READY?
MISSED CALL KIG

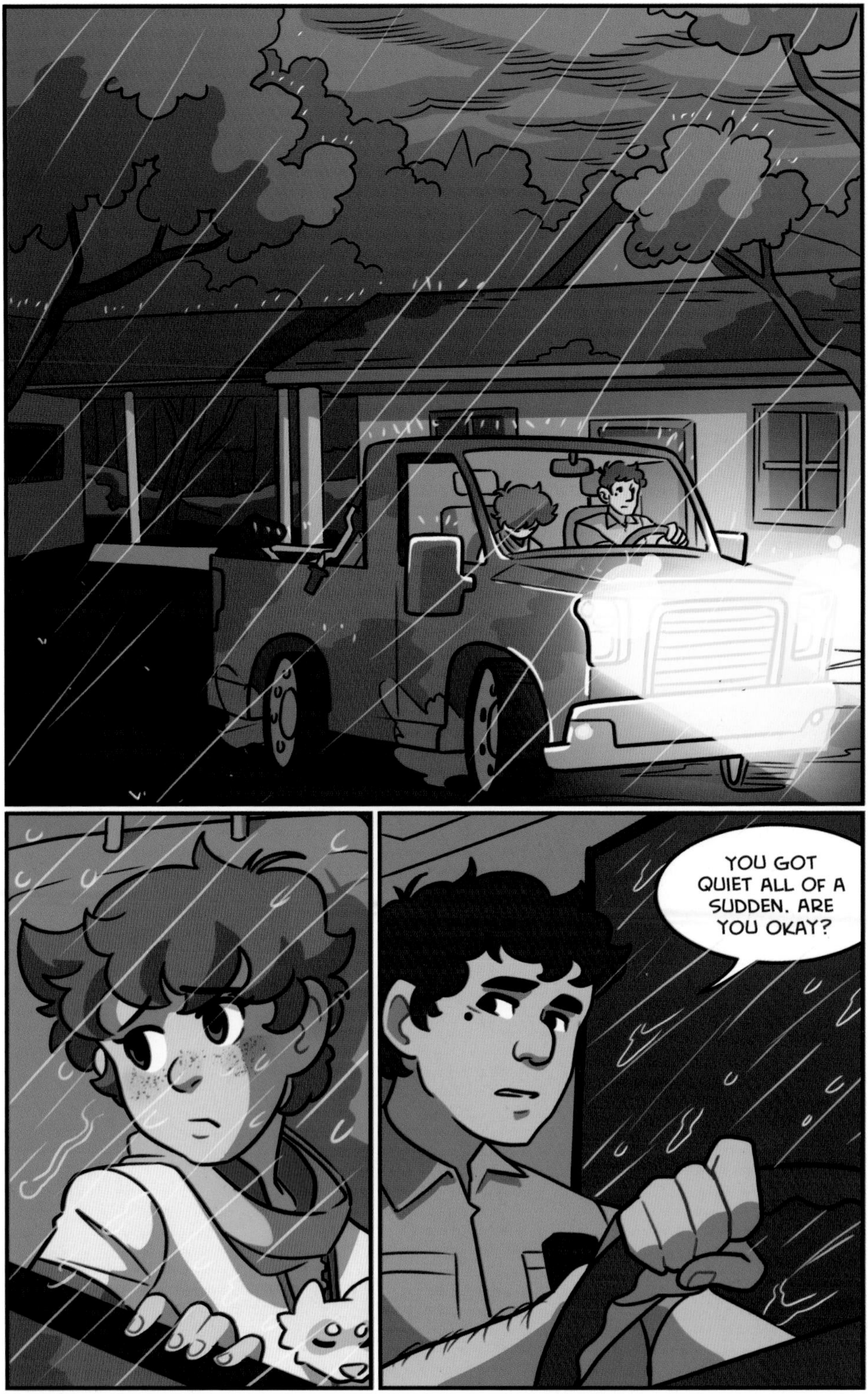
YOU GOT QUIET ALL OF A SUDDEN. ARE YOU OKAY?

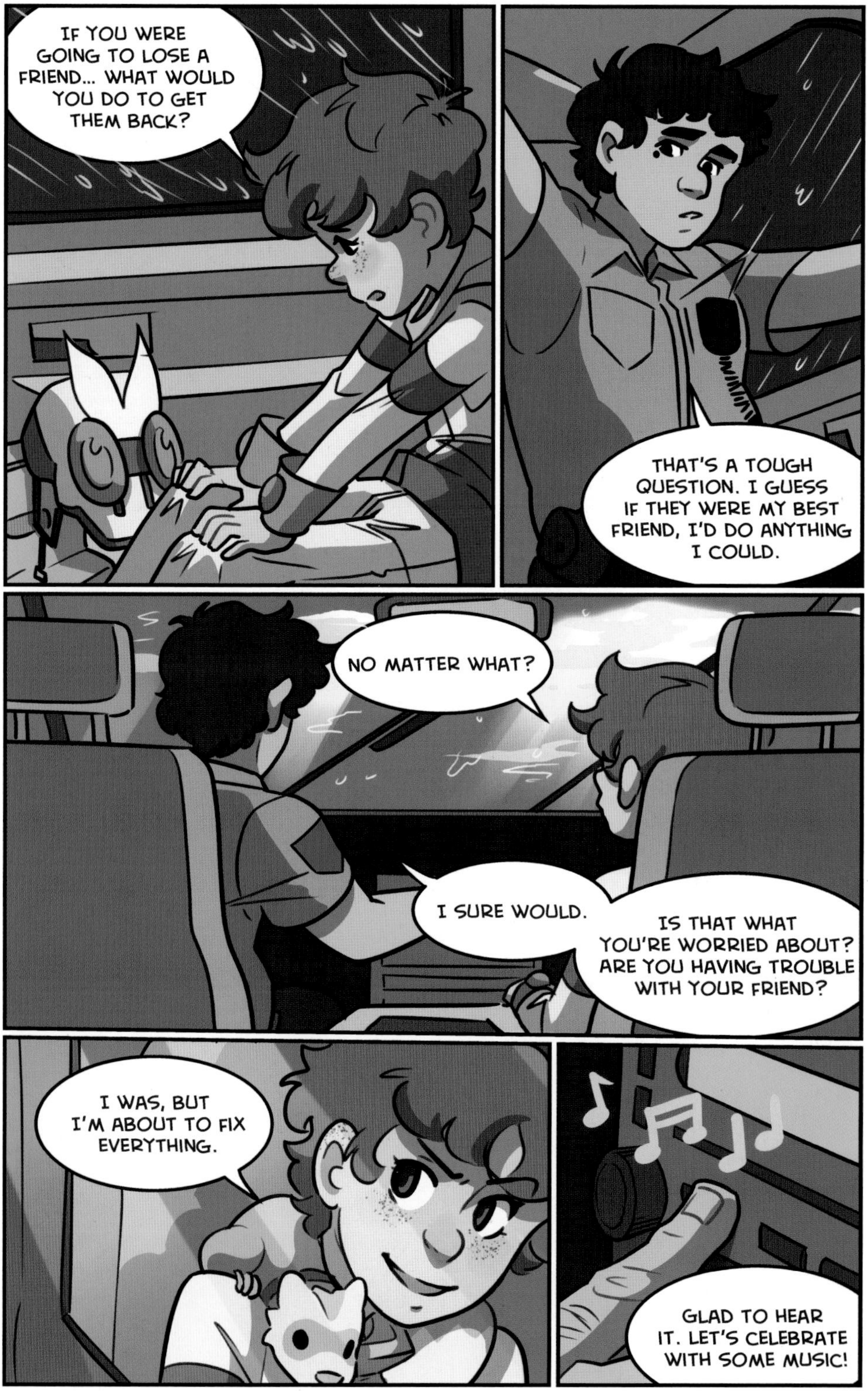
IF YOU WERE GOING TO LOSE A FRIEND... WHAT WOULD YOU DO TO GET THEM BACK?
THAT'S A TOUGH QUESTION. I GUESS IF THEY WERE MY BEST FRIEND, I'D DO ANYTHING I COULD.
NO MATTER WHAT?
I SURE WOULD.
IS THAT WHAT YOU'RE WORRIED ABOUT? ARE YOU HAVING TROUBLE WITH YOUR FRIEND?
I WAS, BUT I'M ABOUT TO FIX EVERYTHING.
GLAD TO HEAR IT. LET'S CELEBRATE WITH SOME MUSIC!

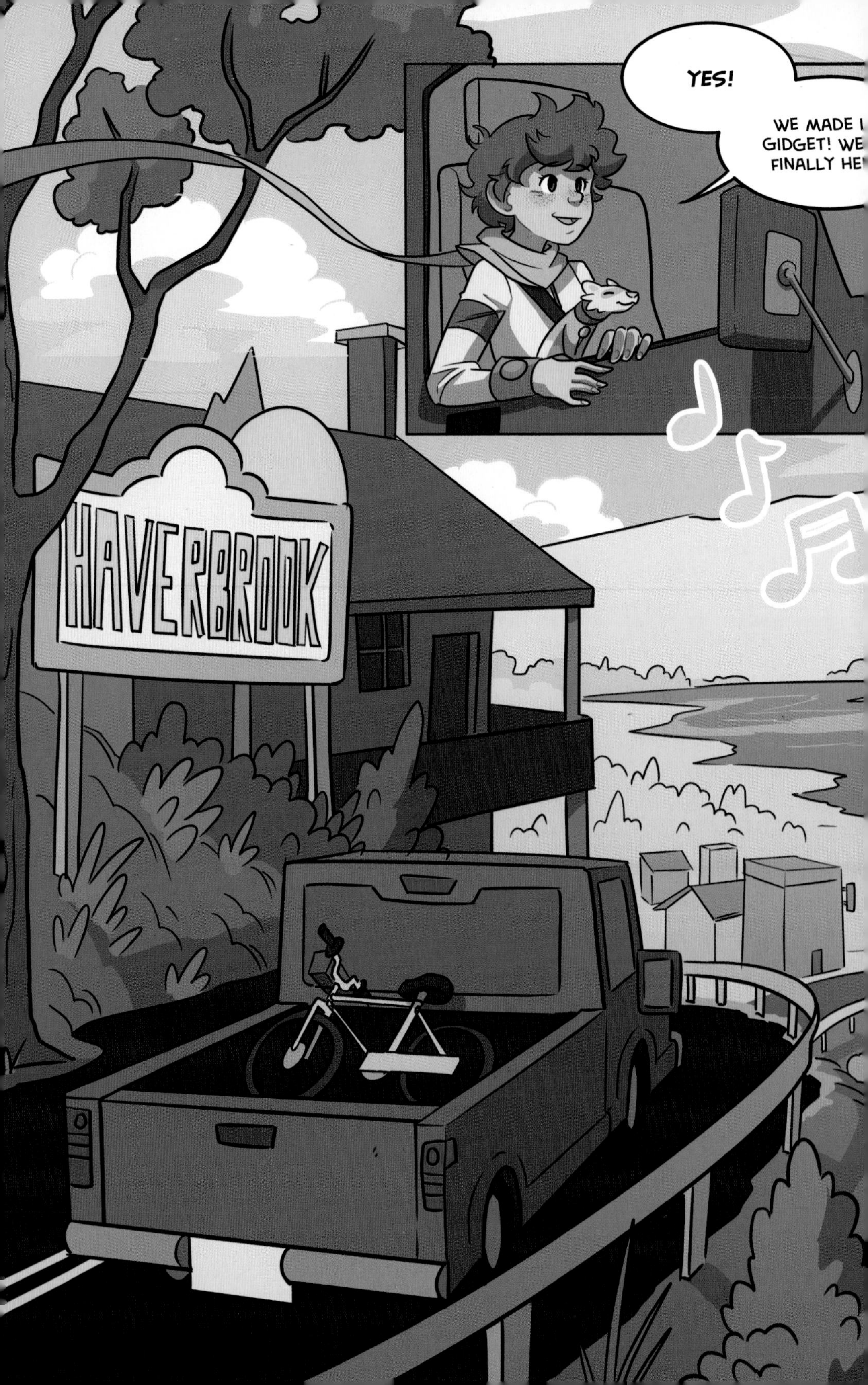
YES!
WE MADE I GIDGET! WE FINALLY HE
HAVERBROOK

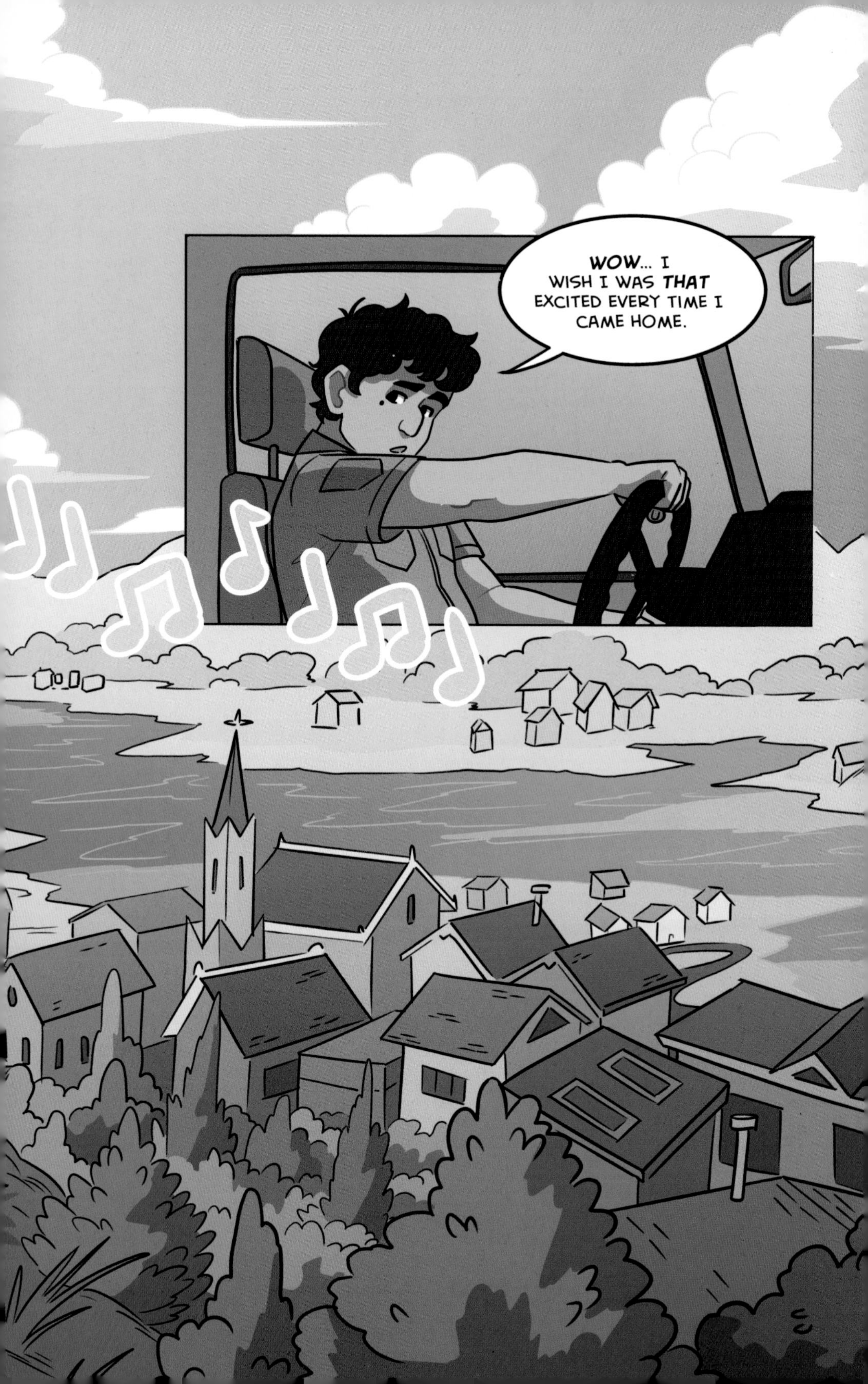
WOW... I WISH I WAS THAT EXCITED EVERY TIME I CAME HOME.

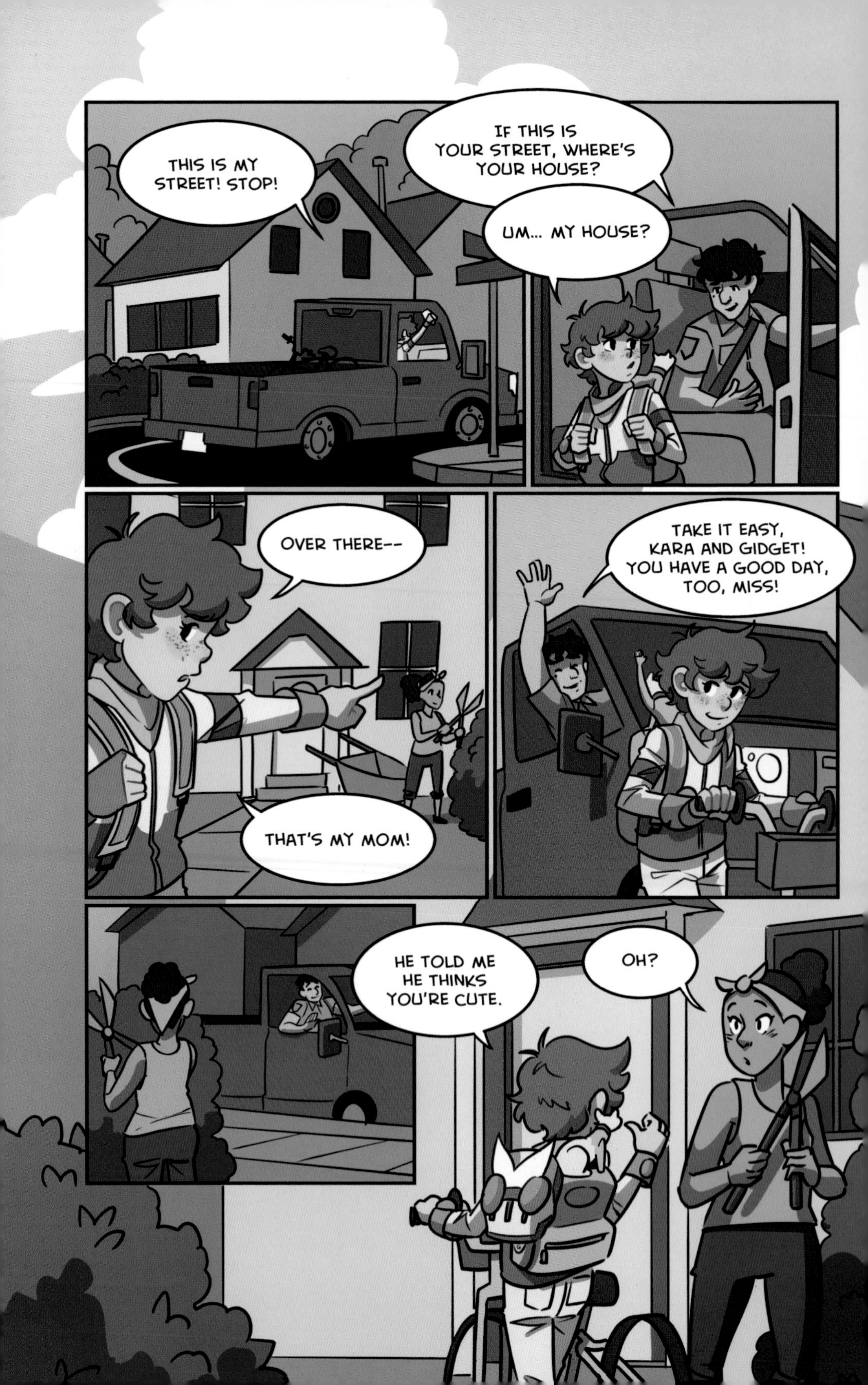
THIS IS MY STREET! STOP!
IF THIS IS YOUR STREET, WHERE'S YOUR HOUSE?
UM... MY HOUSE?
OVER THERE--
THAT'S MY MOM!
TAKE IT EASY, KARA AND GIDGET! YOU HAVE A GOOD DAY, TOO, MISS!
HE TOLD ME HE THINKS YOU'RE CUTE.
OH?

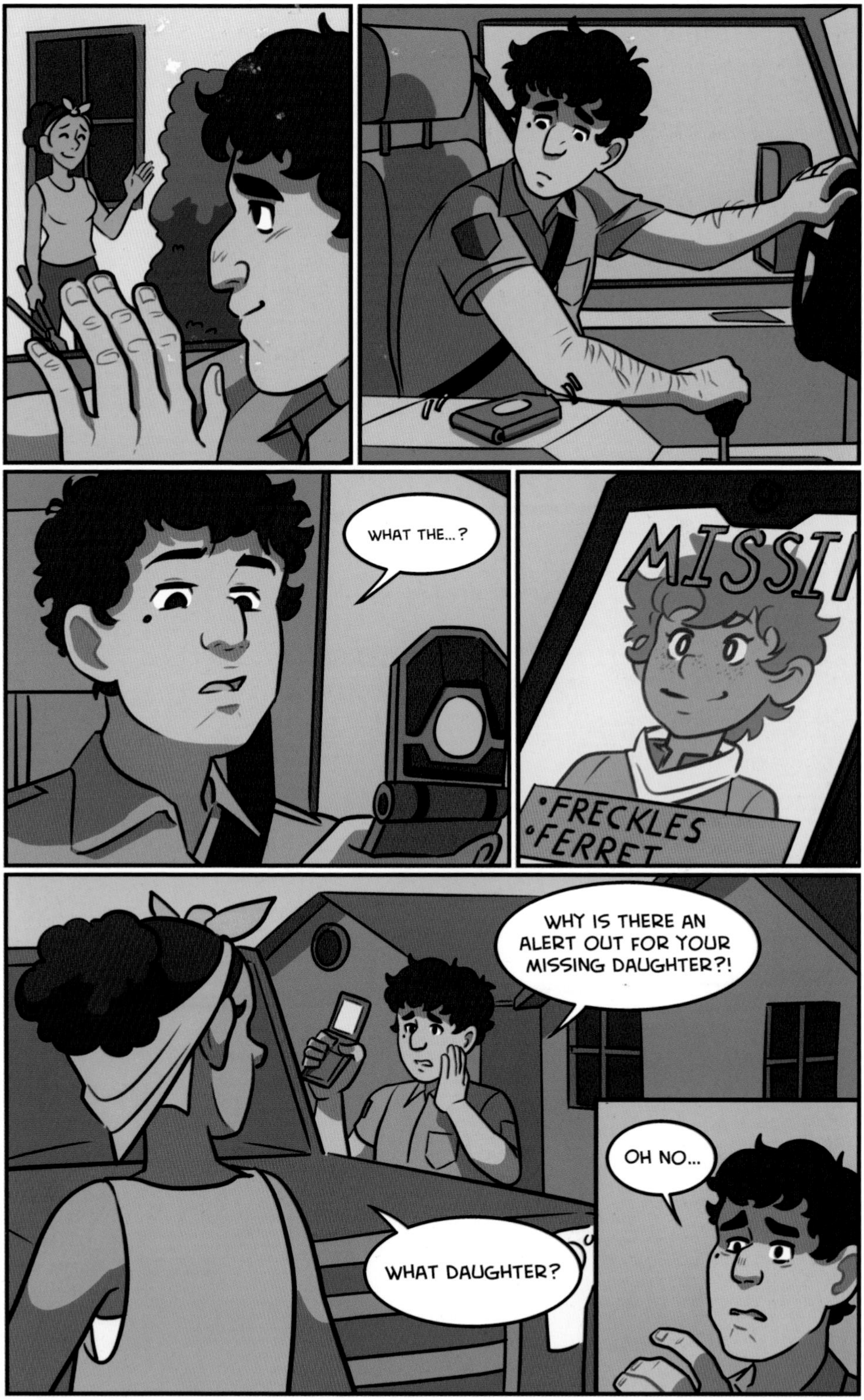
WHAT THE...?
MISSI
•FRECKLES
•FERRET
WHY IS THERE AN ALERT OUT FOR YOUR MISSING DAUGHTER?!
WHAT DAUGHTER?
OH NO...

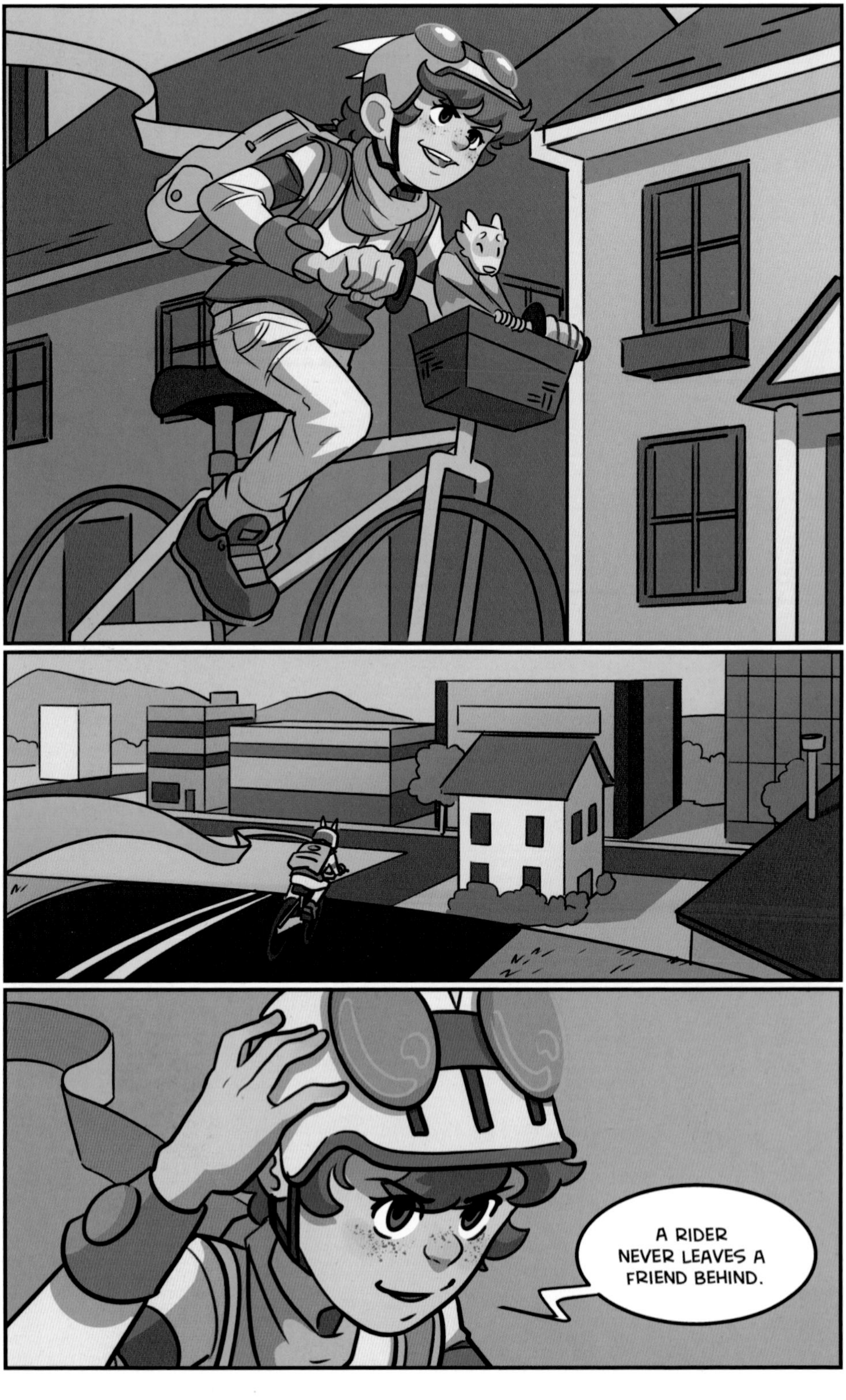
A RIDER NEVER LEAVES A FRIEND BEHIND.

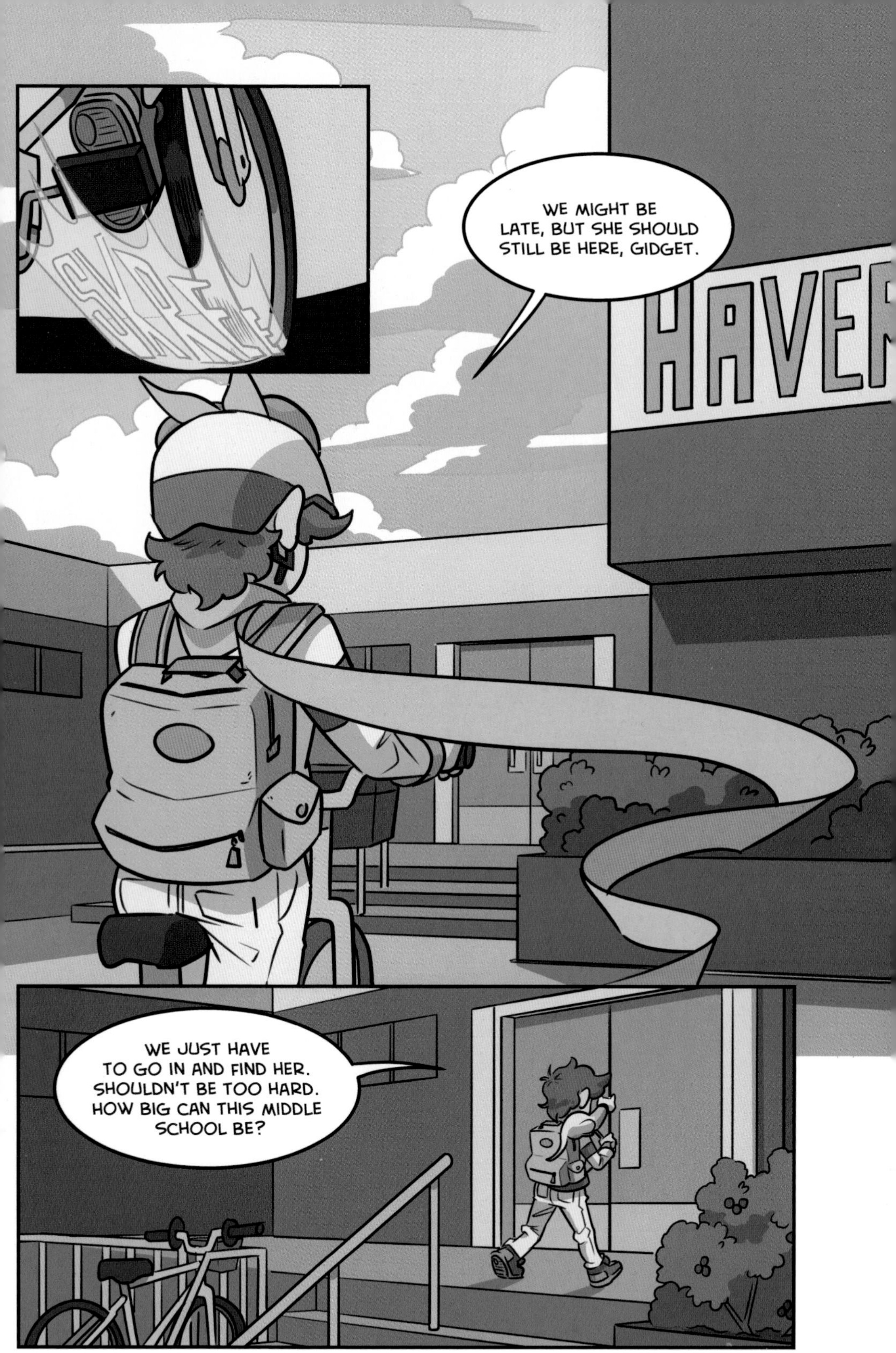
WE MIGHT BE LATE, BUT SHE SHOULD STILL BE HERE, GIDGET.
HAVER
WE JUST HAVE TO GO IN AND FIND HER. SHOULDN'T BE TOO HARD. HOW BIG CAN THIS MIDDLE SCHOOL BE?

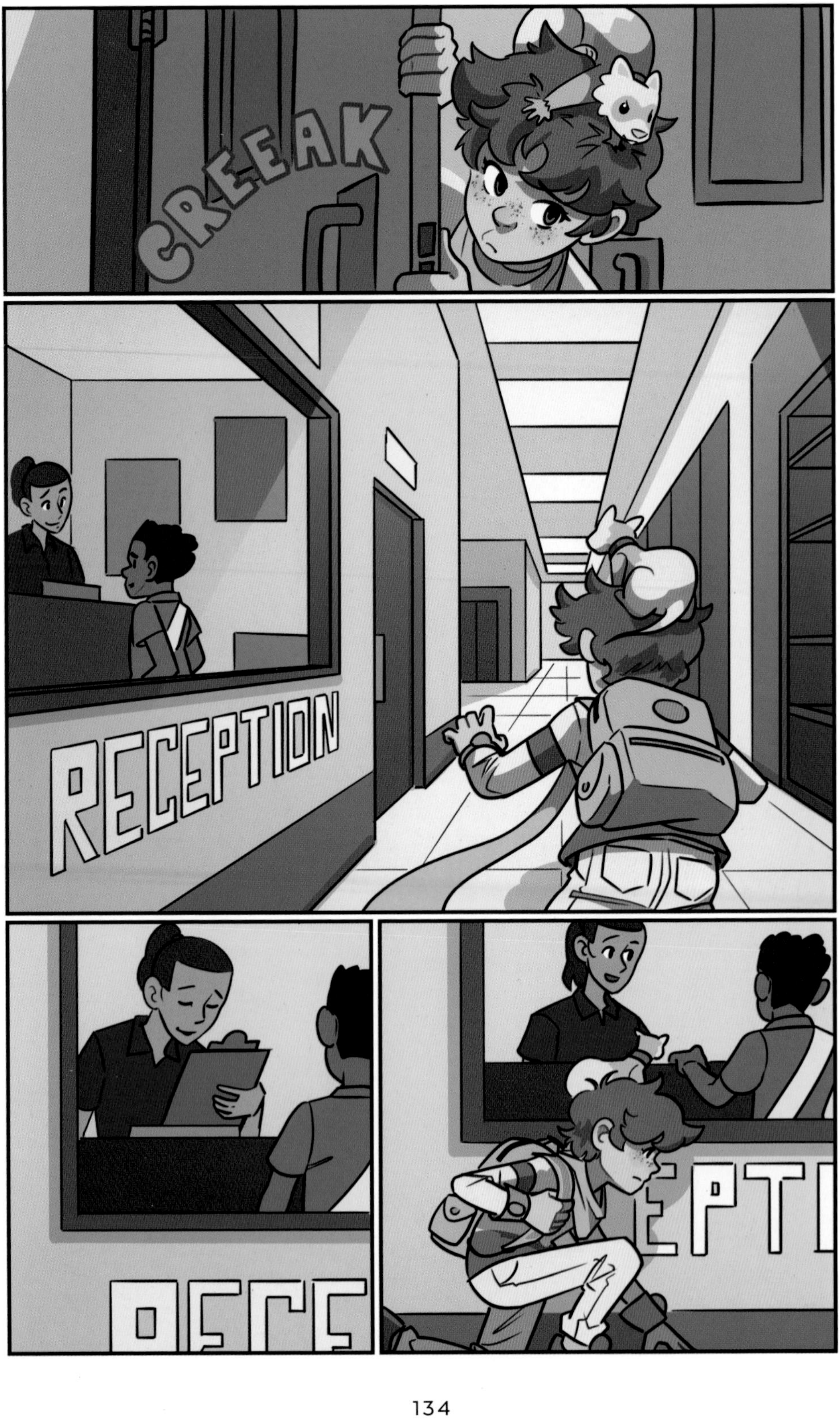
CREEAK
RECEPTION

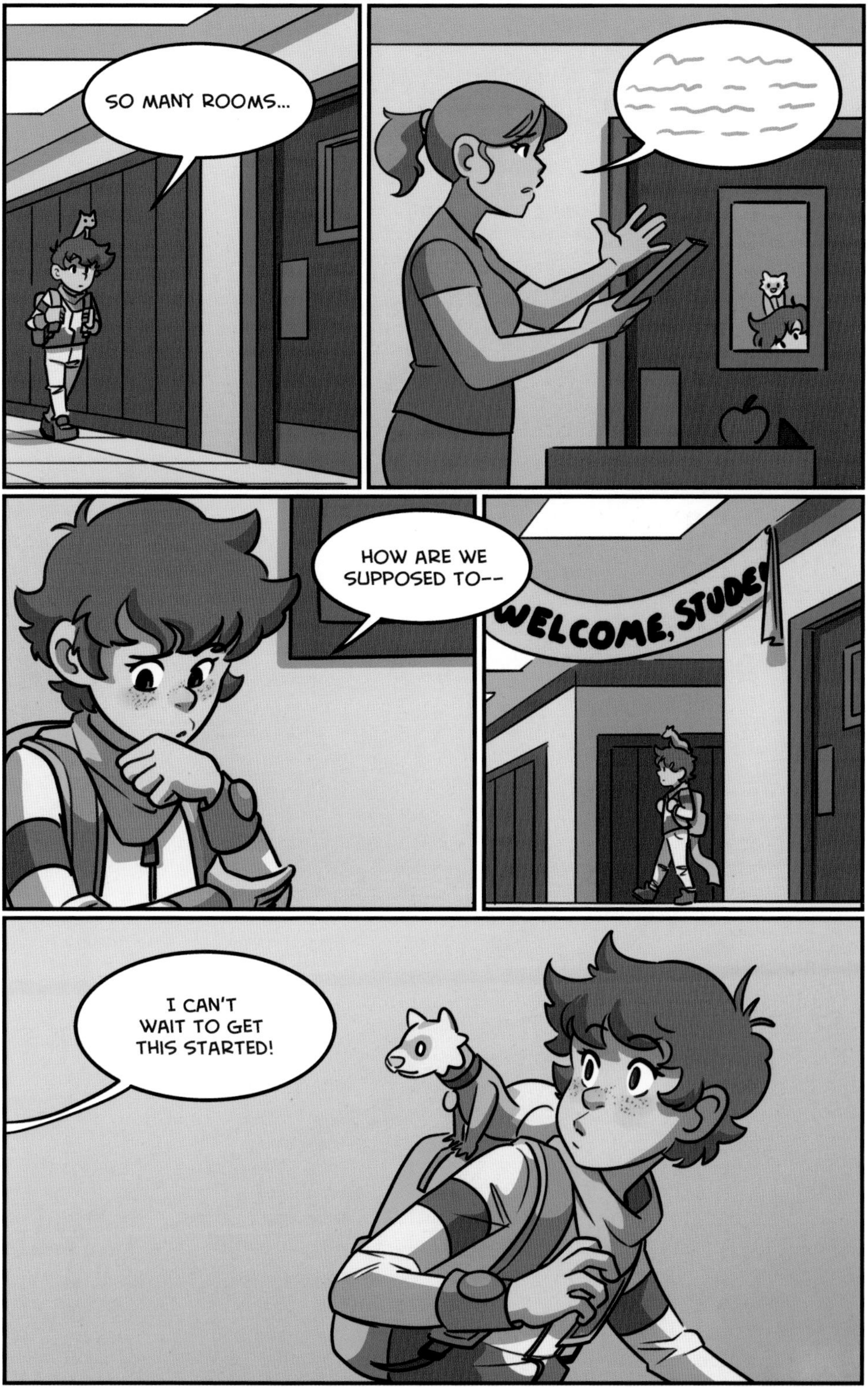
SO MANY ROOMS...
HOW ARE WE SUPPOSED TO--
WELCOME, STUDE
I CAN'T WAIT TO GET THIS STARTED!

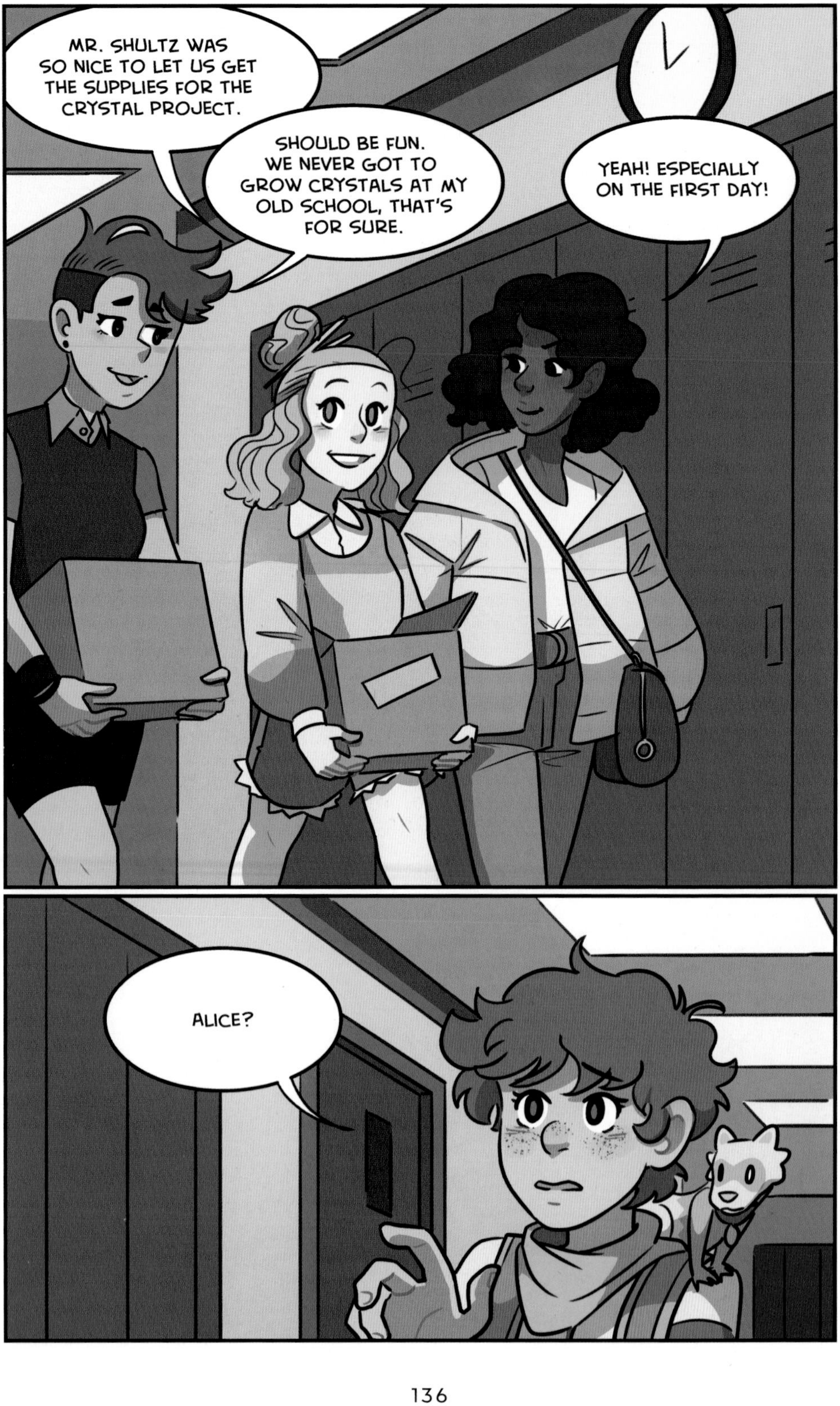

MR. SHULTZ WAS SO NICE TO LET US GET THE SUPPLIES FOR THE CRYSTAL PROJECT.
SHOULD BE FUN. WE NEVER GOT TO GROW CRYSTALS AT MY OLD SCHOOL, THAT'S FOR SURE.
YEAH! ESPECIALLY ON THE FIRST DAY!
ALICE?

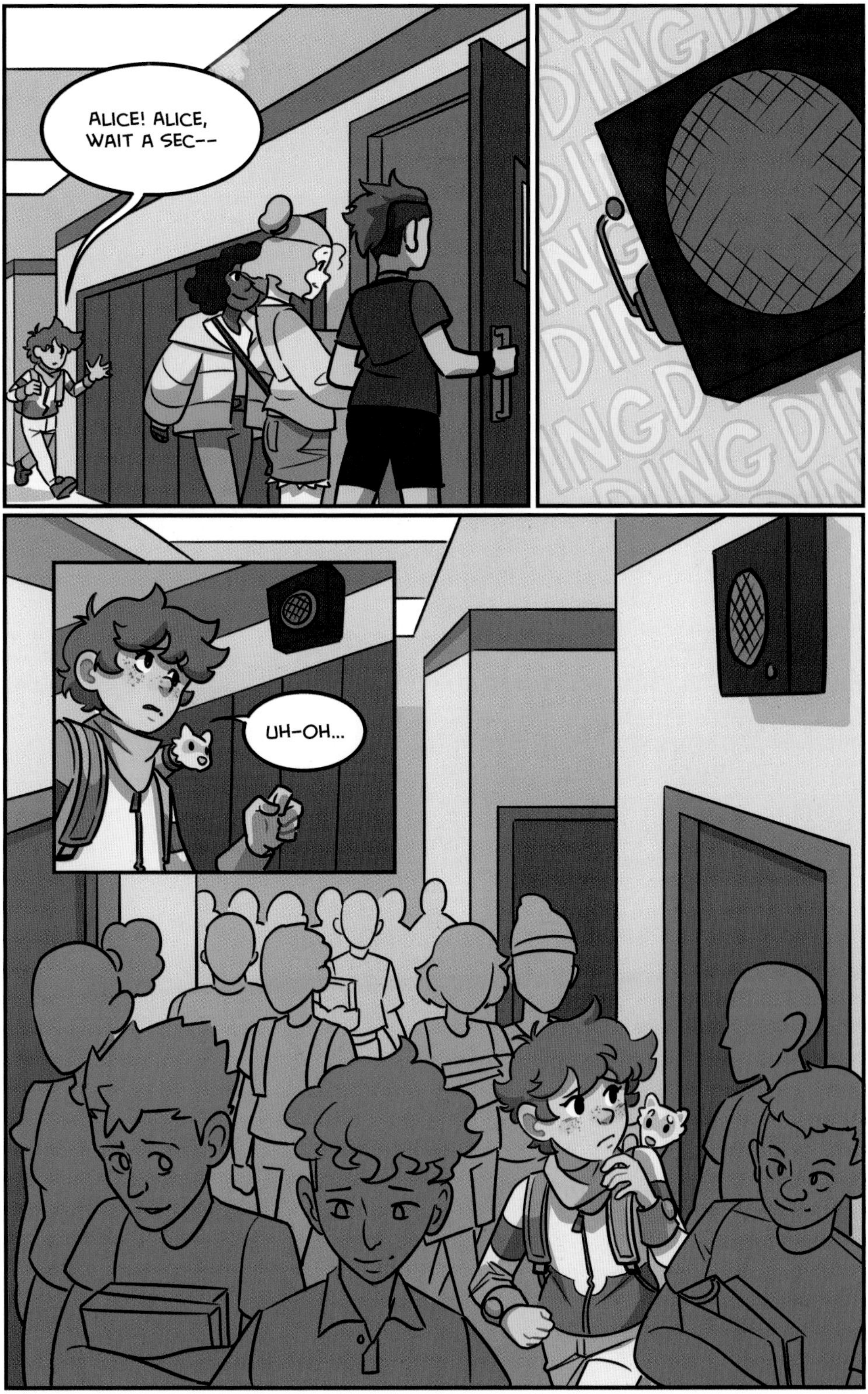
ALICE! ALICE, WAIT A SEC--
DING DING DING DING
UH-OH...

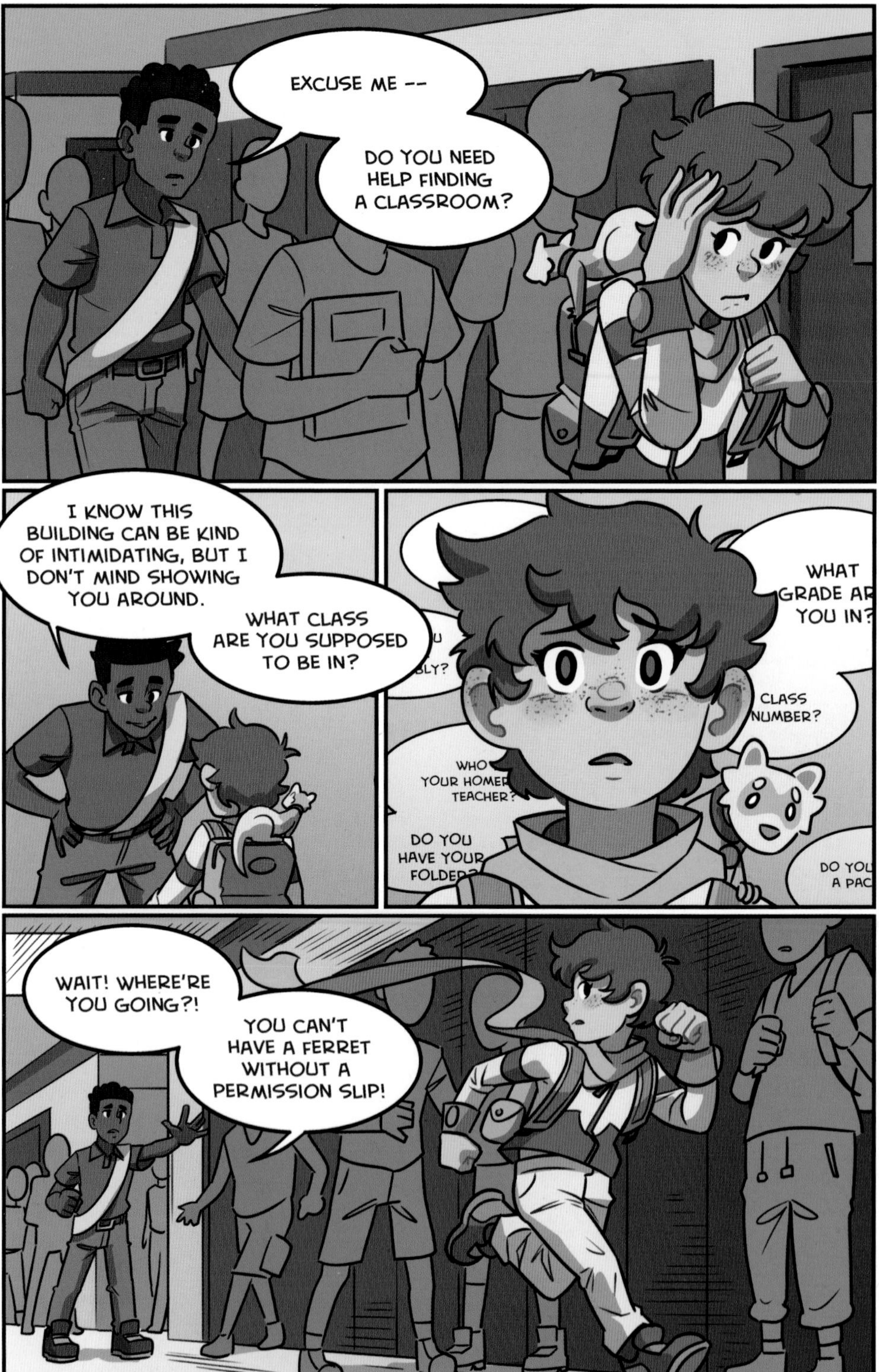
EXCUSE ME --
DO YOU NEED HELP FINDING A CLASSROOM?
I KNOW THIS BUILDING CAN BE KIND OF INTIMIDATING, BUT I DON'T MIND SHOWING YOU AROUND.
WHAT CLASS ARE YOU SUPPOSED TO BE IN?
WHAT GRADE AR YOU IN?
CLASS NUMBER?
DO YOU HAVE YOUR
WAIT! WHERE'RE YOU GOING?!
YOU CAN'T HAVE A FERRET WITHOUT A PERMISSION SLIP!

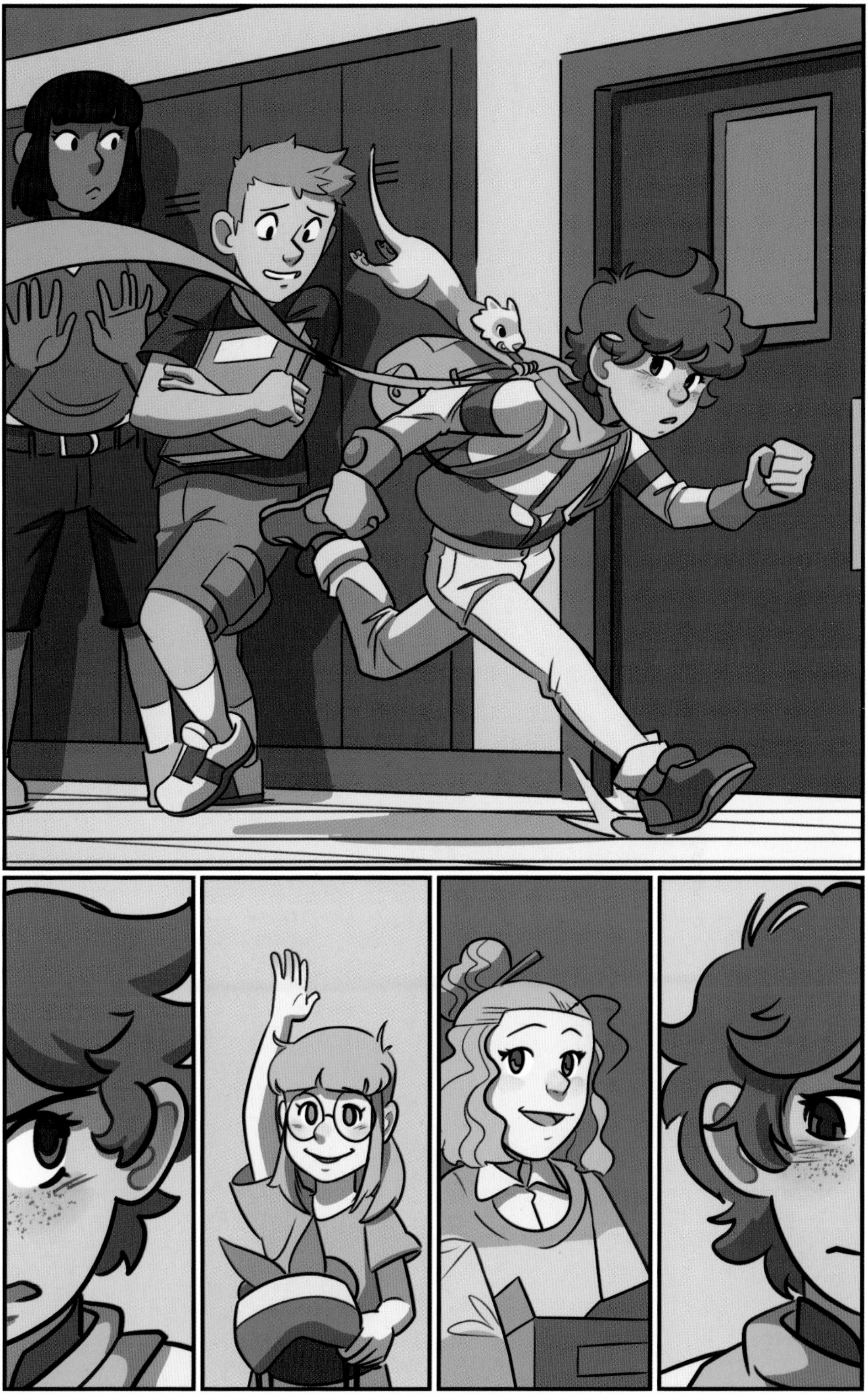

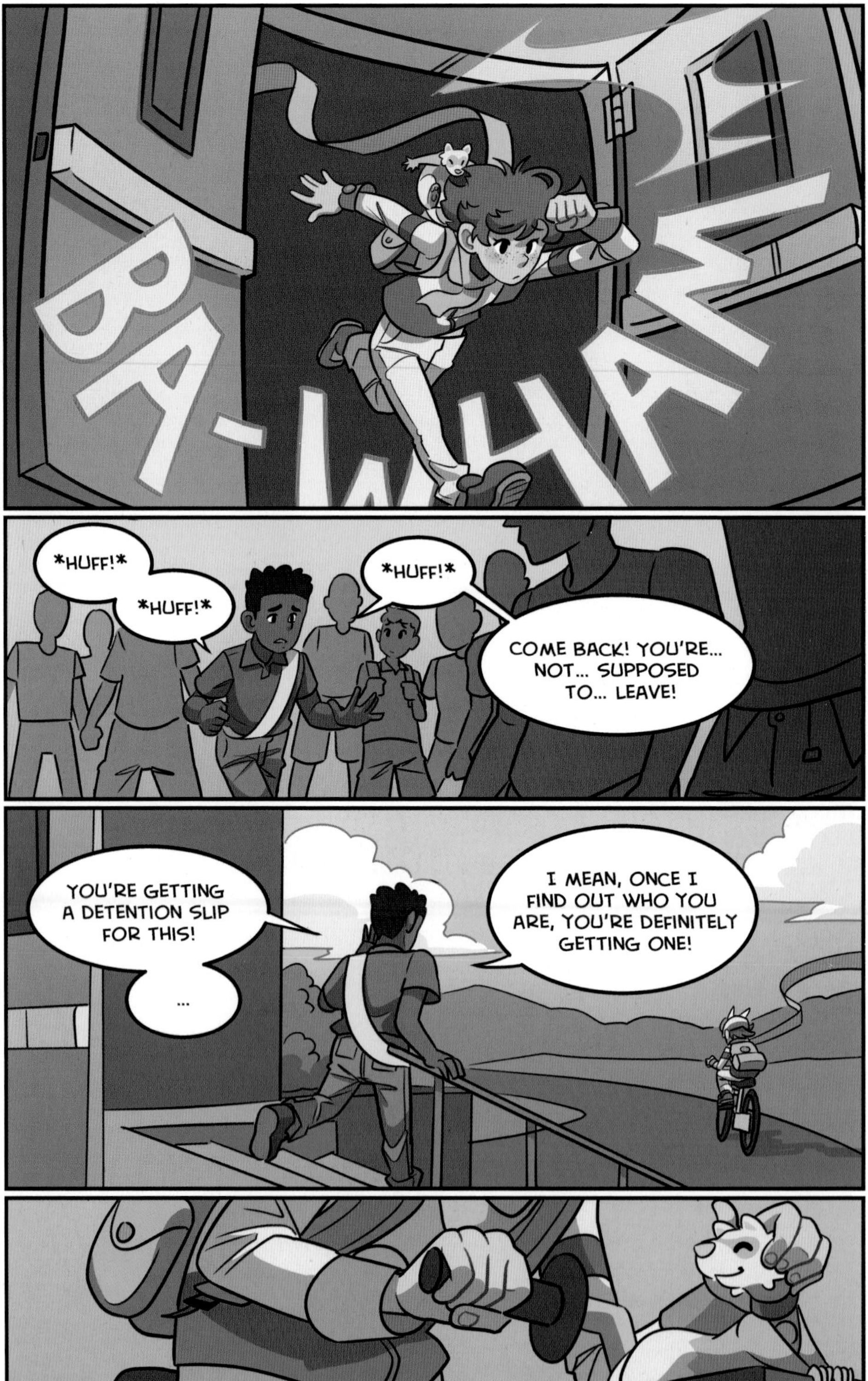
BA-WHAM!
HUFF!
HUFF!
HUFF!
COME BACK! YOU'RE... NOT... SUPPOSED TO... LEAVE!
YOU'RE GETTING A DETENTION SLIP FOR THIS!
...
I MEAN, ONCE I FIND OUT WHO YOU ARE, YOU'RE DEFINITELY GETTING ONE!

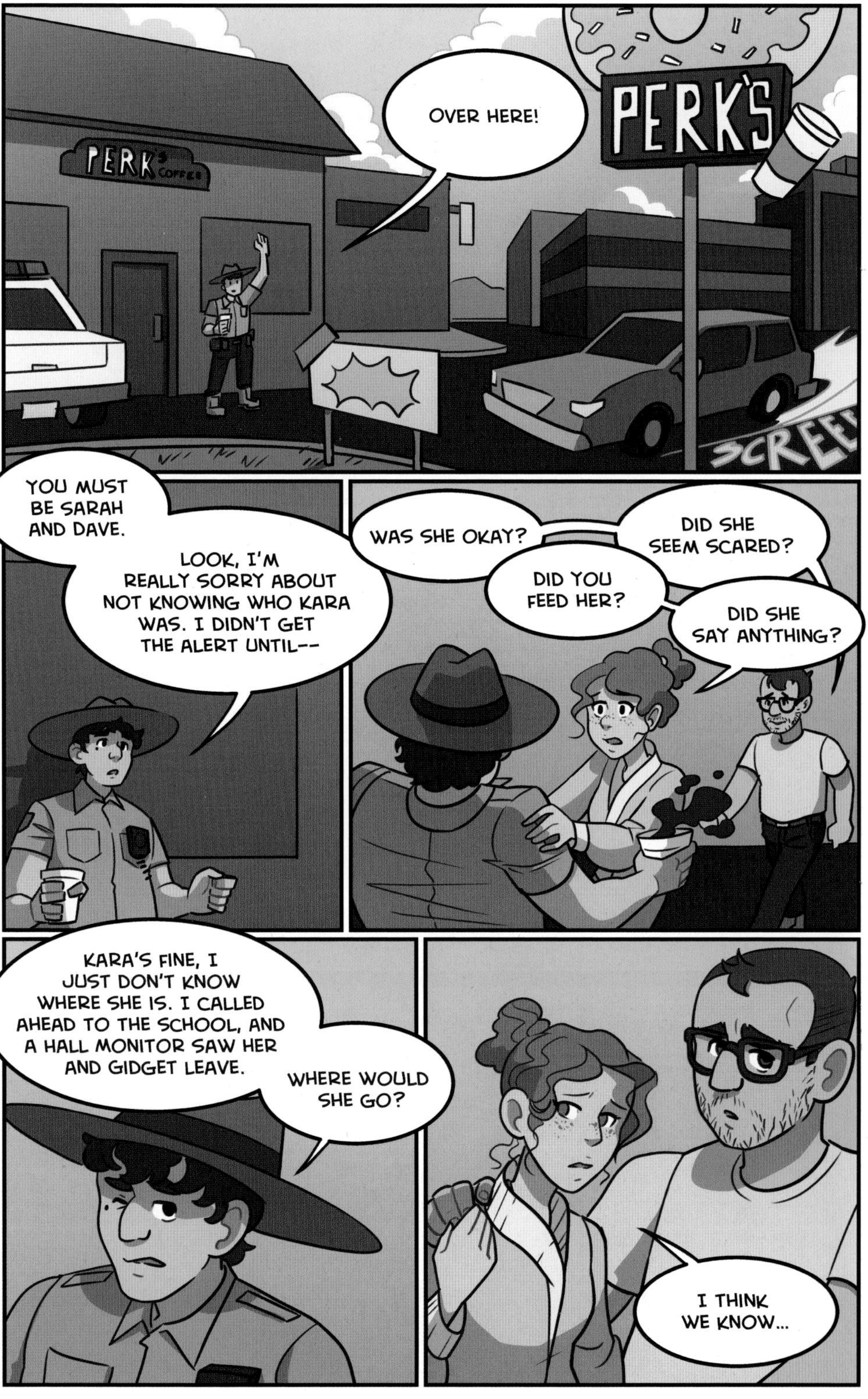
PERK'S COFFEE
OVER HERE!
PERK'S
SCREE
YOU MUST BE SARAH AND DAVE.
LOOK, I'M REALLY SORRY ABOUT NOT KNOWING WHO KARA WAS. I DIDN'T GET THE ALERT UNTIL--
WAS SHE OKAY?
DID SHE SEEM SCARED?
DID YOU FEED HER?
DID SHE SAY ANYTHING?
KARA'S FINE, I JUST DON'T KNOW WHERE SHE IS. I CALLED AHEAD TO THE SCHOOL, AND A HALL MONITOR SAW HER AND GIDGET LEAVE.
WHERE WOULD SHE GO?
I THINK WE KNOW...

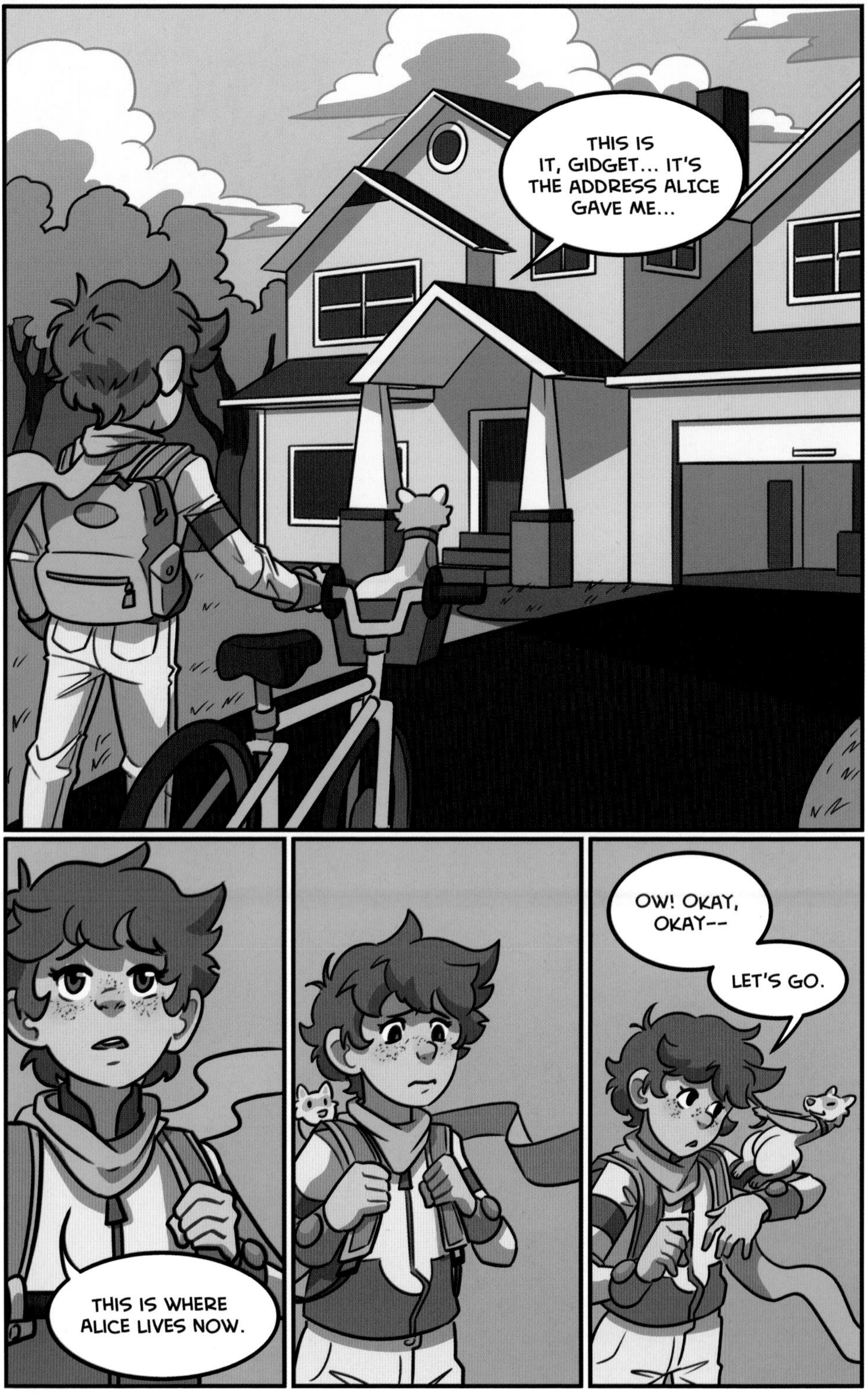
THIS IS IT, GIDGET... IT'S THE ADDRESS ALICE GAVE ME...
THIS IS WHERE ALICE LIVES NOW.
OW! OKAY, OKAY--
LET'S GO.

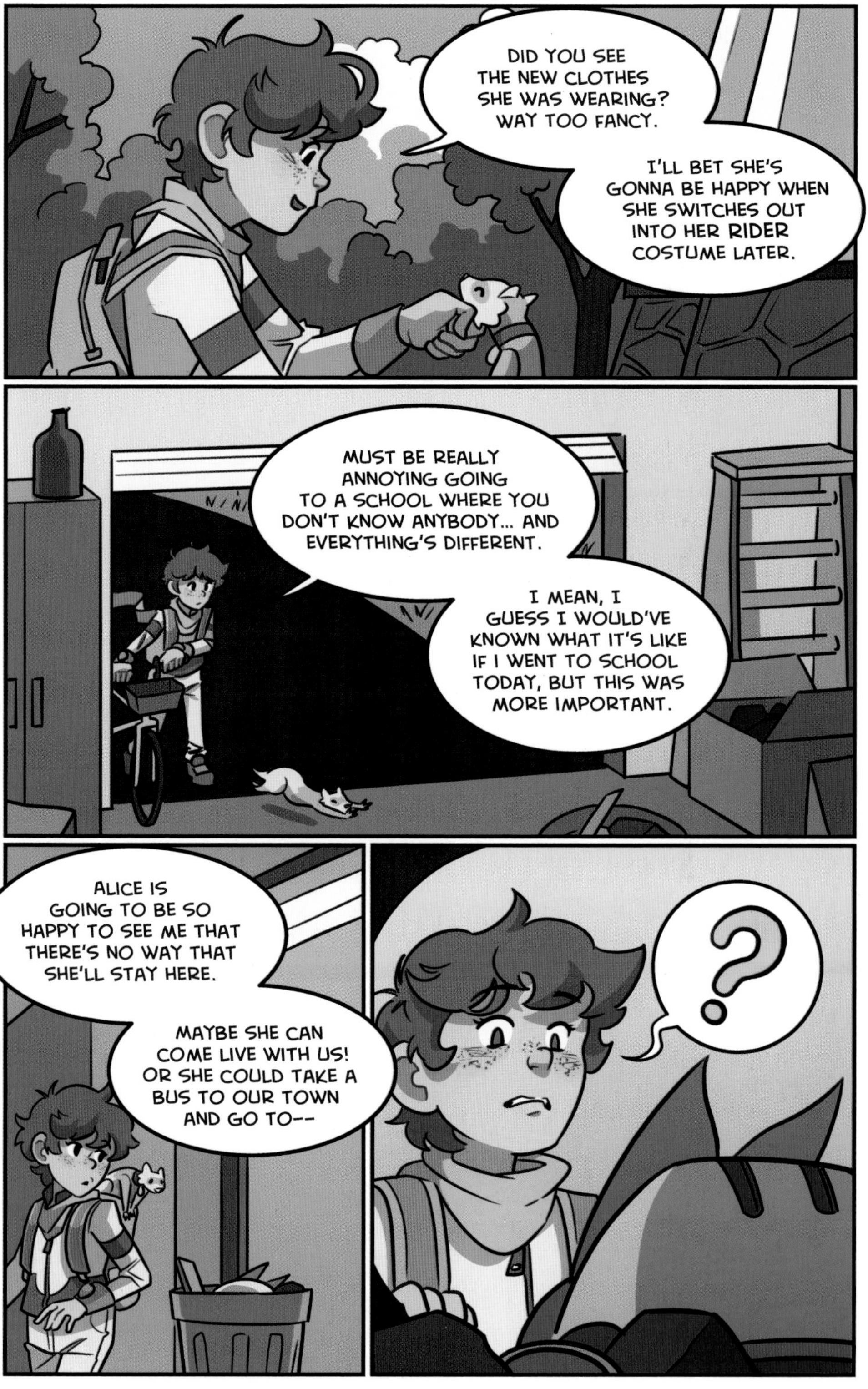
DID YOU SEE THE NEW CLOTHES SHE WAS WEARING? WAY TOO FANCY.
I'LL BET SHE'S GONNA BE HAPPY WHEN SHE SWITCHES OUT INTO HER RIDER COSTUME LATER.
MUST BE REALLY ANNOYING GOING TO A SCHOOL WHERE YOU DON'T KNOW ANYBODY... AND EVERYTHING'S DIFFERENT.
I MEAN, I GUESS I WOULD'VE KNOWN WHAT IT'S LIKE IF I WENT TO SCHOOL TODAY, BUT THIS WAS MORE IMPORTANT.
ALICE IS GOING TO BE SO HAPPY TO SEE ME THAT THERE'S NO WAY THAT SHE'LL STAY HERE.
MAYBE SHE CAN COME LIVE WITH US! OR SHE COULD TAKE A BUS TO OUR TOWN AND GO TO--
?

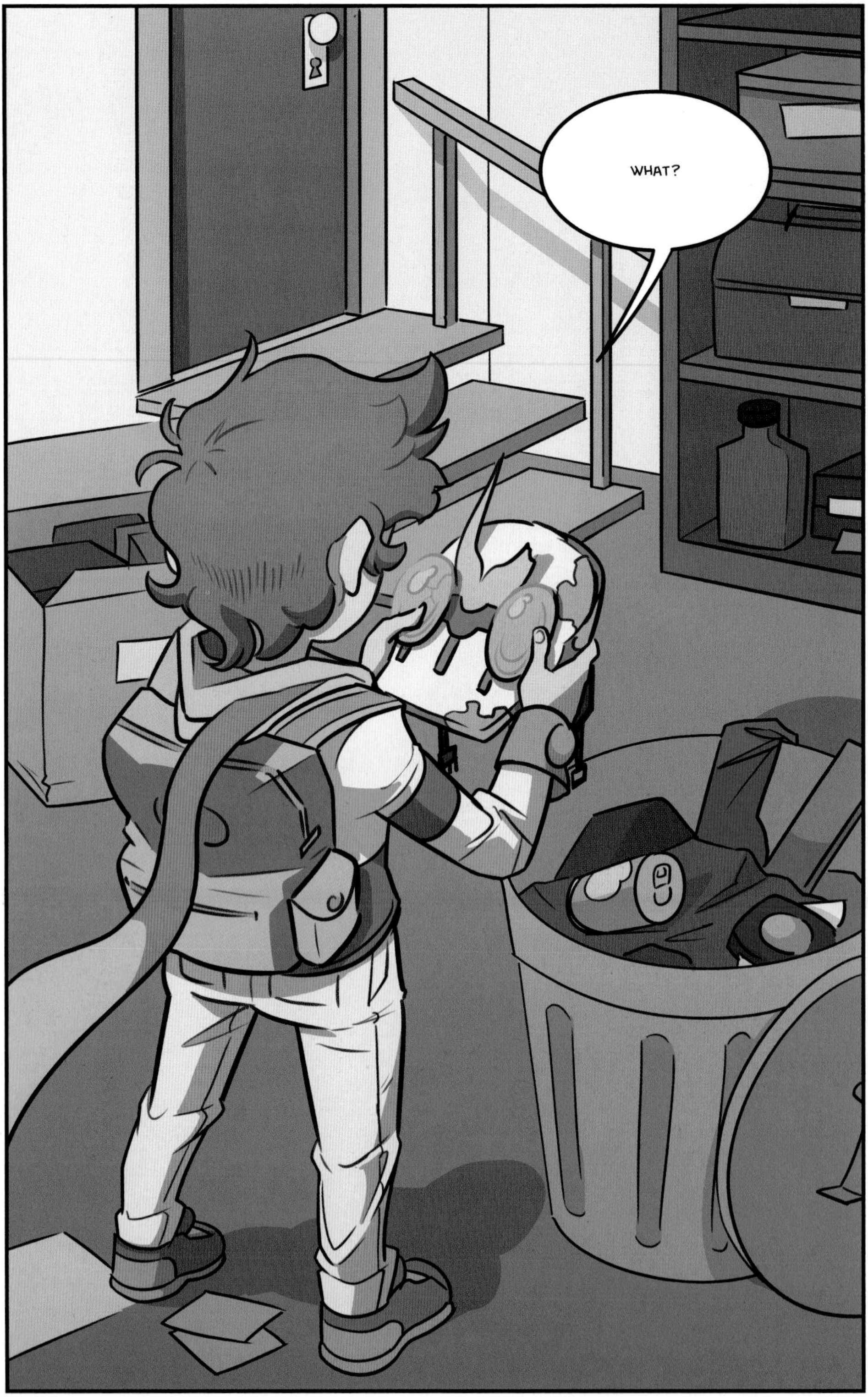
WHAT?

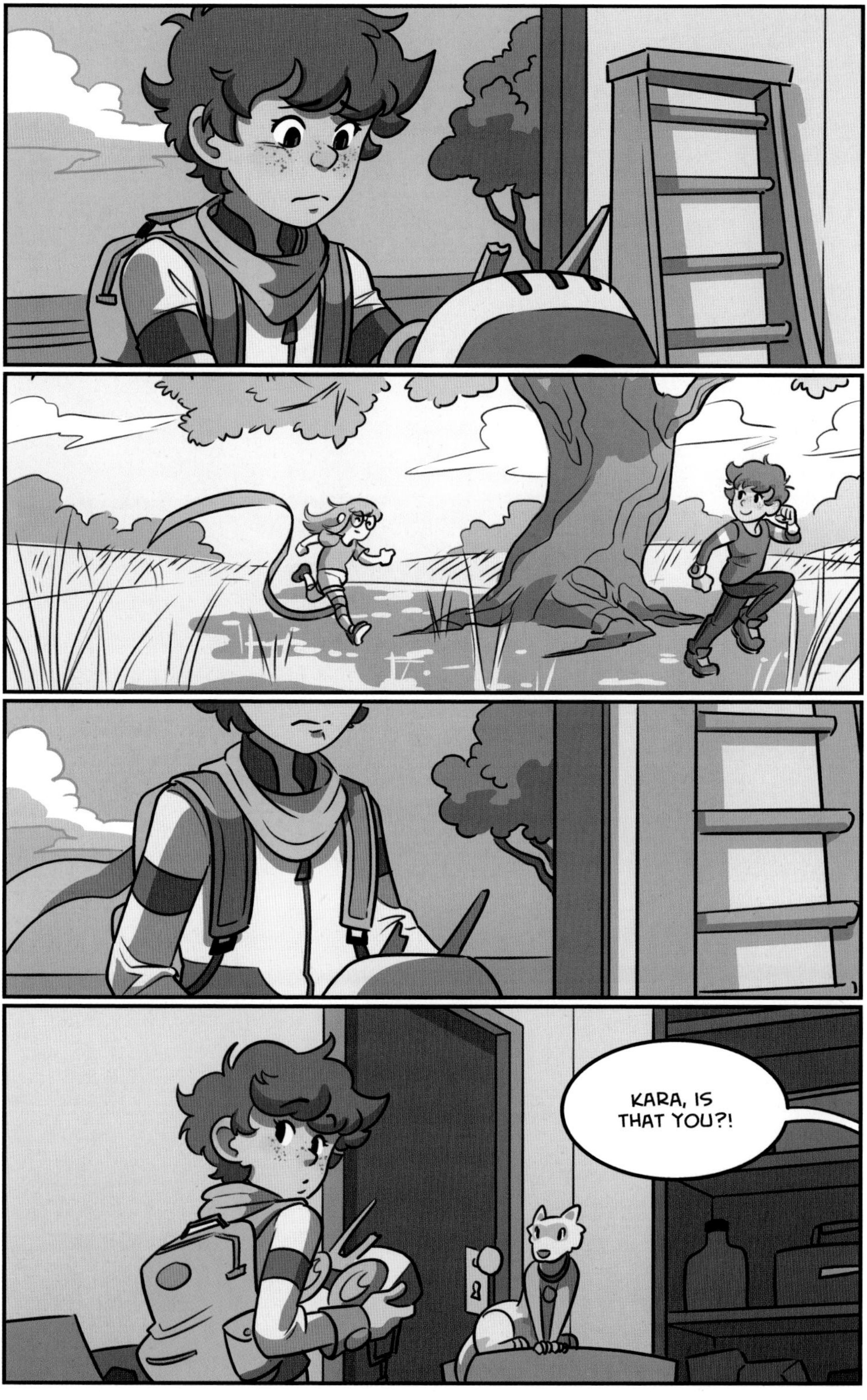
KARA, IS
THAT YOU?!

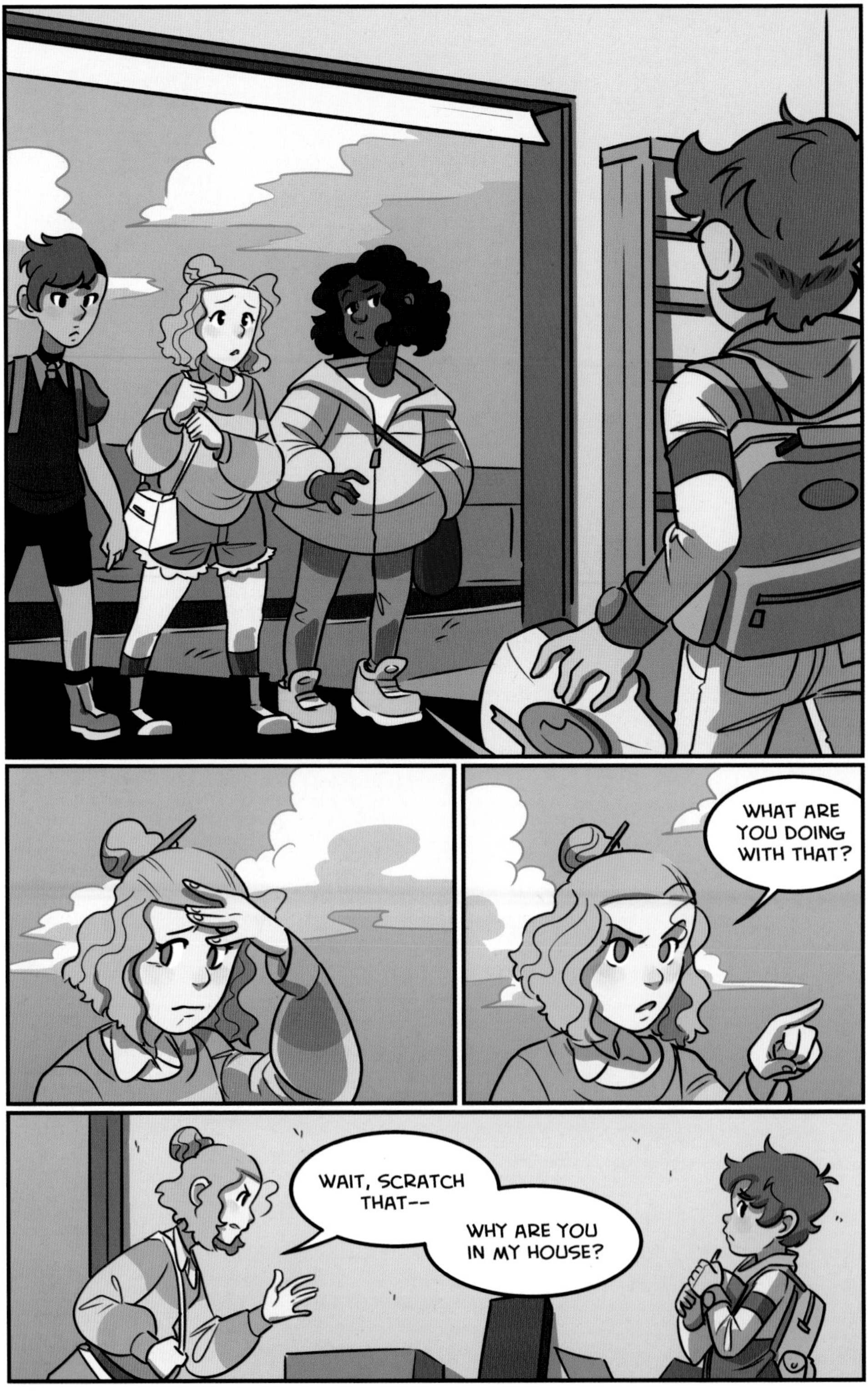
WHAT ARE YOU DOING WITH THAT?
WAIT, SCRATCH THAT--
WHY ARE YOU IN MY HOUSE?

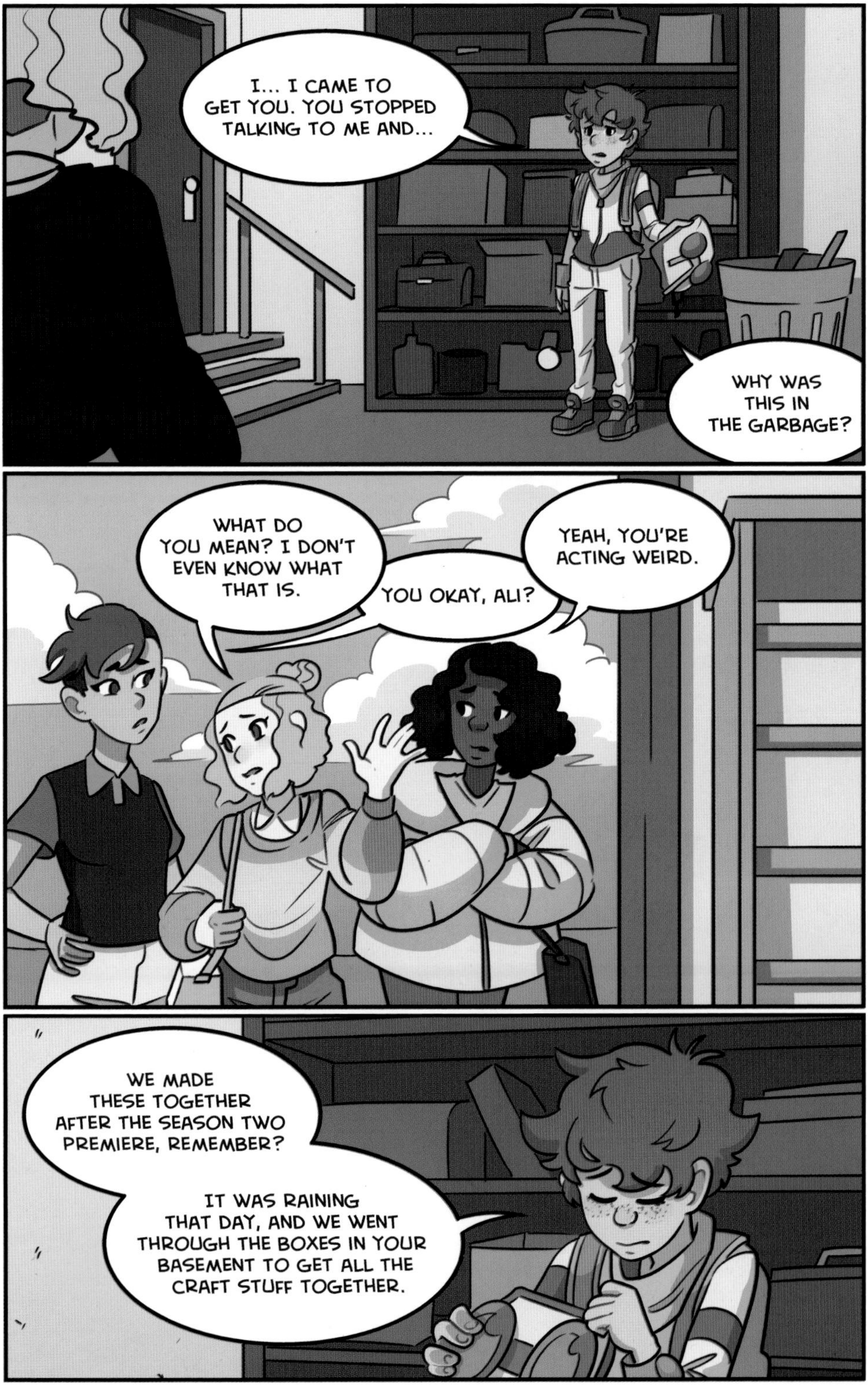
I... I CAME TO GET YOU. YOU STOPPED TALKING TO ME AND...
WHY WAS THIS IN THE GARBAGE?
WHAT DO YOU MEAN? I DON'T EVEN KNOW WHAT THAT IS.
YOU OKAY, ALI?
YEAH, YOU'RE ACTING WEIRD.
WE MADE THESE TOGETHER AFTER THE SEASON TWO PREMIERE, REMEMBER?
IT WAS RAINING THAT DAY, AND WE WENT THROUGH THE BOXES IN YOUR BASEMENT TO GET ALL THE CRAFT STUFF TOGETHER.

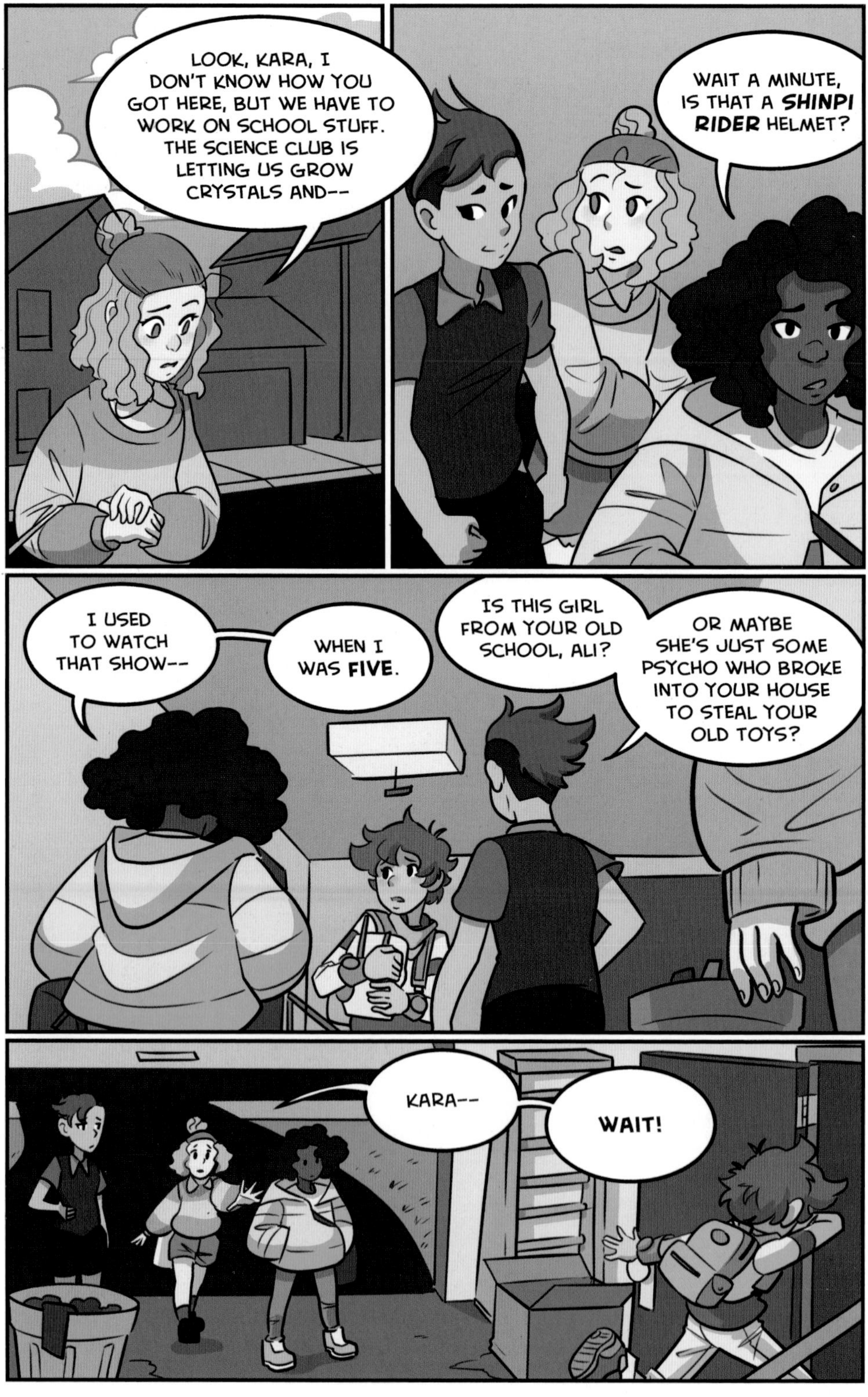
LOOK, KARA, I DON'T KNOW HOW YOU GOT HERE, BUT WE HAVE TO WORK ON SCHOOL STUFF. THE SCIENCE CLUB IS LETTING US GROW CRYSTALS AND--
WAIT A MINUTE, IS THAT A **SHINPI RIDER** HELMET?
I USED TO WATCH THAT SHOW--
WHEN I WAS **FIVE**.
IS THIS GIRL FROM YOUR OLD SCHOOL, ALI?
OR MAYBE SHE'S JUST SOME PSYCHO WHO BROKE INTO YOUR HOUSE TO STEAL YOUR OLD TOYS?
KARA--
WAIT!

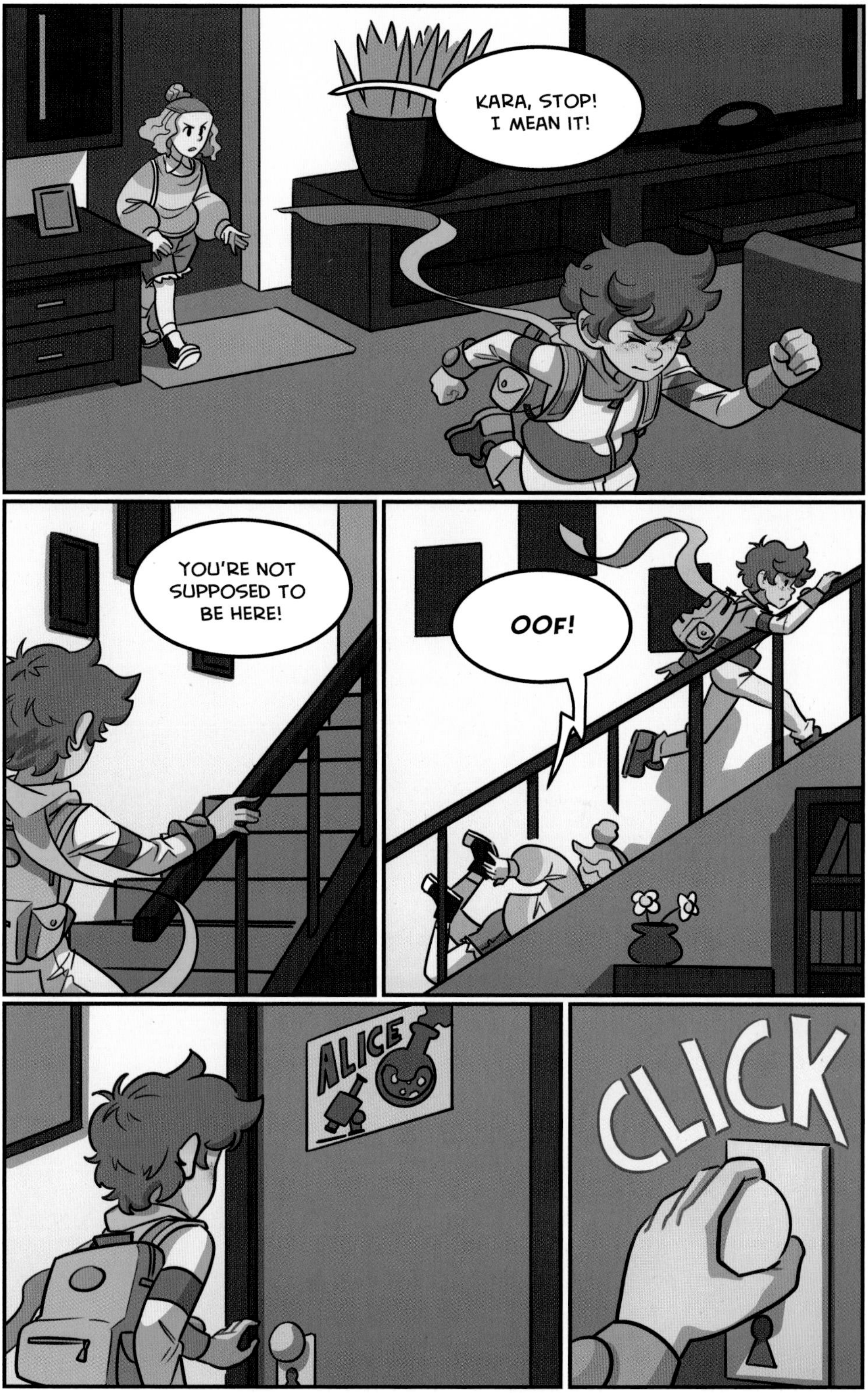
KARA, STOP! I MEAN IT!
YOU'RE NOT SUPPOSED TO BE HERE!
OOF!
ALICE
CLICK

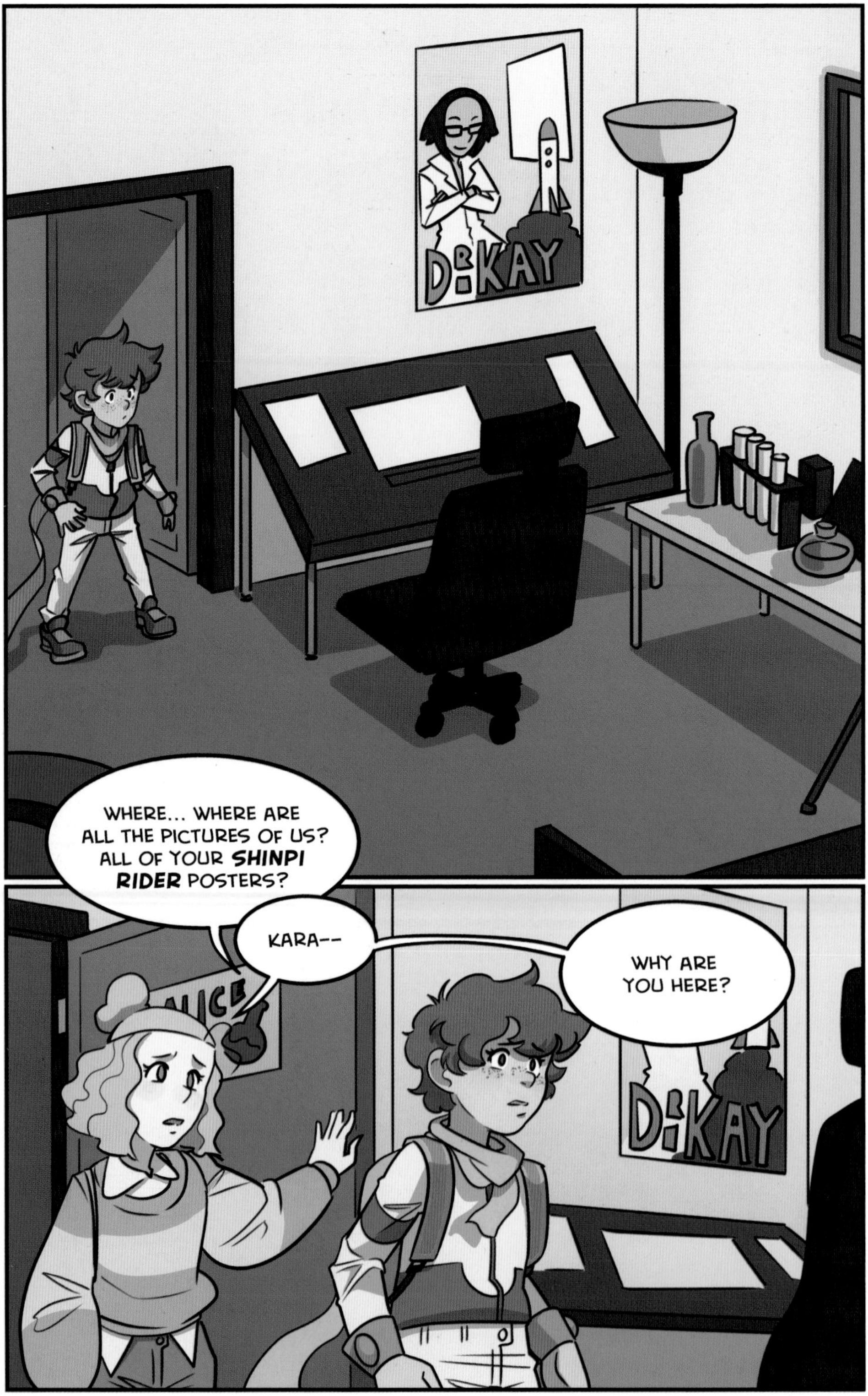
D.KAY
WHERE... WHERE ARE ALL THE PICTURES OF US? ALL OF YOUR **SHINPI RIDER** POSTERS?
KARA--
WHY ARE YOU HERE?
D.KAY

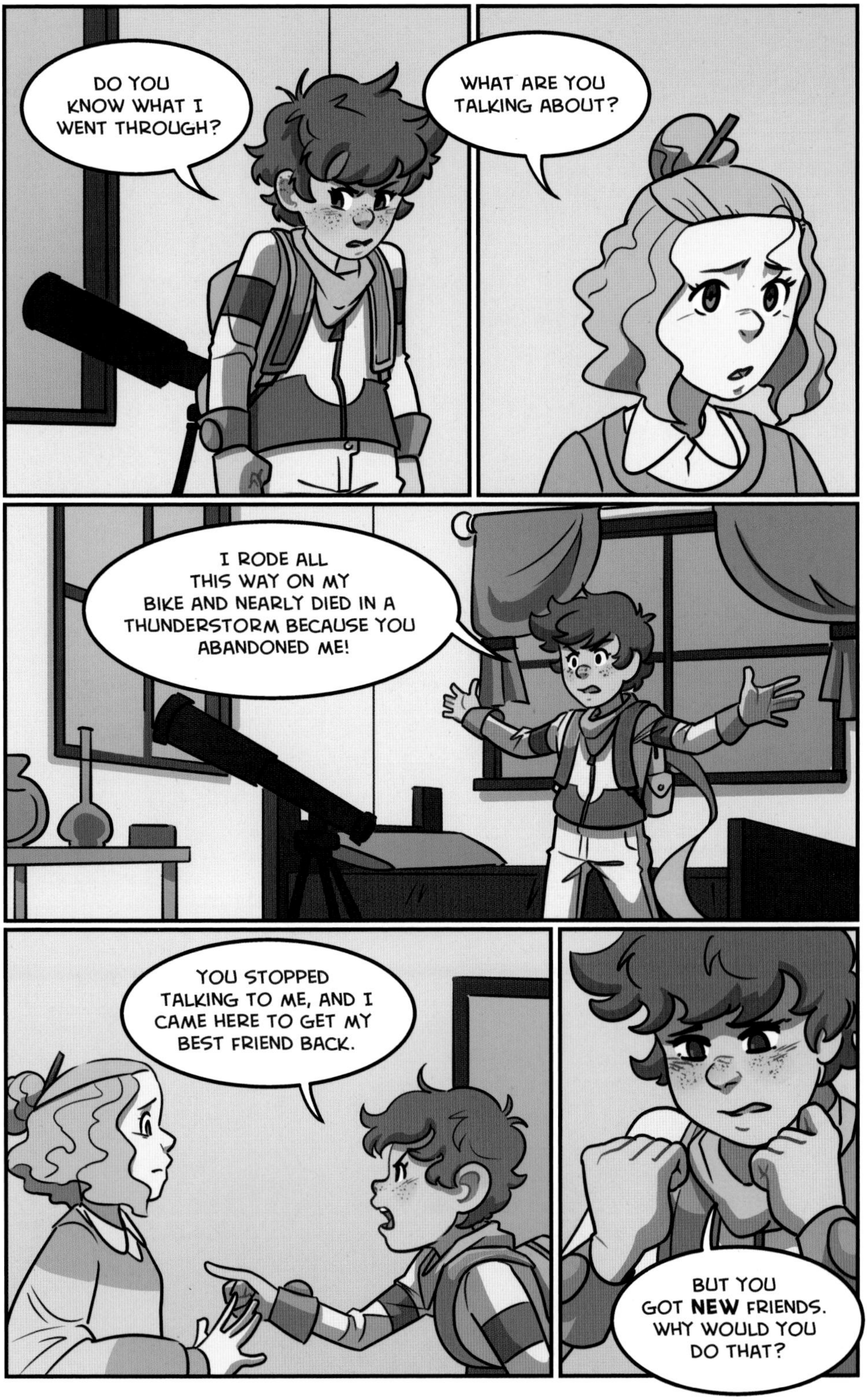
DO YOU KNOW WHAT I WENT THROUGH?
WHAT ARE YOU TALKING ABOUT?
I RODE ALL THIS WAY ON MY BIKE AND NEARLY DIED IN A THUNDERSTORM BECAUSE YOU ABANDONED ME!
YOU STOPPED TALKING TO ME, AND I CAME HERE TO GET MY BEST FRIEND BACK.
BUT YOU GOT **NEW** FRIENDS. WHY WOULD YOU DO THAT?

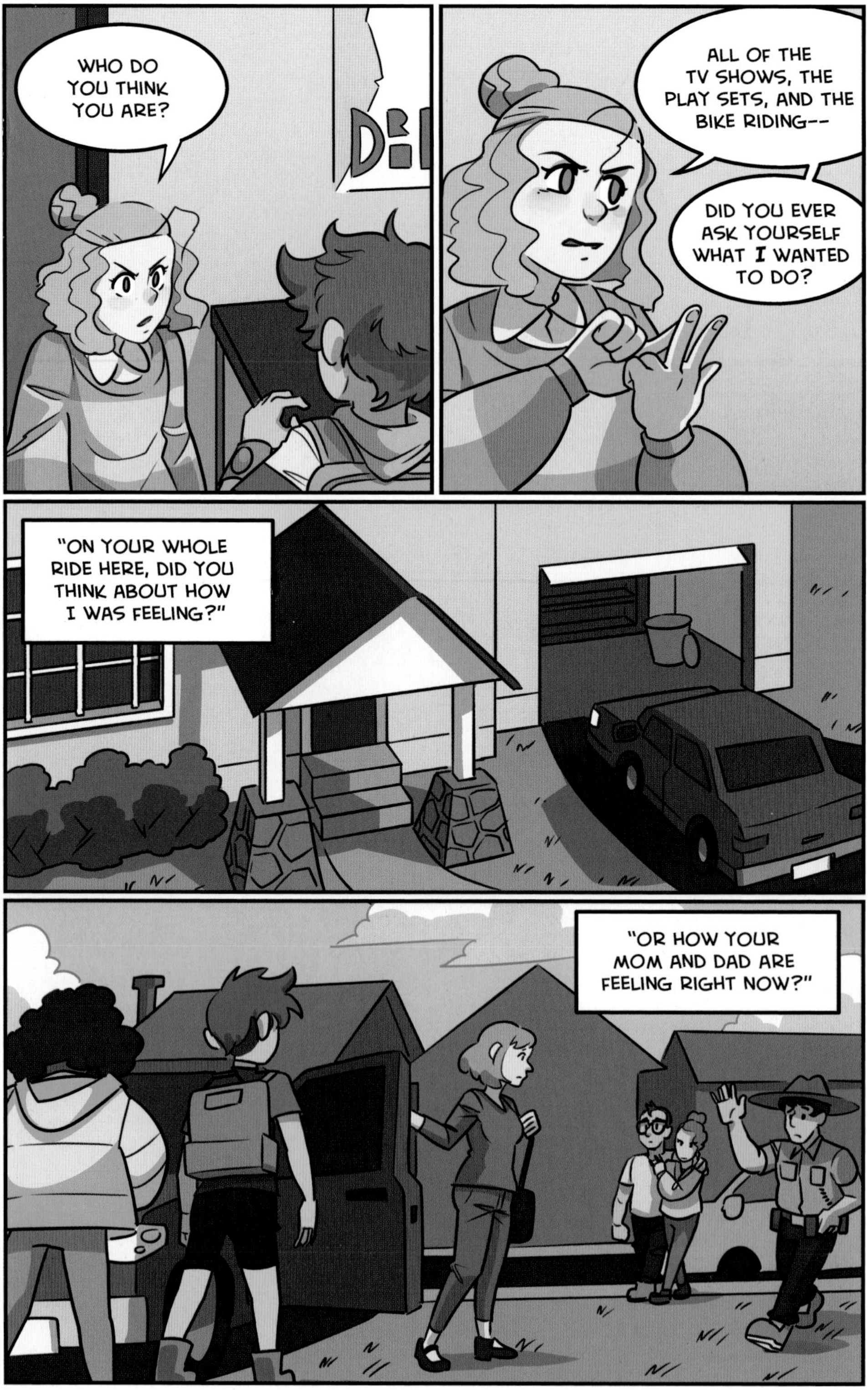
WHO DO YOU THINK YOU ARE?
ALL OF THE TV SHOWS, THE PLAY SETS, AND THE BIKE RIDING--
DID YOU EVER ASK YOURSELF WHAT *I* WANTED TO DO?
"ON YOUR WHOLE RIDE HERE, DID YOU THINK ABOUT HOW I WAS FEELING?"
"OR HOW YOUR MOM AND DAD ARE FEELING RIGHT NOW?"

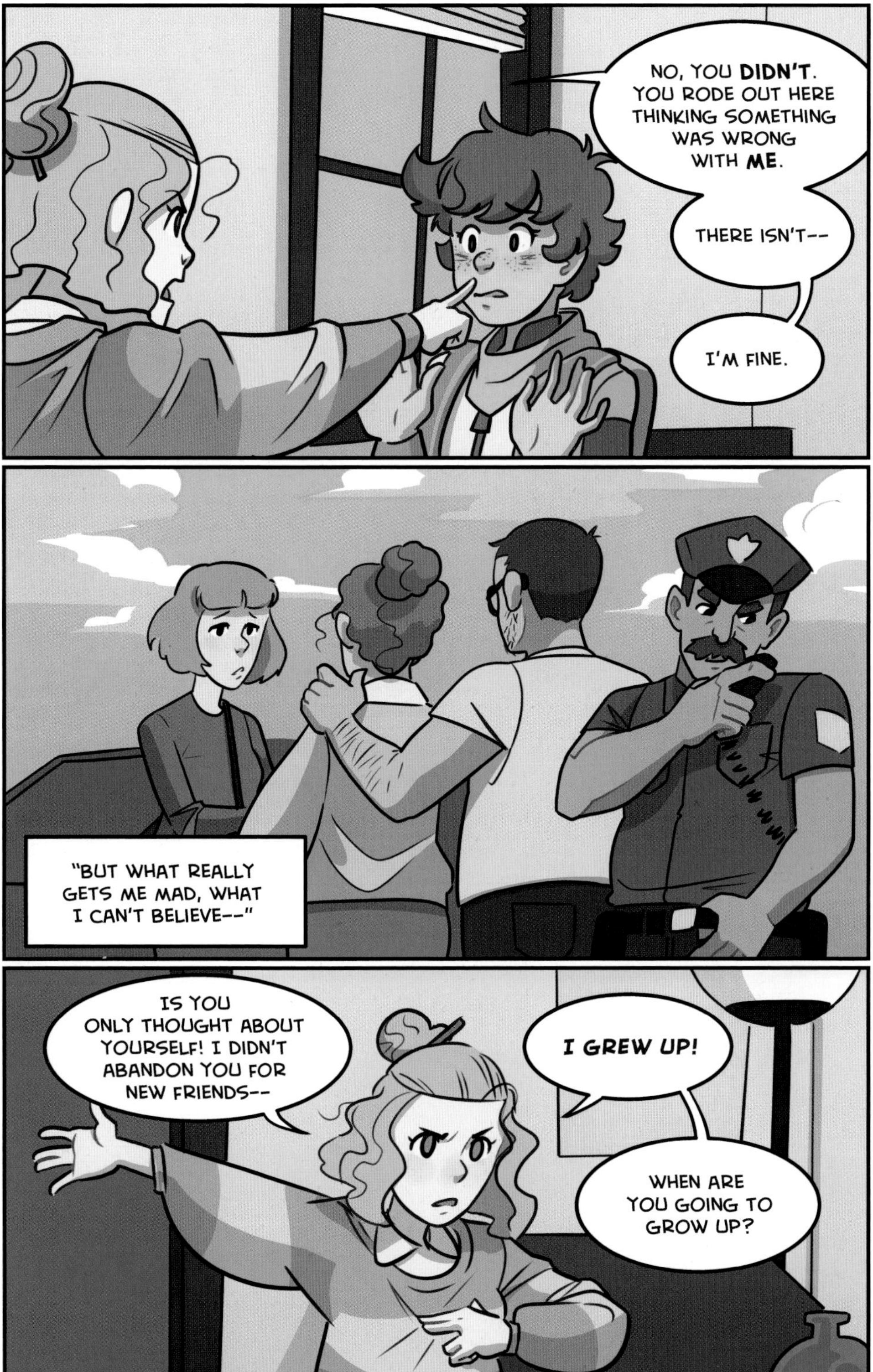
NO, YOU **DIDN'T**. YOU RODE OUT HERE THINKING SOMETHING WAS WRONG WITH **ME**.
THERE ISN'T--
I'M FINE.
"BUT WHAT REALLY GETS ME MAD, WHAT I CAN'T BELIEVE--"
IS YOU ONLY THOUGHT ABOUT YOURSELF! I DIDN'T ABANDON YOU FOR NEW FRIENDS--
I GREW UP!
WHEN ARE YOU GOING TO GROW UP?

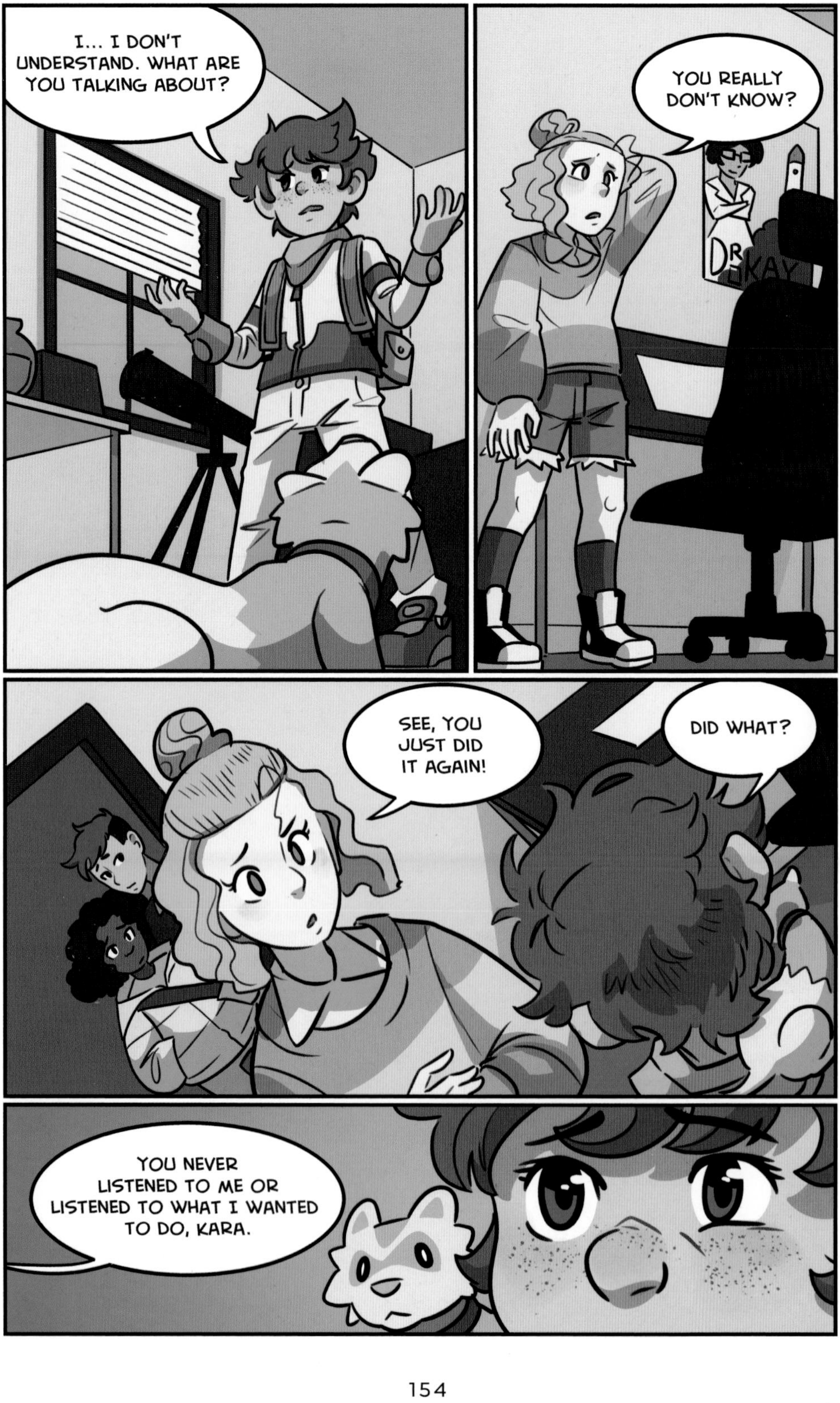
I... I DON'T UNDERSTAND. WHAT ARE YOU TALKING ABOUT?
YOU REALLY DON'T KNOW?
SEE, YOU JUST DID IT AGAIN!
DID WHAT?
YOU NEVER LISTENED TO ME OR LISTENED TO WHAT I WANTED TO DO, KARA.

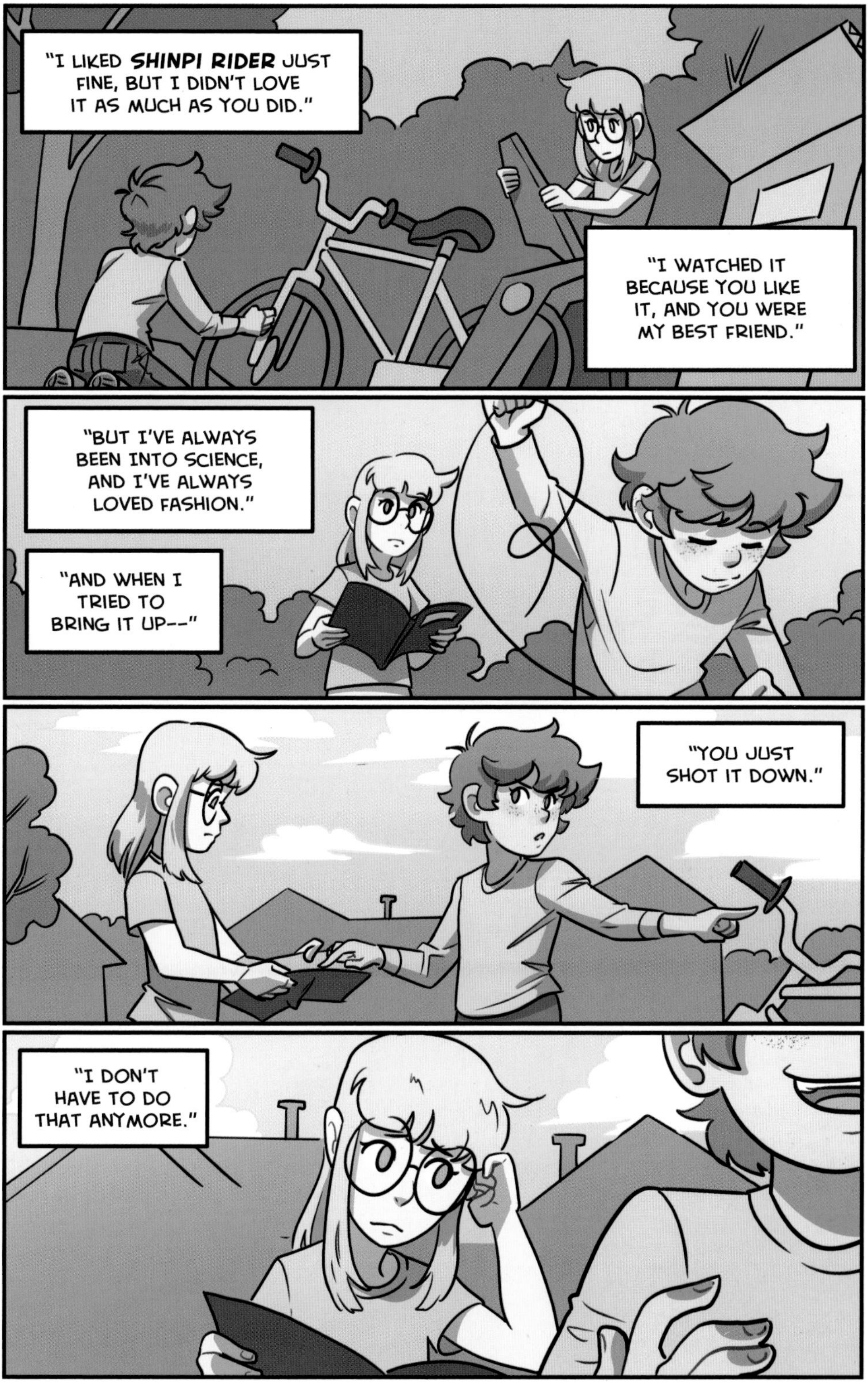
"I LIKED SHINPI RIDER JUST FINE, BUT I DIDN'T LOVE IT AS MUCH AS YOU DID."
"I WATCHED IT BECAUSE YOU LIKE IT, AND YOU WERE MY BEST FRIEND."
"BUT I'VE ALWAYS BEEN INTO SCIENCE, AND I'VE ALWAYS LOVED FASHION."
"AND WHEN I TRIED TO BRING IT UP--"
"YOU JUST SHOT IT DOWN."
"I DON'T HAVE TO DO THAT ANYMORE."

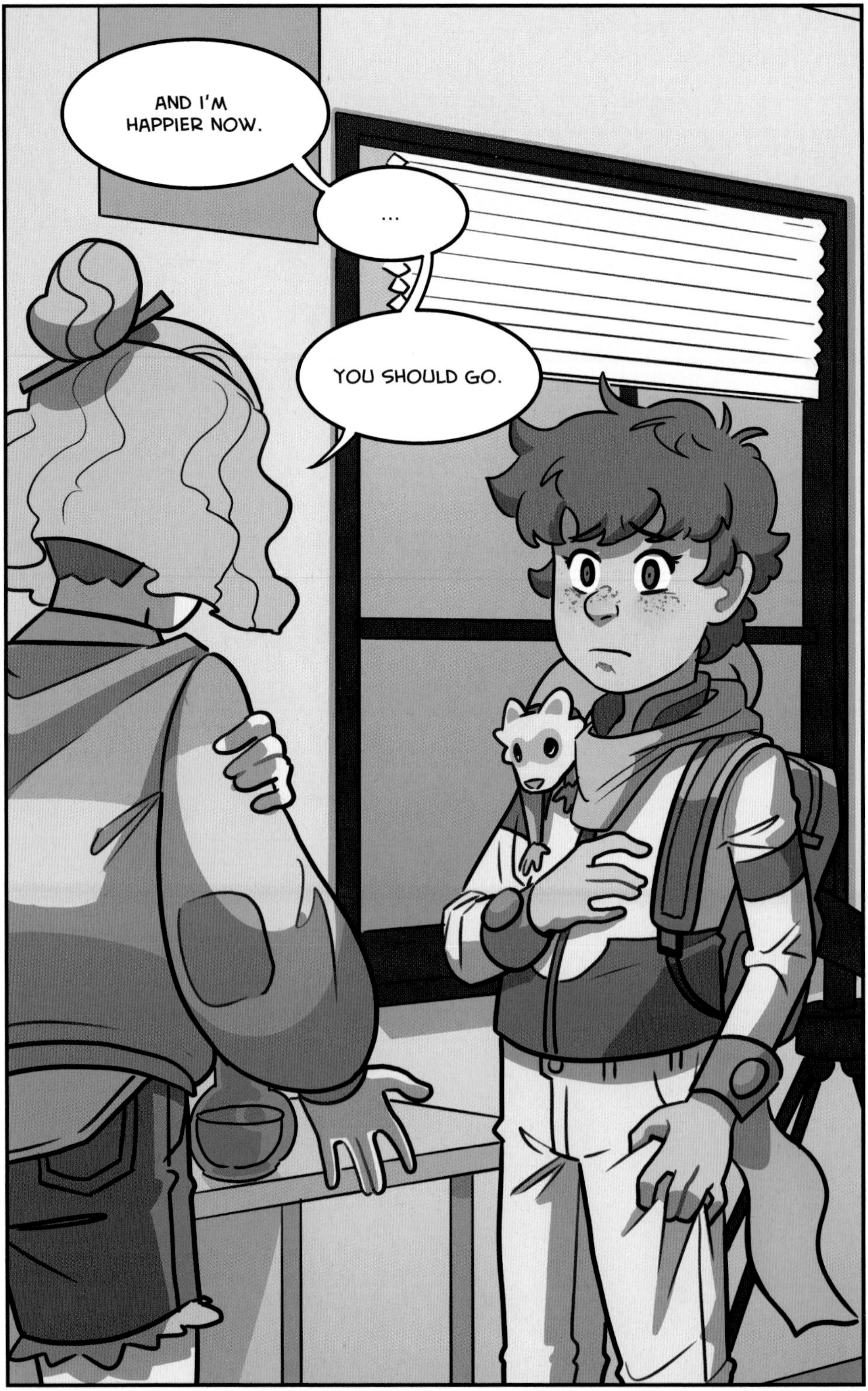
AND I'M HAPPIER NOW.
...
YOU SHOULD GO.

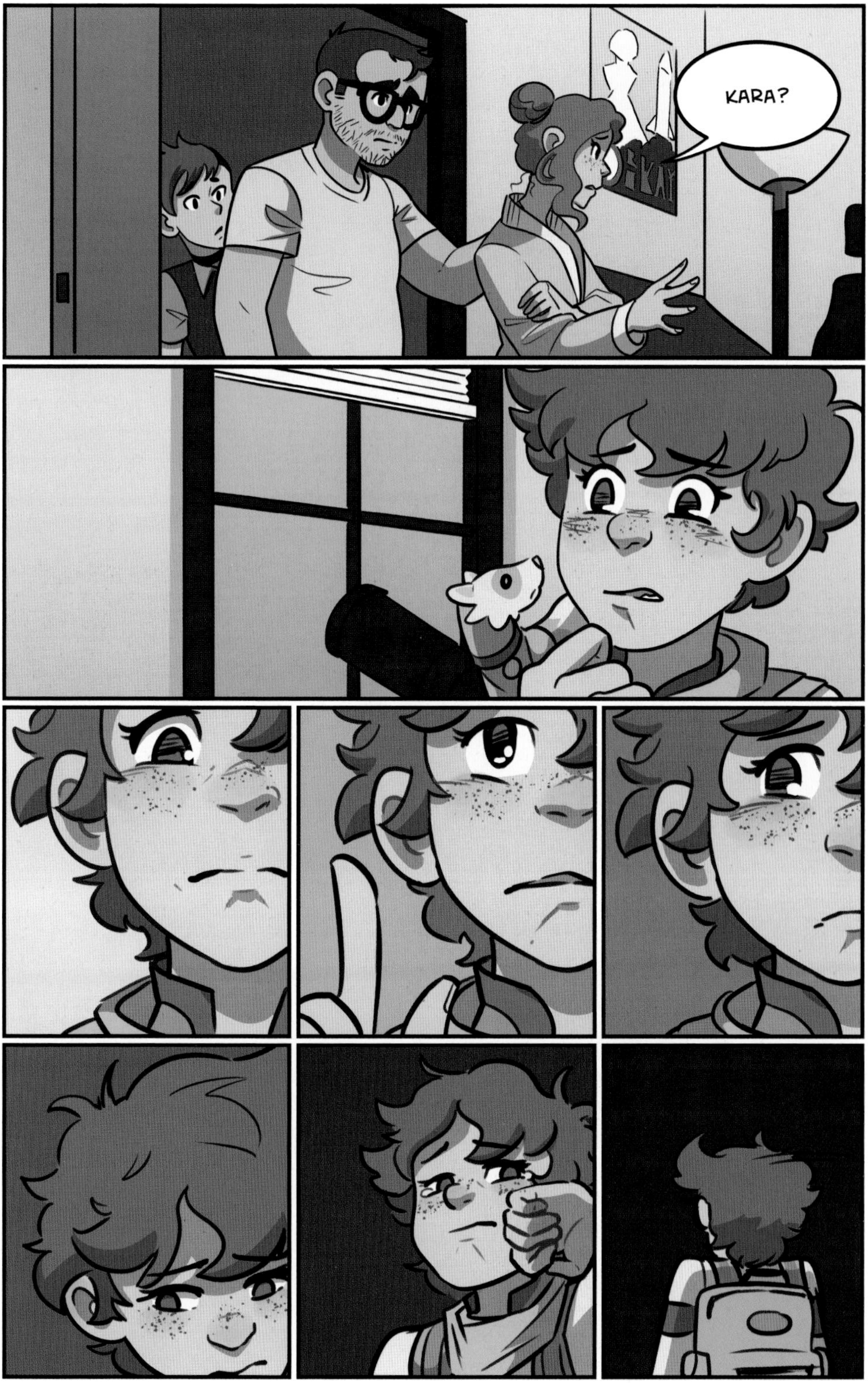
KARA?

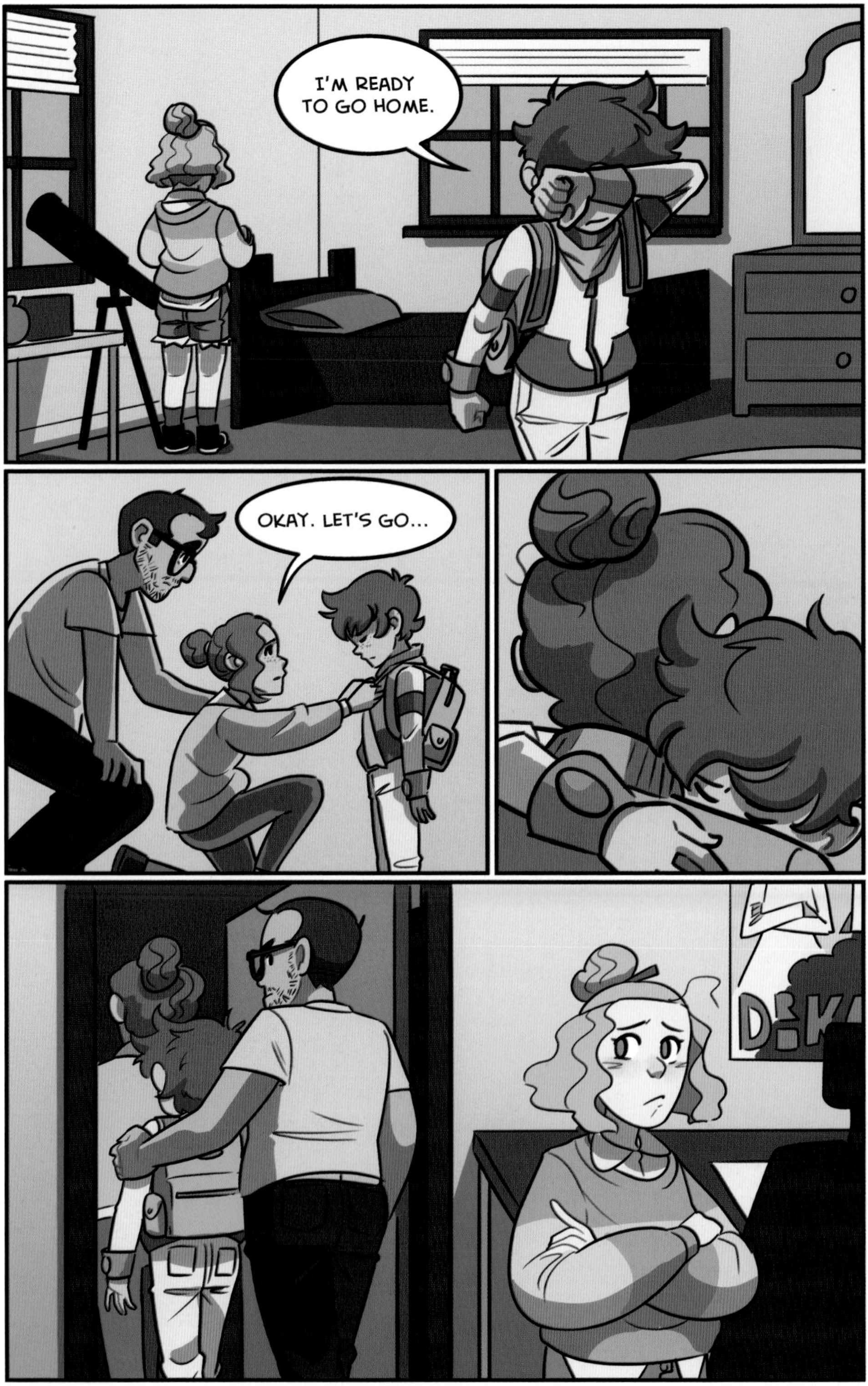
I'M READY TO GO HOME.
OKAY. LET'S GO...

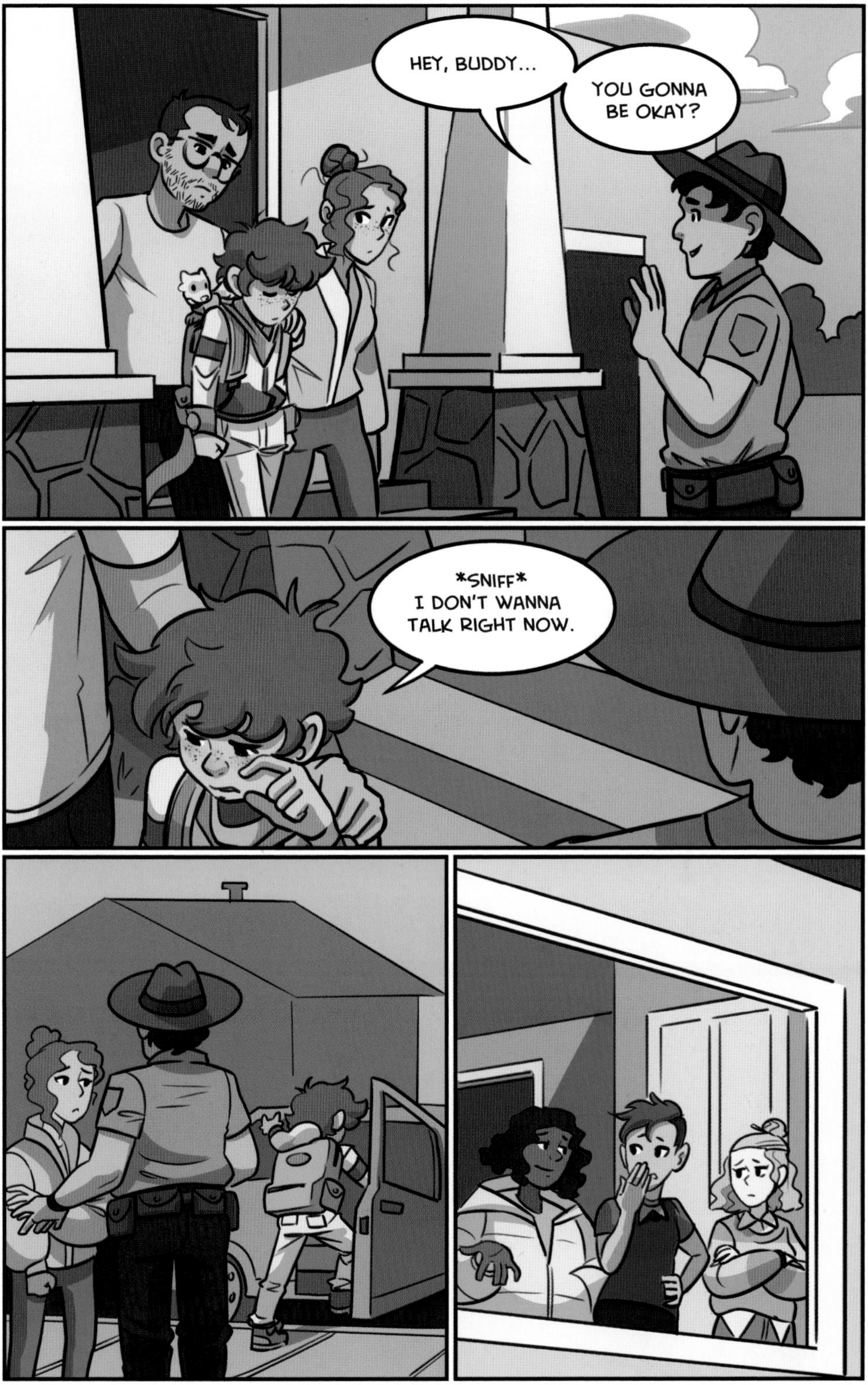
HEY, BUDDY...
YOU GONNA BE OKAY?
SNIFF I DON'T WANNA TALK RIGHT NOW.

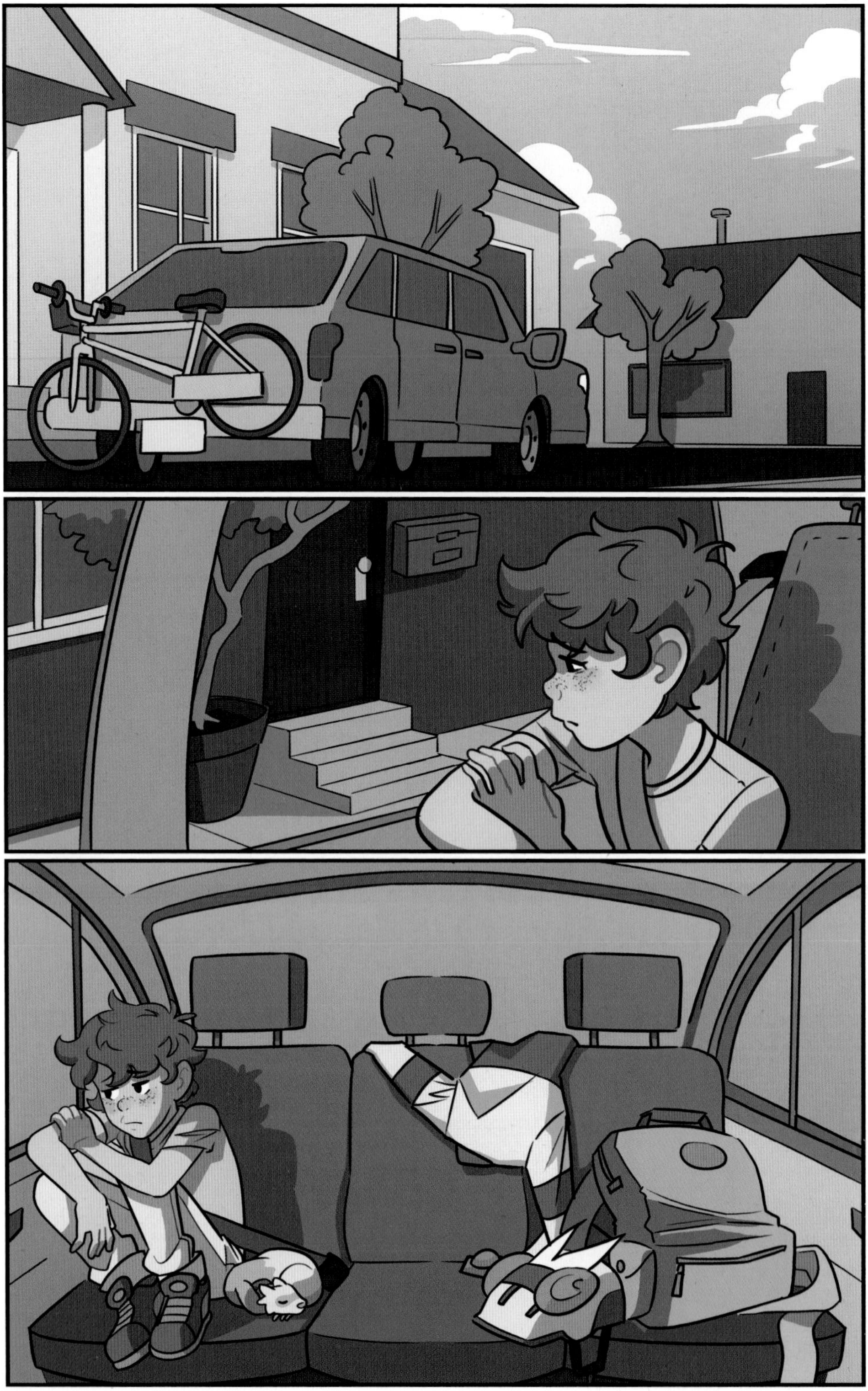

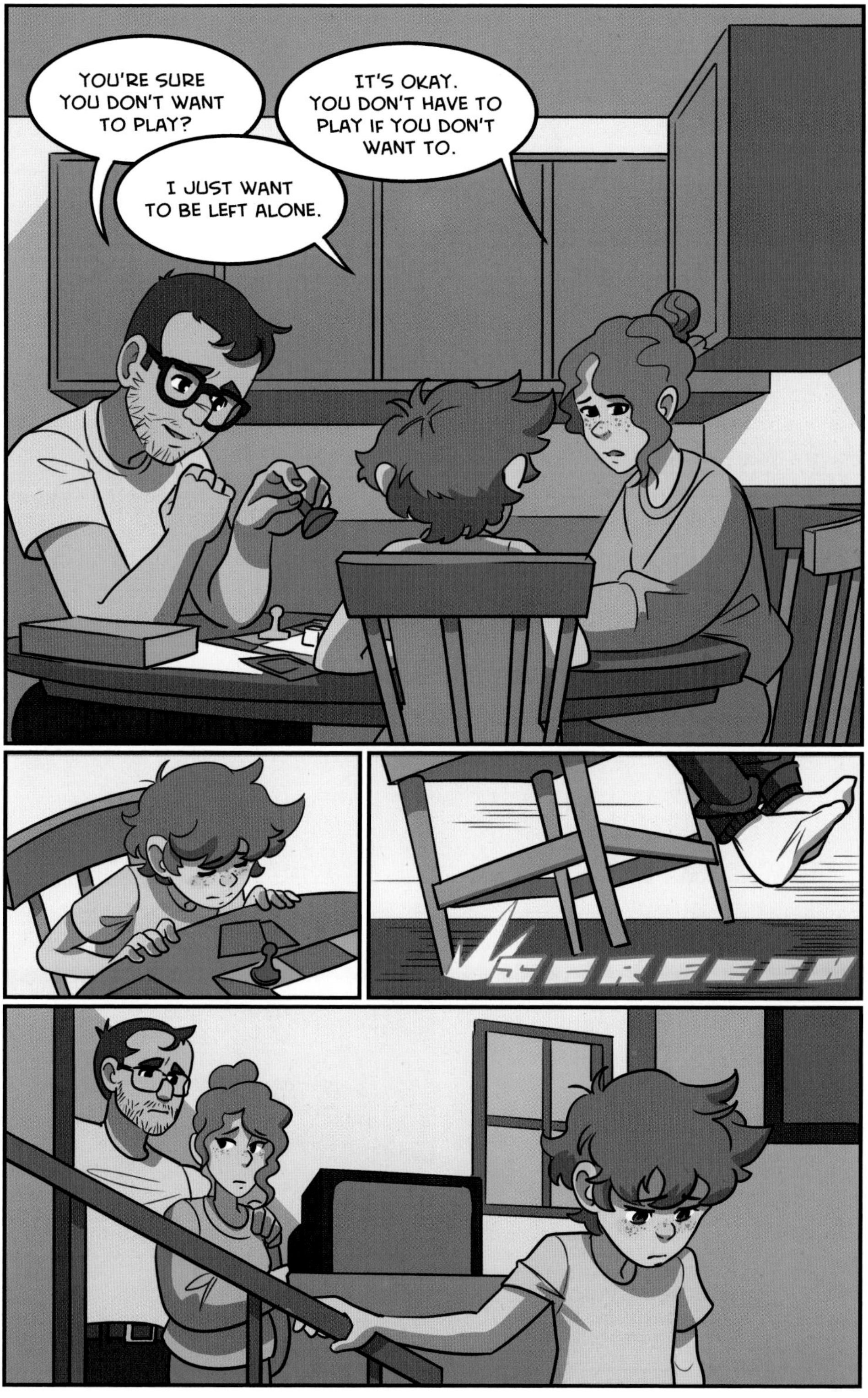
YOU'RE SURE YOU DON'T WANT TO PLAY?
IT'S OKAY. YOU DON'T HAVE TO PLAY IF YOU DON'T WANT TO.
I JUST WANT TO BE LEFT ALONE.
SCREEECH

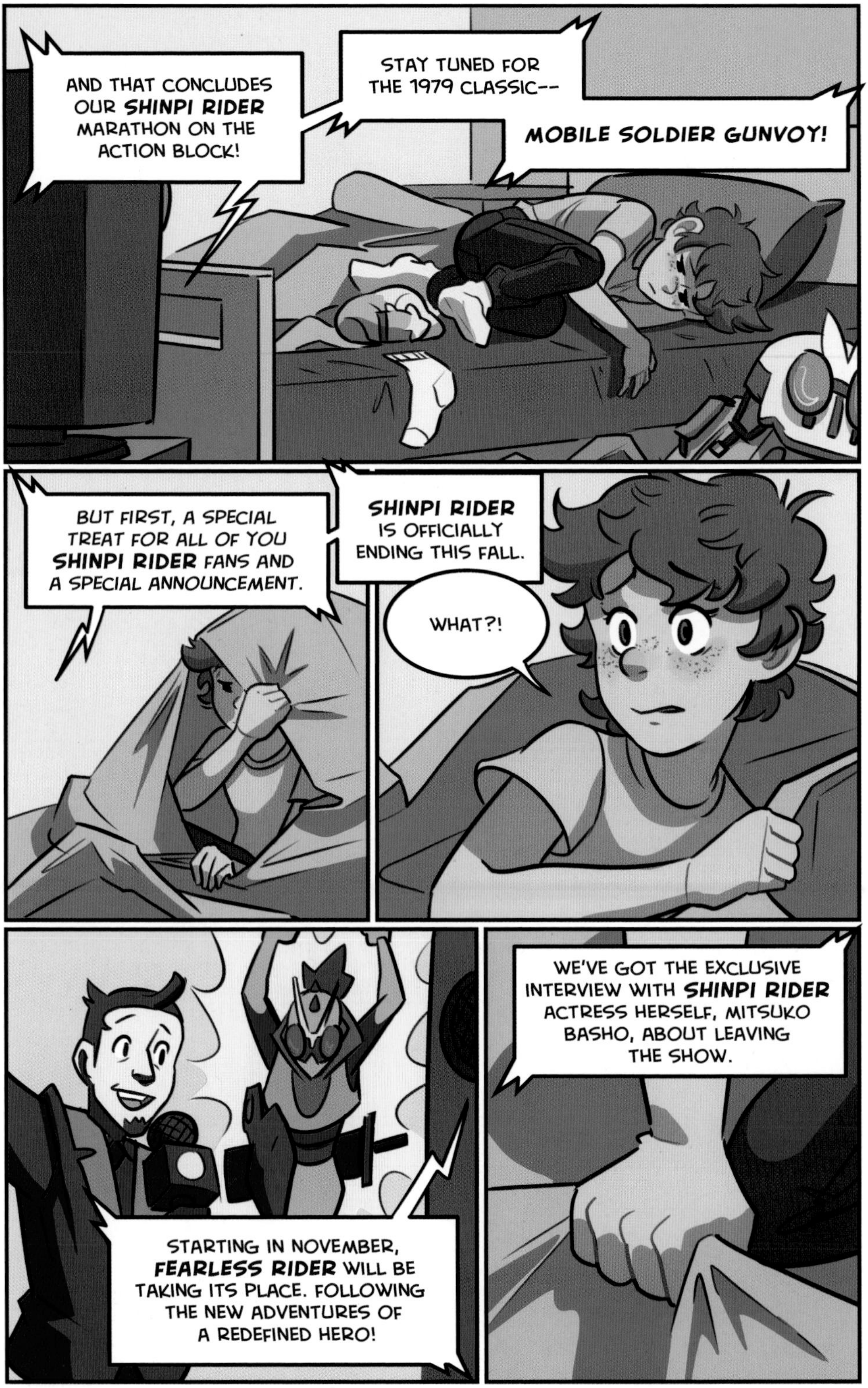
AND THAT CONCLUDES OUR **SHINPI RIDER** MARATHON ON THE ACTION BLOCK!
STAY TUNED FOR THE 1979 CLASSIC--
MOBILE SOLDIER GUNVOY!
BUT FIRST, A SPECIAL TREAT FOR ALL OF YOU **SHINPI RIDER** FANS AND A SPECIAL ANNOUNCEMENT.
SHINPI RIDER IS OFFICIALLY ENDING THIS FALL.
WHAT?!
STARTING IN NOVEMBER, **FEARLESS RIDER** WILL BE TAKING ITS PLACE. FOLLOWING THE NEW ADVENTURES OF A REDEFINED HERO!
WE'VE GOT THE EXCLUSIVE INTERVIEW WITH **SHINPI RIDER** ACTRESS HERSELF, MITSUKO BASHO, ABOUT LEAVING THE SHOW.

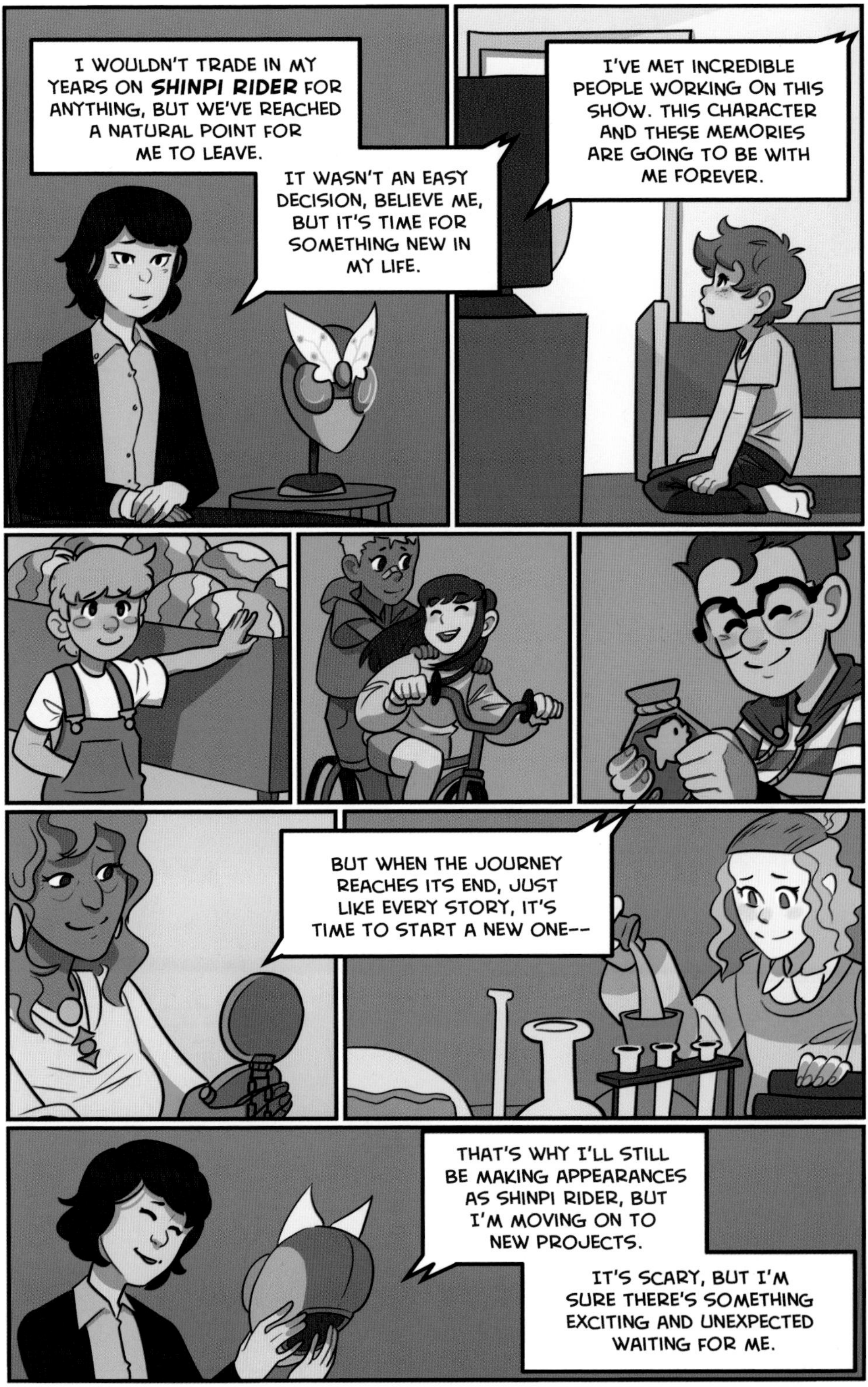
I WOULDN'T TRADE IN MY YEARS ON **SHINPI RIDER** FOR ANYTHING, BUT WE'VE REACHED A NATURAL POINT FOR ME TO LEAVE.
IT WASN'T AN EASY DECISION, BELIEVE ME, BUT IT'S TIME FOR SOMETHING NEW IN MY LIFE.
I'VE MET INCREDIBLE PEOPLE WORKING ON THIS SHOW. THIS CHARACTER AND THESE MEMORIES ARE GOING TO BE WITH ME FOREVER.
BUT WHEN THE JOURNEY REACHES ITS END, JUST LIKE EVERY STORY, IT'S TIME TO START A NEW ONE--
THAT'S WHY I'LL STILL BE MAKING APPEARANCES AS SHINPI RIDER, BUT I'M MOVING ON TO NEW PROJECTS.
IT'S SCARY, BUT I'M SURE THERE'S SOMETHING EXCITING AND UNEXPECTED WAITING FOR ME.

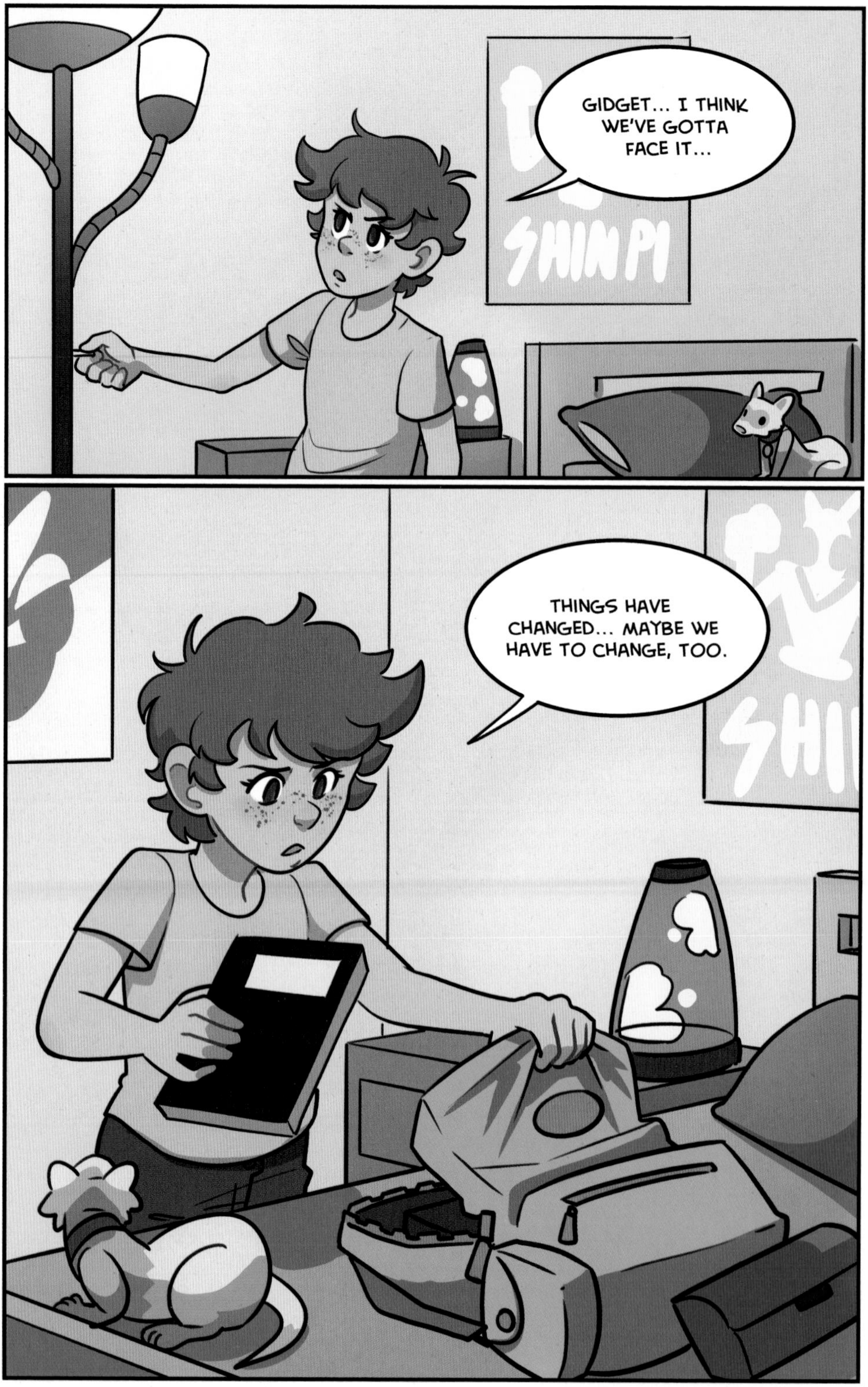
GIDGET... I THINK WE'VE GOTTA FACE IT...
SHINPI
THINGS HAVE CHANGED... MAYBE WE HAVE TO CHANGE, TOO.

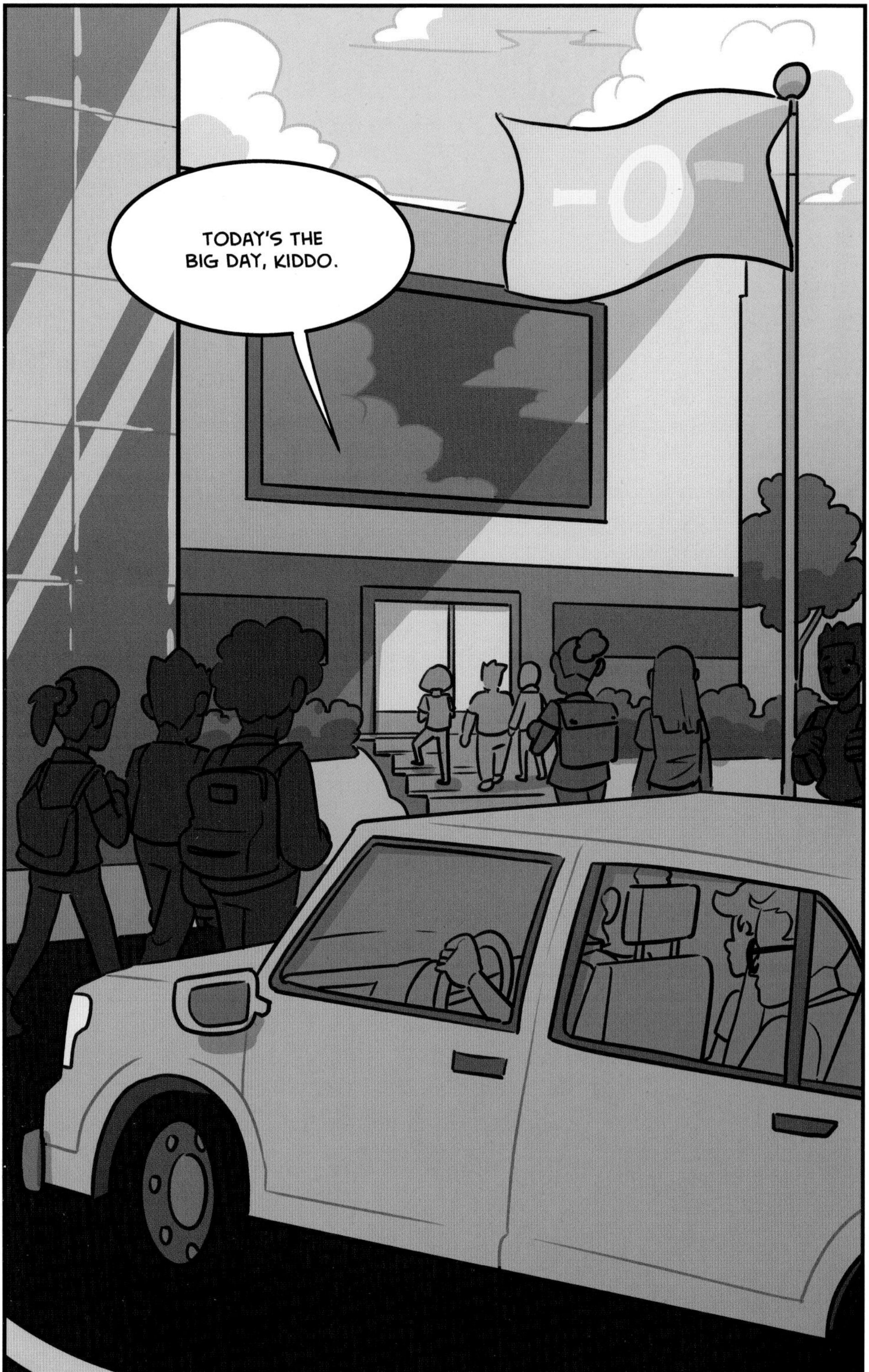
TODAY'S THE BIG DAY, KIDDO.

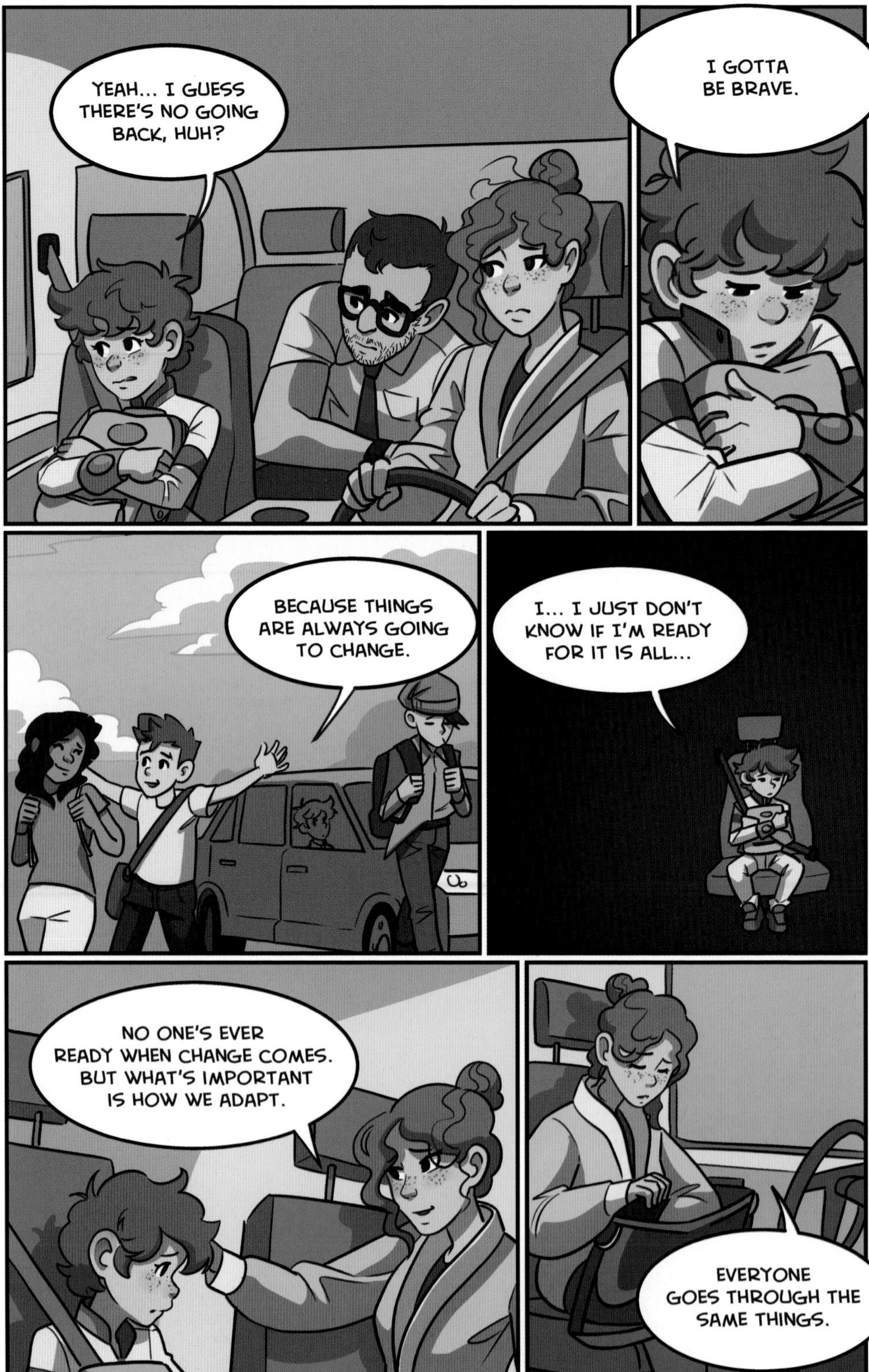
YEAH... I GUESS THERE'S NO GOING BACK, HUH?
I GOTTA BE BRAVE.
BECAUSE THINGS ARE ALWAYS GOING TO CHANGE.
I... I JUST DON'T KNOW IF I'M READY FOR IT IS ALL...
NO ONE'S EVER READY WHEN CHANGE COMES. BUT WHAT'S IMPORTANT IS HOW WE ADAPT.
EVERYONE GOES THROUGH THE SAME THINGS.

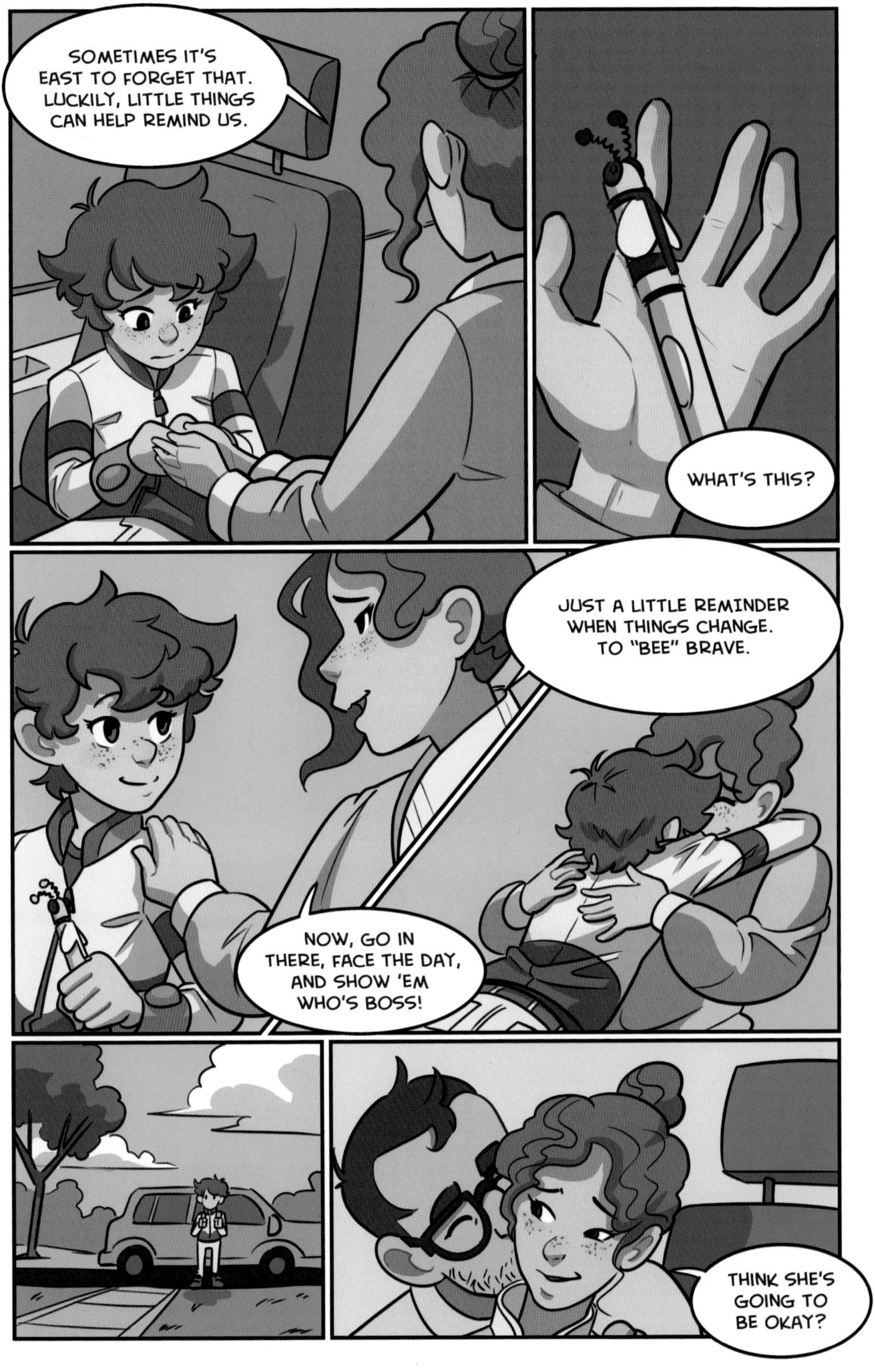
SOMETIMES IT'S EAST TO FORGET THAT. LUCKILY, LITTLE THINGS CAN HELP REMIND US.
WHAT'S THIS?
JUST A LITTLE REMINDER WHEN THINGS CHANGE. TO "BEE" BRAVE.
NOW, GO IN THERE, FACE THE DAY, AND SHOW 'EM WHO'S BOSS!
THINK SHE'S GOING TO BE OKAY?

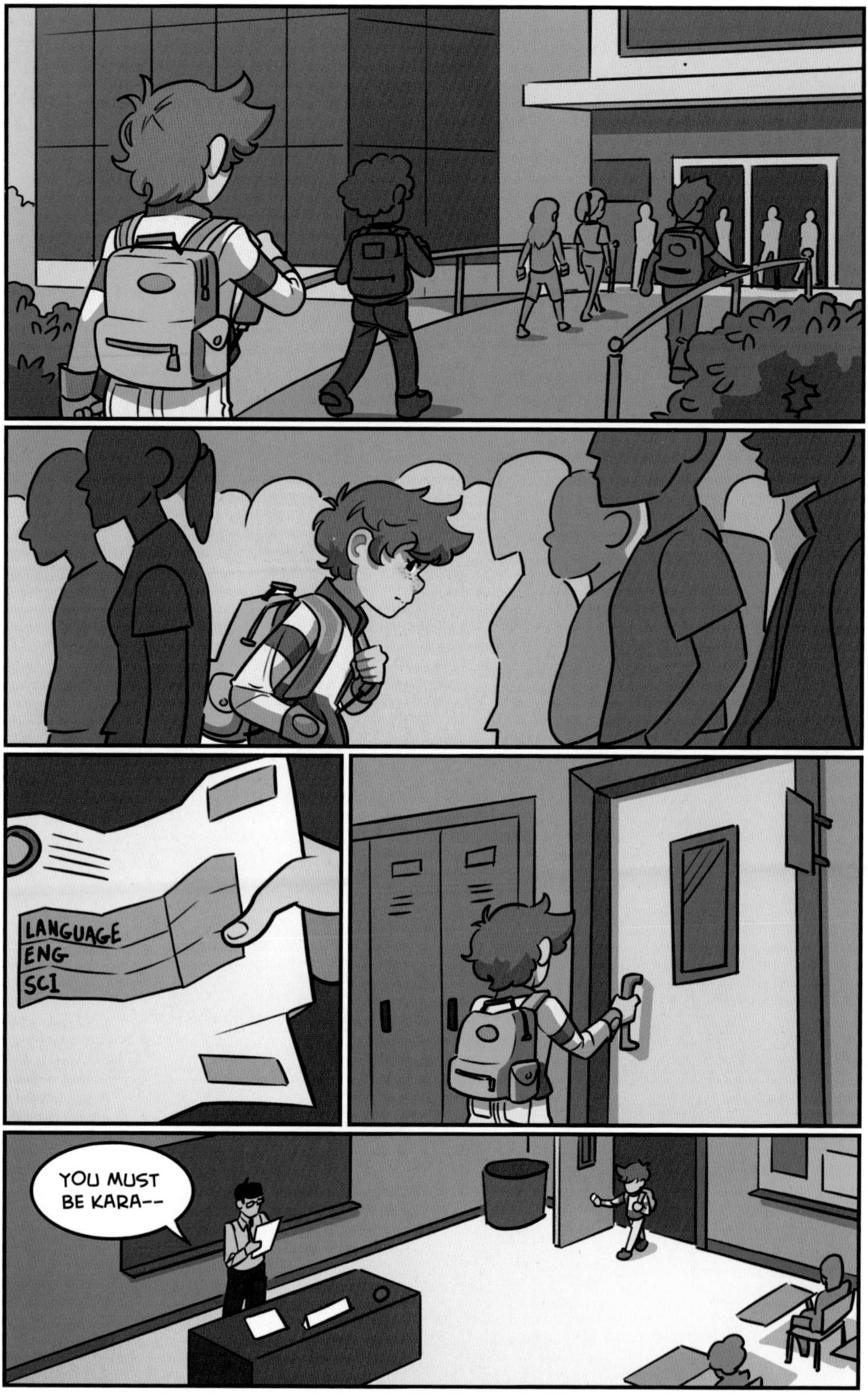
LANGUAGE
ENG
SCI
YOU MUST BE KARA--

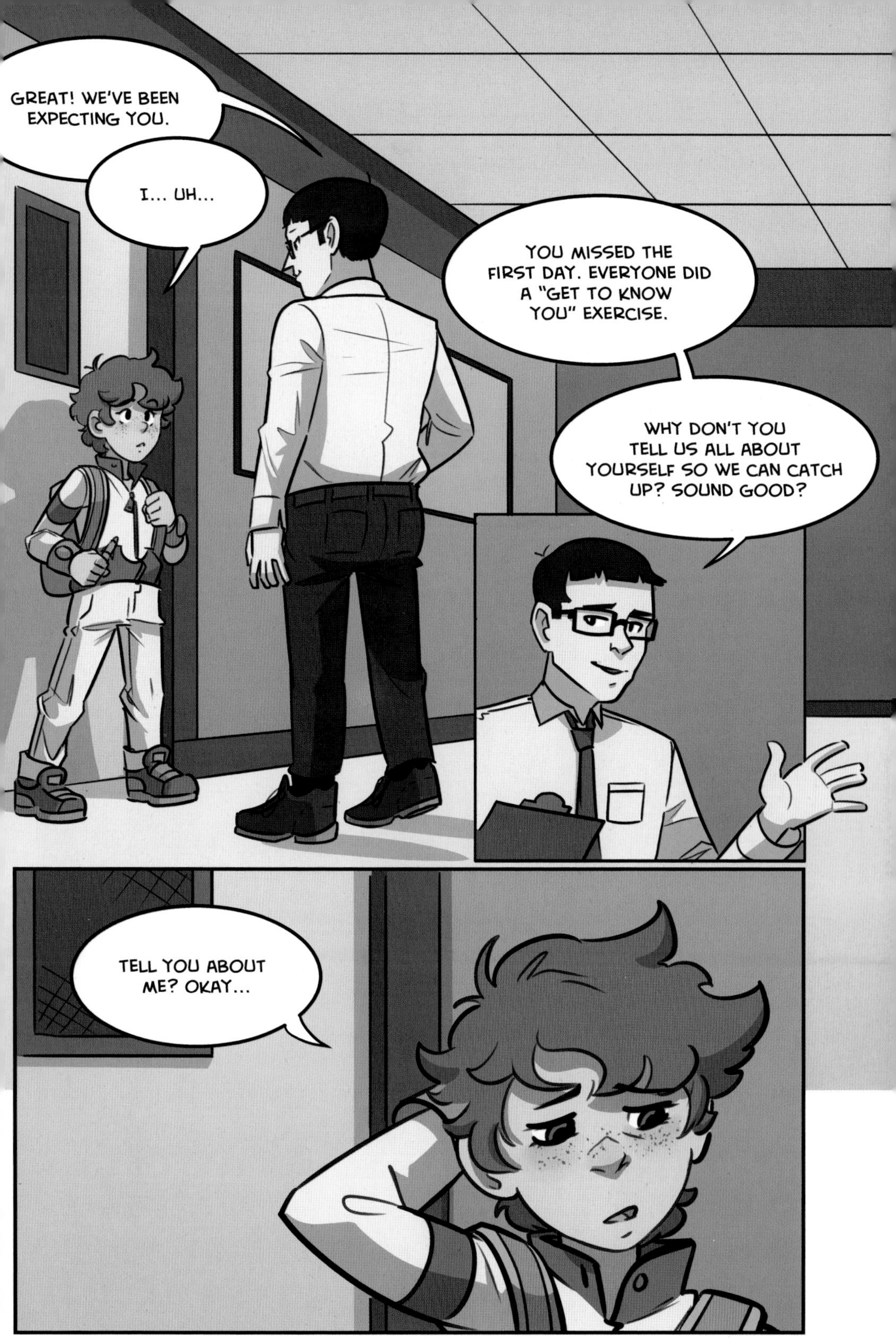
GREAT! WE'VE BEEN EXPECTING YOU.
I... UH...
YOU MISSED THE FIRST DAY. EVERYONE DID A "GET TO KNOW YOU" EXERCISE.
WHY DON'T YOU TELL US ALL ABOUT YOURSELF SO WE CAN CATCH UP? SOUND GOOD?
TELL YOU ABOUT ME? OKAY...

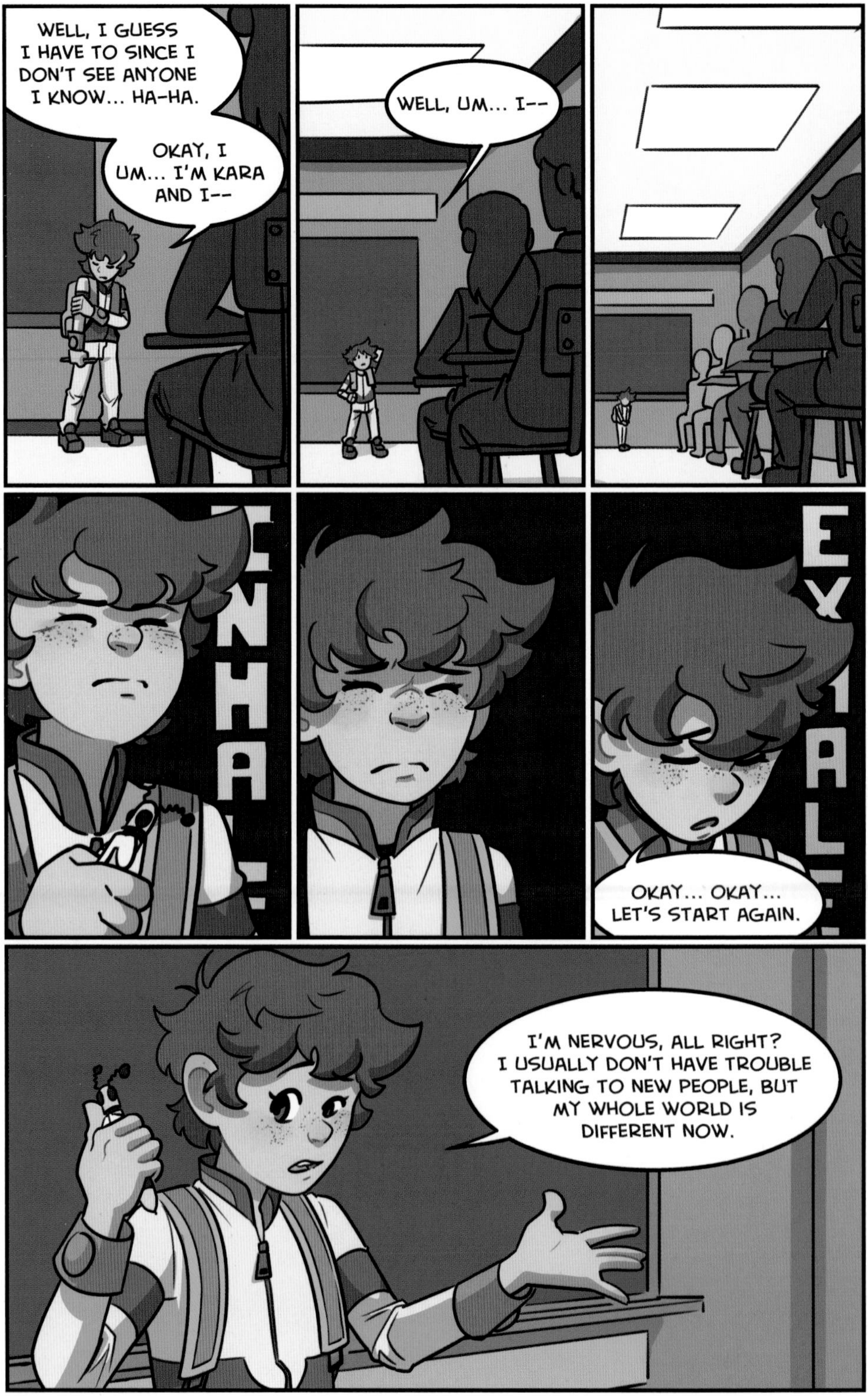
WELL, I GUESS I HAVE TO SINCE I DON'T SEE ANYONE I KNOW... HA-HA.
OKAY, I UM... I'M KARA AND I--
WELL, UM... I--
OKAY... OKAY... LET'S START AGAIN.
I'M NERVOUS, ALL RIGHT? I USUALLY DON'T HAVE TROUBLE TALKING TO NEW PEOPLE, BUT MY WHOLE WORLD IS DIFFERENT NOW.

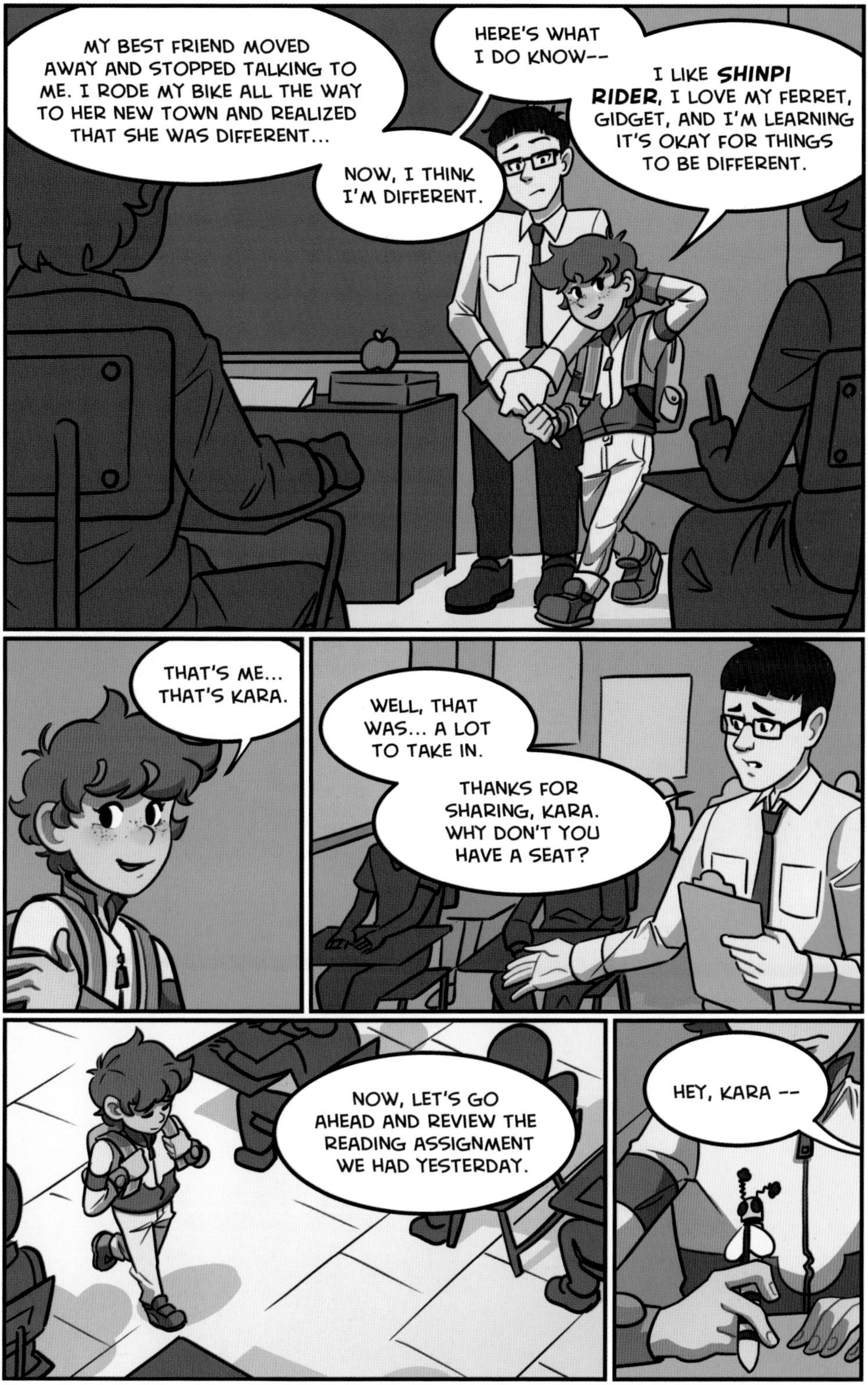
MY BEST FRIEND MOVED AWAY AND STOPPED TALKING TO ME. I RODE MY BIKE ALL THE WAY TO HER NEW TOWN AND REALIZED THAT SHE WAS DIFFERENT...
NOW, I THINK I'M DIFFERENT.
HERE'S WHAT I DO KNOW--
I LIKE **SHINPI RIDER**, I LOVE MY FERRET, GIDGET, AND I'M LEARNING IT'S OKAY FOR THINGS TO BE DIFFERENT.
THAT'S ME... THAT'S KARA.
WELL, THAT WAS... A LOT TO TAKE IN.
THANKS FOR SHARING, KARA. WHY DON'T YOU HAVE A SEAT?
NOW, LET'S GO AHEAD AND REVIEW THE READING ASSIGNMENT WE HAD YESTERDAY.
HEY, KARA --

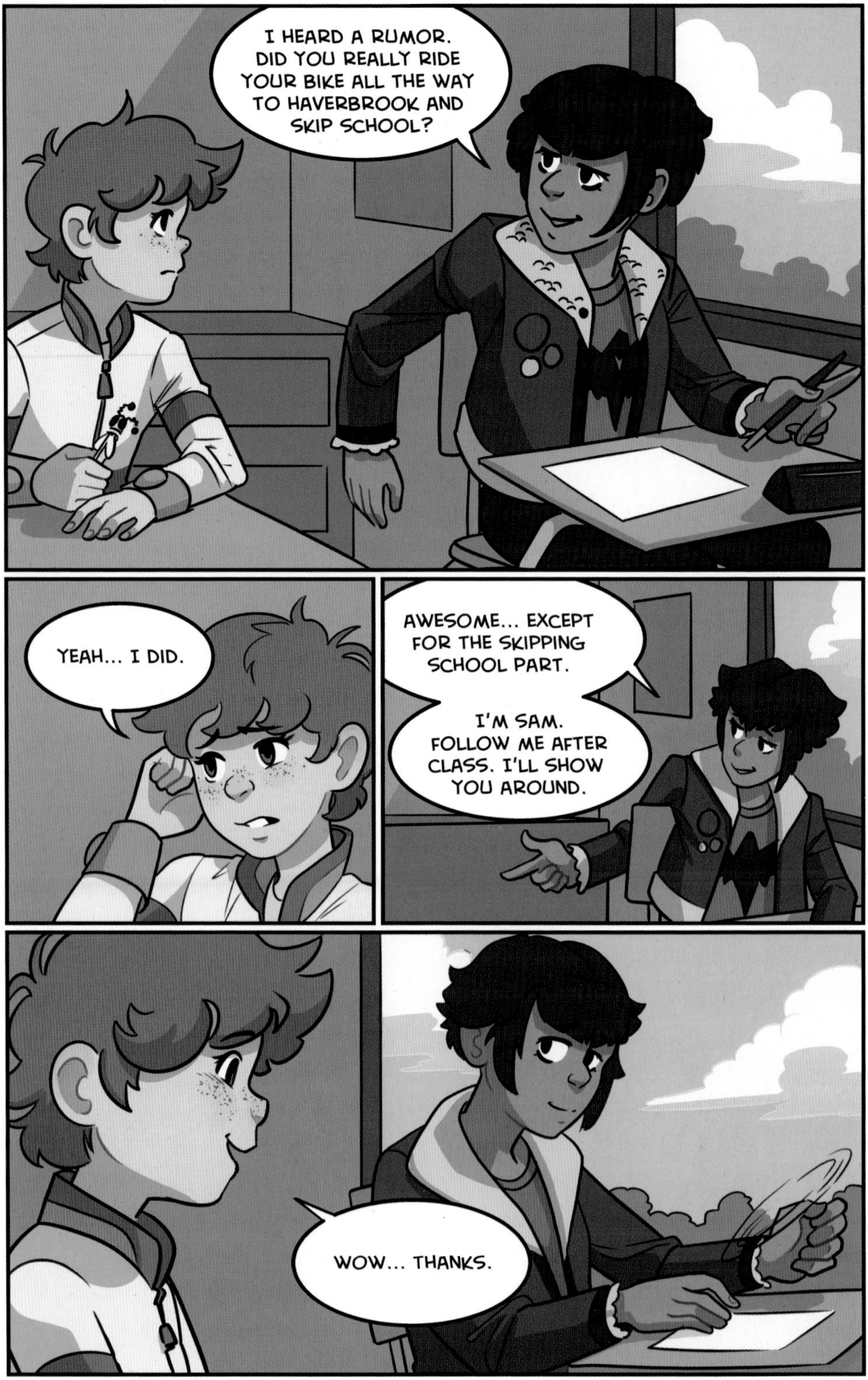
I HEARD A RUMOR. DID YOU REALLY RIDE YOUR BIKE ALL THE WAY TO HAVERBROOK AND SKIP SCHOOL?
YEAH... I DID.
AWESOME... EXCEPT FOR THE SKIPPING SCHOOL PART.
I'M SAM. FOLLOW ME AFTER CLASS. I'LL SHOW YOU AROUND.
WOW... THANKS.

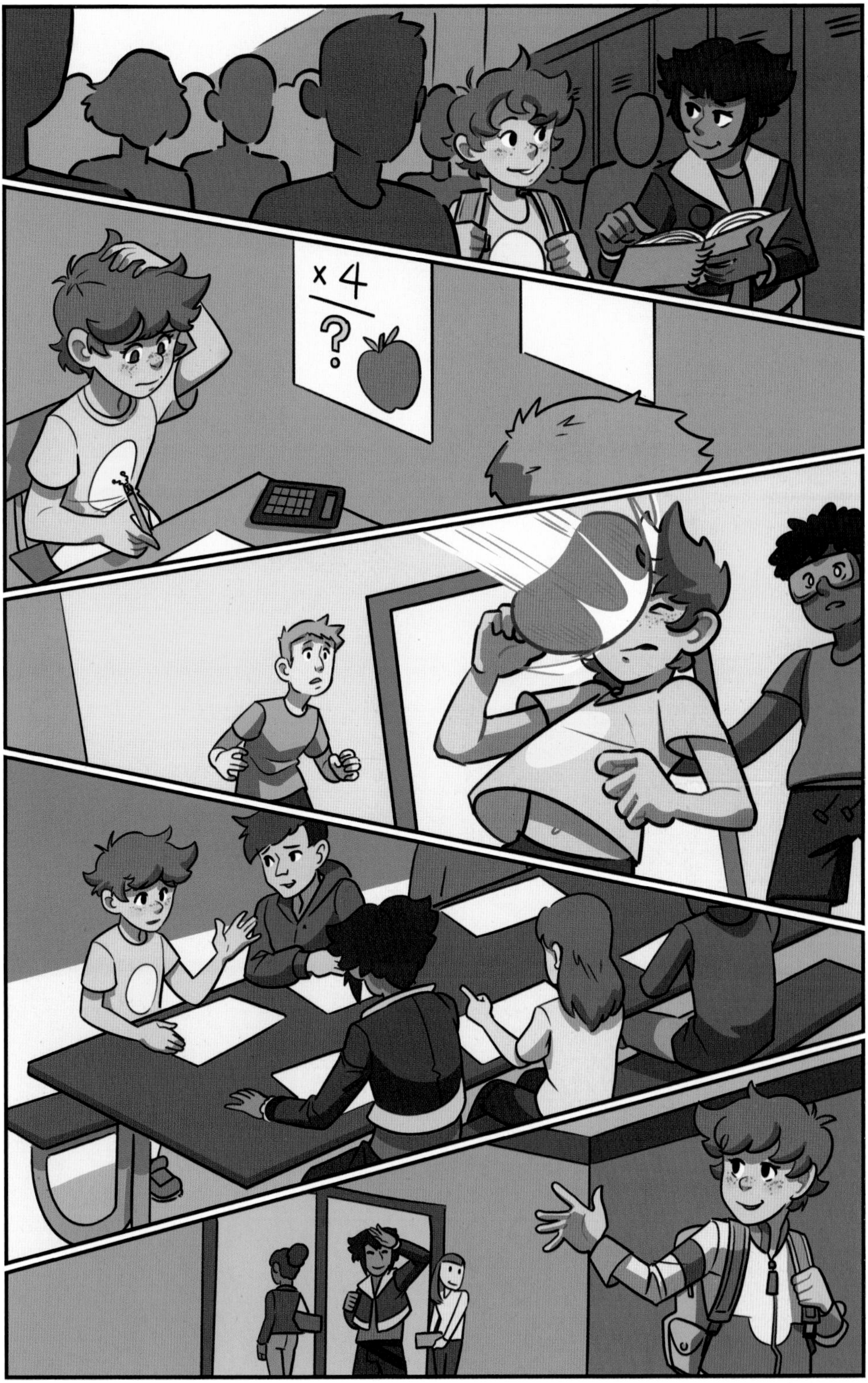
x 4
?

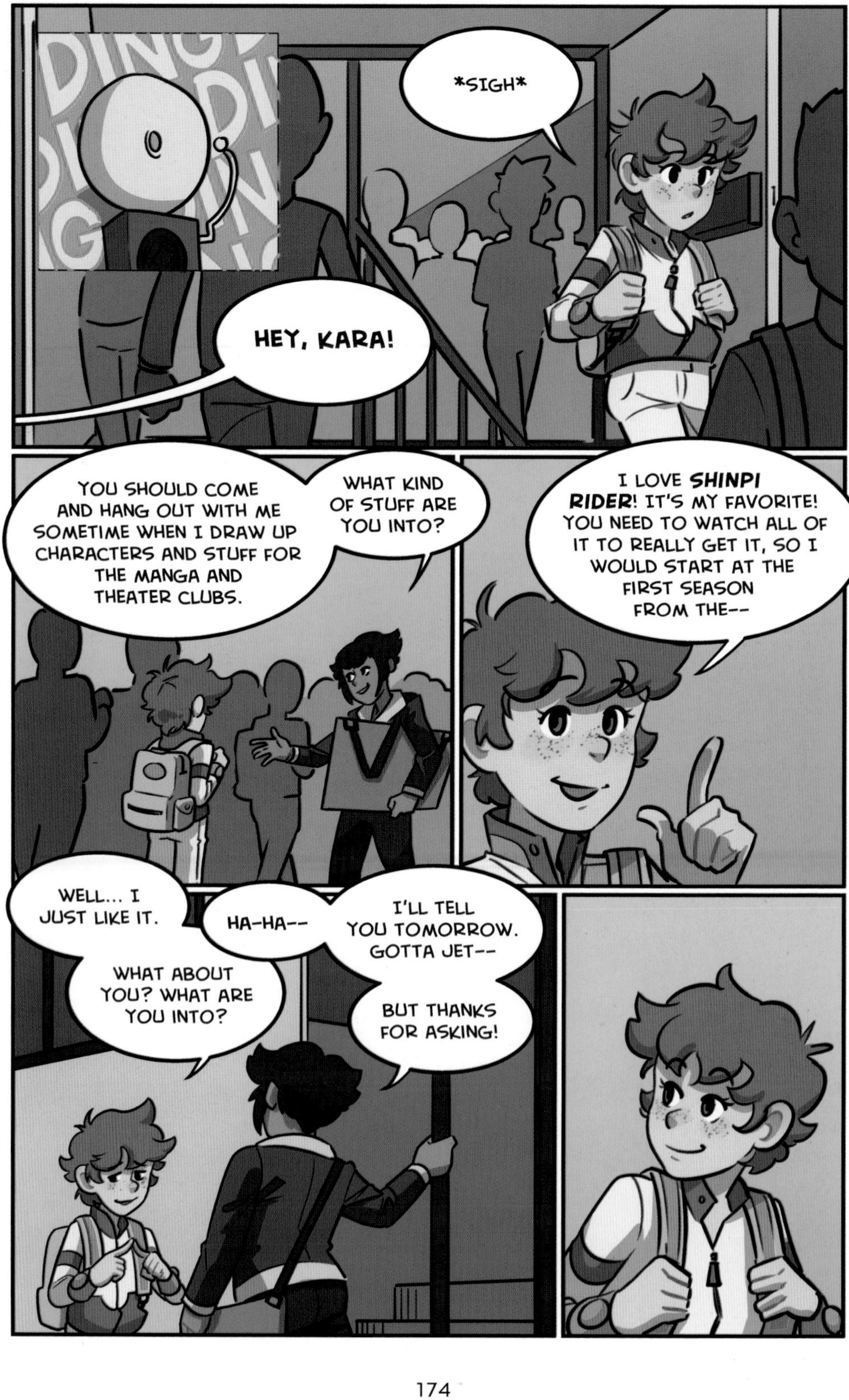
DING DING DING
SIGH
HEY, KARA!
YOU SHOULD COME AND HANG OUT WITH ME SOMETIME WHEN I DRAW UP CHARACTERS AND STUFF FOR THE MANGA AND THEATER CLUBS.
WHAT KIND OF STUFF ARE YOU INTO?
I LOVE SHINPI RIDER! IT'S MY FAVORITE! YOU NEED TO WATCH ALL OF IT TO REALLY GET IT, SO I WOULD START AT THE FIRST SEASON FROM THE--
WELL... I JUST LIKE IT.
WHAT ABOUT YOU? WHAT ARE YOU INTO?
HA-HA--
I'LL TELL YOU TOMORROW. GOTTA JET--
BUT THANKS FOR ASKING!

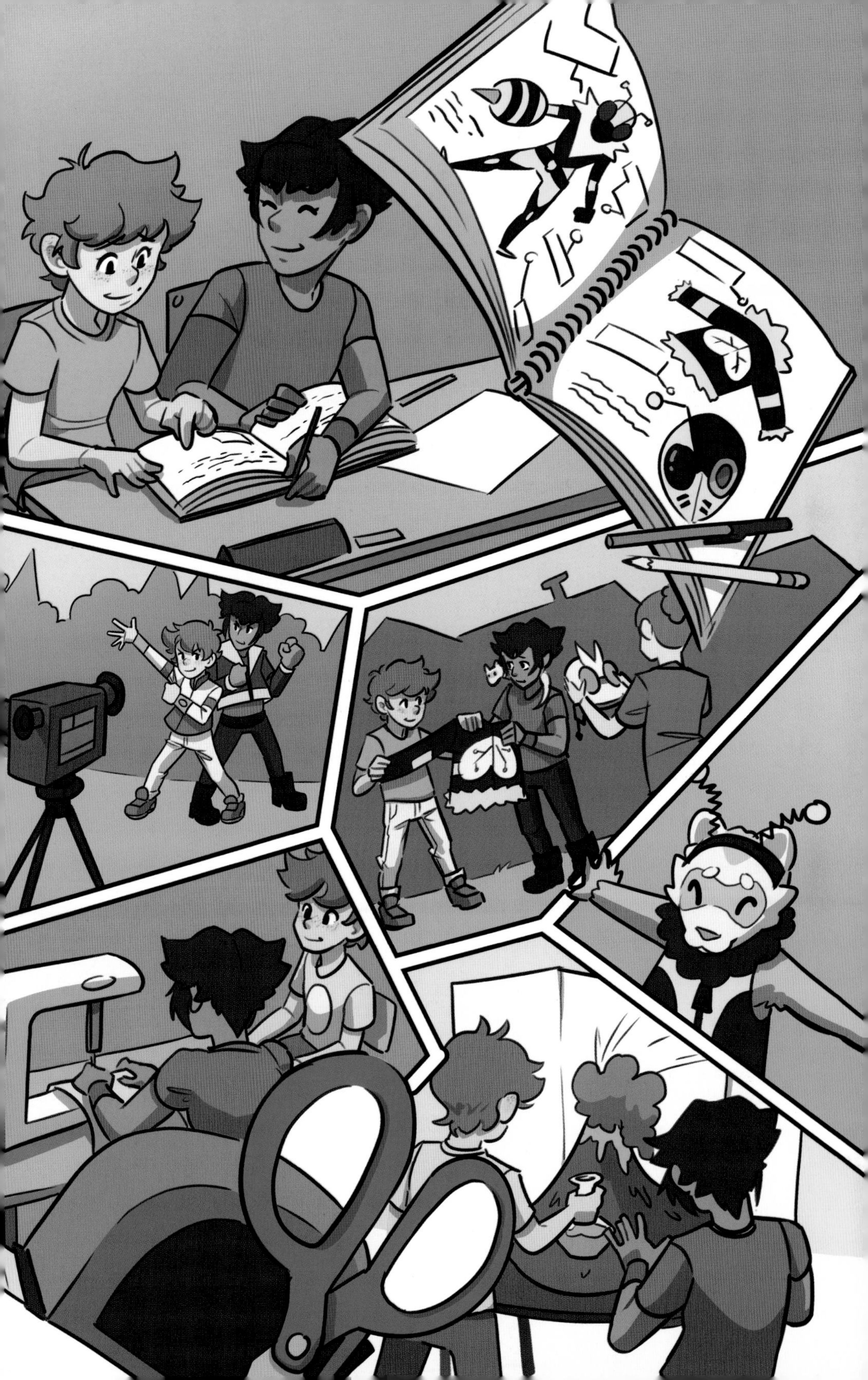

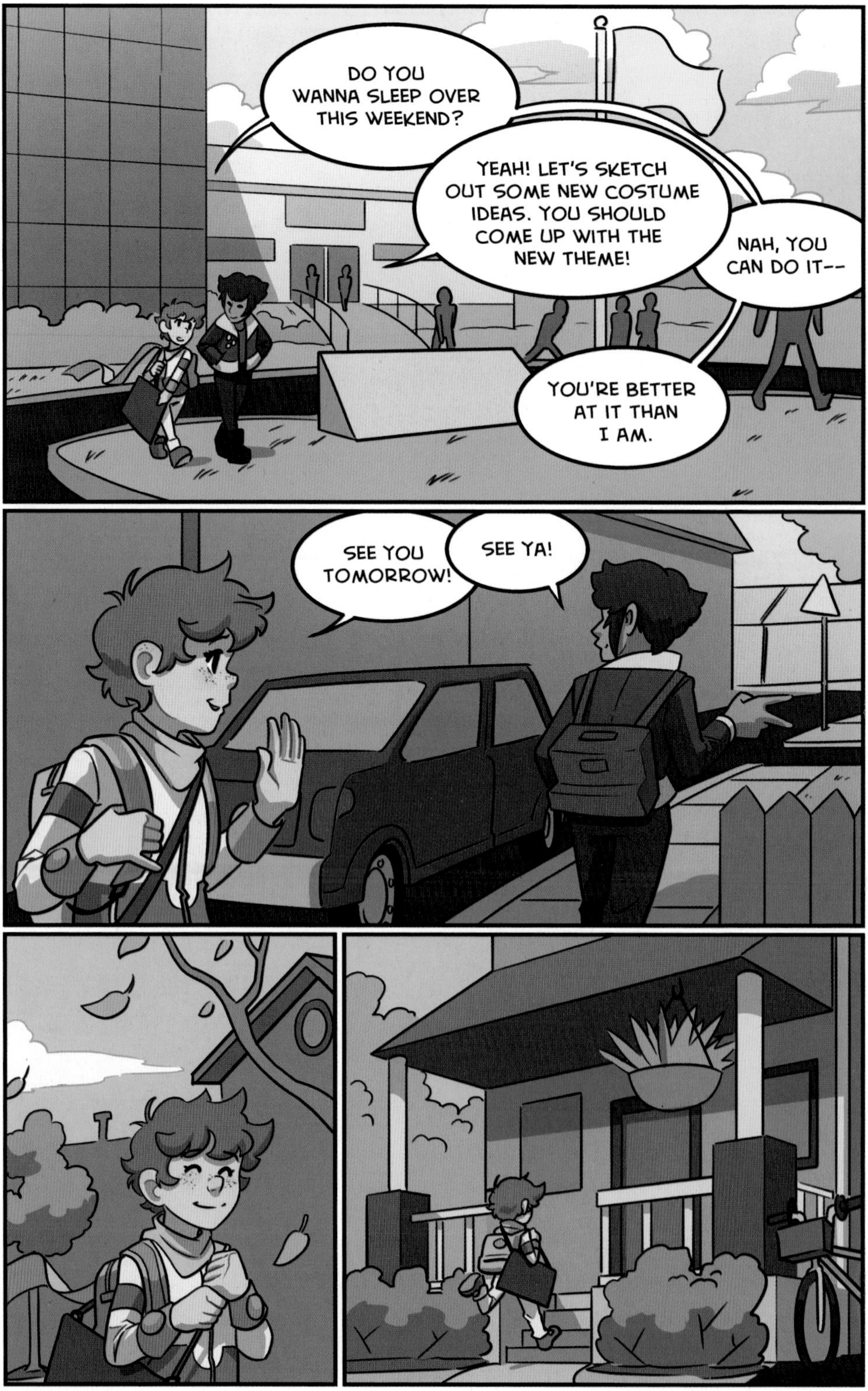
DO YOU WANNA SLEEP OVER THIS WEEKEND?
YEAH! LET'S SKETCH OUT SOME NEW COSTUME IDEAS. YOU SHOULD COME UP WITH THE NEW THEME!
NAH, YOU CAN DO IT--
YOU'RE BETTER AT IT THAN I AM.
SEE YOU TOMORROW!
SEE YA!

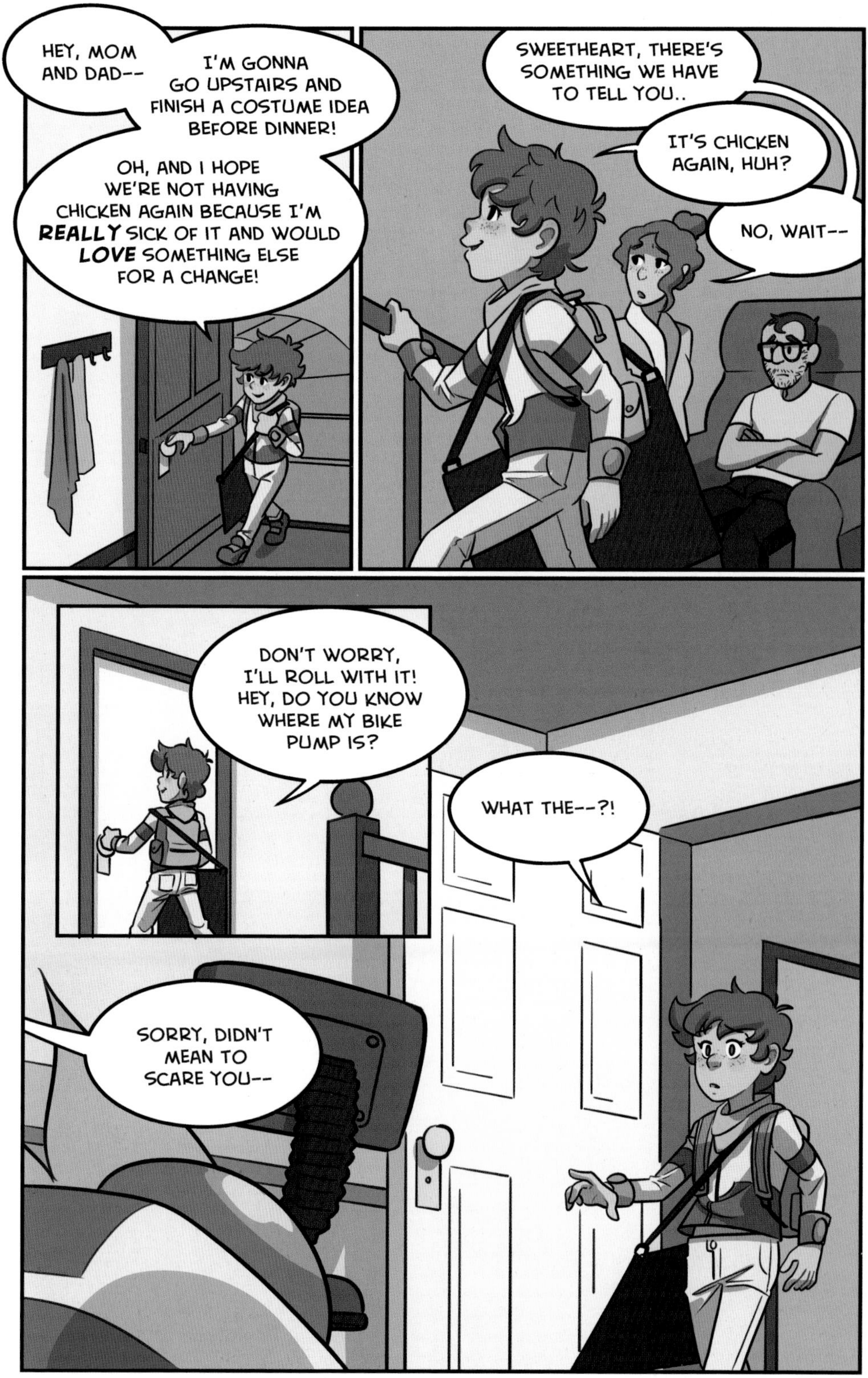
HEY, MOM AND DAD--
I'M GONNA GO UPSTAIRS AND FINISH A COSTUME IDEA BEFORE DINNER!
OH, AND I HOPE WE'RE NOT HAVING CHICKEN AGAIN BECAUSE I'M **REALLY** SICK OF IT AND WOULD **LOVE** SOMETHING ELSE FOR A CHANGE!
SWEETHEART, THERE'S SOMETHING WE HAVE TO TELL YOU..
IT'S CHICKEN AGAIN, HUH?
NO, WAIT--
DON'T WORRY, I'LL ROLL WITH IT! HEY, DO YOU KNOW WHERE MY BIKE PUMP IS?
WHAT THE--?!
SORRY, DIDN'T MEAN TO SCARE YOU--

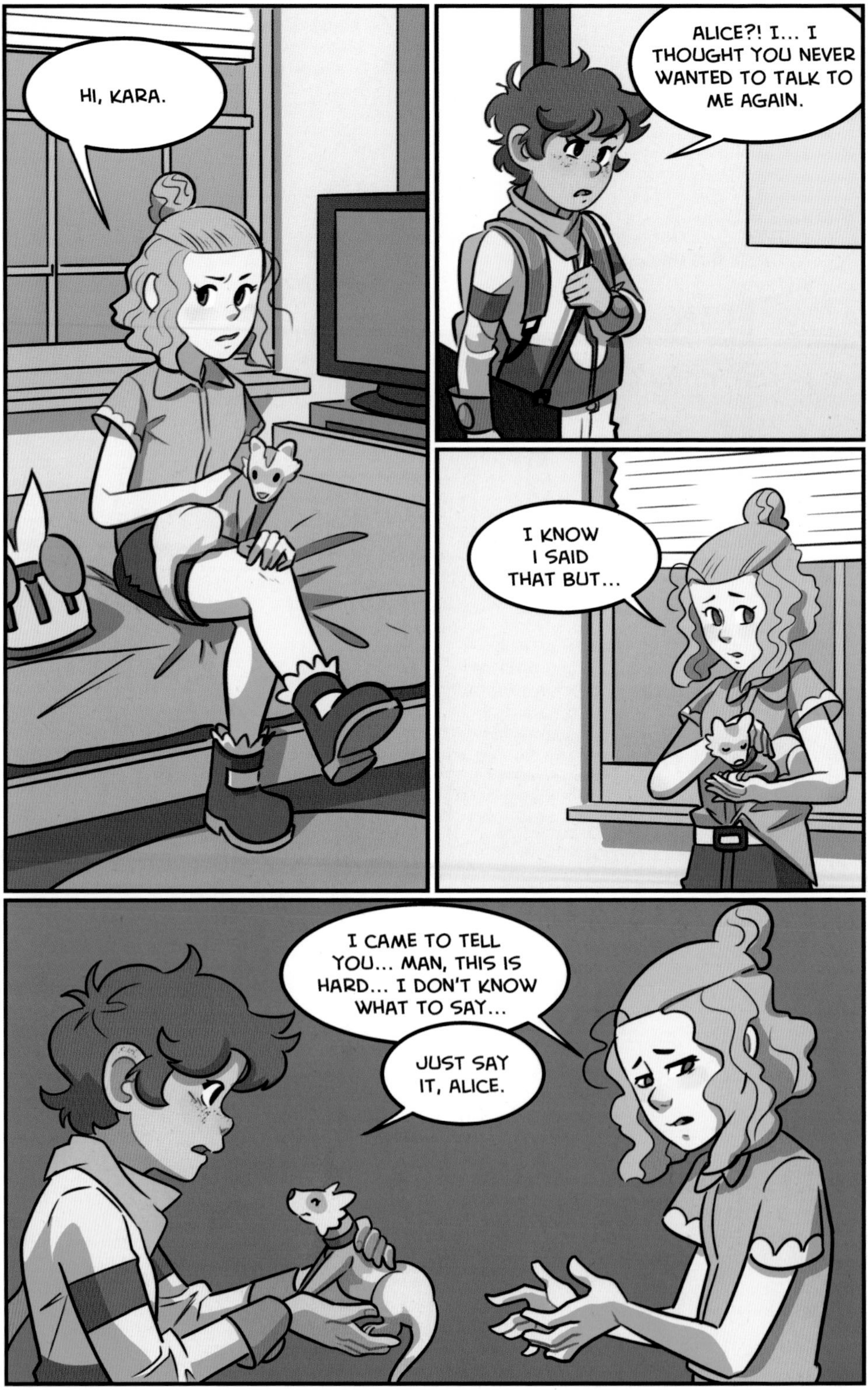
HI, KARA.
ALICE?! I... I THOUGHT YOU NEVER WANTED TO TALK TO ME AGAIN.
I KNOW I SAID THAT BUT...
I CAME TO TELL YOU... MAN, THIS IS HARD... I DON'T KNOW WHAT TO SAY...
JUST SAY IT, ALICE.

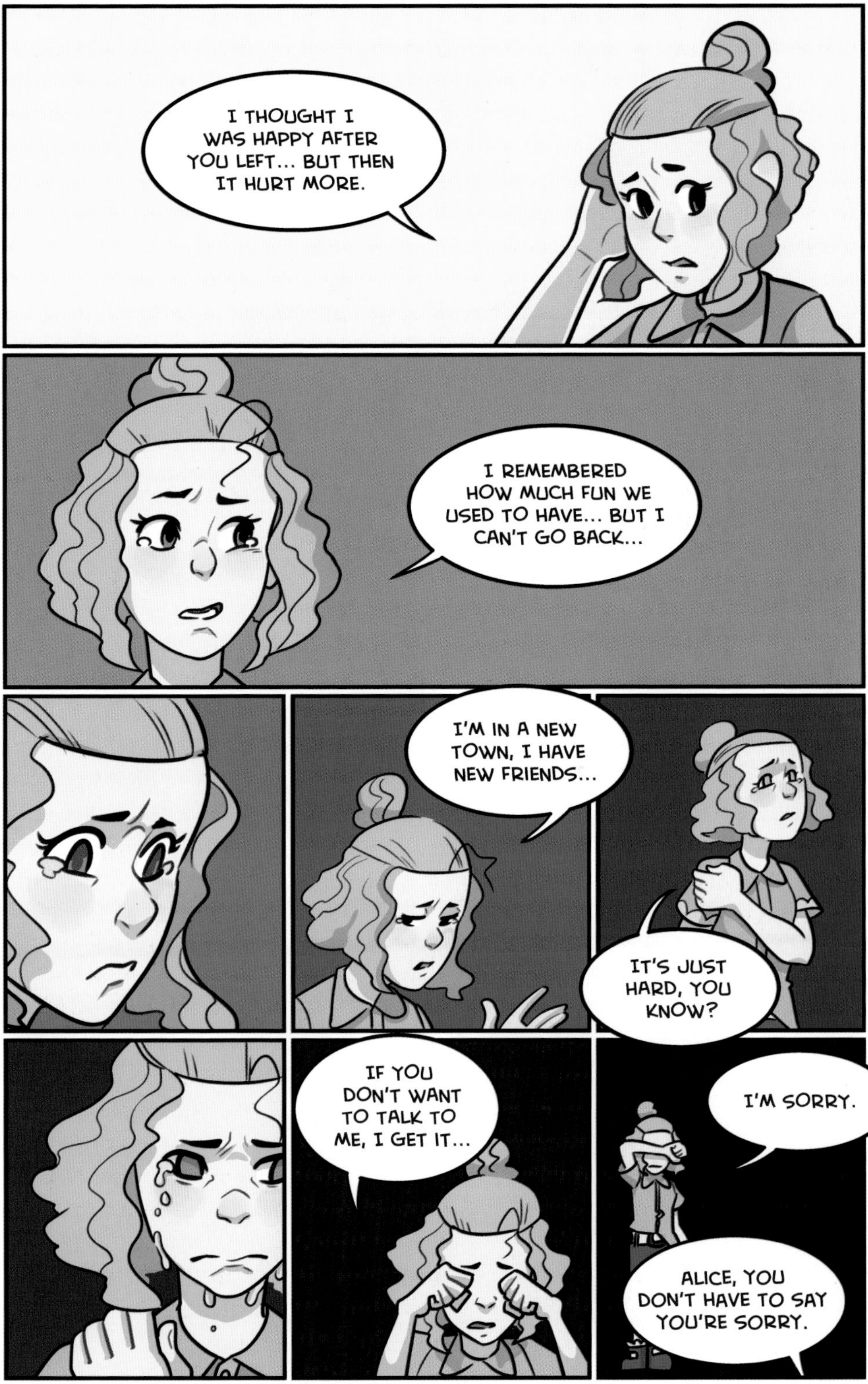
I THOUGHT I WAS HAPPY AFTER YOU LEFT... BUT THEN IT HURT MORE.
I REMEMBERED HOW MUCH FUN WE USED TO HAVE... BUT I CAN'T GO BACK...
I'M IN A NEW TOWN, I HAVE NEW FRIENDS...
IT'S JUST HARD, YOU KNOW?
IF YOU DON'T WANT TO TALK TO ME, I GET IT...
I'M SORRY.
ALICE, YOU DON'T HAVE TO SAY YOU'RE SORRY.

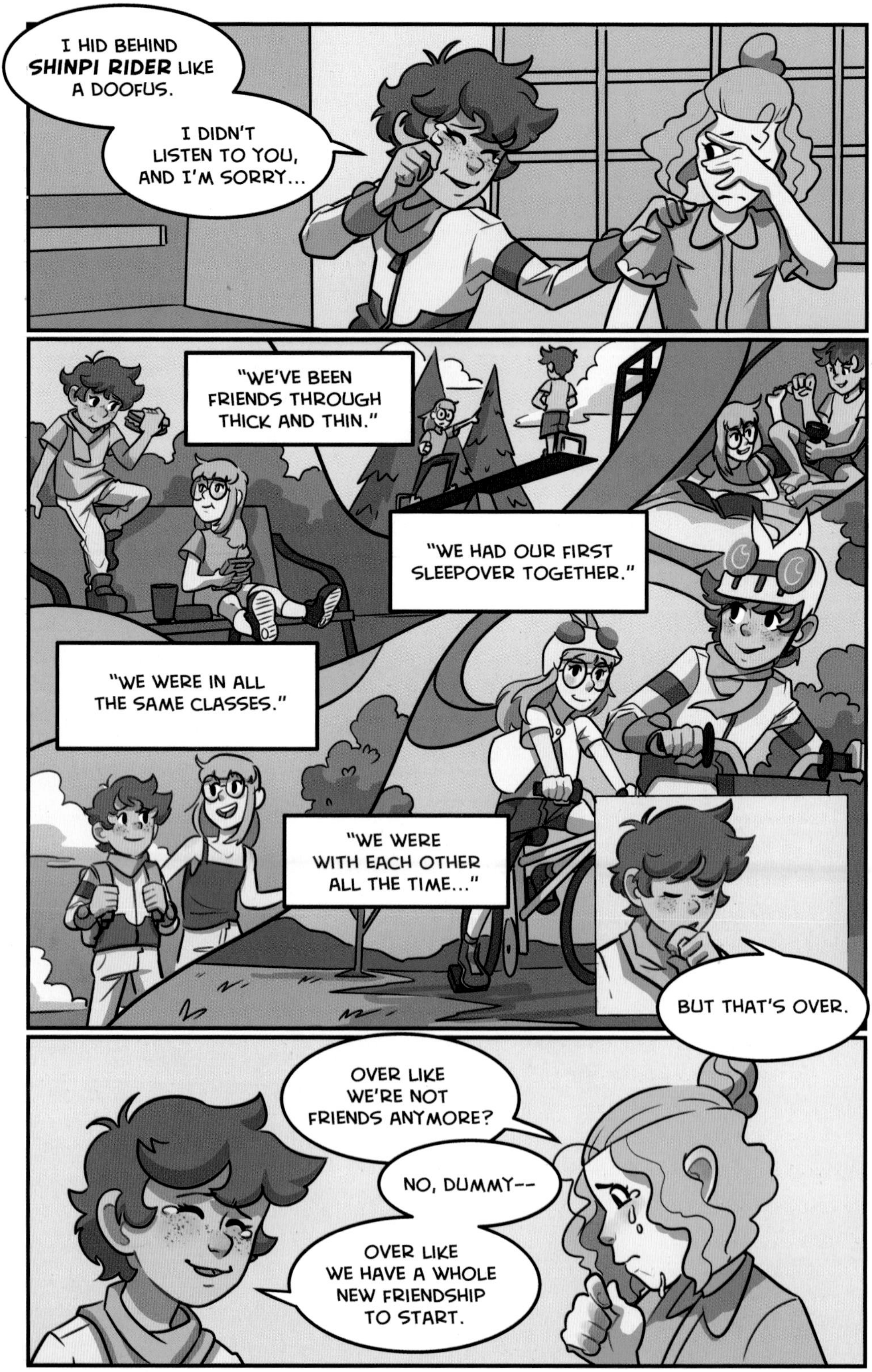
I HID BEHIND SHINPI RIDER LIKE A DOOFUS.
I DIDN'T LISTEN TO YOU, AND I'M SORRY...
"WE'VE BEEN FRIENDS THROUGH THICK AND THIN."
"WE HAD OUR FIRST SLEEPOVER TOGETHER."
"WE WERE IN ALL THE SAME CLASSES."
"WE WERE WITH EACH OTHER ALL THE TIME..."
BUT THAT'S OVER.
OVER LIKE WE'RE NOT FRIENDS ANYMORE?
NO, DUMMY--
OVER LIKE WE HAVE A WHOLE NEW FRIENDSHIP TO START.

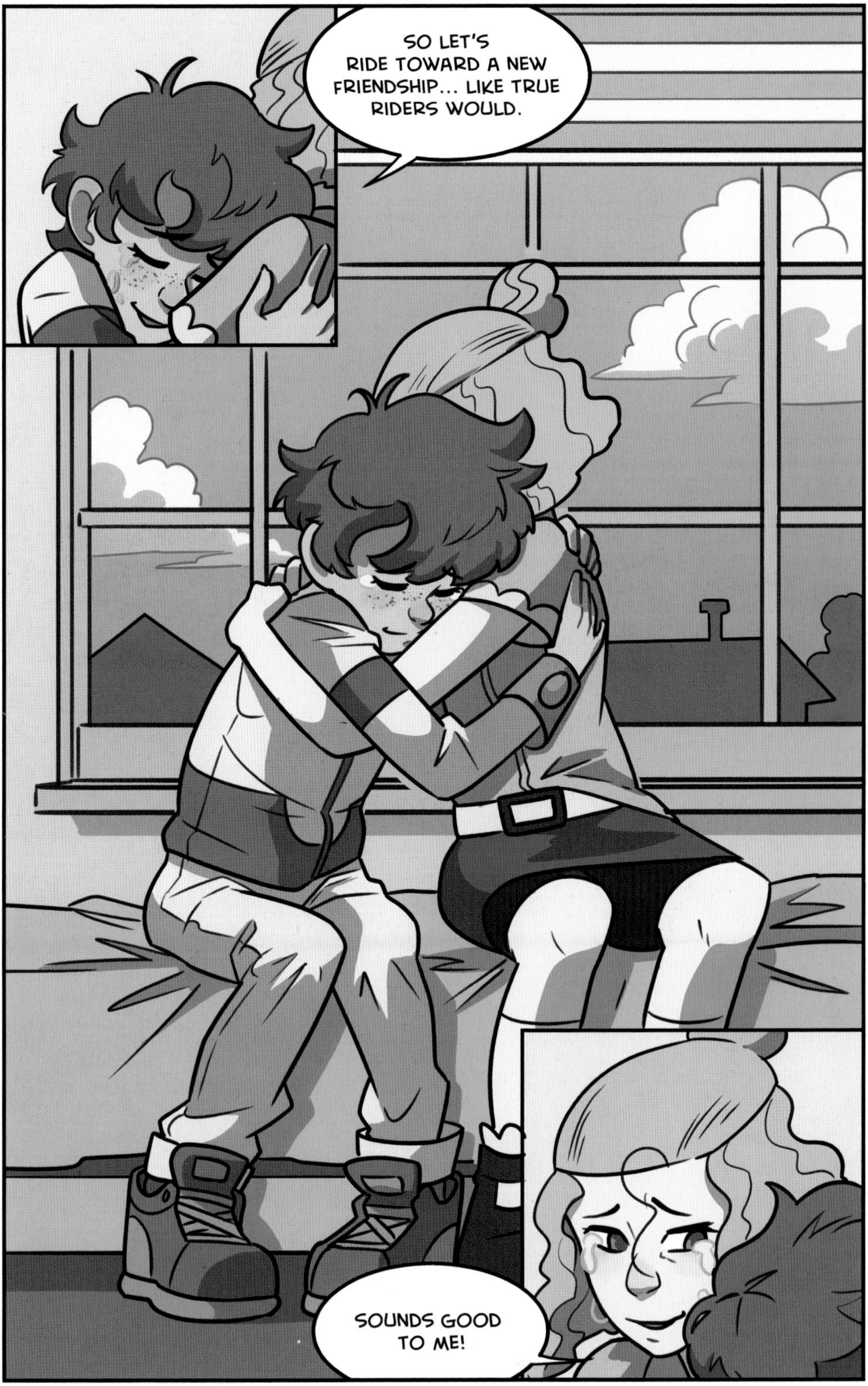
SO LET'S RIDE TOWARD A NEW FRIENDSHIP... LIKE TRUE RIDERS WOULD.
SOUNDS GOOD TO ME!

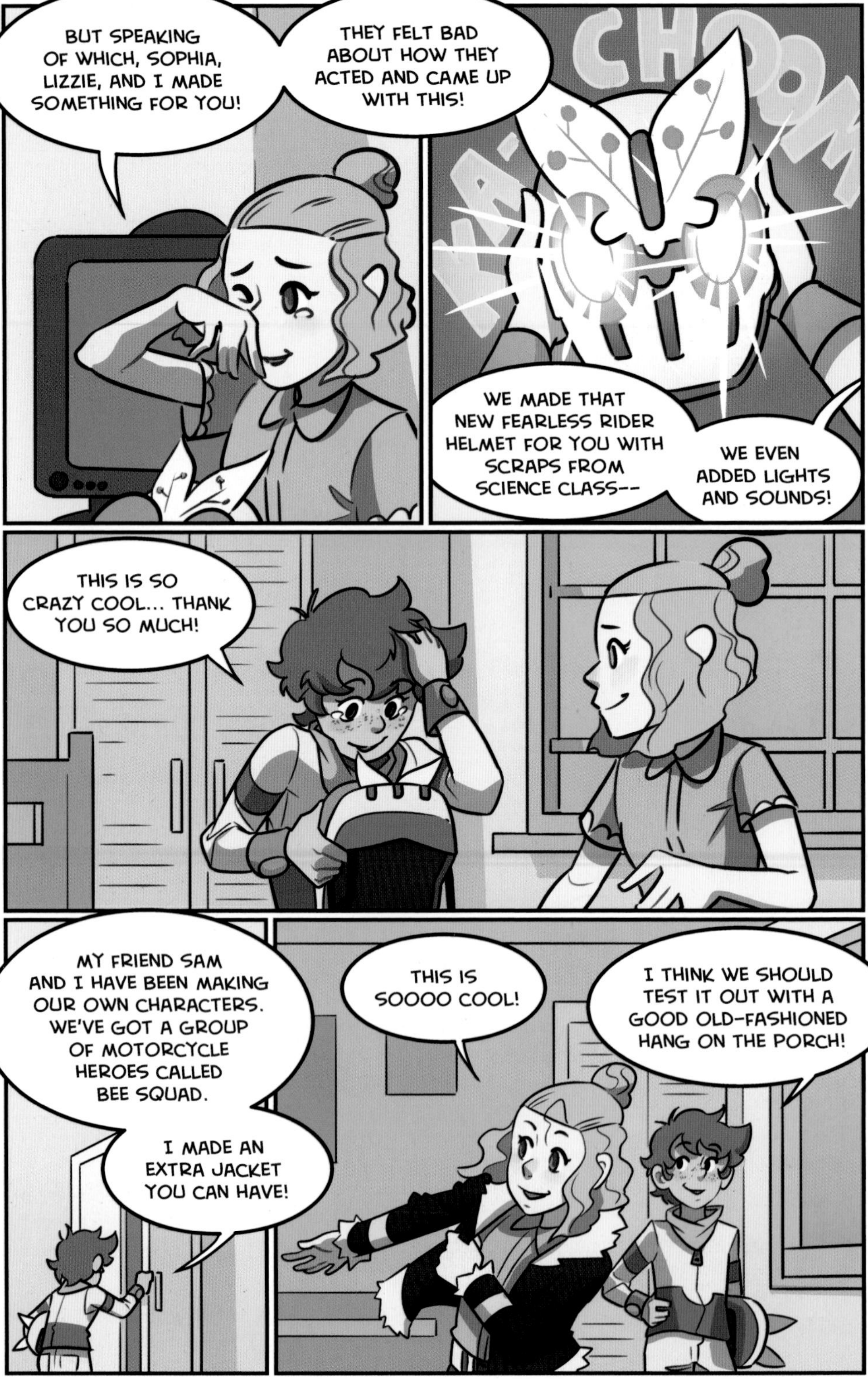
BUT SPEAKING OF WHICH, SOPHIA, LIZZIE, AND I MADE SOMETHING FOR YOU!
THEY FELT BAD ABOUT HOW THEY ACTED AND CAME UP WITH THIS!
KA-CHOOM
WE MADE THAT NEW FEARLESS RIDER HELMET FOR YOU WITH SCRAPS FROM SCIENCE CLASS--
WE EVEN ADDED LIGHTS AND SOUNDS!
THIS IS SO CRAZY COOL... THANK YOU SO MUCH!
MY FRIEND SAM AND I HAVE BEEN MAKING OUR OWN CHARACTERS. WE'VE GOT A GROUP OF MOTORCYCLE HEROES CALLED BEE SQUAD.
I MADE AN EXTRA JACKET YOU CAN HAVE!
THIS IS SOOOO COOL!
I THINK WE SHOULD TEST IT OUT WITH A GOOD OLD-FASHIONED HANG ON THE PORCH!

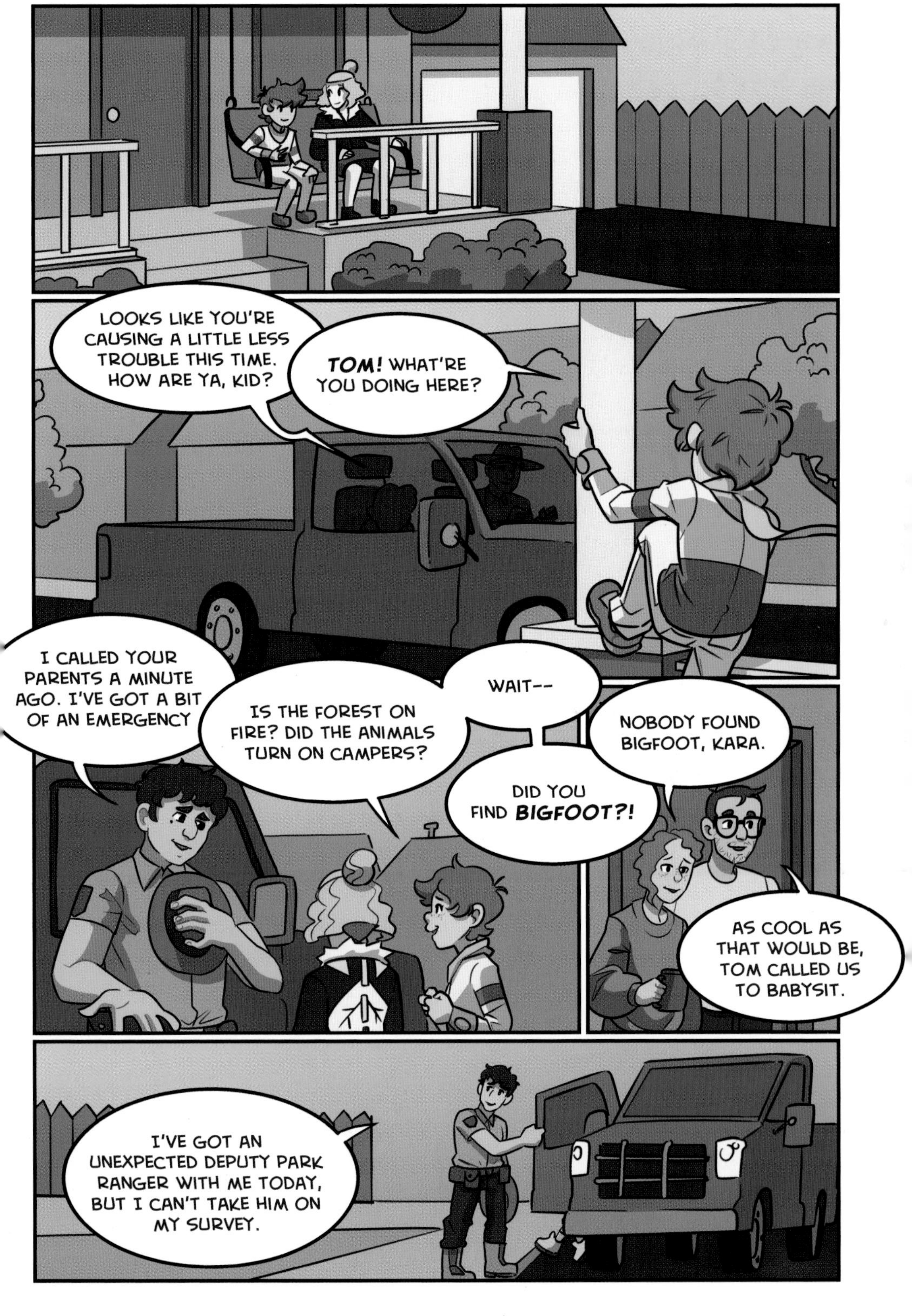

LOOKS LIKE YOU'RE CAUSING A LITTLE LESS TROUBLE THIS TIME. HOW ARE YA, KID?
TOM! WHAT'RE YOU DOING HERE?
I CALLED YOUR PARENTS A MINUTE AGO. I'VE GOT A BIT OF AN EMERGENCY
IS THE FOREST ON FIRE? DID THE ANIMALS TURN ON CAMPERS?
WAIT--
DID YOU FIND BIGFOOT?!
NOBODY FOUND BIGFOOT, KARA.
AS COOL AS THAT WOULD BE, TOM CALLED US TO BABYSIT.
I'VE GOT AN UNEXPECTED DEPUTY PARK RANGER WITH ME TODAY, BUT I CAN'T TAKE HIM ON MY SURVEY.

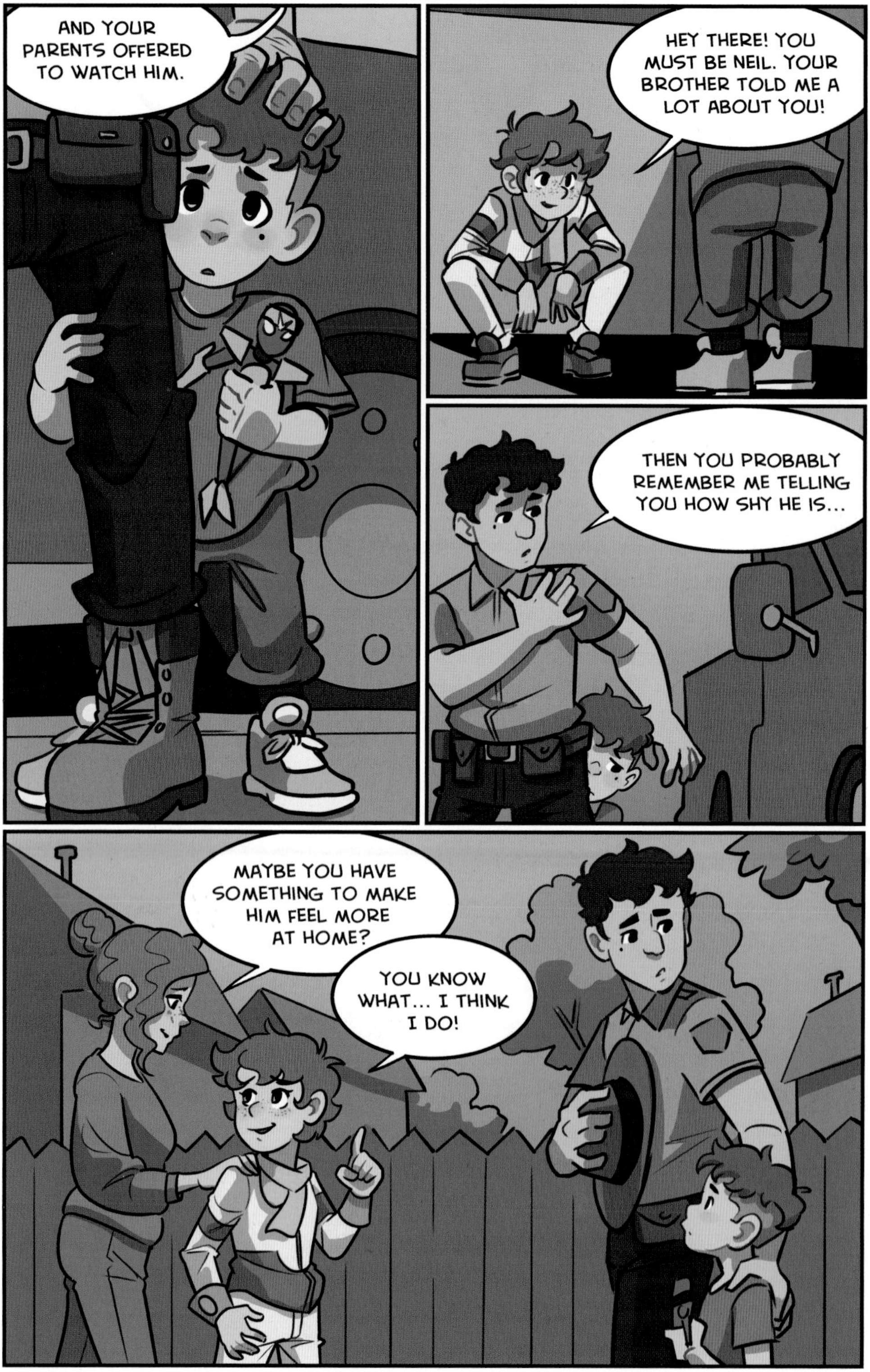
AND YOUR PARENTS OFFERED TO WATCH HIM.
HEY THERE! YOU MUST BE NEIL. YOUR BROTHER TOLD ME A LOT ABOUT YOU!
THEN YOU PROBABLY REMEMBER ME TELLING YOU HOW SHY HE IS...
MAYBE YOU HAVE SOMETHING TO MAKE HIM FEEL MORE AT HOME?
YOU KNOW WHAT... I THINK I DO!

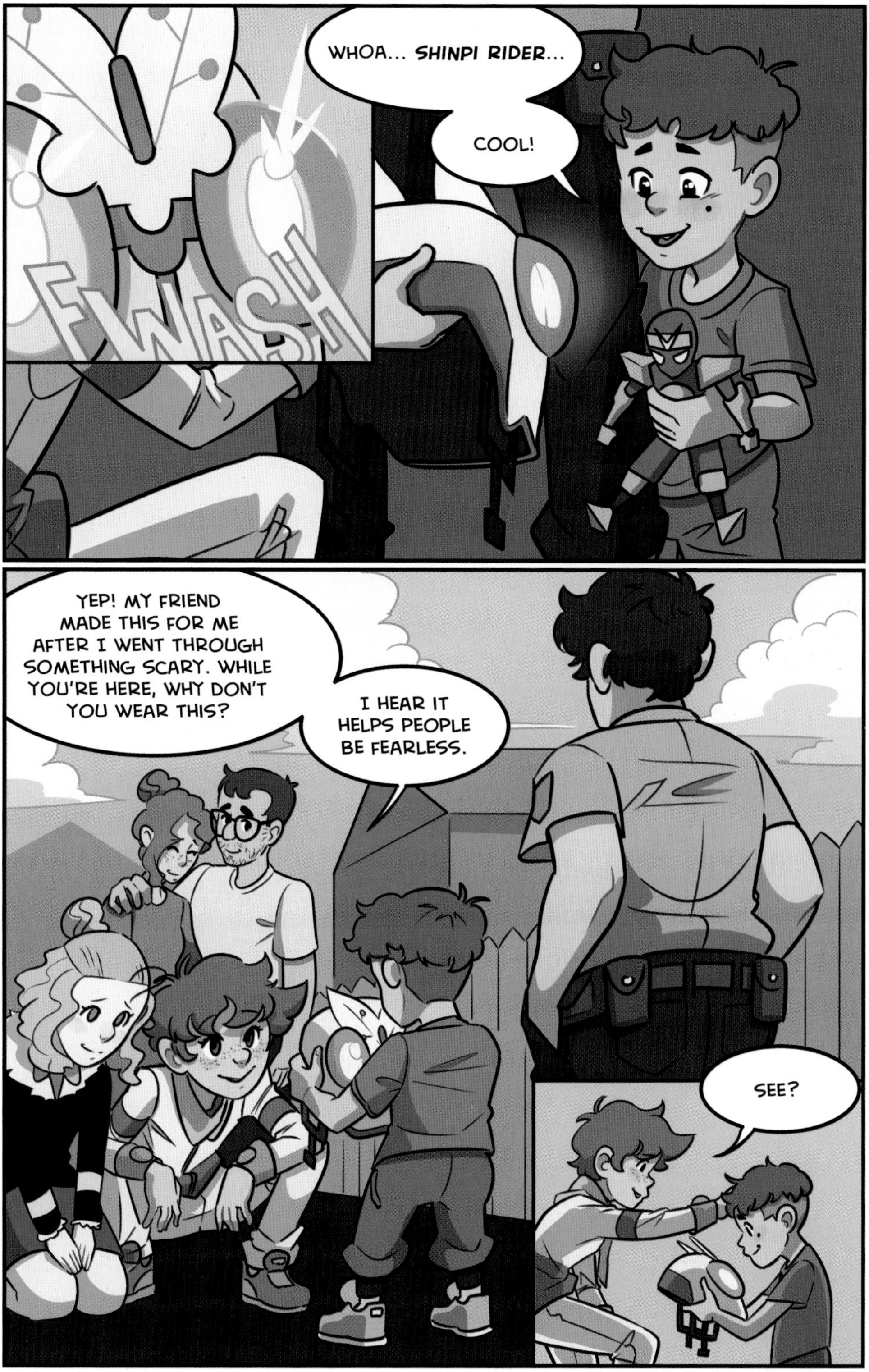
FWASH
WHOA... SHINPI RIDER...
COOL!
YEP! MY FRIEND MADE THIS FOR ME AFTER I WENT THROUGH SOMETHING SCARY. WHILE YOU'RE HERE, WHY DON'T YOU WEAR THIS?
I HEAR IT HELPS PEOPLE BE FEARLESS.
SEE?

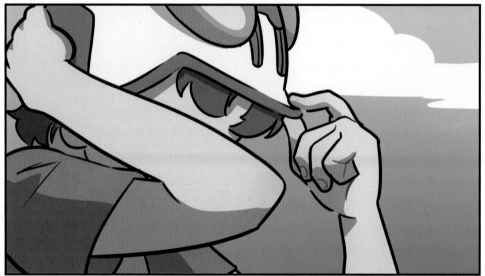

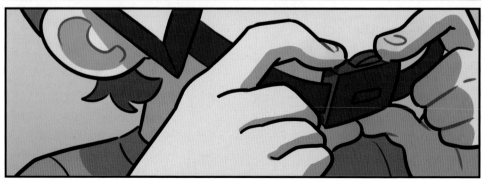

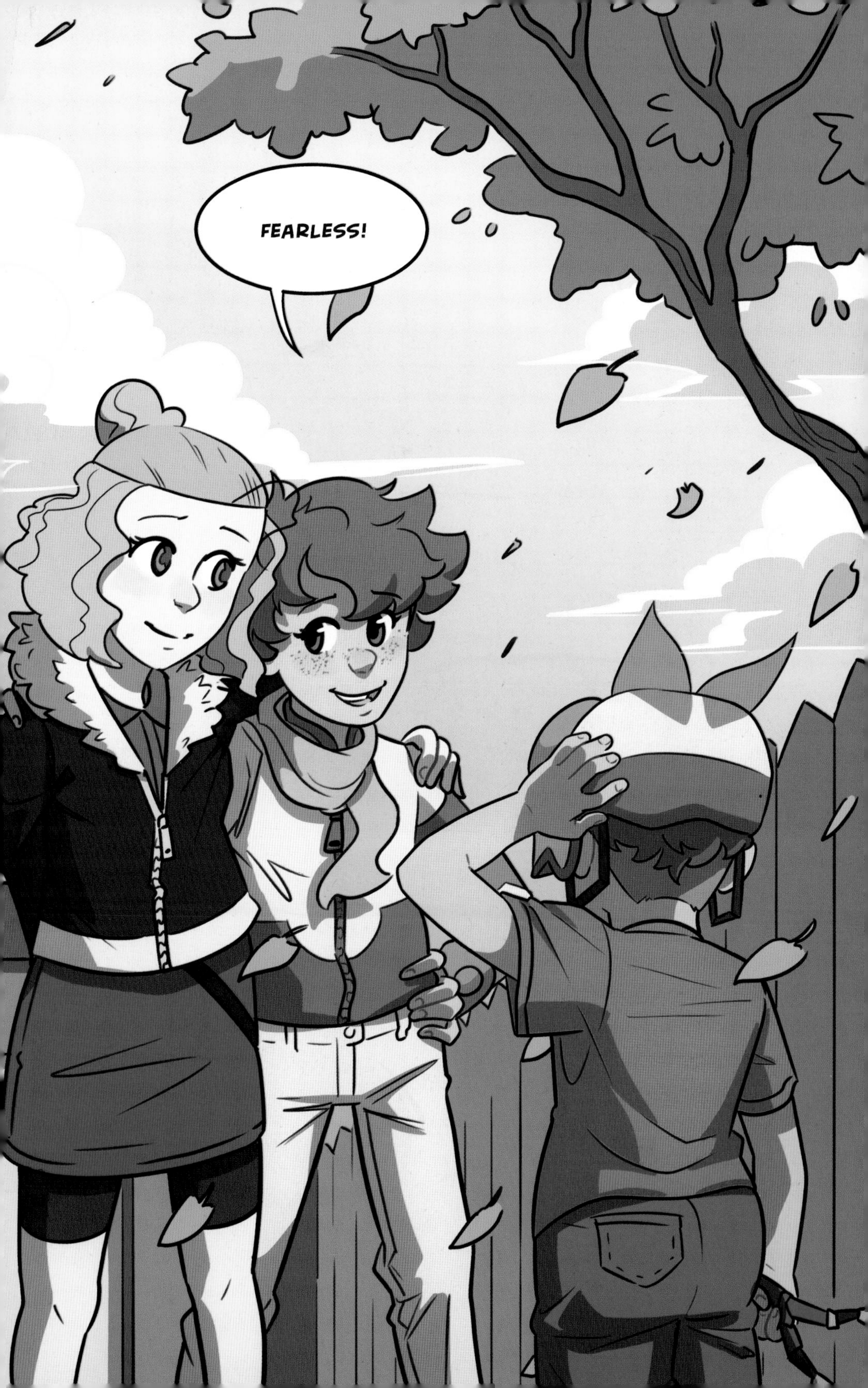
FEARLESS!

KENNY PORTER is a comic book writer living in Grand Rapids, Michigan. He's writen for DC Comics, SEGA, Image/Top Cow, and more. He graduated with a BA in writing from Grand Valley State University. You can find him at portercomics.com.

ZACH WILCOX is a Philadelphia-based artist. He has a master's degree in fine arts for sequential art from Savannah College of Art and Design and a BS in digital media from Drexel University. He specializes in comics, illustration, concept art, storyboards, and animated GIFs. You can learn more about him at zachwek.com.